Juli Anne Lindsey is an obsessive reader who was onc orn between the love of her two favourite genres: toe- irling romance and chew-your-nails suspense. Now she ets to write both for Mills & Boon Heroes. When she' not creating new worlds, Julie can be found car oling her three kids around northeastern Ohio and plot ng with her shamelessly enabling friends. Winner of t e Daphne du Maurier Award for Excellence in My ery/Suspense, Julie is a member of International Thr er Writers, Romance Writers of America and Sisters in Crime. Learn more about Julie and her books at j ieannelindsey.com

Ka n Whiddon started weaving fanciful tales for her you er brothers at the age of eleven. Amid the gorgeous Cat ill Mountains, then the majestic Rocky Mountains, she uelled her imagination with the natural beauty sur nding her. Karen now lives in north Texas, writes ful me and volunteers for a boxer dog rescue. She sha s her life with her hero of a husband and four to five do depending on if she is fostering. You can email K n at kwhiddon1@aol.com. Fans can also check out he website, karenwhiddon.com

D1343978

Also by Julie Anne Lindsey

SVU Surveillance
Deadly Cover-Up
Missing in the Mountains
Marine Protector
Dangerous Knowledge
Shadow Point Deputy
Marked by the Marshal
Federal Agent Under Fire
The Sheriff's Secret

Also by Karen Whiddon

The CEO's Secret Baby
The Cop's Missing Child
The Millionaire Cowboy's Secret
Texas Secrets, Lovers' Lies
The Rancher's Return
The Texan's Return
Wyoming Undercover
The Texas Soldier's Son
Texas Ranch Justice
Snowbound Targets

Discover more at millsandboon.co.uk

PROTECTING HIS WITNESS

JULIE ANNE LINDSEY

COLTON 911: SOLDIER'S RETURN

KAREN WHIDDON

MILLS & BOON

All rights reserved including the right of reproduction in whole or in part in any form. This edition is published by arrangement with Harlequin Books S.A.

This is a work of fiction. Names, characters, places, locations and incidents are purely fictional and bear no relationship to any real life individuals, living or dead, or to any actual places, business establishments, locations, events or incidents. Any resemblance is entirely coincidental.

This book is sold subject to the condition that it shall not, by way of trade or otherwise, be lent, resold, hired out or otherwise circulated without the prior consent of the publisher in any form of binding or cover other than that in which it is published and without a similar condition including this condition being imposed on the subsequent purchaser.

® and ™ are trademarks owned and used by the trademark owner and/ or its licensee. Trademarks marked with ® are registered with the United Kingdom Patent Office and/or the Office for Harmonisation in the Internal Market and in other countries.

First Published in Great Britain 2021
by Mills & Boon, an imprint of HarperCollins*Publishers* Ltd
1 London Bridge Street, London, SE1 9GF

www.harpercollins.co.uk

HarperCollins*Publishers*
1st Floor, Watermarque Building,
Ringsend Road, Dublin 4, Ireland

Protecting His Witness © 2021 Julie Anne Lindsey
Colton 911: Soldier's Return © 2021 Harlequin Books S.A.

Special thanks and acknowledgement are given to Karen Whiddon for her contribution to the *Colton 911: Chicago* series.

ISBN: 978-0-263-28330-3

0321

MIX
Paper from
responsible sources
FSC™ C007454

This book is produced from independently certified FSC™ paper to ensure responsible forest management.

For more information visit: www.harpercollins.co.uk/green

Printed and bound in Spain
by CPI, Barcelona

Chapter One

Maisy Daniels shifted uncomfortably on the hard kitchen chair, rubbing the curve of her once decidedly flat abdomen, which had morphed into a watermelon in her third trimester. She smiled at the thought, not missing her thinner shape at all. Not yet, anyway. Right now her body was doing an amazing feat that many couldn't, and Maisy was honored by the opportunity.

Her baby was stronger by the day, and she couldn't wait to meet the little one soon. She imagined her labor and delivery. The deep, practiced breathing, a positive attitude and classical music playing through each contraction. Her birth plan was perfect, laid out in excruciating detail. Though all that truly mattered was that her baby arrived safely into Maisy's loving embrace, preferably without anyone trying to kill them. In other words, under near-opposite circumstances than those in which her baby was conceived.

"Hey." US Marshal Clara Spencer popped into the small and toasty kitchen with her usual encouraging smile. Her smart blond bob was streaked lightly with gray and tucked behind her ears. Laugh lines hugged the edges of her mouth. "Sorry. I had to take that call. Things are still a go for the move today. We're even moving the timeline up a little. How are you feeling?"

"Good." Maisy straightened in her chair, scrutinizing the woman before her, someone fate had made her dearest friend. One part lawman and two parts Mary Poppins, Clara had become everything to Maisy these last few months, including one of the only people she ever got to see. "The call went okay?" Maisy asked, sensing an odd uncertainty in Clara's normally cheery eyes.

"Mmm-hmm." She patted Maisy's shoulder on her way to the stove, where she'd set a kettle to boil before leaving the room to take a call. "The other marshal will be here within the hour. Then we'll transport you back to your hometown for the trial. You and I will be sharing subpar room service cheeseburgers together in some high-rise hotel by nightfall."

"Wow." Maisy stifled a grimace, forcing a curt laugh instead. "You make it sound so tempting. I might start walking right now." She curled her arms protectively over her middle, cradling her baby bump. Much as Maisy longed for the trial to be over, her testimony given and Sam Luciano behind bars for life, she would fear for her safety, and that of her baby, until the day officially arrived. Until then, anything could happen, and most of the possibilities running through Maisy's mind were grim.

Sam Luciano was an organized crime boss with reach and influence most celebrities never achieved. She'd come to understand he was involved in every manner of awfulness, but the crime that mattered most to Maisy was the murder of her twin sister, Natalie. And with a little luck, Maisy's testimony would secure Luciano's permanent resident status at the Castle on Cumberland, aka Kentucky State Penitentiary, the state's maximum security and supermax prison.

Clara set a steaming mug of tea on the table before Maisy, its chipped edge and floral pattern worn from age and washing. "Just breathe," she said gently, taking the seat beside her, a second mug cradled in her hands. "You've made it. All the way to the end, and in less than two weeks, you'll be free to go anywhere you want, any time you want and with anyone you choose. No more passing time cooped up in a safe house, playing cards and wearing out the Netflix account with me and your other stuffy old guardians."

"You're not stuffy or old." Maisy smiled, sipping her tea and wondering if it was really that simple. After six long months in near-isolation, she'd tell her story to a jury, justice would prevail and she'd return to her life in progress. It seemed impossible. And suddenly, leaving the place she never wanted to live in the first place felt a lot scarier than she'd ever imagined. "Don't tell the other marshals," Maisy confided, "but I'm going to miss you the most."

Clara set her tea aside. She reached for Maisy and wrapped her in a warm hug. "I'm going to miss you, too, kiddo. But just think, after this is over, our time together will be on your own terms and at your leisure instead of for your protection and under duress."

Maisy nodded, a lump of emotion rising in her throat. The little cottage on Elmwood Lane had been a safe haven for her and the baby she hadn't even known she was carrying on the day she arrived. "I couldn't have survived this without you."

Clara had been everything Maisy needed to get through life in voluntary captivity, through the shocking realization she would soon be a mother and the oppressive grief of a twin sister lost. She'd been a buoy on days Maisy was sure her testimony wouldn't be enough to make a difference. And she'd found the perfect obstetrician to care for Maisy throughout her pregnancy. She'd driven her to every appointment and nursed Maisy through three long months of morning sickness. She'd done it all without ever being asked.

Maisy wiped a renegade tear as the hug ended, determined to stay strong. "Thank you. For everything."

Clara's brown eyes misted. "Stop that. If you cry, then I'll cry, and the escorting marshal will get here and think we're both nuts."

Maisy did her best to pull herself together, though pregnancy had her emotions thoroughly heightened and her hormones wholly out of whack. "I'll try," she promised, lifting her mug and inhaling the sweet steam before taking a long, soothing sip.

"Good." Clara watched Maisy closely, a small smile budding on her lips. "Did I tell you I was able to poke around a little like you asked?"

"No." A thrill shot through Maisy as she straightened. "Learn anything good?"

"Mostly that I was right, of course. The trial postponements have been in our favor. Prosecution has been building an airtight case. Locating and securing three additional witnesses."

"What?" Maisy set her mug aside so she wouldn't drop it from shock. "There are more witnesses?" A nearly forgotten sense of hope bubbled inside her. She wasn't alone.

"Yes." Clara's grin widened. She'd told her as much before, multiple times, but Maisy had assumed the words were unfounded, meant to make her feel better but with

PROTECTING HIS WITNESS

JULIE ANNE LINDSEY

NEATH PORT TALBOT LIBRARIES	
2300145058	
Askews & Holts	09-Mar-2021
AF	£6.99
NPTPON	

This book is dedicated to my Private Eyes,
you know who you are, and I can't thank you enough.

no real basis. "So, it's just like I told you," Clara continued. "Everything is going to be just fine."

"Thank you." Maisy let the tears roll this time, embracing the relief and joy along with a sliver of guilt for asking Clara to nose around outside the scope of the case. "I hope you won't get into trouble for snooping."

"I was careful. And besides, you're being transferred today. The trial is almost here, and this will all be over soon. It was worth the risk just to see that smile on your face." Clara's phone rang, and she glanced at it briefly. Her smile wavered but rallied. "Our ride will be here soon. You should probably finish packing while I take this call."

Maisy rose with her tea and headed to the small rear bedroom she'd practically lived in since spring, riding on a surge of hope and possibilities. Four witnesses sounded like a pretty strong case to her. Surely no jury would side with Luciano now. And there would be justice for Natalie and all his other victims. Like Aaron.

Maisy sat on the soft twin bed a moment before her trembling legs gave out, and a fresh wave of grief rushed over her. Natalie shouldn't have volunteered to visit Aaron's house that day. He and Maisy had only been on a handful of dates, and he'd nearly thrown Maisy out after taking a private phone call she'd assumed was from a girlfriend. He'd been hiding something, and Maisy had sensed it. She'd left in a huff and forgotten her book. A tattered old copy of *Little Women* she rarely went anywhere without.

Natalie went to retrieve it.

And now she was dead. Her life traded for a ten-dollar paperback.

Maisy's paperback.

She wiped her tears and worked to calm her breathing, fighting to regain control. The unexpected bouts of grief weren't good for her blood pressure, and she needed to think of her baby. "Aunt Natalie was my personal defender," she whispered to her swollen abdomen, imagining her perfect child inside. "Our mama left me that book. She'd read it to us a dozen times and it was her favorite to the end, even through endless rounds of chemo."

Sam Luciano had been at Aaron's house when Natalie arrived. She'd snapped a photo of his car, license plate included, and texted it to Maisy before circling around to the back deck without ringing the doorbell. She'd assumed the car belong to the suspected other woman in Aaron's life, and she'd called to let Maisy know.

"That's how I met your father," Maisy told the bump, now shifting slightly with each stretch of an arm or leg. "He made me feel loved even when I hated myself. He made me smile when all I wanted to do was cry. And he tracked that monster down then arrested him for what he did to Aunt Natalie and Aaron." For the final reason alone, Maisy would love Blaze Winchester until the day she died.

And she'd see him again soon. Seven months pregnant with his child. She'd wanted to tell him sooner but wasn't allowed. Communication with the outside world was limited, and communication with anyone from her past was forbidden, at least until the trial. So Maisy had spent countless nights planning how to break the news. And now she wouldn't have to. A single look at her would say it all.

She pushed onto her feet, forcing Blaze's handsome face from her mind. Whatever he would think of her pregnancy was up to him, and no amount of planning on her part would change it. Until then, she had packing to do.

She'd moved the bulk of her things into a set of plastic bins against the wall when she heard a car outside. A black SUV with tinted glass and a government plate was visible in the driveway, just beyond her first-floor window. The marshal from her home county had arrived to escort her and Clara back to the town where the trial would take place.

A man climbed out from the driver's side, closed his door, then examined the home carefully as he moved toward the porch. He was older, with a dusting of gray at his temples and a scowl in his expression that unsettled Maisy's stomach. Not that it took much for that these days. Blustering November winds tussled his hair and split his unzipped jacket up the center, exposing a sidearm at his hip.

Maisy shivered. Her expression reflected in the windowpane said it all. There was fear and apprehension in her clear hazel eyes and a downward turn to her lips. Even the flush of her pale, freckled skin gave her away. She didn't want to leave. Too many terrible things could happen outside her protected walls, and in her current condition, she was helpless to do more than let them happen if they did.

Cold seemed to seep in from outside, under the locked window and around the reinforced frame. Leeching into Maisy's skin and frosting her bones. According to local news reports, the entirety of northern Kentucky was in for relentless rains this week, followed by dropping temperatures and a heavy late-season snowfall next.

Maisy gave her bare feet, yoga pants and tunic top a regretful look, then headed into the hallway for a coat and her favorite fur-lined boots. The last thing she wanted was to be this pregnant in a snowstorm, but at least she could stay warm while she got through it.

Bang!

The first gunshot sounded before she'd reached the coat hooks in the narrow rear hall.

Clara's voice erupted from the silence a moment later, calling orders and relaying details. Including a description of the man Maisy had seen in the driveway.

Maisy turned, eyes wide and heart pumping as she realized what was happening. Clara was calling for help. The cottage was under attack. "Clara!"

The next gunshot ended Clara's commands.

Fear rooted Maisy in place, freezing her limbs and turning her mind to mush.

The shots began again, this time coming rapidly. Splitting the woodwork of a nearby archway and tossing bits of drywall into the air.

"Clara!" Maisy cried again, this time with all the strength and volume she could muster.

"Run!" Clara answered, weak and frantic. "Run! You know what to do! Go!"

Maisy turned on autopilot. They'd practiced this a dozen times, weekly at first, maybe more. If the cottage was under attack, the marshal on duty would call for backup and hold down the fort. It was aisy's job to escape. It was her only job in the event of a crisis. *The most important job*, Clara always said. *Because if I die trying to save you, and you're killed anyway, then what was the point?*

Hot tears trailed over Maisy's cheeks, blurring her eyes and stinging her nose as she shoved swollen feet into waiting, unlaced sneakers, swept the go-bag out from beneath the bench at the back door and burst into the frigid windy day, gunshots blazing behind her.

Chapter Two

West Liberty homicide detective Blaze Winchester
dragged his weary, aching body away from the precinct
where he'd turned a seasoned gangbanger over for book-
ing. The number of kills under the banger's belt was
well into double digits, and it felt good to get him off
the streets. It had felt less good, however, chasing him
eleven blocks through a rival gang's territory, and being
sucker punched twice. Blaze's head hurt. His leg muscles burned, and his gut was loudly demanding dinner.
Thankfully, his shift was up and there was beer, a mari-
nating rib eye and a warm bed waiting for him at home.

"Hey, Winchester!" Blaze's younger brother's voice
rang out behind him. "Wait up."

Lucas waved. The youngest detective with the special victims' unit, he'd been riding the highs of a long-
overdue arrest and unexpected reunion with his college
sweetheart for months. It was equally good for him and
annoying.

Blaze wasn't in the mood.

"Where are you headed?" Lucas asked.

"Home."

"Any news on the Luciano case?" He matched his

pace with Blaze as they moved through the lot toward their waiting trucks.

The air seemed to thicken at the sound of Sam Luciano's name, the world going colder and darker. "No." Blaze hadn't heard anything new and nothing official. Everyone who did know anything was infuriatingly tight-lipped on the matter. But the last time he'd checked in with the guards where Luciano awaited trial, they were distinctly on edge. One guard admitted there was new tension among the inmates but couldn't say why. He described a vague but hostile undercurrent he couldn't quite put his finger on, but he was sure the other guards felt it, too. *Something*, he'd said, *like the brewing of a storm.* The guard felt certain that Luciano was the eye of that storm but had no idea what he was up to. Blaze had a guess, and he didn't like it. Luciano knew the prosecution had him dead to rights this time, and he was surely plotting a way to save his sorry behind. There hadn't been any news after that, if he could call it news at all. And the trial was less than two weeks away.

"You want to hit O'Grady's Pub?" Lucas asked. "I heard you had one hell of a day, and it looks like you're getting a shiner. Beer could help."

Blaze grimaced, his cheekbone aching on cue. "No, thanks."

O'Grady's was a place Lucas spent a lot of time in college and still did on occasion. He and his fiancée liked to hang out there—it reminded them of the old days. Neither brother enjoyed the local cop bars, so they met there a couple nights a week. This week, Blaze had too much on his mind to socialize. When he wasn't working, he was preparing mentally for Luciano's trial, where he would take the stand. "I'm grilling and watching the game tonight. You're welcome to tag along if you want to split a rib eye."

Lucas laughed. "Like you'd ever split a rib eye. Anyway, I've got dinner plans. I just wanted to make sure you're okay."

Blaze waved him off. "I'm fine. Tired. Hungry. Fine." He repeated the initial sentiment slowly for emphasis. Then, before Lucas could push, Blaze let the grouchy expression of an older brother being coddled by his younger sibling creep over his face.

Lucas lifted his palms and stepped back, easing in the direction of his vehicle parked several spots away. "You know Gwen has friends if you're ever interested in going out and acting your age again sometime. Nice friends. Redheads, even." He grinned suggestively.

"Good night." Blaze climbed inside his truck and shut the door. The only redhead Blaze wanted to spend time with was locked away in witness protection and probably hadn't given him a second thought since she'd arrived. He turned over the engine and powered down his window, hooking an elbow over the frame. "Tell Gwen I said hello and that I'm sorry I can't go to O'Grady's. Now she's stuck with you all night. I owe her one."

"Funny," Lucas said, climbing into the seat of his own truck and not looking as if he thought it was funny at all. "You know being alone will make you bitter," he hollered.

"Too late." Blaze closed the window and pumped the heat.

Temperatures had been falling all day, and if the sway of the trees and tint of the sky were any indication, the thin drizzle starting now would soon become a storm.

Blaze followed Lucas as far as the highway before honking his goodbye. Lucas took the on-ramp toward the restored historical home he shared with Gwen. Blaze stayed the course, riding the two-lane road out of town, headed for his cabin outside city limits.

He adjusted his wipers as the rain picked up, his mind wandering back to Luciano's trial the way it always did these days. Blaze had made the arrest no one before him had ever been able to achieve, and his career could be made if the trial went his way. If not, he'd have reason to worry. Luciano was smoke, and he controlled the better part of Kentucky's underground—probably a few cops and officials, too. So, if he got out, or even stayed in his current digs, where he might regain some control on the outside, there would be hell to pay for dragging him through this. And Blaze had more than just himself to worry about.

The trial had already been pushed back twice. Not a good sign, and possibly Luciano's doings. There were rumors of threats made against the prosecution and the judge, but no one would say, officially. No one who knew anything about Luciano wanted to be anywhere near that trial. Fear his crime family would retaliate on participants was strong, but it wouldn't stop Blaze from taking the stand. Nothing would. As far as he was concerned, there wasn't a hole deep enough for Luciano, and he'd do anything to help throw him in it.

Blaze hit the defrosters and cranked the heat inside his truck as homes grew smaller and the streetlights more sparse. Slowly, the two-lane road through town became a winding country route with sporadic traffic and an endless tree line.

By the time he hit the long gravel drive to his cabin, Blaze was well past the need for a beer or a steak. Thoughts of Luciano had wound him tight enough to implode, and with no one around to punch or chase, a good night's sleep was probably what he needed most. He could eat tomorrow when his mood improved. For now he was glad to put the day behind him and mentally mark another off his internal countdown to Luciano's trial.

He left his truck in the drive and turned for his steps, pulling the hood of his jacket higher over his head against the pelting rain. Something moved on his porch, and Blaze's body went rigid, his hand straight to his sidearm. If someone planned to keep him from testifying, they'd quickly regret it. "Who's there?" he demanded, widening his stance and ready to draw.

"Blaze?" a small, familiar voice quavered in the shadows. "It's me. I'm sorry. I should have called."

Blaze blinked against the darkness, his heart pinching tight. "Maisy?"

Maisy Daniels had torn into his life late last year like a bullet, ripping past all his walls and pretenses. She'd helped him track down and arrest Luciano for the murder of a friend and her twin sister, then vanished with a band of US Marshals. Taken in for protection until the trial. Luciano had been the catalyst who'd brought Maisy into his life, then the reason she was taken away. And he hated him all the more for the latter.

Blaze flew onto the porch, drawn by shock and the heartbreak in her voice. She was huddled in the corner, arms curled around herself and thick red hair hanging wet and dark against her cheeks. "What happened? What are you doing here?" He scanned the empty space near his truck for signs of another vehicle he'd somehow missed. Sudden fear clenched his heart and lungs. "Where are the marshals?"

"Dead, I think," Maisy whispered, rolling pleading,

tear-filled eyes to meet his. "I didn't know where else to go."

He reached for her, gut wrenching. "Let's get you inside. You're soaked, probably frozen and…" His words were lost as she stretched onto her feet and her distended silhouette registered in his addled mind. "Pregnant?"

MAISY FOUGHT AGAINST the urge to throw herself at Blaze, to thank him in tears and hugs and sobs for not turning her away. She knew, logically, of course, that as the arresting detective for Sam Luciano, Blaze would never turn away a witness who could help the case. But Blaze was so much more than some detective to her, and the intimate physical connection they'd once shared made everything deeply, illogically personal, even now. She forced her chin up as he led her inside.

The small, familiar cabin hadn't changed. She'd loved the open floor plan the first time she'd visited, but after months in a highly compartmentalized safe house, the cabin's layout seemed dangerous. There was nowhere to hide. Only a single bedroom and bathroom at the back of the home had doors to block an intruder's view. The living room, dining room and kitchen were all visible from the welcome mat where she stood.

She took a tentative step forward, marveling at how well the scene before her matched her memories. The ashy evidence of an appreciated fireplace. Piles of paperwork on the desk in the corner. Blaze's cologne woven into the fabric of his furniture, curtains and rugs. It was as if his home had been frozen in time. As if she'd never left.

If only that was true.

Blaze locked the door behind her, checked the window,

then ran a heavy hand through sopping brown hair. The wind had knocked his hood off as he'd run to her, and he hadn't seemed to notice. His long legs had eaten up the space between them. His expression had been fearful, but exuberant. Until she'd stood. And everything had changed. "Let's take care of you first," he said. "Then we'll talk about what's happening. Obviously you weren't followed. If you had been, you wouldn't still be here." He grimaced, then stripped out of his coat, dropping it onto the arm of his couch as he darted through his living room then vanished into the bathroom. "Are you hurt? Sick?" he called, riffling through the linen cabinet.

"No."

He reappeared a moment later with a stack of towels. "Hang on."

He opened the door to his bedroom and hurried inside. Dresser drawers squeaked and thumped in the distance while she shivered on the black-and-white-checkered rug inside his door, trying not to make a puddle on the wide-planked wooden floor. "Okay." Blaze reappeared with a pile of clothing stacked on the towels and extended the offering as he crossed the living area to her. "You probably want a hot shower, but I think we should talk first. I can wait if you want to change. I don't want you to be uncomfortable." His gaze moved pointedly to her middle before jumping back to her eyes.

Too late to avoid being uncomfortable, she thought, cradling her belly in her arms. "Thanks."

"Maybe you should sit."

"First I'll change," she said, accepting the towels and clothing. "I'll only be a minute."

He swept one arm in the general direction she was headed. "Take your time. I'll put on the coffee. Oh. Maisy?"

She paused midstep, her heart beating wildly. Was this the moment he would ask about her baby? About *their* baby?

"Is caffeine okay?" He looked to her middle again. "I mean, you know, for…you?"

Maisy sighed, relieved to put off the inevitable a few moments longer. "Whatever you make is perfect. Thank you."

He nodded, and she hurried away.

Inside the bathroom, Maisy stripped out of her things, soaked to the bone from a long walk in the wind and rain. She hung her shirt and pants over the shower curtain rod to dry. There had been a time, however briefly, when she'd showered in this room as often as her own. Her toothbrush had stood with his on the counter, and she'd even kept a few things in a drawer.

Maisy traced a finger along that drawer, then tugged nosily, wondering if maybe… But no. Apparently some things at Blaze's home had changed after all. The drawer was empty. Nothing inside but her memories, and she wondered for the millionth time if Blaze had thought of her at all while she was gone.

She dried herself with the towels, mopping rain from her hair before sliding into the clothes he'd provided. Elastic-waisted sweatpants, a large T-shirt and hoodie. She tugged white athletic socks over her frozen feet, then gave her flushed face a long, appraising look in the bathroom mirror. The day had been awful, and it showed. Every part of her ached, from her heart to her toes, and now, on this worst day of all, she had to explain her pregnancy to Blaze. She'd hoped that the news would make him happy, but how could this moment ever feel good or right in the shadows of such loss and desperation?

A soft rap on the door startled her back to the moment. "You okay in there?"

She wiped hot tears from her cheeks, then pulled in a steadying breath before opening the door. "Sorry. It's been a tough day."

He nodded, giving her a once-over, then offering a steaming cup. "I decided against coffee."

She batted back another round of tears as she inhaled the familiar scent of chamomile tea. The same tea Clara had made her only hours before. "Thank you."

"I called around while you were changing, but no one's talking about what happened to you today." He stepped aside to let her out of the bathroom. "Luciano's determined to stop this trial. He's been making threats from behind bars, and I'm willing to bet he's moved on to taking action." He turned worried gray-blue eyes on her as they moved toward the kitchen together. "Did you tell anyone about us? About our relationship before?"

"Just Clara," she said, feeling his words like a punch to the gut. Was he embarrassed? Ashamed? "She was the marshal who was with me today." A wedge of grief lodged in her throat, and she had to work to force it away.

He shook his head. "I'm sorry."

Maisy sipped her tea, longing for the warmth of it to erase her bone-deep chill. "We shouldn't tell anyone if no one is talking," she said. "We can't trust the marshals. It was a marshal who attacked today. There's no way to know who can be trusted. If you ask too many questions, someone will figure out I'm with you."

"If they haven't already," he said. "You're sure you never told anyone about us?"

"Only Clara," Maisy repeated, more firmly this time. "Lucas knew about us," she said, biting into her lip and begging the pain in her heart to relocate. She stopped when she tasted blood, then winced.

"Yes, and he's digging into this for me. Quietly. Until he calls back, let's go over everything you can remember. Walk me through your day. Are you hungry?"

"No." Maisy's stomach growled in protest of the lie.

"How do you feel about steak?"

She shrugged, unsure she could manage anything so heavy and hoping the tea would stay down. "Do you have toast?"

"Sure. I'll cook. You talk," he said, pushing up the sleeves on a navy thermal shirt and washing his hands.

Maisy took a seat at Blaze's small kitchen table, then steeled herself to relive the events of her day. She covered it all, from the sweet moments shared with Clara to the marshal's morning phone calls. Two in the time it had taken to have a cup of tea. The arrival of the second marshal. The shooting. And the running.

Maisy had escaped with her go-bag, bare feet stuffed into sneakers, a tunic top and yoga pants only, through icy winds and falling temperatures to the bus stop at Fourth and Walnut. Clara had forced her to memorize the schedules of buses nearest the safe house. "It was already after one when I left," she said, "so I'd missed the bus on Frank by ten minutes. I had to double back and cross the block to Fourth. I used the alley entrance to a dry cleaner's as cover until I saw the bus approaching."

The gunshots had echoed in her ears as she'd run. Police cruisers and emergency vehicles had raced past, responding to Clara's calls. Hoping to save her and arrest the male marshal whose face Maisy would never forget. "I took the local bus to a stop near the Greyhound station, then bought a ticket to Cincinnati," she continued.

"Clara said that if I did that, anyone who was following me would assume I was planning to hide, trying to disappear across state lines. I took taxis from there. A few miles at a time, walking as far as I could in between rides so that even the cabbies wouldn't know where I went once they dropped me off. When I made it back to West Liberty, I got out at the church on Mogadore Road and walked the rest of the way."

Blaze pressed the lever on his toaster, lowering two slices of bread into the heat. "You walked from St. Peter's? I live nearly four miles from there."

"And it took me the rest of the day," she said. Her blistered feet could attest. "I stopped as often as possible to get off my feet and have something to drink."

"Drink?" he said. "Not eat?"

She shook her head. "There was only a little cash left once I'd paid for the buses and cabbies."

Blaze opened the refrigerator and took out a carton of eggs, a bag of shredded cheese and pile of vegetables. "You still like omelets?"

"Yes." Heat rushed to her cheeks as she answered. Several mornings when she'd worn his T-shirt and little else flashed to mind. Just Blaze in pajama bottoms, pushing eggs around a skillet while she did her best to tease and distract him.

She'd held on to those memories tightly during her time at the safe house. The time she'd spent with Blaze had been intense, hot and all-encompassing. A necessary release and distraction when emotions had ruled her life. Grief, shame and guilt over the loss of her sister, who'd been doing a simple favor. Anger, anguish and fear related to Luciano, what he'd done to Natalie and Aaron and what he would do to Maisy if given the chance. She'd knotted all those things up tight and shoved them down deep in order to stay strong and help Blaze locate the psychopath. But they'd leaked out in the forms of need and desire. Her lust for Blaze had created an outlet so emotionally satisfying and physically exhausting that she'd held herself together between the rounds just to get her next hit. Then, before she'd realized, months had passed, Luciano was under arrest and she was on her way to an undisclosed location, where she would await her time to testify. Now, here she was, faced with all the emotions again, and without an outlet. Feeling alone in a room with the man who'd once been her refuge.

Blaze worked efficiently at his counter, making her meal exactly as he used to and checking his phone regularly between chops and stirs. He delivered the toast when it popped up, with a mini tub of butter and a knife, then turned on the evening news.

"Thank you." She bit into the first slice of warm toast before bothering to add butter. Her mouth watered and her stomach groaned in appreciation. She rested a hand over her bump as she felt her baby begin to stir. "This is delicious."

Blaze cocked a brow as the eggs cooked. "It's toast."

The phone rang and he stilled. "It's Lucas." He accepted the call, then flipped the omelet that was slowly filling the small home with heavenly aromas of salty cheese and all the best veggies. Onions. Sweet peppers. Mushrooms.

Maisy finished the first slice of toast and moved quickly to the second.

Blaze spoke in acronyms and painfully short sentences for several seconds before disconnecting the call. He plated the eggs, then made his way to the table, setting one plate before her, keeping the second for himself. "The marshals made the official announcement," he said. "Two units assigned to the protection of a Luciano witness failed to check in. They've alerted local police to the situation and given a physical description of a male marshal, still missing."

"And Clara?" she asked, her stomach turning.

He shook his head. "Eat. You need the fuel." His gaze traveled to her hand, resting on her rounded middle. "And the nutrition."

She squirmed under his scrutiny, trying desperately not to think of Clara, hoping there was a chance she wasn't really gone.

Blaze narrowed his eyes, squinted at Maisy's bump, and she could see him doing the mental math. Working out if the baby could be his, or if she'd somehow gotten involved with another man after leaving town. Maisy nearly laughed.

Blaze lifted his fork. "Lucas is calling back when he knows something more."

"You told him I was here?" she asked, knowing the truth. There were few secrets between the Winchester brothers.

"Yeah." Again his attention lowered to the hand resting on her abdomen.

"And you told him I'm pregnant?"

He gave one short, stiff dip of his chin in answer, then dragged his gaze to meet hers. "You want to tell me about that?" he asked, his expression guarded and mildly hostile. Or maybe that was her projecting.

"I learned I was pregnant about two weeks after I arrived at the safe house."

His furrowed brows relaxed slowly. "Two weeks."

"Yes." She took her time forking a bite of omelet before meeting his eye once more. "At first I didn't realize what was happening. All the grief and guilt and emotion I'd been avoiding hit hard once I had nothing to do but think. Then I got a stomach bug." Her lips twitched as the evening round of in utero kickboxing began.

"Morning sickness," he guessed.

"Yes."

He lowered his fork to his plate. "Is the baby mine?" he asked carefully, voice wary.

"Yes."

Blaze covered his mouth with one big hand, scrubbing it across his lips and cheek before dropping it into his lap. "A boy? Girl?"

Maisy shook her head. "I don't know." She'd forgone the information in favor of waiting for Blaze. He'd already missed so much by the time the baby was old enough to determine the gender, she'd wanted to save something for him to experience with her instead of after the fact. She'd wanted to include him, if he wanted to be included, because she knew it would break her heart if the tables were turned and she was the one finding out at the last minute that she would be a mother and that she'd missed everything leading up to that moment.

"What are you waiting for?" he asked.

"You." The word was barely more than a whisper on her tongue. Her eyes stung with the truth and vulnerability in that single word.

Their gazes locked for one brief moment, the way they had so many times before.

"Why didn't you tell me?" he asked, looking crestfallen. And sounding a little angry.

Maisy recoiled. "How could I?" She searched his expression for a hint on how to proceed. Was he truly upset? With the news? With her? The prospect unnerved her further, and her spine straightened. "I wasn't allowed to use a phone. I couldn't leave the house for days. I've spent the last six months in a one-thousand-square-foot home, under constant guard of strangers. I looked forward to the doctor appointments just so I could get out, see and talk to people who weren't bound by their job and an oath to protect me. It's not as if I've been living it up. Laughing about the big secret I was keeping. I was isolated, Blaze, and you know it. You're the one who sent me there."

His jaw clenched. "I made the arrangements to keep you safe."

"Yeah?" she laughed humorlessly, pushing away from the table. "How did that work out?"

Maisy walked away as calmly as she could manage while fighting a scream and possibly more tears. Back to the bathroom where she could close the door and press her hands against her ears, where Clara's voice still rang. *If I die trying to save you, and you're killed anyway, then what was the point?*

It was a good question, because Maisy couldn't see the point in any of this.

Chapter Three

Blaze watched Maisy walk away, his heart pounding and thoughts racing. Aside from the shocking realization that she was in serious danger again, maybe even more danger than when she left town to start with, now she was pregnant. With his baby.

His head spun as the bathroom door snapped shut behind her, and he let his head fall forward into waiting palms. A torrent of frustration and curses poured from his lips. No surprise she'd taken his anger personally. He could barely put two coherent thoughts together, let alone a decent encouraging sentence. Was that what she needed? Encouragement?

He raised his head with a groan. How could he possibly know what Maisy needed beyond protection? They'd been apart longer than they'd ever been together. And the fact that she'd gone through this much of her pregnancy alone, displaced, afraid, and now with a lunatic gunning for her all over again. *Not just her*, he thought, *them. Maisy and our baby.* His hands curled into fists at the final thought. And the curses started once more.

Why hadn't the marshals in charge of her contacted him about the baby? How had they watched her, with his child growing inside her, and not found a way to pass the message along? He was a detective, for crying out loud. He understood the stakes and the system. He wouldn't have done anything to give away her position or put her in harm's way. He'd do anything to protect her. *Them*, he corrected himself with the shake of his head. Sure, he would've wanted to pass a message back to her. Tell her he was happy and that she shouldn't be afraid. He might've tried to arrange a call to be sure she knew he meant it, or a visit…

Maybe they were right to keep him in the dark. Because how could he have sat idly by when he wanted to write in stone that he was all in for his kid? No matter what happened between him and Maisy.

The sound of running water drew his attention back to the bathroom, where it seemed Maisy had taken him up on the offer of a hot shower. Good. She needed time to warm up and unwind. He needed time to cool down and make a plan.

Soapy scents of his cheap, drugstore shampoo crept under the door as he began to pace. It was easier to think when he was in motion. Maisy would hate the subpar, nearly empty selection of bath products jammed into the caddy. He'd packed up her things months ago, hating the way remnants of the fruity, floral soaps and lotions seemed to linger. For weeks, she'd been everywhere he looked, and he couldn't stand it when she wasn't. So, he'd packed her up, memories, toiletries and all. And put it all in a box, out of sight and out of mind, where he wasn't tempted to dwell on things he couldn't change.

It had been stupid and unprofessional of him to get involved with a witness. He knew it then, and he knew it now, but there had always been something about that woman. Something that had tangled his thoughts, then his body, with hers so easily and intensely. Something he could never put a name to. Then she was gone. He'd never felt that way before or since. And darn if that same whatever it was wasn't back full force at the sight of her. It wasn't right, or fair, that all his wishes to see her one more time had been granted by a cruel twist of fate. Wasn't fair that Maisy was back, but she was in danger.

And probably naked in his shower.

The idea of her new, fuller silhouette looming behind his shower curtain flashed into his imagination, and his jaw dropped.

He dialed Lucas.

"Hey," his brother answered before the first ring had finished, as if he'd already had the phone in his hands. "I was just about to call you. The word is officially out on Maisy. Marshals contacted the precinct. You'll be getting a call any minute. Sergeant Maxwell's freaking out. Luciano's conviction was supposed to be a gold star on his career right along with yours."

Blaze paused to consider that. "It's not over yet. We'll still get Luciano. What do you think happened to get the marshals talking?" Surely they hadn't simply changed their minds on sharing the fact one of their own attacked a safe house today.

"I don't know, but Blaze," Lucas began, hesitant. "Is the baby yours?"

His mind snapped back to the moment, torn between all-encompassing fear and elation. "Yeah." He cleared his throat against the strange thickness and marveled briefly at the way his chest filled with pride.

"Congratulations, big brother," Lucas said. "How's that going so far?"

Blaze flicked his attention to the closed bathroom door. "Not great."

His phone buzzed with an incoming call, and he checked the number on the screen. "That's Maxwell. I've got to go." He disconnected with Lucas, shifting easily between the calls and noting the shower had stopped in the background. "Winchester."

"I've got some tough news on the Luciano case," Sergeant Maxwell began, skipping the customary greeting and unnecessary introduction. "The witness you moved into protection this spring is missing, along with the US marshal assigned to assist in her transportation. Another marshal, who we believe was protecting her at the time of the disappearance, was fatally wounded."

Blaze returned to pacing. "You're sure the protective marshal is dead?" he asked, deciding how much of what he knew to tell his sergeant.

"Yes," Maxwell answered. "Marshal Clara Spencer suffered multiple gunshot wounds to the chest and torso. She was already gone when backup arrived. We're hoping the other marshal was able to get Miss Daniels to safety, but considering it's been hours since he last checked in, no one is holding out a lot of hope."

Blaze slowed his orbit around the kitchen table. "You think the transporting marshal saved the witness from the shooter?"

"It's the best-case scenario," Maxwell said, his voice low and unsure. "So, that's what we're hoping. I'll keep you posted."

"Great." Blaze pressed the palm of one hand to his forehead. "I'd appreciate that."

"I know your shift just ended, but I want you doing whatever you can to stay on top of this. We can't let this case fall apart. So let's be proactive. Find out where Miss Daniels might go or who she might talk to if she's separated from the marshal. The trial's coming up fast, and we're down two witnesses. You need to get Daniels back into protective custody."

Blaze ground his teeth. "Protective custody didn't work so well earlier today. How do we know she'll be safe if we go that route again?"

The bathroom door opened, and Maisy stepped out. The mirror was steamed behind her. She'd redressed in his clothes, filling out the tops in the center now, sleeves hanging low over her small hands and baggy sweatpants bunched up at the ankles of her short legs. Her skin was flushed from the warmth of the water. Her hair damp and wild.

"I don't know, Winchester," he bellowed. "But I've got protocols to follow, and so do you. So start working every angle."

Blaze lifted a finger to his lips when he caught Maisy's eye, suddenly certain of how much he wanted to share with Maxwell.

Nothing. Not yet.

"Sergeant?" Something the older man had said returned to Blaze with a snap, and he felt his brows pulling low. "Did you say we're down to two witnesses?" He hoped he'd misunderstood. The prosecution's case relied on the presence and credibility of their witnesses. "There were four." Losing two would be devastating.

Blaze watched as the beautiful redhead drifted closer to him, fearful for new reasons now. Losing more than one witness meant something bigger than he'd imagined was afoot, and that was no good for Maisy.

She stopped moving. Tension stiffened her posture, and fear flashed in her eyes.

"That's the other update we were given," Maxwell said. "William Hanes was found dead in his SUV this morning. Outside his office in Louisville. Hanes was an informant from Luciano's batch of thugs. No one was supposed to know he was turning on him at trial."

Blaze felt his muscles lock. This was more than Luciano becoming privy to Maisy's location and taking a chance to silence her. This was a multitiered attack. "Luciano's eliminating the witnesses."

MAISY LOWERED HERSELF onto Blaze's worn-out sofa and pulled the quilt off the back, a gift, she remembered, from his mother. "Luciano's killing witnesses," she said, raising her eyes to Blaze as he moved into the living room, having ended his call.

He took a seat at her side. "It appears that way."

Her arms went around her middle on instinct, and she told herself to breathe.

"According to my sergeant, the local marshals think the man who came to transport you might've taken you away with him for your protection."

"What?" Maisy's jaw sank open. "If that guy saved me, then who do they think was the shooter?"

Blaze lifted his shoulder slightly, lips pursed. "Didn't say."

Anger rushed in Maisy's veins. "That guy's not a hero. He's a killer."

Blaze's knee began to bob, and he kneaded his hands on his lap. His gray-blue eyes were soft and compassionate when he turned to her. "I asked about your friend Clara."

"She didn't make it," Maisy guessed, reading the grim expression on his brow.

"I'm sorry. No."

The introductory notes of a special report interrupted the evening news, and Maisy and Blaze turned to it in unison. "This just in," an anchor proclaimed from his position on the courthouse steps. Behind him, an enormous American flag waved in the wind and rain.

Maisy's pulse thumped between her ears as the reporter recounted details of the Luciano case. And she cringed as he relayed facts from her nightmarish day. Tears welled as Clara's death was announced, matter-of-factly, and backdropped by a photo of her with her family.

"Maisy," Blaze said softly, the sound of her name on his lips spilling goose pimples over her flesh. "Are you okay?"

She nodded quickly, fighting tears. The concern in his voice nearly broke her, but she'd already lost too many hours to grief today.

Now it was time to be strong. She'd assumed earlier that if the safe house ever came under siege, she'd be helpless. But she'd proven herself wrong. She'd run. Executed the plan the marshals had put in place. Though, she'd improvised at the end, seeking Blaze's protection instead of calling the local marshals' office as she'd been taught. After a marshal had killed Clara, Blaze was the only person she knew she could trust. Still, Maisy had saved herself and her baby. She would keep being strong and help Blaze make sure Luciano was punished for the lives he'd taken. The crime boss probably thought he was saving himself with this sudden strike of aggression, but in reality, he was digging his own grave. Or supermax jail cell, as it may be.

"You don't have to testify, you know," Blaze said. "No one would blame you if you decided not to. You have a baby to think about now, someone else to put first. And seeing Luciano punished isn't worth risking your life. Or the life of your baby."

Maisy smoothed the soft material of his hoodie over the curve of her middle, inhaling the scent of him and trying not to scream. "I'm absolutely testifying," she said, forcing her shoulders back and her frustrations down. "I owe it to Natalie. To Aaron. To Clara. And to all the other people whose lives were taken because of Luciano." And she owed it to all the people who'd eventually become his victim if he wasn't locked away for good. "You said the prosecution is down a witness. That leaves me and two others, and it means my testimony is more important than ever now."

His jaw clenched. "And what about the baby?"

"What about the baby?" She bristled. "I'm doing this for the baby. Because what kind of mother would I be if I didn't do the right thing now, when it matters the most? And lives are on the line?"

"You'd be the kind of mother who's alive to raise her baby," he said. "One who has a child to raise because she kept them both out of harm's way."

Her blood boiled at the suggestion. And at the words *her baby*. Hers. Not his. "Don't you dare do that," she snapped. "Don't make me out to be selfish or careless. I'm not either of those things. And what about you, Detective Winchester? Are you out of harm's way? Or is your life on the line every day that you get up and put on that badge?" She crossed her arms and narrowed her eyes. "What kind of father does that make you?"

"I'm not pregnant," he snapped.

"And I'm not helpless. The least I can do is show up at court, like I promised, and tell Natalie's story. In fact, that's the one and only thing I can do to get justice for my sister. And I'm sure as heck going to do it. With or without your help."

His expression soured, then ran the gamut of emotions, from suppressed outrage to something resembling compassion, before going flat. Settling on the blank cop expression she hated.

"A marshal came into my safe house and killed my friend," she went on, sternly, determined to make him see things her way. "Luciano knows who I am and that I planned to testify. He won't stop coming for me if I promise not to. I made his list, which means I'm in danger until his hands are permanently tied. I don't know who I can trust, and I don't know who will help me if you won't, but I'll still try because I have to."

The forgotten newscast returned from a commercial, and the anchor, still poised on the courthouse steps, said her name. A photo of Maisy lodged in the bottom right corner of the screen.

Blaze cursed. He fished the remote from a basket on the table and pumped up the volume. "Looks like news travels fast."

"West Liberty local Maisy Daniels," the reporter continued, "set to testify in the Sam Luciano trial late next week, has allegedly gone missing from her safe house. Daniels was scheduled to return to town today for preparation with the prosecution, but neither she nor the US marshal assigned to her have reported to their destination."

A second photo appeared on screen, taking up residence in the opposite corner. "Gene Franco, a longtime member of the US Marshals service and local resident, was sent to collect Miss Daniels," the reporter explained. The smiling man in the photo wore an official uniform jacket and hat. Happy eyes stared joyously into the camera, a striking jolt of blue against the backdrop of ivory skin and a mass of white hair. Clean shaven with a full, round face, this man could've been anyone's dad or grandpa, maybe a neighbor or friend, but he definitely wasn't the one who'd come to her safe house. "That's not him," Maisy whispered, confusion circling in her chest.

"What?" Blaze's bouncy knee stilled. "What do you mean?"

"I mean that's not the man who came for me." She swung a pointed finger toward the screen. "It wasn't him."

Blaze stretched onto his feet, rubbing a hand over his mouth, then locking the open palm onto his hip. "So this guy isn't corrupt."

"I don't know about that, but he's definitely not the man who shot Clara." Maisy stared back at the jolly-looking man in the photo, suddenly saddened by what his disappearance likely meant for him. "And he's probably dead."

Blaze laced his fingers on top of his head. "If we don't have a murderous marshal on our hands, we're probably dealing with a hired gun."

"A hit man?" Maisy squeaked. Were those even real? Criminals, yes. Corrupt lawmen, sure. But hit men?

"Maybe," he said. "Luciano's facing life in the supermax, and it looks like he's pulling out all the stops to make sure that doesn't happen."

Chapter Four

Maisy woke to the scents of eggs and bacon. She curled and stretched beneath the thick down comforter, content and utterly at peace. For one blissful moment, before opening her eyes, she was back at the safe house, counting the last few days before she would return to West Liberty and give testimony that would finally put Sam Luciano in prison. Her dreams of pending freedom and safety, for her and for her baby, grew with each new breath. She could almost hear her dear friend Clara humming in the kitchen.

Clara.

Maisy's heart kicked and reality snapped her eyes wide. The familiar ache of grief wedged in her throat and weighted her chest. She wasn't at the safe house, and Clara would never again make breakfast. Not for Maisy, and not for the family she'd left behind. A too-big sacrifice made in the name of protecting Maisy and her baby.

Tears blurred her vision as the wave of emotion crashed over her. Another woman was dead because of Maisy. First Natalie. Now Clara. And the gaping holes left by their absences were too much to bear.

She pressed her face into the pillow, willing back the breakdown that had been looming since she'd opened the safe house door and run. Since she'd left Clara behind, Maisy owed Clara's family everything for their loss, but how could she even begin to repay that debt? She released the pillow on a long, shuddering breath. Maisy would have to carry this grief with her, like the rest, because there would be no amends for the devastation she'd caused. She'd just have to make sure her shoulders were strong enough to carry the burden.

Her heart ached as she swung her feet over the bed's edge and onto the floor. She couldn't rewind time, and she could never thank Clara's family properly or enough. But she could make sure her sacrifice meant something. She could follow through with her testimony and see Luciano punished.

She could stop him from taking more lives.

Her stomach grumbled in response to the savory-scented breakfast down the hall, and she forced herself upright. Then shuffled into Blaze's bathroom to prepare for the day, whatever it would bring. She'd slept deeply for the first time in months, thanks to the emotional stress of a narrow escape and the physical exertion of many miles walked. The haystack masquerading as her hair and sheet marks pressed into her cheeks confirmed it. She looked longingly at the shower, dreaming of the hot water against her skin, but her baby had other plans, twisting and kicking in a rhythm that could only be interpreted as a plea for bacon.

She brushed her teeth and hair, warmed by the fact Blaze had kept her old things after all, then followed the scents of breakfast to the kitchen. Her steps faltered when her abdomen tightened and the ache of a false contraction rippled over her. She leaned against the wall and rubbed her bump, breathing slowly through the dull pain. Braxton-Hicks contractions were the newest in a long line of bizarre things her body had done these last few months, each meant to accommodate and one day deliver her baby. "I know you're excited to get out here and meet me," she whispered, catching her breath and soothing her infant, "but I need you to wait until this trial is over." It was a conversation she'd been having more and more. "You're going to be just fine where you are until then, okay? Don't rush."

Eager as she was to finally see and kiss her baby's perfect cherub face, she really didn't want to give her testimony from a delivery room. Though she suspected a hospital gown might be the only thing that would fit her if she got any bigger.

Still, a hospital wasn't safe. Nowhere was. Not if Luciano had gotten to her at a federal safe house. Going into labor before the trial would mean becoming a sitting duck. An immobile target. Easy pickings. And if she survived long enough to safely deliver her baby, then be released, she'd be on the run with a newborn, and that was her personal nightmare.

She peeled herself off the wall and went to greet Blaze.

"Morning," she said, taking a moment to savor the perfection of him at the stove, a fitted heather-gray T-shirt and low-slung jeans clinging in all the right places. His hair was damp and mussed from a shower. His feet were bare. And that smile when he saw her sent her heart into an erratic sprint.

"Hey." He flipped off the stove's burners, then let his gaze slide over her. "Hungry?"

She nodded, hoping he couldn't read her mind. The food smelled amazing, but her body was suddenly craving more than breakfast.

"Have a seat. It's ready," he said, plating the meal onto matching dishes, then delivering them to the table. "Tea or water?"

"Tea?" she asked, scanning the stove for signs of a kettle.

Blaze delivered a pot and mug with tea bag. "Hot and ready when you are."

Heat rushed across her cheeks, and she couldn't stop a little grin from curling her lips. "Ready. Thanks." Her tummy fluttered with the pleasure of his attention. She poured a cup, trying uselessly to concentrate on anything besides the memories of just how attentive Blaze could be.

"Sleep well?" he asked, joining her at the table.

Her mind raced with faded images of him. Memories from another life, when he'd lavished her with his undivided attention and unhurried time. Their bodies tangled and sliding together beneath his sheets.

"What are you thinking about?" he asked.

Maisy paused her chewing, cheeks flashing hot once more. She took her time before answering. First sipping, then swallowing her tea. "Everything's delicious," she said. "I dropped into your lap yesterday, on the run from a psychopath and carrying your child. And you're handling it all with complete Zen."

"Maybe I have you fooled," he said, flashing a brief, but brilliant smile. "Maybe breakfast is just a ploy for your time and information."

She shook her head slowly. "You always made me breakfast."

His head tipped slightly over one shoulder, and his gaze darted to her mouth. "I've always wanted your time."

Maisy didn't bother to hide her smile. "Okay. So, what can I do for you?"

He pulled his eyes back to meet hers. "When are you due?"

"Ah." She sipped her tea, pleased he was interested in the baby. Terrified he wasn't happy about it. He hadn't really said one way or another. "Six weeks. Give or take."

His eyes widened momentarily, then dropped to her middle before returning to meet hers. "That's soon. When did you find out and how?"

"A couple weeks after I got to the safe house. I'd been sick. I mentioned that last night."

He nodded. "I remember. Tell me more."

She squared her shoulders and settled her hands on the bump. "I assumed all my symptoms were stress related. It was a tough time for me. Fatigue, lack of appetite, heightened emotions." She shook her head. "Even when I realized I was late for my cycle, I dismissed it as stress related. It was another week or two before I was willing to face the fact I could be pregnant. We'd been so careful." She shivered at a flash of them together, joined by hearts and bodies. She'd been falling in love. Fast, deep and powerless to stop it. "I had to ask one of the marshals to buy a home test kit for me. That was humiliating, because they all knew my previous few months were spent trying to find Luciano, and always with you, the detective assigned to my twin's murder case." The words soured on her tongue, turning her stomach, hating the reminder Natalie was gone. "I knew they'd assumed I was either easy or stupid, because getting involved with you was…"

"Stupid?" he asked, voice and eyes hard.

"Frowned upon," she continued. "But I needed to know if I was pregnant more than I could afford to care what the marshals thought. Clara was the only one of my armed guards unafraid of making the purchase. She waited outside the bathroom door while I went in to see the results, and she held me up every step of the way afterward."

Blaze worked his jaw, eyes tight. "I'm glad you had someone there for you."

"Me, too."

"Have you had any issues with the pregnancy? Are you getting good prenatal care?" he asked.

Maisy nodded. "The best. I've got an OB in Myersville who's amazing. She understands my situation fully and has been a blessing to me and to our baby."

Blaze's pressed lips parted, and he pulled in a little breath.

Maisy gave herself a big mental push, then forged ahead with the speech she'd practiced a thousand times in her head, in the shower, in her sleep. "I know this is strange for you. I remember how shocked I was when I found out about the pregnancy, but I've had months to get my head around it, and since it's happening inside my body, I've had a constant reminder. But this has been completely sprung on you. I knew the minute I saw the little pink plus sign that I wanted to have this child. It's okay if you don't. You should take as long as you want to decide. I don't expect anything from you. And I'm fully prepared to raise our baby on my own, if that's what you choose. Though I could definitely use your help staying alive until Luciano is in prison," she improvised.

No matter how many times she'd planned to tell Blaze he could choose his level of involvement, none of those scenarios happened while she was on the run. "I can walk away after that, if you'd like," she continued, "but even then, my door will always be open for your visits, if you change your mind. Because, bottom line, Blaze. This is your baby, too. He or she is as much a part of you as me, and while I want our child to know you, and see what an amazing man you are, that will be up to you." She exhaled deeply, satisfied to have said the bulk of what she'd planned, if not quite as eloquently as she'd hoped.

Blaze blinked, then rubbed a heavy hand over his face.

"But those are conversations for another time," she said, pressing on. "Right now, we should probably figure out who's trying to kill me, and shut that down, so I make it to the trial."

BLAZE STARED ACROSS the table, mind reeling. He'd waited months to see Maisy's face again. Dreamed of it. Longed for it. But he'd never imagined she'd be pregnant when that day came. And now that she was, how could she consider for a second that he wouldn't take 100 percent responsibility for his child? Did she really think he wouldn't be all in for his kid? Did she not understand him at all?

He ground his teeth, keeping the emotions in check. She was right about one thing. They could talk about this later, after he was sure she and his baby were safe. The threat against them was real and present. They had the rest of their—hopefully long—lives to celebrate the unexpected gift. Right now, he needed a plan.

Maisy raised an eyebrow. "You doing okay over there?"

"Never better."

She laughed, and his chest tightened. Maisy was just so damn beautiful. He'd forgotten the extent of it. Thick red hair, luminous hazel eyes. Porcelain skin and full pink lips. She'd stolen his breath at first sight, but he'd quickly learned not to let her beauty fool him. Maisy was smart, fast on her feet and fierce. She'd been formidable and single-minded in her quest to help locate Luciano all those months ago, and none of that had changed. The expression *whiskey in a teacup* had always come to mind when he thought of her. Sheer tenacity. Hell or high water. Packed in an incredibly distracting disguise. Even sitting here, in her last trimester of an unexpected pregnancy, with others being killed around her, she was still determined to see the criminal punished. Maisy would do whatever it took to honor the lives Luciano stole. There wasn't likely any stopping her, so he got on board.

"I've been thinking about the missing marshal," she said, as if on cue. "I saw the man who shot Clara. I think you should take me to the station and let me work with a sketch artist to get his image down. Then at least you'll know who you're looking for."

Blaze nodded. "I can use the image to find out if he's actually a marshal." Whoever the shooter was, he belonged behind bars, but if he was a US marshal, things would get a lot worse for Maisy fast. Marshals had access to files and details a typical criminal wouldn't, no matter how networked he or she was. And a marshal had something even more dangerous—the trust of other lawmen.

"Right," Maisy agreed. "Once we get a name to go with the face, we can track him down and stop him before he hurts any more witnesses."

Blaze leaned forward, pressing his forearms to the table and leveling her with his most intimidating expression. "Why don't we compromise," he suggested. "You describe him to me, then I'll meet with the sketch artist. The best thing you can do right now is lie low and let me handle this." He laced each word with heavy caution. A tone that had scared more than a few local thugs and gangsters. A tone he hoped would convey the importance of her going along with his request.

Maisy curled a thin, protective arm over her rounded middle, hazel eyes flashing in response. "Not a chance."

Chapter Five

Blaze dialed Sergeant Maxwell while Maisy cleaned up after breakfast. She'd insisted on splitting the duties. He'd made the meal, so she'd cleared the table, then refused his help washing dishes.

The call connected, and Blaze cleared his throat before leaving a message. "Hey, Sarge," he began, watching Maisy from across the room. "This is Blaze. I'm working in the field this morning, trying to make some progress on that task you gave me last night. Nothing so far, but I've got a few ideas I hope will pan out. I'll check in as information becomes available. I've got my phone on me if you need to reach me, or if you learn anything new I can work with." He disconnected, then ran a hand through his hair, hoping to hell his sergeant would recognize Blaze's intentional lack of details as a need to speak in person.

Maisy looked over her shoulder as she set the final plate into the drying rack. "That was a pointedly vague message."

"I can't be sure who's listening." Blaze tucked the phone into his pocket. "Sergeant Maxwell asked me to find you and figure out what happened. He knows that will take time, so we've got some leeway to work with.

He won't expect to see me around the office for a day or two."

"But I want to go in," she said, turning her back to the sink, and fixing her full attention on Blaze. "I want to talk with a sketch artist."

Blaze grinned at the wet line across her abdomen.

"Don't laugh," she said, curving loving arms around her bump and hiding the wet spot. "It's not as easy to reach things as it used to be. I practically have to climb onto the counter just to turn on the faucet."

He shook his head. "Don't move. I'll be right back." He strode into his laundry area, amused, among other things, by Maisy's growing middle. He pulled her clothes from the dryer and shook the pieces out.

"What are you doing?" she asked.

He turned slowly to smile at her. He hadn't heard her following him, though he should have expected as much. "You're stealthy."

"For someone my size?" she asked, curling thin fingers over newly rounded hips.

"Just stealthy," he corrected. "For anyone."

"Smart answer," she teased. "But, really, what are you doing? We were talking."

Blaze handed her the outfit. "I found these in my bathroom and washed them. I thought you'd want your own clothes to go out in today."

Maisy stared at the maternity shirt, pants and underthings she'd arrived in. A pretty blush spread across her ivory skin. "You washed my clothes?"

"I assumed you wouldn't want to go anywhere in my sweatpants and hoodie."

She accepted the offering, and Blaze stuffed his fingers into his jeans pockets. "Thank you."

"You're welcome."

Maisy nodded, eyes glistening with emotion as she raised the outfit to her nose and inhaled. "Care if I hit the shower?"

"Go for it."

"Then we'll go see the sketch artist?" she asked.

He laughed. There was no sidetracking her. That hadn't changed. "I need to make a few calls to coordinate your visit, but once I know I can keep you safe there, we'll go."

"Okay," Maisy agreed. "Thank you." She turned to leave, and Blaze caught her elbow.

"Hey." A jolt of electricity shot through him as their nearness registered, stirring emotions he thought he'd tucked neatly away. "One more thing before you shower. I have something on my desk I think you should keep." He stepped into the hall, releasing her when he wanted to pull her against him.

Maisy followed silently across the open space outside the laundry room.

He lifted the department-issued Taser and held it between them. "I pulled it from my gun safe this morning. It's charged and ready. I want you to keep it on you at all times."

She reached for the device tentatively. "You want me to use a Taser on someone?"

"Yes." He nodded, widening his stance and crossing his arms. "And I want you to respond immediately. Don't waste time thinking. Trust your instincts, release the safety, here, then press the trigger. Here." He pointed to each feature as he spoke. "Feel threatened? Pull trigger. Got it? I don't even care if you accidentally tase a harmless citizen. I'll make the necessary apologies later."

He put his hand over hers and fixed her with a pointed stare. "I'd rather you zap a dozen innocent men than hesitate and not zap a killer."

Maisy raised her brows. "I'm not sure how I feel about all that, but I promise to act in the spirit of your request."

"I accept. But I meant what I said. Better safe than sorry."

She rolled her eyes. "Sure. As long as you're not one of the innocent people I zap."

He frowned. "Should we give it a practice run?"

"I think I've got it. Now, I'll take a shower so we can get started on this day and hopefully figure out where the man who killed Clara is now. He's our link to Luciano."

Blaze's gaze lowered to Maisy's distracting new curves at the mention of her in the shower.

"Call the sketch artist," she said, then disappeared with her clothes and the Taser.

Blaze took a moment to enjoy the sweet tension in his muscles as she walked away. He couldn't be sure what Maisy thought of her new figure, but the fact she carried his baby was unequivocally the hottest thing he'd ever known.

He gave a soft whistle, then liberated his phone and dialed Sarah at the station.

When Maisy emerged from the bathroom, she looked like something off a billboard. Her tousled, towel-dried hair hung down her back in auburn waves. Her skin was pink from the steamy shower, and her lips shone with what he guessed to be a layer of her old lip gloss. One he was intimately familiar with. One that tasted like his best memories.

"Did you make the appointment?" she asked.

"Four o'clock," he said. "She normally leaves at three,

but she was booked all day, and I didn't want to wait until tomorrow. I told her this was a special circumstance situation, and that I needed her to keep the appointment under wraps. She agreed and fit us in at the end of the day."

Maisy tugged the hem of her tunic top. "Thank you. For everything."

"Whatever you need," he said, flashing a wicked smile. "West Liberty's finest. At your service."

"I hoped you'd say that."

Blaze mentally skated backward over his words, half-afraid to ask. "Why?"

"I appreciate you washing my clothes, but I can't keep wearing this same outfit every day," she said. "I need the rest of my things from the safe house. I thought we could make a trip over there today. Now we have time before seeing the sketch artist."

Blaze checked his watch, then gave Maisy and her rounded middle a long look. "The house is probably sealed as a crime scene," he said, working through the possibility of liberating her wardrobe. "If the house wasn't fully processed yesterday, we could run into a forensics team. And even if the place is empty, and we can get in, Luciano could have someone watching. Either for your return, or to pick up leads from visiting law enforcement."

She chewed her lip, easily drawing his attention there. "I had to leave everything when I ran. It'd be really nice to have more of my things. My mom's book is still there. Photographs of Natalie and me."

Blaze teetered, weighing the options. The maternity clothes were something he could replace. Her personal keepsakes were not. He sighed, recognizing defeat as it registered. Protecting and pleasing Maisy didn't always line up, and this was a prime example of one of those times. But he knew what her mother's book meant to her. Her sister had unintentionally died retrieving it. Losing the treasure to Luciano now seemed wrong. "I'll agree to a drive-by only. If we see any activity at the house or anyone loitering in a car nearby, we leave."

"Deal."

MAISY CLIMBED INTO Blaze's truck, wearing his gray hooded sweatshirt and black motorcycle jacket over her maternity shirt. Every strand of her long hair was tucked carefully inside a ball cap.

"Ready?" he asked, grinning as she grappled with her seat belt.

It wasn't easy to fit the safety measure below her bump and across her hips where it belonged, or guide it properly across her chest these days. The bulky layered coats didn't help. "Stop smiling," she said, laughing at the ridiculousness of her shape and seat belt predicament.

A sharp pain stilled her hands and twisted her expression into a grimace. She fastened the seat belt, then rubbed the alien-looking bulge on her abdomen. A tiny elbow, knee or foot had rammed against her ribs, temporarily stealing her breath.

"What's wrong?" Blaze asked, panic flashing in his dark eyes.

She exhaled as the infant moved again. "It's okay. The baby is running out of room and likes to use my organs as a trampoline park."

Blaze cringed, then started the truck with a nervous laugh. "Maybe it's better that I haven't been around. I'd probably have raced you to the hospital a dozen times by now."

Maisy watched as he shifted into gear and headed down the driveway. "It's not better," she said softly. She would've gladly made those unnecessary trips if it'd meant having him around.

Pleasure twinkled in his eyes as they turned onto the road.

"I was afraid, too, at first," she said, dragging her gaze back to the road. "Dr. Nazir has been great. She gave me her personal number, and I called her a lot those first few months." Maisy chuckled. "I was terrified something would go wrong, but she told me which symptoms to watch out for and what was considered normal. She advised on everything from diet and exercise to sleep positions and my birth plan. Basically, she's held my hand every step of the way. Clara, too. Clara has kids of her own, so she…" Maisy froze. "Had," she corrected. "Clara had kids of her own." But now those kids were orphans so Maisy's baby wouldn't be.

"Hey." Blaze set a broad palm over her hand on the seat between them. "This isn't your fault. None of it. We've talked about this. Remember?"

She tried to force a smile but failed. Blaze had spent countless moments in the months she'd shared with him assuring her the only person to blame was Luciano. On the whole, she knew it was true, but deep down, she couldn't help acknowledging that Natalie and Clara would be alive if it wasn't for her. So, maybe Aaron's death was all on Luciano, but Maisy's sister and her assigned marshal were only in his path because of her.

Blaze stole glances at her as he drove, maybe waiting for her to respond, but she couldn't. "I'm sorry I've missed your pregnancy," he said, flicking his gaze briefly to her bump. "I would've been there. Every step. If I could've."

She smiled, a genuine feeling of warmth spreading through her. "I know."

She'd prepared herself for the worst when she told him he could walk away last night, but it would've surprised her if he had. Family meant everything to the Winchesters, especially Blaze. That's just who he was. Whether or not he still wanted her was another story, but they had bigger things to figure out first. Like where Clara's killer went, and if he knew Maisy was with Blaze. As for a future with the father of her child, Maisy didn't expect him to want that. Their romance had been based on heightened emotions and circumstances. And any foundation built on sex, especially when she was currently the size of a barn, was sure to collapse.

"Have you heard the baby's heartbeat?" Blaze asked, drawing her attention back to the moment.

"Sure. At every visit for the last few months." She chewed her lip, collecting her nerve. "I see Dr. Nazir every two weeks now. My next appointment is in a few days. If you'd like to come, you can stay with me during the exam." Maisy had talked to the doctor about Blaze an embarrassing amount, but she could hardly help herself. Blaze had come to represent her old life, her freedom and a time when she'd never felt more cherished. "I know she'd like to meet you."

His lips parted, and his eyes widened. "Yes. Please. I'd like that. Very much."

"Okay." She nodded, fighting a too-broad smile. "Good, but you should probably lower your expectations. The appointments aren't as exciting as you might think."

"I doubt that." Blaze squeezed her hand. "Thank you."

The drive to the next county passed in a mix of electric energy and companionable silence. The butterflies in Maisy's stomach gave her acrobatic baby some real competition for room and overall flutters.

The turn onto her old street, and the appearance of her temporary home erased all the good feelings in the space of a heartbeat.

Her eyes stung with grief and heartbreak.

Blaze released her hand, curling long, steady fingers around the steering wheel instead. "Let's make another pass or two before we stop."

She stared in silence as they rolled past the familiar driveway. The small white cottage with its pale blue shutters and cheery yellow door twisted her heart painfully. She imagined Clara planting perennials in the spring. Beautiful things to look forward to, she'd claimed. Because everyone needed those. She'd been sure the symbolism matched perfectly with Maisy's situation. She only had to plant some seeds of hope and dream of new beginnings. When she emerged from protective custody, the worst would be behind her. She'd have a new baby and a beautiful new beginning.

Oxygen seemed to rush from her lungs as an onslaught of uglier, more recent memories overtook her. Too raw and too recent to manage.

Blaze eased his truck into the driveway several minutes later, then settled the engine. "You okay?"

"Nervous," she admitted, casting a quick glance his way. "The last time I was here, someone came to kill me."

Blaze scanned the scene beyond the window. "Well, let's get in and out. No reason to hang around in case that guy comes back."

She blew out a steady breath, then reached for her door handle.

"At least the shooter didn't get a look at you. The image shared on the news was from last year. Your hair was shorter and straightened in the photo. You had bangs, and you weren't pregnant."

"Well, thank you for this shapely disguise," she said, setting her hands on the enormous bump with an awkward smile. "Honestly, I barely recognize myself half the time, so I guess you're right. It would be hard to pick me out from an old photo."

Blaze nodded, then climbed down from the cab, his blank cop expression in place. He rounded the truck's hood and met her on her side, offering her a hand when she opened the door.

They moved to the home's front door in tandem, then paused at the broken crime scene seal on the door.

Blaze pulled his gun from the holster, looked at Maisy and frowned.

"I'm not staying out here alone," she said. "If that's what you're thinking. No way."

Blaze pressed his lips tight, weighing the options. He swore under his breath, then turned his back to her and placed one of her hands on his lean, sculpted side. "Stay close. Consider me your shield."

He opened the door, and they entered the small cottage together, navigating the space. Blaze cleared each room as unbidden tears rolled over Maisy's cheeks. Bloodstains marred the living room walls and carpet where she'd last seen Clara, gun drawn and calling for backup. Everything in sight had been overturned, dumped or destroyed.

"Why would they do this?" Maisy asked. "What evidence can be found by tearing a home apart?"

"This isn't the work of a crime scene team," Blaze said, putting his gun away. "Someone came in when they left. Whoever did this broke the seal on the door and then, apparently, searched for something."

"Like what?" Maisy shivered at the thought of strangers ripping through her things, pawing at her little cottage life.

Blaze fixed her with an icy stare. "You."

Chapter Six

Blaze loaded Maisy's belongings into the bed of his pickup truck. Three lidded plastic totes. Two duffel bags and a few boxes of books. The entire contents of what was left of her life amounted to less, materially, than his personal collection of fishing gear.

She'd given up everything in her quest to find justice for Luciano's victims, and it both filled and pained Blaze's heart. He needed to make sure she got the chance to complete her mission.

He pulled a heavy tarp over her things and secured it, then joined her in the cab. "You okay?" he asked. He couldn't imagine how tough it must've been, seeing the place again so soon, especially in that condition. Her expression as she'd packed had said plenty. She was angry and afraid, but more than that, Maisy was tired. It was written on her face, but she was too darn stubborn to admit it or lean on him for support. He just didn't understand why.

"Not going to lie," she said. "Being here wasn't great." Her voice shook as she spoke, and Blaze longed to fold her into his arms.

Instead, he started the engine and shifted immediately

into gear, getting out of there as quickly as possible. In case whoever tossed the place returned.

"I'm glad to have my stuff back, but I'd hoped to find some kind of clue that would help us track the killer. Instead the whole cottage was trashed and the trip was a 50 percent bust."

Blaze turned to her as she stared dejectedly through the window. "The crime scene tape was broken, so we can assume officials had already done their job before it was overturned. Most likely, whatever clues the shooter left behind were already collected before the home was sealed."

"Maybe," she muttered. "Hopefully that wasn't done by a member of the crime scene to destroy or cover up the evidence."

Blaze tried to smile or muster any level of encouraging expression and failed miserably. He couldn't blame Maisy for her lack of faith in the system. Not when a man dressed as a marshal had killed her friend and guardian. It wasn't fair that she'd been through so much. Had given up so much. And he hated that she was only six weeks from delivering her first child, and she only had one tiny box of baby things. She should have a whole nursery set up by now, and a closet full of clothes. The pregnancy should've been celebrated, not hidden, and his family should have smothered her with love and attention so she could laugh about it with him each night. Maisy and their baby should be safe. Not on the run.

His grip tightened on the steering wheel.

"I'm fine, Blaze," she said, drawing his attention to her. "I hate that look, so do me a favor and don't use it on me."

"What look?" he asked, straightening his spine and

doing his best impression of someone handling the situation better than he was. "I was thinking. That's all."

"You were thinking that you pity me," she said, "And I don't want it. So, knock it off."

He bit the insides of his cheeks, fighting the urge to argue and knowing she wouldn't listen anyway. They'd both get all wound up, throwing their misplaced frustrations and anger at one another until someone said something they didn't mean and couldn't take back. They'd both regret their parts immediately and miserably afterward. He and Maisy had had a few of those explosive debates in their heyday. Each had ended in explosive makeup sex and hours of profuse apologies. The possibility of makeup sex was clearly out of the question. He'd be lucky if Maisy ever let him touch her again after he'd gotten her pregnant and left her alone for half a year. He definitely couldn't argue with her right now. He had enough regrets already and wasn't in the market for more.

She kept her attention focused through the window at her side, stroking her bump, comforting the child inside her.

Blaze longed to do the same. Wanted to caress the place where his baby grew and touch the woman who'd once stolen his heart. A woman who'd yet to give it back. But he kept his hands to himself, certain she thought he'd touched her enough already. "It's empathy," he said, finally, unable to let her think he pitied her. "I'm saddened by what you're going through because I care about your happiness, and I think it sucks that you're stuck in this psychopath's storm. You gave up everything because of him, including your freedom. For months. And now that you've made it to the finish line, he's pulled the rug and set you back at the beginning. On the run all over again.

Scared. Unsure who to trust. I don't pity you, Maze. I'm angry for you."

She turned heated hazel eyes on him. "I know who I can trust. You. And I know you'll get me through this, whatever it takes. You'll keep me safe until I can do what I set out to do. Be the voice that Natalie, Clara and all Luciano's other victims no longer have."

The return drive passed in a flash of trees and small-town blurs outside his window. Maisy was quiet until a dime store appeared in the distance just outside the West Liberty city limits. "Do you think they have a restroom?" she asked. "I could use a break, and probably a bottle of water."

"It's worth a try if you need one," he said, pulling the truck into a long, narrow lot, glad for the opportunity to meet at least one of her needs. If the business didn't have a public restroom, he'd use his badge to temporarily change the policy.

He snagged a spot near the door and gave the place a long, careful look. The building was large, some sort of renovated warehouse or repurposed pole barn, not uncommon outside the city limits. A vinyl sign hung from the rooftop with the words *Now Open* scripted in red.

He scanned the area carefully before unlocking the truck doors and heading around to help Maisy down from the cab.

Thankfully, the ladies' room was clearly marked at the back of the building, and Blaze didn't have to pull rank on a retail worker. On the off chance anyone stopped here to ask about Maisy, it wouldn't be good for employees to remember she'd been with him.

Blaze lingered outside the closed restroom door, an aisle of baby things stretching before him. A smattering of shoppers perused the selections. Blaze's feet pulled him forward without conscious intent, into the foreign, brightly colored world. Images of happy children stared back from every baby-based product imaginable, and many he'd never imagined. The brands, sizes and options in diapers and formula were infinite and intimidating. There was a section of special laundry soaps, medicines with droppers and little silicon finger puppet–style toothbrushes for cleaning babies' gums.

His gut tightened, and his skin prickled with fear and enthusiasm. This was his future. All these things he'd never seen before were about to become his everyday normal. A growing bud of panic gave way to an unexpected rush of joy as that beautiful truth settled in. He was going to be a father.

In six weeks.

He read labels and dragged his fingertips across lace bonnets and terry-cloth bibs. Tiny shirts with adorable sayings like *Daddy's Little Princess* had images of shiny crowns. Blue overalls with cartoon chicks were embroidered with the words *Chick Magnet*. It was all too tiny and cute. There were booties printed to look like athletic shoes and cowboy boots.

He wanted to buy it all.

"First time?" a man asked, both startling and horrifying Blaze.

He blinked unfocused eyes, shocked that he'd allowed a stranger to get so close without him knowing. "Sorry. What?" He smiled apologetically as he assessed the man. Harmless. Young. His unbuttoned uniform shirt tagged him as a local mechanic.

The guy grinned. "New dad?" he asked. "You've got

that look. I'm on number four. I can help you choose a diaper. How old's your kid?"

Blaze shook his head. "No, not yet. Thank you."

The man puckered his brows.

"Excuse me." Blaze rushed back to the restrooms, unsure how long he'd been in the aisle, lost in thought.

The ladies' room door was open when he arrived. The single-occupant unit empty.

A flood of panic ripped through him. "Maisy?" he said, turning to scan the store in search of her wild red curls. "Maisy?" He hurried along the rear wall, peering down each aisle into the faces of strangers. "Maisy!"

"Blaze?"

He spun in place, heart hammering painfully against his ribs.

Maisy waved tentatively back from several feet away. He hadn't recognized her, dressed in his bulky jackets, her hair stuffed into his ball cap.

Relief hit like a baseball bat as he closed the distance between them and wrapped his arms around her.

"Are you okay?" she asked, hugging him loosely, and with only one arm.

He laughed, embarrassed as he stepped back and scrubbed a hand over his mouth.

"You look a little bewildered." She frowned awkwardly, a crooked smile on her lips.

"I'm fine," he said. Hooking a hand on his hip and pulling himself together. "Where were you?"

"Shopping. I thought I should change my look, so I don't have to masquerade as a pregnant man until the trial ends." She dragged a palm over his motorcycle jacket in illustration.

"Right." Blaze peeked into the plastic shopping basket in her grip. Hair dye, makeup and glasses cluttered the bottom of the little carrier. "Sounds like a plan. May I?" He tugged the thin metal handles, and Maisy released the basket.

She slipped her arm around his as they made their way to the checkout counter. "Thanks. I could've carried it myself, but I appreciate the gesture."

His racing heart settled easily under her touch. "How about we agree you're as strong as an ox, but I'll do the lifting anyway for the next six weeks? It'll make me feel useful."

"Only if you never compare me to an ox again."

"Y'all find everything all right?" a portly middle-aged woman asked from behind the counter. She wore a blue vest with the store logo and half glasses over small brown eyes. A name badge identified her as Theresa.

"Yes, thank you," Maisy said, releasing Blaze in favor of winding both arms over her bump.

Blaze set the basket on the counter.

"When are you due?" Theresa asked, cheerfully scanning the selections. "Boy or girl?"

"Soon," Maisy said. "We're keeping the gender a surprise."

The clerk's eyes widened, and she belted out a laugh. "Well, I don't hear that much these days. Folks like to plan every little second of their lives. Good for you. Enjoying the moments as they come." She totaled the bill and dropped the final item into a bag.

Blaze offered her a few bills and waited for change.

"Well, good luck with everything," she said. "You sure are one nice-looking family. Bring that baby back around here when I can meet it."

"Will do," Blaze promised, chest puffing with pride as he lifted the bags and led Maisy back to the truck.

MAISY SET THE blow-dryer onto Blaze's bathroom countertop and stared at the reflection before her. Gone were the long red curls. Present was a blunt, poker-straight, shoulder-length bob with heavy bangs in a deep mocha brown she hated. She'd followed the guidance of an online makeup tutorial to generate a dramatic smoky-eye look and enhance her cheekbones. Her full pink lips were painted in matte crimson instead of the neutral gloss she'd used since high school.

"I look like a pregnant hooker," she told the alternate version of herself looking back at her through cat-eye glasses. Then she pressed the tip of an eyebrow pencil into the skin near her upper lip. "Right down to the fake beauty mark."

Thankfully, she still had her own clothes. A simple, long-sleeved red T-shirt and maternity jeans.

"Maze?" Blaze called, rapping softly on the semiopen door.

"Nope." She turned to wait as Blaze peeked inside. "There's no one by that name in here."

His lips parted as he stepped into the threshold and leaned against the doorjamb. "Whoa."

"Yeah." She turned back to the mirror. "At least Luciano's henchmen won't recognize me. I barely recognize myself."

Blaze locked eyes with her reflection. "You look like a hot librarian. Or a naughty schoolteacher."

Maisy turned to face him, dragging the glasses to the tip of her nose. "Well then, how about a ride to the station before I give you detention?"

Blaze flashed a wicked grin before peeling himself away from the jamb. "Yes, ma'am."

THE POLICE STATION was busy as they made their way to an office near the back.

A pretty blonde with blue eyes and graphite-smudged fingers popped up to greet them. "Detective Winchester." She reached for Blaze, eagerly shaking his hand, before turning her attention to Maisy. "I'm Sarah. It's lovely to meet you."

"Hi," she answered, reluctant to share her name. "Thank you for agreeing to meet me on such short notice. I understand you usually go home by now."

"It's no problem," Sarah assured. "I'm glad to help. Have a seat."

Maisy sat opposite Sarah and rested her hands on the table.

Sarah stared openly a moment before blushing. "Sorry," she said, looking immeasurably guilty. "It's just that you don't look anything like the picture on the news. I hope you don't mind. Lucas filled me in."

Maisy looked to Blaze, hoping his brother knew what he was doing by sharing her identity with the sketch artist.

Blaze offered a nearly imperceptible nod.

"Well, that was the goal," Maisy said, answering the woman's comment about her appearance. "It's a little much, right?" She waved her hands in a small circle around her hair and face.

Sarah laughed. "You're obviously beautiful either way, but this is a great cover. The bump was a brilliant touch."

"The bump is real," Maisy said, wrapping her arms around her middle.

Sarah's brows rose. "Oh. Sorry. I didn't know."

"It's okay. Most don't."

"Well, congratulations?" Sarah offered.

Maisy grinned, feeling the warmth of her well-wishes spread through her.

Blaze rocked back on his heels. "Thank you." He set a hand on Maisy's shoulder, his thumb stroking the fabric of her jacket.

Sarah's jaw dropped. "No. You two? Really?"

Maisy laughed, a shock of pleasure and electricity coursing through her. "True story."

"Winchester!" A man's voice boomed outside the door.

Blaze pulled his hand away as if he'd been burned. "Sergeant," he returned, spinning toward the door.

Maisy twisted in her seat for a look through the open doorway, but she didn't recognize any of the faces outside.

"Will you two be okay without me?" Blaze asked, moving toward the door. "I want to brief Sergeant Maxwell on the situation and talk to the marshals if they're here."

Maisy smiled. "I'm sure we can manage on our own awhile."

"Go for it," Sarah said. "I'm going to need at least thirty minutes."

Blaze nodded, stepping into the hallway. He smiled at Maisy before pulling the door shut behind him.

"So the rumors are true," Sarah said, grinning as she lifted her pencil to the paper. "Blaze Winchester is officially off the market."

"Oh no." Maisy blanched. "It's not like that between us anymore. Until yesterday, I hadn't seen him since they took me into protective custody. He didn't even know about the baby until I showed up on his doorstep." She bit her lip, hating the unnecessary overshare. She cleared her throat and tried again. "Right now we're just… I don't know. Trying to stay alive, I guess." She laughed to alleviate the awkward moment she'd created, but only felt more uncomfortable.

Sarah leaned over her sketch pad, still waiting to make the first line. "I hate to break the news, but that man is clearly lost for you. I know you're in a tough place right now. A crazy crime boss is trying to kill you and all that, but I work with these guys all day. Every day. And that bright-eyed detective who just strode out of here isn't the same man I've watched mope and skulk around for the past six months. That guy right there—" she pointed to the door, as if Blaze was still visible through it "—he's a man who just found his way home."

Maisy's heart swelled nonsensically. She didn't know Sarah, or have a clue how well Sarah knew Blaze, but she really liked the woman's opinion. "I'll take your word for it," she said, hoping she was right.

"You can take it to the bank," she said. "Now, what do you say we get the safe house shooter's face all over the news and shut Luciano down?"

Maisy beamed. Exactly what she was there for.

She and Sarah worked diligently until the sketch of Clara's shooter was nearly perfect. Maisy marveled at the way Sarah's hand moved confidently over the page, adding lines and curves, then dragging skilled fingertips across the work, blending to create depth, shade and shadow. The result was remarkable and could easily be mistaken for a black-and-white photograph.

Maisy's abdomen tightened unexpectedly, and she grunted in response to the sudden pain.

"Maisy?" Sarah asked, eyes wide with instant concern.

"False contractions," she answered softly, puffing short, labored breaths. She stretched onto her feet as the pain subsided, then paced the small room in slow, even strides, smoothing her palms against the hardened sides of her middle. "Sorry. I'll just walk it off."

Sarah offered an understanding smile. "Braxton-Hicks can be the worst," she said. "So painful and such a tease. You'll be praying for the real thing in a month or so, and these jokers will get your hopes up for nothing."

Maisy laughed. "I can't wait for that." Praying for labor would mean the trial was over and she'd survived.

Another sharp pain cut the relief short, and Maisy gritted her teeth.

"Do you need a break?" Sarah asked. "There's a restroom in a little alcove a few doors down from here. A water fountain and snack machines, too. Across from Detective Winchester's office. Out this door and to the left. You can't miss it. Go stretch and breathe."

Maisy bobbed her head, inhaling long and slow through her nose as she straightened her spine. She released the air through open lips. "Okay. I won't be long." She hooked her purse over her shoulder, then gritted her way through another punch of pain.

"I'll finish up, then come and check on you," Sarah promised. "Remember, go left. Right is the way back to the main lobby, and the door will lock behind you if you leave."

Maisy turned left, then checked over her shoulder to be sure there wasn't any miscommunication amid the pain.

Sarah gave a thumbs-up, and Maisy shuffled away, eyes locked on a blue-and-white sign identifying the restrooms and vending area.

Blaze's office door was open, but the room was empty.

The hall ended in a bullpen of sorts, lined in desks and filled with people in uniforms, suits and street clothes. Voices rose into a cloud of noise, punctuated with ringing phones and the click-clack of a dozen hands on keyboards. She suppressed the pinch of fear rising in her. Everyone in sight appeared to be official in one way or another. Even a man dressed as a homeless person had a badge on a chain around his neck.

You're safe, she told herself as she hurried into the ladies' room, cringing and breathing like a lunatic.

She jammed a wad of paper towels under running water, then squeezed out the excess before pressing the cool compress to her forehead. She wiped her temples, then repeated the process, holding the towels against the back of her neck.

The door to the bathroom opened, and Maisy bowed her head farther, balancing the towels and avoiding eye contact.

The scent of men's cologne sprang her upright.

"No." Terror choked the word as she looked Clara's shooter in the eye.

He grabbed her in one swift move, pulling her to him with powerful arms. A broad, leather-gloved hand clamped over her lips, and he lowered his mouth to her ear. "We're walking out of here," he whispered. "And you aren't going to fight me on it, or I will hurt your baby. Got it?"

Maisy sucked in a ragged breath, nodding wildly and fumbling for her purse.

The man's icy blue eyes met hers in the mirror, and she stilled as her fingers reached their goal. "Think of that baby," he said, the words filled with warning and resolve. "Don't be a hero."

He turned her toward the restroom's exit with a forceful jerk, then shoved her forward. "Down the hall and to the right. We're leaving through the back door."

Maisy whimpered, then groaned, bending slightly forward with the sound.

When he attempted to wrench her upright, she pulled the Taser from her purse and pressed the trigger.

Chapter Seven

Blaze scanned the space outside his sergeant's office; the normally busy area was borderline chaos. Officers, detectives and a collection of men and women far above his pay grade filled every nook, corner and cranny. The entire county population of law enforcement seemed to be on hand, plotting, planning and conspiring to get a location on Maisy, the missing witness, and her marshal. Thankfully, Blaze had Lucas on board to run interference as needed, and a sergeant who'd protect Maisy with his life, once Blaze had the chance to fill him in.

Getting Maxwell alone, long enough to bring him up to speed, however, wouldn't be easy. Even members of administration and guards from the jail where Luciano was being held had shown up to make sense of what was happening and to form a collaboration to stop him. Thanks to Luciano's long list of crimes and extensive network, every agency from the IRS to the FBI had a dog in the fight. And every agency wanted to be the one who broke the case.

Sergeant Maxwell pressed his palms against the desk, leveling a pair of local marshals with his most resolute stare. "I appreciate your determination to take the Luciano situation off our hands here, but Maisy Daniels is our witness. She's a West Liberty citizen who worked in direct cooperation with Detective Winchester for four months when Luciano went underground. She's the reason there will even be a trial. That young woman lost her twin sister to that piece of garbage. She willingly gave up her freedom in exchange for the marshals' protection and a chance to testify against him."

The marshals narrowed their eyes in defiance, knowing Maxwell was right but not wanting to take full responsibility for what had happened at the safe house. "How could we have known something like this would happen?"

"Because it's your job to know," Maxwell retorted. "You botched her protection. Now I'm ready to accept whatever help we can get to assure she's found and protected until she can do what she set out to do, which is make your case for you."

The marshal smirked, hands clasped before him. "Thanks, but we've got this covered."

Maxwell's face went from an irritated red to a ready-to-explode purple. "She trusted us, and we trusted you. Now a marshal is dead, and our witness is missing days before the trial. Not to mention the other witnesses are dropping like flies. So, you'll excuse me if I want all hands on deck. That means my men are on this, and staying on it."

The marshal in charge glared, deep-set brown eyes flashing. "I'm sure you mean well, Sergeant, but watch your step here. It sounds as if you're making unwarranted accusations about our abilities to perform our jobs, or worse, that we have a dirty marshal. I won't stand here and put up with that. What happened at that safe house was a tragedy, but it wasn't something anyone could've prepared for. Including you, so I suggest you stop glowering and pointing fingers."

Blaze bit his tongue, knowing more than he could share. That Maisy had confirmed the missing marshal from the news wasn't the man who'd shot Clara. The shooter had been an impostor, and the true marshal sent for her transport was likely dead. He checked his watch, eager for the marshals to leave so he could confide Maisy's appearance quietly to Maxwell and decide what to do from there. He'd already been away from her too long. Sarah had to be finishing the sketch by now.

A sharp scream pierced the white noise outside Maxwell's door, and the room fell silent for a lingering heartbeat.

Blaze's feet were in motion instantly, as if the scream had triggered his fight-or-flight system, and every fiber of his being already knew Maisy was the woman who'd screamed.

And he was ready to fight.

The thick collection of bodies in the busy central space parted as he ran toward the sound. Toward the restroom, he realized, not the office where he'd left her with Sarah.

Maisy appeared in the next second, pale and terrified, racing through the crowd, every member of which was suddenly on high alert. She collided with him, tears streaming, breaths coming short and fast. "I tased him!" she panted. "In the bathroom. The ladies' room. Clara's shooter."

Blaze didn't have to speak. Uniformed officers broke away without question, jogging toward the women's restroom as Blaze wrapped Maisy in his arms.

He caught Lucas's eye in the commotion as he led her to his office, only a few yards away.

She nearly collapsed onto the chair as Blaze shut the door. She curled inward, rolling her shoulders over her bump and wrapping protective arms around it as she began to sob.

His muscles ached to hold her. And also to take care of whoever had dared lay a hand on her. "Hey. You're okay." He crouched on the floor before her chair, seeking her eyes with his. Fury and terror raced in his veins. However much he wanted to get ahold of the man who'd attacked her, Maisy needed him, and her needs would always trump his. Her happiness and safety were integral to his own. "You're safe now," he said softly. "Did he hurt you?"

She shook her head as she cried, dark eye makeup twisting black rivulets over bright red cheeks. "It was him, Blaze! The safe house shooter reached me here. At the police station. How long can I possibly stay alive if there's no place he can't get to me?"

"Hey." He raised his palms tentatively, cupping her jaw and brushing strands of freshly dyed brown locks away from her wet cheeks with his thumbs. "You'll survive as long as you have to because you are who you are," he said. "You're tough and you're resilient. And you're not going to let Luciano or one of his henchmen change that."

She lifted puffy eyes to his, her long lashes soaked with tears. "Okay."

"Good." He smiled. "Now, are you hurt?" he asked again. "Take a minute and think beyond the adrenaline. Is the baby okay? Do you need a medic?"

He gritted his teeth behind the smile, aching to tear in half the son of a gun who'd caused this. He scanned her pretty face, her neck, limbs and middle. She was too covered, long sleeves. Jeans. Dressed for the falling temperature outside. Even if he could confirm there were no scratches or bruises, how could he have any idea what kind of damage might've been done internally? This kind of stress couldn't be good for her or their baby.

"I'm not hurt," she said. "Shaken, but that's all." She rubbed her wrists, then ran shaky palms over her arms, presumably attempting to scrub away the effects of her attacker's touch. "He only had ahold of me for a second, thanks to your Taser."

Blaze pulled the cell phone from his pocket. "I'd feel better if Isaac took a look at you. We don't have to go to the hospital if he doesn't think it's necessary, but I don't want to take any chances. You remember Isaac? You liked him."

Isaac was the youngest Winchester, a fairer-skinned, lighter-haired, first-cousin, practically raised in Blaze's family home. They weren't brothers by birth, but they were unequivocally brothers, and Blaze trusted Isaac's medical opinion more highly than any other medic's in the county.

Maisy gave a shaky nod. "I remember." Her bump seemed to move, and she settled a hand over the spot where Blaze had seen the small pulse point. "Okay," she said. "Thank you."

Blaze forced his eyes away from her middle, heart thundering for a new reason now. It was easy to think of the baby abstractly, like an idea more than reality, until he saw evidence of its movement. Its life. His throat thickened and his head filled with questions. Was she carrying a boy or a girl? His son? Or his daughter? "You did good, Maze," he said, barely choking back the emotion. "You protected yourself and the baby. All on your own. And I swear I won't ever make you do that again."

She reached a small hand out to him, gliding her palm against his cheek. "This isn't your fault. This is all Luciano, and we need to stop him."

Blaze covered her hand with his, then, winding long fingers around her narrow wrist, he pressed a kiss against the soft skin of her palm. "I was wrong to think any place was safe. I knew the guy impersonated a marshal. I should've known he could be anywhere, pose as anyone. Clearly, he has connections." The words led to another sobering thought. "Someone let him in here. And I'm going to find out who."

A heavy knock rattled the door, standing Blaze at attention, one hand on his gun and prepared to draw. "Blaze?" His brother's voice called from the hall outside.

He opened up and urged Lucas inside. "What'd you learn?"

Lucas glanced from Blaze to Maisy, then back. "The bathroom was empty, but we got him on the security feed, using the rear entrance for his escape. Tech's working backward now, watching to catch him coming in. My best guess is that someone left the door ajar for him, maybe with a stopper of some kind."

Maisy twisted on her seat, eyes wide. "So someone here is definitely dirty."

"Looks like," Lucas said. "Problem is, half the lawmen in the county are here. We've got marshals and jail personnel on top of our uniforms and detectives on-site right now. And assuming I'm right about the door being left ajar, who's to say the person who did that didn't leave the premises afterward? The dirty one might not even be here anymore."

Blaze groaned. "There's no camera pointed at the door from the inside, either. Just from the lot."

"Maxwell's working with tech services," Lucas said. "He thinks the exterior camera could have picked up an image in the glass. We might still be able to find out who helped the guy get in here."

"Knock, knock," Sarah called from outside the door. "It's Sarah."

Lucas opened the door and pulled her inside. "Hey."

"Hey," she answered, her eyes darting to Maisy as she pushed onto her feet. "Oh thank goodness!" The women met in a hug.

"I'm okay," Maisy assured.

"I'm not," Sarah said, shaking her head. "I think I had a heart attack when I heard you scream. Then everyone was running around, and no one knew where you went."

Lucas's eyes widened at the sight of Maisy's round middle, which had been somewhat hidden until she stood and turned to face them.

Blaze grinned despite himself. Knowing she was pregnant and seeing the evidence were two different experiences. "How's the sketch?" he asked, changing the subject.

"Finished." Sarah turned the image around to show them.

Lucas pointed at the paper. "That's him. From the security footage."

Maisy nodded, going pale, then returning to her seat. "Yeah. He's the one who attacked the safe house."

Tension rippled through the room. Blaze shot a text to Isaac, requesting he stop by the station and take a look at Maisy, then returned his attention to her. "Isaac's on the way."

"Are you hurt?" Lucas asked, a thread of panic around the words.

"No, I'm fine," she assured. "We're just being cautious. Plus, I doubt Blaze would let me leave this office until I agreed to an exam."

Lucas edged closer, smile widening. "I don't blame him. You're carrying precious cargo, I hear."

Maisy laughed, hands going to her middle. "That's pretty obvious these days."

Lucas grinned. "You've undergone quite a makeover."

"Unfortunately," she said, pulling a wad of tissues from the box on Blaze's desk and running them over her makeup-drenched face. "I didn't fool that guy, whoever he is. Thankfully Blaze armed me with a Taser this morning."

"Where is it?" Lucas asked, voicing the words before Blaze could form them.

"I dropped it when I ran."

Nonsensical pride bubbled in Blaze's chest. She hadn't wanted to take the Taser, but she had, and she'd promised to use it in the spirit he'd intended. And she'd done a bang-up job.

Blaze's desk phone rang, and he nearly yanked it off the base, eager for an update. "Winchester."

"We're tracking the intruder through local surveillance cameras," Sergeant Maxwell said. "And we've collected a Taser from the floor of the women's restroom. Any idea why I'm calling you about that?"

Blaze waited.

"The weapon was department issued," he said. "To you. Got anything to say about it?"

Blaze looked to his brother before dragging his gaze to Maisy.

"I'll take your silence as a big fat yes, and trust you're going to fill me in on things as soon as you get Maisy

Daniels to safety," Maxwell said. "I can only presume that's what's going on here, though I can't imagine why you'd bring her to the station considering our concerns about a leak at this level."

"You're absolutely right, sir. I intended to talk to you sooner, but the marshals—"

"Are a pain in my backside," he interrupted. "Fine. I'll stop by your office for an update as soon as I can. If you need to leave before I can get there, do it. Meanwhile, there's something more you should know."

Blaze froze, and his breath seemed to stop as he waited for the update.

"There's something I didn't get the chance to tell you earlier, too." Maxwell released a heavy sigh against the receiver. "We lost another witness on the Luciano case early this morning. That makes two in two days. And two consecutive attempts on Miss Daniels, as well. We're down to her and one other witness. Without them, Luciano's lawyers won't have any trouble getting him off these charges, per their usual. So, however you came to be back in touch with Maisy Daniels, you've got my permission to do whatever you need to keep her safe. Time off. Airfare to the moon. You got it. Just protect her."

"With my life, sir."

Chapter Eight

Maisy eased onto Blaze's couch, exhausted by the emotionally depleting day. From their visit to the safe house, where the memories and destruction had pushed her to request a bathroom break halfway home. So she could stand in a public restroom and cry. To her direct attack at the police station, where the psychopath who'd killed Clara had threatened her baby. It was all just too much, and she was certain she could sleep until her due date if the universe would let her.

Though, given her string of awful luck, she'd be happy with a thirty-minute power nap.

Thankfully, the police, marshals service and public at large had a face to go with the attacks now, and the man would be on the run. Unlikely to come for her again. Though that didn't mean another of Luciano's henchmen weren't on their way.

Blaze clattered around in the kitchen, cleaning up after a wonderful meal of steaks and baked potatoes. He'd insisted she rest instead of help, and she hadn't had the energy to protest.

She turned the television to the local news and let her eyelids slip shut, attempting to center herself in the moment and trust that she was safe again for now. The pair of Tylenol Isaac had recommended during her exam had taken the edge off her sore muscles, mostly aching from the tension she'd carried there for too long. Isaac had further prescribed plenty of rest, water and time off her feet. She'd always liked him.

"All right," Blaze said, sweeping into the room and heading for the couch. "What are you watching?"

"News," she said, as if anything else was an option for them. "Maybe the police captured the lunatic assigned to kill me and no one has bothered to call and tell you."

Blaze tented his brows. "That would be a serious inside scoop." He lifted her feet off the little cushion she'd propped them on, then tossed the pillow aside, easily taking its place. "Is this okay?" he asked, resting her ankles across his lap.

"I can sit up," she offered, squirming to attempt the task.

"No way." He gripped her calves gently, urging her to be still. "You were comfortable, and I interrupted."

"But it's rude of me to take up your whole couch," she countered.

"Let's compromise. You can have the couch back, and I'll put the little pillow under your feet again. Or we can share the couch, and I'll hold your feet. Lady's choice."

Maisy bit her lip, enamored by his grin. She enjoyed the exchange more than she should and especially liked the feel of his hands on her. "Fine. If you insist," she said. "You made me dinner. The least I can do is let you touch my feet."

His eyes went dark with faux mischief. "I can touch them?"

Maisy snorted. "You are touching them. They're on your lap."

Blaze stretched his fingers in the air above her fuzzy socks, then lowered his hands to her ankles, peeling the polka-dotted fleece away. She shivered as he pressed the pads of his thumbs against her tender arches, working in small, muscle-melting circles.

She groaned unintentionally, and his big hands closed over her feet in response.

"I'm doing okay?" he asked, a note of pride and more than a little smugness in his tone.

"Mmm-hmm." Maisy braced herself against a flash of other times Blaze had been smugly responsive to her little moans.

He watched her as he massaged, his gaze gliding over her body, lingering on her parted lips before looking into her eyes. "Feeling more relaxed?"

"Very." Her cheeks went hot again, this time with clear and perfect memories of his hands all over her in the very best ways. "Don't stop," she said, allowing her head to drop against the pillow behind her and her eyes to fall shut. She'd said those same words to him more times than she could count. She wasn't sure when a foot rub had ever gotten her so worked up, but she liked it. And she blamed the pregnancy hormones.

"Can I ask you something?" Blaze's voice was low and smooth.

"Anything."

His fingers stilled for a half heartbeat before falling back into rhythm. "Do you have a name picked out?"

Her eyes opened, and she raised her face to look at him. "Natalie, if it's a girl." To honor her sister. "Blaze, if it's a boy." She pressed her lips together as a flicker of shyness cooled her thoroughly. "If that's okay with you."

He nodded. "Yeah."

"Yeah?"

Blaze cleared his throat, head bobbing and smile growing. "I'd like that. A lot, actually."

The familiar tones of a breaking news story drew their attention to the television, where Sarah's drawing of the man who'd attacked Maisy and killed Clara appeared onscreen.

Maisy used the remote to increase the volume. Sergeant Maxwell had been immeasurably kind to her when he'd arrived in Blaze's office. He'd promised to have the sketch distributed to every major news channel and media outlet possible before dinner. And it looked as if he'd gotten that done. According to Maxwell, the attacker's image was also being run through facial recognition software. A match would provide law enforcement with a name and profile to use in tracking him, including known associates and addresses.

"We're going to find him," Blaze said, sliding his hands over her ankles and tightening his grip once more.

Maisy had changed into her pajamas while Blaze made dinner. Now, his confident fingers were making their way up the soft cotton material, kneading and massaging her tired calves as they went.

"Still okay?" he asked.

She fixed him with a disbelieving stare. "You know I love this. You know I'm a sucker for all forms of massage. So, what exactly are you up to, Blaze Winchester?" Certainly not a trip to the bedroom. Unless he found women the size of tugboats, and roughly shaped like one, sexually arousing.

He grinned. "I'm just trying to be a good host. Make you comfortable. Show you I'm glad you're here." His expression went serious. "Maybe show you how incredibly sorry I am that you were ever in danger on my watch."

That made more sense. This was an apology massage.

"Not your fault," she said for the tenth time since she'd been attacked. "It is your fault I'm alive, however. Because you had the forethought to arm me with a weapon I could easily access and use. It's also your fault I have a full stomach of nutritious food right now. That all my things are under this roof. And I have a safe, warm, dry place to sleep. Those things are 100 percent on you."

Blaze shook his head in disagreement as she spoke. "You're smart," he said, his magic hands determinedly erasing the stress of her day, and possibly the bones in her body. "Not everyone could have acted as quickly. Thought as clearly. Made the move to escape before being taken." He worked the muscles of her calves with impressive care and expertise, fuzzing up her thoughts. "And it was your idea to talk to Sarah today. You're the reason this guy's face is on television. Now he's on the run." Blaze tipped his head toward the newscast without breaking her stare. "You did that."

A zealous onscreen reporter recapped the uglier details of Maisy's last two days.

"Someone will recognize him," Blaze assured. "People will call in and testify to seeing him at the local gas station or serving him at a sandwich shop. Maybe they'll know his cousin's girlfriend, but they will call." Blaze smiled. "And then we've got him. If we're lucky, he'll flip on his employer in exchange for a plea bargain. Then his testimony can be added to our case at Luciano's trial."

Maisy rubbed her stomach where the muscles began to bunch and tighten across her abdomen. "So, I did okay," she said, working her lips into a little smile. "I guess we make a good team."

"The best," he said, voice thick with promise and nostalgia. "The way I recall it, you and I were good in every way."

Maisy bit her bottom lip and shifted as heat rose through her chest and pooled in her core. Her breasts tightened, and she ached for the complete intimate connection they'd shared so many times before.

But that would have to wait until she could see her feet again, if that was what he was thinking about. Everything else in her life had to wait until the day Luciano was behind the bars of a maximum-security prison, cut off from his network. A day when she no longer had to worry a killer lurked nearby, tasked with her murder.

Until then, she needed to get her head on straight. She had to stop getting lost in the past, wishing things were like they were before. Because everything had changed.

BLAZE WATCHED MAISY, loving her shy smile and the sweet blush across her cheeks. He especially enjoyed knowing he'd put that expression on her face and incited the heat. Being there with her, so comfortably, so casually, was all that he'd dreamed of for a very long time.

Now, here they were. Together again. Despite the hurricane trying to tear them apart.

And he was touching her.

And she was enjoying it.

And the connection felt so powerful, he had to force himself not to press his luck and scare her away. If she still cared for him the way he cared for her, one day soon their life together could be like this every night, minus the danger. He and Maisy could be teammates, conquering whatever life threw at them. Because he and Maisy were great together.

He cradled her feet on his lap, working his fingers over the soles then the tender muscles of her calves, willing to comfort her for as long as she would allow it. He'd truly missed these simple moments with her, and he hoped selfishly she felt the same way. Everything was easy with Maisy, comfortable and familiar, even when they'd been new to one another. The connection between them was like nothing he'd ever felt before.

And now they had a baby on the way.

There was no denying his incredible physical attraction to her. He doubted any amount of time or distance could have changed that. But it was impossible to know if the feelings were one-sided. Or if she could ever want him again the way she once had. After all, he'd gotten her pregnant, then vanished from her life. Logically, he couldn't have done anything differently, because he hadn't known about the baby, but logic didn't always matter where emotions were involved.

He ran his hands over her calves, stopping to grip the sensitive space behind her knee.

Maisy sucked in a breath, and their gazes locked.

The familiar heat in her eyes sent flames licking through him, spreading like wildfire and tightening his jeans.

"Maisy?"

"Uhm." She averted her eyes, red scorch marks slashing both cheeks. "I should get to bed. I've had a long day, and Isaac said I should rest. Is that okay?" She swung her legs away from him.

"Of course," he said, lifting his hands.

She paused after she stood, apparently conflicted.

"Maybe I should sleep on the couch this time. You suffered out here last night."

"I'm fine," he said, dropping his hands to his lap. "How about I walk you to your door?"

She rolled her eyes and huffed a laugh as he stood and followed her toward his room.

She stopped after only a few paces and gripped her middle.

"What's wrong?"

She grimaced, bracing a palm against the wall. "False contraction. I'm fine. It'll pass." She smiled, breathing in strange little puffs. "I just wish these practice runs weren't quite so realistic."

Blaze moved in closer, brushing hair away from her face. "Here." He looped an arm around her shoulders and turned her to him.

She went easily, rubbing her middle and letting Blaze keep her upright as she navigated the evident pain. "I was supposed to begin Lamaze classes by now," she said. "Dr. Nazir recommended them last month, but I put off registering. I figured I'd wait and take the classes once I got back home instead."

"Lamaze?" he asked, gears turning in his head. Classes to prepare women for labor and delivery.

She nodded, expression still tight with discomfort. "I have a birth plan," she said. "I want a natural delivery with dim light and soft music. Lamaze will help me manage the pain."

"Do you need a partner for those classes?" he asked, almost certain most women did. Not that Maisy had ever seemed like any other woman to him.

"Yeah," she said, cautiously. "Usually. Why?"

"I'd like to be your partner," he offered.

Her face snapped up, curiosity and surprise on her brow. "Okay."

He smiled.

Maisy stepped away, breathing a little more naturally. "I should lie down now. I'll see you in the morning?"

Blaze stuffed his hands into his pockets, hating the chill left in her absence. "I'll be here if you need anything."

And just like that, he watched her walk away again.

And he hated it even more this time around.

Chapter Nine

Maisy slept poorly, despite her fatigue, stealing short bits of rest between longer bursts of paranoia and anxiety. The last forty-eight hours had overwhelmed her, and the more frequent Braxton-Hicks had her further on edge. Being pregnant for the first time came with its own amount of subtle panic, and without Clara to reassure her, the fear for her baby was mounting. If she went into labor before her life settled, she wouldn't even know how to handle it. Obviously her painstakingly prepared birth plan wasn't going to happen the way she'd hoped. And she hadn't even had her Lamaze classes yet. With a killer stalking her until the trial, she wasn't sure when she'd ever have the chance to do anything normal again before her baby's birth.

She waited impatiently for the sun to rise and trace a path across the windowsill, then she climbed out of bed. She took her time getting ready for the day, unsure if Blaze was awake and not wanting to disturb him if he wasn't. He'd probably stayed up well into the night, keeping watch and waiting for updates from his sergeant.

When she opened the bathroom door, the scent of brewing coffee and something rich and buttery wafted in to greet her on the air. She followed the sounds and scents of breakfast through Blaze's home, trying not to drool. "You made pancakes," she accused a moment before entering the kitchen.

He peeked over one broad shoulder as she approached, then whistled. "You wake up looking like that?"

"In full makeup and wearing the only outfit I don't completely hate?" she asked. "Absolutely. My hair blew itself out."

He grinned. "The curls are back. I approve."

And Maisy approved of his nicely fitting jeans and simple white T-shirt. His hair was rumpled, and his cheeks were stubble-covered. He looked like the definition of sexy and casual.

"Are you getting used to it?" he asked, reminding her they were still talking about her awful hair.

"No. As usual, I jumped the gun and caused myself trouble." Quick reactions were her specialty. They'd saved her life once or twice lately, but for the previous twenty-six years, her act-now, think-later personality had gotten her into more than one bind. Overpaying for things. Overcommitting to social engagements. And that belly button piercing on her twenty-first birthday. "I could probably get on board with the length, but I don't like the color." She rolled her eyes, then moved to his side, pouring a mug of coffee while he flipped another pancake. "It's a little dumb, but I don't look like Natalie anymore." She inhaled the warm, bitter steam. "I kind of liked that I could still see her in the mirror."

He adjusted the flame under his skillet, then offered a warm smile. "I don't think it's dumb. I don't think she would, either." His gaze slid to the cup in her hand. "Is that okay for you?" he asked, a small crease forming between his brows. "For the baby?"

She narrowed her eyes as she blew across the hot surface of her drink. "Yes." She'd stuck to decaf and herbal tea for months, but she hoped a little caffeine would help clear the fog of fatigue from her brain.

He moved the final pancake to a plate piled ten high. "Right," he said sheepishly. "How about I let you take care of Bun while I take care of you?"

"Excuse me?" she asked. "Did you just call my child Bun?"

"Our child," he said, a flash of intense pleasure in his soft blue eyes. "And yeah, like a bun in the oven."

Maisy squinted, lips pursed.

"Not that I'm calling you an oven," he backpedaled. "Hey, look, I made pancakes."

She took a seat at the table, warmed by his insistence at calling the baby theirs. "This all looks and smells amazing," she said. "Sorry if I'm being cranky. None of the bad stuff is your fault, and I'm really glad I'm here. And that you're here. It didn't occur to me until I'd walked all the way to your doorstep that you could have moved. Or acquired a live-in girlfriend while I was gone. I was stuck in the safe house, but your life was marching on."

Blaze watched her cautiously as he ferried the platter of hotcakes to the table, along with butter, syrup and silverware. Plates were already waiting. "I love this place. I can't imagine leaving it. And my life didn't move on the way you're implying."

"No girlfriend?" she asked, knowing it was unlikely he was seeing anyone and the woman hadn't called or stopped by in two days. Though, she could be traveling, or maybe they'd spoken privately while Maisy was showering or in bed. Anything was possible, and it was better to assume he was taken than assume he was single and learn she was wrong. Her traitorous heart had already imagined them raising their child together, watching the baby age as they grew old in one another's lives.

Blaze settled on the seat across from hers and selected a pancake. "I haven't dated." He shifted uncomfortably, casting a quick gaze in her direction. "I'm guessing you didn't sleep well." He pointed his fork at her coffee when she stared blankly back.

He hadn't dated? In all these months? She took a bigger drink of coffee, busying her mouth against the urge to ask why and if, maybe, it was because of her. "Not really," she said instead, answering his question about her sleep. "It's hard to get comfortable these days. Add everything that has been going on to that, and it's practically impossible. I was lucky the night I got here. I slept like a baby. Did you get any rest?"

"Some. I did a little research after you went to bed. I was curious about the contractions you were having."

She paused, watching him more closely as she helped herself to a pancake. "Yeah?"

He inclined his head. "From what I understand, Braxton-Hicks are par for the course, but I also learned that the amount of physical and emotional stress you're under can cause preterm labor. Which is scary, so we should keep a close eye on the contractions in case one of these days they become more than just little practice runs. And definitely ask your doctor about what you're going through when we see her."

Maisy smiled. "I appreciate that you're a problem solver, civil servant and all-around hero, but I think you're overreacting a little."

He smirked. "You think I'm an all-around hero?"

She laughed. "We'll ask Dr. Nazir about the contractions and see what she thinks."

He released a long sigh, as if he might've been holding his breath before. "How do you stay so calm all the time? Do you know how many things can go wrong in a pregnancy?"

"I'm aware." She forked a bite of pancake and dragged it through a puddle of syrup. Between fears for her baby's health and the possibility of a lurking assassin, she'd rather think about the assassin. Avoiding him was at least something she could control. Or try to. "Any word on the runaway shooter? I don't suppose someone saw him pumping gas and called the police? Maybe he's behind bars right now?"

"Afraid not," Blaze said. "But everyone in the state is probably looking for him. Maxwell texted earlier to say the FBI put a bounty on his head. One hundred grand to anyone with information leading to his arrest," Blaze said. "So, the public is looking for him just as diligently as law enforcement now. He will turn up."

Maisy breathed easier. "Let's hope someone finds him before he finds us."

A sudden thump on the porch sent a bolt of panic through the air, and Maisy's fork clattered to her plate.

Blaze was on his feet before she took her next breath, gun drawn.

Her gaze darted across the front windows, searching for shadows, for signs the killer had found her.

"Stay here," Blaze instructed, and he moved carefully toward the door.

BLAZE BRACED HIMSELF to defend Maisy and their child. The urge to fight tightened his muscles as he moved. The desire to rain a world of hurt down on whoever dared to come for her fueled his steps. He leaned a shoulder against the wall and peered around the edge of his curtains, scanning the empty gravel drive out front. A puff of dust drew his attention to the bicycle making its way back to the road. "Newspaper," he said, chuckling lightly before opening the door.

Maisy heaved a sigh behind him.

He carried the paper to the table and returned his gun to his holster.

"I don't need any more coffee," she said pressing both palms to her chest. "I think I just had three consecutive heart attacks."

Blaze went back to his pancakes, smiling, but on edge. If he'd somehow missed the paper boy driving up to the porch, how could he keep a trained killer off his property?

"What do you know about the other witness who died?" Maisy asked. "We never talked about that. One was killed the day my safe house was attacked, then another was lost yesterday. Was he in witness protection, too?"

"No." Blaze set his fork aside. "This guy was a middle-aged banker who'd laundered money for Luciano a bunch of times over the years. He also witnessed him murder two businessmen who owed him money. One of them was your friend Aaron."

Maisy's jaw sank open. "He wasn't alone that day?" The day she'd lost her sister.

"Seems not, though it's the first I'm hearing about it. Turns out the marshals have been working on a need-to-know basis with information on this case. And they haven't felt the West Liberty PD needed to know much."

Maisy rubbed her forehead. "I will never understand the weird tension between law enforcement entities. Or why criminals like Luciano kill people who owe them money. He can't get money from a dead person. Why not keep him alive? Murder seems counterintuitive to his cause."

Blaze had no real answer to her first question, but he could take a stab at the second. "Once someone like Luciano decides the guy can't or won't ever pay up, killing him sets a precedent for others in his debt."

"Pay or die," she mused. "I suppose that would be a powerful motivational tool for anyone on the fence about running off with his money."

Blaze nodded. "Pretty much."

"So, the man who died yesterday was one of Luciano's own? How do you think he found out the guy was going to testify?"

"That's the question of the day," Blaze said. "No one was supposed to know. Everyone hates the thought of a dirty lawman, but there's a hole in our fence somewhere. We've got too many infiltrations happening right now for anyone to keep claiming coincidence."

Maisy's shoulders slumped. "So we have to hope the shooter is captured, then agrees to turn on Luciano."

"His testimony would really help." Blaze tried to imagine a scenario where the shooter could be located, captured, then turned before the trial began next week.

Maisy unrolled the morning paper, then shook it open and blanched. "Well, new plan needed." She pushed her plate aside and smoothed the paper onto the table between them. An article with Sarah's sketch and a photo of the same man centered the page. Underscored by a headline announcing he'd been found. Dead inside his car.

Blaze swore, then hunted down his cell phone. He'd left it on his couch when he went to make breakfast. He'd silenced the device before falling asleep, to avoid waking Maisy. Until he'd walked away and left it on the sofa cushions, he'd still heard it vibrate with every incoming message.

He scrolled the missed notifications. The notification of the shooter's death had come from Maxwell an hour ago.

He dialed his sergeant, and the call went to voice mail.

"This isn't good, right?" Maisy asked.

Blaze lifted troubled eyes to her and shook his head. "No." He dialed Lucas next.

"Because, if this guy is dead, it's because some bigger, badder guy is taking over his work?" Maisy asked, attention back on the paper before her.

Lucas's phone rang through to voice mail.

Blaze redialed. Fairly certain as usual that Maisy's theory was correct. And that wasn't good news. "Pick up," he whispered, willing his brother to answer the damn phone.

"How is Luciano doing this?" Maisy asked, her pale skin going a little green. "He's pulling all these strings from jail? He got a second shooter to shoot his original shooter? Who does that? How big is his network?"

"Winchester," Lucas finally answered on a yawn.

"Have you seen the paper?" Blaze asked rhetorically, skipping over the small talk. He had no doubt that Lucas would've called him if he'd seen the headline.

"I just got home three hours ago. I was called back in after dinner last night. Why?" His voice cleared on the final word, as if his brain was finally waking up. "What happened? Are Maisy and the baby okay?"

"Yeah, but the man who attacked her yesterday is dead. Shot inside his car."

Lucas swore, a little more colorfully than Blaze had.

"I'm putting you on speaker," Blaze said, pressing the option on his phone screen, then setting the device on the table. "Lucas. Maisy."

The pair exchanged tense pleasantries.

Blaze pulled the newspaper across the table and skimmed the rest of the small article. Maisy's questions were valid. How powerful was Luciano? And was Blaze being naive to believe he could protect her at his home? "It might be time to take Maisy off the grid somewhere."

"What?" she asked, eyes wide, as his brother wondered, "Where?"

"I don't know yet, but if her attacker's dead this morning, I've got to consider whoever shot him is looking for her now. Someone has surely shared the fact she was with me at the station yesterday. If not, I'm sure they'll be looking at me anyway. Maisy was in my care while we searched for Luciano last year, until she went into protective custody."

Lucas grunted.

Maisy pressed her lips together, brows furrowed. "I'll do whatever you think is necessary, but I have to see Dr. Nazir for my appointment this week. I can't miss that."

"All right," Lucas said. "Let me get dressed and make some coffee. I'll think of some ideas for relocation and call you back."

Blaze disconnected the call, then reached for Maisy's hand. "We won't miss the appointment," he vowed. "And I don't want you to worry. The move is strictly precautionary. We'll find a nice place with everything you need to be comfortable. Check in under fake names, then relax until the trial. It'll be an adventure. No one will know where we are, and all we'll have to do is pass another week or so playing cards and watching television."

The tension in her jaw and across her forehead lightened. "When you said off grid, I pictured myself eating cold corn out of a can and peeing in the woods."

Blaze barked a laugh. "I swear I will not let things get that bad. We'll spend the rest of today making plans then slip away after dark. How about that?"

She squeezed his hand. "Okay."

"Until then," he said, working up a brighter voice and smile, "I found something I want to show you." He stood and pulled her up with him, then led her into the living room, where his laptop sat open on the coffee table. "When I was reading up on your contractions last night, I found these videos on YouTube that I think you're going to like."

"What videos?" she asked, caution creeping into her voice. "I don't want to watch another woman deliver a baby. I've seen it, and it's terrifying."

Blaze moved the laptop to the end of the table, then sat on the floor in front of it. "Sit with me?" he asked, patting the floor in front of him, then opening his legs in a V.

She frowned.

"Trust me." He reached for her, and she sighed before following him onto the floor.

"Will you start the video?"

She dragged a fingertip over his laptop's touch pad, then clicked once before settling between his open legs, folding hers before her. "Lamaze," she said softly. "You found me an online Lamaze class?"

"There were a few with good reviews," he said, "but this one had the most views. That has to count for something, right? If you don't like it, we can watch a different one."

Maisy was still as the woman onscreen introduced herself, listing her experience and qualifications, then gushing over the miracle of motherhood, pregnancy and birth.

"Now you won't have to risk going anywhere to take the class," Blaze said softly, trying not to talk over the class leader. "I can be with you. You'll be prepared, and from what I've read, you can use the breathing techniques to help with pain from your Braxton-Hicks."

He pulled her hair over one shoulder, peeking around for a look at her face.

Maisy leaned against him, tilting her head to reveal a teary-eyed gaze. She pulled his arms around her and smoothed his palms over her bump. "Thank you," she whispered.

And Blaze knew whatever happened between them now, there would never be another woman in his life, because his heart forever belonged to her.

Chapter Ten

Maisy completed her first Lamaze class with Blaze as her partner. The moment was satisfying beyond her wildest dreams. Despite all the bad things that had happened, she could never have imagined seventy-two hours ago that she'd be in Blaze's home again, in his arms and completing a Lamaze class that he'd found online for her.

The smile on her face could possibly be permanent.

"That was good," he said. "What did you think?"

Maisy turned to face him where they sat, then rose onto her knees and framed his face in her hands. "This was the most perfect thing you could have done. It was exactly what I needed. And having you by my side was icing on the cake."

His eyes widened briefly before dropping their focus to her lips and going dark with something that looked a lot like hunger. "You're welcome."

She leaned forward, pressing her forehead to his and basking in the perfect moment. For the first time in what felt like forever, she was relaxed, grounded and at peace.

His hands rose to her waist, tugging her down to him, before slipping his fingers into her hair.

She started at the jolt of electricity that pulsed through her. Blaze's nearness had always affected her that way.

He cupped the back of her head, cradling her, and Maisy's inhibitions fell away.

Lost in the spell he'd always had on her, she pressed her lips to his and let everything else go. Warmth spread through her at the scents of his shampoo and cologne. The gentle scrape of his unshaven cheeks against her palms. The strength of his arms. Breadth of his chest.

His lips parted beneath hers, and she easily opened to receive him. Her heart pounded enthusiastically as he deepened the kiss.

When he moaned into her mouth, lavishing her generously with bone-melting caresses of his tongue, she worried there'd soon be little more than a puddle left of her.

Until then, she embraced it. Allowing joy to ping-pong inside her, erasing all the bad memories and replacing them with red-hot need and want and hope. Her head fell back as Blaze moved his mouth over her chin and down her neck, suckling and nipping in sweet, erotic bites.

She smiled at the ceiling, truly happy and completely relaxed for the first time in months. She soaked up the heat of his lips on her throat and his hands on her breasts until a rush of unbidden and unwanted worries returned. Ruining everything.

Her heart sank, then broke with memories of what had brought her back to him. And reminders that they would soon be on the run from her would-be killer. The icy blast cooled her heated core.

"What's wrong?" Blaze panted, sliding his hands over the curves of her hips. Concern and tenderness warred with want in his eyes. "Are you okay?"

She nodded, biting her lip and hating herself for inciting the kiss, only to pull away. "I'm sorry. I can't."

"Can't kiss me?" he asked. "Or something else?" He

released her when she pulled back, stroking her arm and reaching for her hand instead. "You were doing one hell of a job." He grinned, attempting to let her off the hook. "But it's okay if you don't want to anymore."

She nodded, unable to form the right words, if there were any, to explain herself. She just couldn't afford to get lost in another whirlwind relationship with Blaze, easy as that would be. She had more than herself to think about this time. There was a baby on the way who would need 100 percent of her. Whatever she and Blaze were doing, it couldn't continue, and losing him had nearly torn her apart the last time.

A peppy rap on Blaze's front door broke the tension, turning them both toward the sound. The shadow poised beyond the front window leaned forward and pressed cupped hands to the glass.

Blaze groaned. "Derek," he muttered, relaxing his posture as he turned back to Maisy, gentle eyes fixed on hers.

She held her breath in anticipation of whatever he might say.

Instead, he pressed a kiss against her forehead, then rose gracefully and offered her his hand, bringing her up with him.

She went to the kitchen table, thankful for the interruption, while Blaze answered the door. Her hands moved instinctively to her neck and collarbone, tracing the paths of his touch. Her fingertips glided over trembling lips, still sensitive from his kiss. She'd blame her hormones for turning a Lamaze class into a reason to make out on the living room floor, but she was certain her heart had as much to do with that as anything. Why did her life and love have to be so complicated?

A sharp wolf whistle drew her eyes to Derek, the oldest of the Winchester brothers, striding confidently in her direction. His arms were already open to embrace her. "Well, look at you."

Derek, Blaze and Lucas were what Maisy's grandmother called Irish triplets. The younger two were conceived within weeks of the previous boy's birth, keeping their poor mother pregnant for nearly three years straight. A predicament Maisy couldn't imagine. And didn't want to. But she could surely sympathize with any woman married to a Winchester. How could she possible keep her hands to herself?

Despite their close ages, Lucas, the youngest, was distinctly more easygoing than the others. Blaze tended to brood. And Derek had never met a woman he couldn't immediately relieve of her clothing.

"Hi, Derek," she said, tugging nervously on her shorter, now brown hair.

"Miss me?" he asked, wrapping her into a careful hug, as if he might somehow hurt her, or catch her pregnancy.

"Every minute," she said. "How'd you know I was here?" She looked around him as he released her, seeking Blaze's face.

"Blaze called everyone the minute he heard the good news." He grinned, gaze dropping to her middle.

"Everyone?" she asked, fighting a proud smile.

"Everyone listed under *W* for Winchester in his contacts list, I suspect," Derek said with a wink. "Our mama's fit to die if she doesn't get a look at you soon. She's planning a baby shower for immediately outside the courtroom following your testimony, I believe. I'm bringing potato salad."

Blaze laughed, arriving in the kitchen a moment later, arms loaded with what looked like groceries and a box of doughnuts. "I only called my brothers and parents. Mama did the rest. And Derek brought you food because apparently he didn't think I was feeding you."

"Pregnant women have cravings," Derek said.

"You came over to bring me doughnuts?" Maisy asked, enjoying the simple moment of normalcy. She couldn't wait to see Mr. and Mrs. Winchester again. They'd been so kind to her when they'd first met. They hadn't treated her as if she might break, despite the fact she was mired in guilt and grief. They'd called her strong and courageous.

"While I'm here, I thought we could work up a plan to hide you both for another week or so until the trial," Derek said. "I have strong connections to local law enforcement that keep me informed without obligating me to do anything I don't want to."

"They can order you to butt out," Maisy said, grinning.

"They can try."

"Sounds good," Blaze agreed, setting the doughnut box on his table and the sack of groceries beside it.

"Have you thought about reaching out to the judge or prosecuting attorneys?" Derek asked. "Maybe you can get the trial moved up or find a way for Maisy to give her testimony from a secondary location. Livestream it for the jury."

Blaze reached into the grocery bag, brows furrowed. "The trial's been pushed back three times already. There's no way they'll move it up, but we can ask about a live feed testimony."

"Be prepared for some pushback from the lawyers," Derek said. "They'll claim the jury needs her to be physically present, but the judge knows the situation. He'll have to consider her safety in all this and remember she's one of only two witnesses left."

"You're both assuming the judge isn't dirty," Maisy said, a knot of fear growing in her gut. "Someone definitely is."

The brothers traded pointed looks, then Blaze turned back to the groceries.

She watched in unexpected amusement as he lined up Derek's offerings on the table next to the doughnuts. Licorice and lemon candies. Crackers and ginger ale. A tub of rocky road ice cream. "Two jars of pickles?"

Derek shrugged. "One's dill. One's bread and butter."

"Very thoughtful."

"Thanks. So, when are you due?" he asked, apparently unable to stop staring at her middle. "Blaze was quick to deliver the news. Not so much with the details."

"About six weeks," she said. Luck willing.

"Boy or girl?"

"I don't know yet."

He scrunched his smug, handsome face. "Why not?" He hiked his brows when she only shrugged in response, then crossed his arms and leaned against the counter to stare at her.

She laughed. "I'd nearly forgotten how shy and unintrusive you are."

Blaze hauled the pickles to the refrigerator. "We'll know when we know, brother. For now, let's work on that plan for anonymous lodging, then set up arrangements for check-in, wherever we're headed."

Derek grinned wickedly. "All right. One more question."

Maisy crossed her arms and glared back. "If you ask me what I weigh, I will force-feed you all those dills."

"Have you thought of Derek for a boy name?" he asked, a hint of sincerity in his normally cocky tone.

"Hey," Blaze answered, smiling broadly as he slipped into the space at Maisy's side. "Get your own baby. This one is mine."

Maisy laughed. "How about we buy you a World's Best Uncle mug?" she suggested. "We can have Derek put on that."

Derek considered the offer briefly. "Make it a shot glass, and I'm in."

"Done." Blaze poured his brother a cup of coffee and ferried it to the table. "I'm open to suggestions on locations. We can stay under an alias without trouble and pay in cash," he said. "Not too far outside the city limits. She needs to be within fifteen minutes of a hospital. I don't want to take any chances if she gets hurt or sick."

Derek accepted, then sipped the coffee. "You also don't want to be too close to town, or anywhere a series of traffic cams or storefront surveillance videos could give you away."

Maisy listened as the brothers volleyed ideas. They were so much alike, yet so different. It reminded her of her relationship with Natalie. They'd been identical in appearance, but cut from two completely different cloths. Natalie had always been brave and bright, a wild little flame, ready to catch the world on fire. Maisy had been content to observe, never interested in sharing the spotlight. Too afraid of getting burned.

"There are some older motels on the edge of town," Blaze continued. "What do you know about those?"

"Nothing good," Derek admitted. "Prostitutes. Petty crime. Terrible dining options. What about that ritzy spa in the mountains? It's a little farther away, but they've got a doctor on staff."

Maisy's toes curled in hope. She'd never been to an actual overnight spa, but she could get behind spending a week at one.

Blaze lifted his brows, not seeming to hate the idea, either.

The sudden explosion of his front window elicited a scream from Maisy's core. Confusion overtook her as shards of glass cascaded across the wooden floor, skittering in jagged luminescent splinters. Something hard landed in the entryway and rolled in their direction, emitting a thick, acrid smoke.

Both brothers drew their weapons as Maisy fought to make sense of what was happening.

"Get down," Derek called, marching stealthily forward, gun drawn.

Maisy crouched, hands over her head and eyes tearing as the smoke began to fill Blaze's cabin. Nothing made any sense, yet it was all incredibly clear.

Blaze's home was under attack.

"Smoke bomb," Blaze growled, opening one arm wide as he positioned himself in front of Maisy, eyes trained through the growing cloud.

"He's coming in," Derek said, crouched low and gun raised. Acknowledging the obvious.

The only reason to use a device like this was to gain easy access. Soon he, Maisy and his brother would be blind, disoriented and gasping for air. Easy pickings for whoever had thrown the bomb. That person surely had a gas mask and planned to simply walk inside and kill them all.

But this guy had picked the wrong cabin.

The front door burst open a moment later, barely visible now. The sound of splintering wood assured him the barrier had been kicked in.

Derek vanished in the thick gray smoke.

"Derek." Maisy coughed the word.

"He's got this," Blaze said, unable to name a time anyone had gotten the drop on his big brother. "Stay with me. We'll get out of here."

Maisy's small fingers curled into the fabric of Blaze's T-shirt, and she coughed against his back.

"Cover your mouth," he instructed, softly, gut clenching and fear gripping his throat. "Stay low. Back door."

They moved together a few feet before Derek barreled into Blaze, arms pinwheeling, curses flying. Maisy screamed, and the sound ricocheted through Blaze's heart.

Derek righted himself, wiping a sleeve across his face with a sneer before launching back into the fog.

Unseen things broke and shattered around them, stirring up the chaos and shooting terror through Blaze's veins. There was more than one assailant, he realized with a start. The shooter had worked alone, but it took more than one criminal to storm a cabin.

A gunshot rang out, and ice washed through Blaze's veins.

Maisy pressed her face into his back, no doubt recalling the last time she'd been under siege like this and lost a friend.

He reached for her arms, pulling her to his side, then rushing her toward the back door. They needed fresh air and the space to dial 911. If they could circle back to the driveway and get Maisy behind the wheel of his truck, Blaze might even be able to come back and help his brother.

The plan was forming in his head when a second explosion stopped him short. Light flowed through the hazy space where the rear door had once been.

And a form appeared in the haze. A fist connected with Blaze's head before he could turn back. He fell against Maisy, pinning her against the wall.

She screamed, then ducked free, coughing as she vanished into the smoke.

Blaze blinked burning, watering eyes, unsure which direction was up when the second hit arrived, knocking him onto the floor. His training kicked in a heartbeat later, spurred by fear of Maisy's absence, and realization of what that absence could mean. His leg shot out on autopilot as years of hand-to-hand combat training jerked into motion. His foot connected hard with his intruder's torso, eliciting a low, guttural response. Blaze jerked upright on the next breath, fueled by rage and resolve. He landed two sharp punches against his assailant before dropping the man like a sack of potatoes. He didn't get back up.

"Maisy!" Blaze turned in the smoke, eyes stinging and blurred. His throat burned with every breath. His lungs screamed in protest of the polluted air.

Something looped around his throat and tightened, cutting off his limited oxygen. And his world began to shimmer.

Blaze clawed at the rope, cutting into his skin, twisting his body in an attempt to break free.

And a hail of gunshots erupted, illuminating the hazy cabin in muzzle flashes. He threw both elbows backward, aiming and missing his attacker, then the rope tightened again. His knees went weak, and his vision tunneled to a pinhole.

Then Blaze's attacker collapsed behind him, releasing the rope as he fell.

Blaze crumpled forward, gulping poisoned air and coughing against the intake.

Maisy dropped an iron skillet before him, then latched onto Blaze's arms and dragged him toward the broken-in door.

Chapter Eleven

Blaze stood beside the open ambulance doors while Isaac examined Maisy. She'd somehow managed to escape the attack on his cabin without any apparent injuries, despite being unarmed, untrained and seven months pregnant. More than that, she'd saved his life.

Blaze had already called her obstetrician to request her appointment be moved up. The doctor had easily agreed to make room for her first thing tomorrow morning. They'd go to the ER now if Isaac thought it was necessary. Otherwise it was time to pack up and get out of town.

"I'm fine," she complained around an oxygen mask while Isaac continued to monitor her vitals. "The baby's having a party, and I feel better than I have in days."

"It's the adrenaline and oxygen," Isaac told her, working the stethoscope out of his ears and looking strangely at Blaze.

"What?"

His brother frowned. "I'm not sure. Come in here a sec."

Blaze climbed into the ambulance, every fiber of him on full alert. "What's wrong?"

Isaac handed the stethoscope to Blaze. "Put this on. Tell me if you can hear this."

Blaze obeyed without question and looked to Maisy, terror-stricken and praying it didn't show.

Isaac pressed the chest piece against her bump, and it jumped.

Blaze's eyes widened. It was the first time he'd seen Maisy's bare stomach since their reunion. The first he'd ever seen a child moving inside its mother. *His child*, he recalled fiercely, and an instant lump formed in his throat. If something was wrong with their baby…

Isaac moved the chest piece, setting it a few inches away, then looked to Blaze. "How about now? Does that sound right to you?"

Blaze glared back. He had no medical training. If Isaac suspected something was wrong, they should be on the road, doubling the speed limit to get help for his family, not running the hunch past an untrained, inept detective.

"Listen, please," Isaac encouraged.

A small thrumming registered.

Blaze felt his lips part and his chest tighten, as if the tiny sound was connected directly to his heart. "That's—"

"Your baby," Isaac said proudly. "A fine, strong heartbeat, for what I can only assume is a completely healthy child. The obstetrician will likely perform an ultrasound tomorrow and look at each finger and toe, but I don't have any reason to think you need an immediate trip to the ER."

Blaze stared at the place where his child squirmed just below the surface, the steady lub-dub, lub-dub, repeating in his ear. He raised blurring eyes to Maisy.

She caught a tear rolling down her cheek and laughed. Her bright smile was pure pride. True joy. He returned the stethoscope to Isaac without taking his eyes off Maisy, then rested his ear against her middle.

Maisy laced her fingers into his hair and stroked the strands from his forehead as he listened for a heartbeat he could no longer hear and enjoyed the subtle motion of their baby inside her.

"I'll give you three a moment," Isaac said, climbing down from the bay.

Outside, a crowd of law enforcement officials had gathered beside a collection of vehicles. Police cruisers. Government SUVs. A fire truck and other ambulances, along with their drivers and passengers, rounded out the heavily armed circus. Two men were in custody—one shot in the shoulder by Derek, and the other with significant head trauma, thanks to Maisy and Blaze's grandmother's wrought iron skillet. Neither man was carrying any form of identification. And they weren't talking.

"Stop me if I'm ruining the moment," Maisy said softly, "but all those lawmen aren't making me feel any safer."

Slowly, Blaze forced himself upright, unsure what to say. There weren't words. He'd thought the same thing more than once since the caravan of vehicles had begun to arrive. Someone involved in this case was dirty. And it could be any one of the men and women outside right now. "Agreed."

Derek strode across the grassy lawn toward the ambulance, a reluctant smile on his smug face. "How are you guys doing?"

"Good," Maisy answered, tugging her shirt over her exposed stomach. "You?"

"Not a scratch on me." He squared his shoulders. "Unlike the goons in the other ambulances."

"You shot someone," she said, softly. The words were thick with compassion and concern. "That's got to be hard."

Derek frowned dramatically. He bent, then straightened, his pointer finger in the air a few times. "Nah. It's pretty easy. You just—" He turned the finger gun toward a nearby medical kit and gave a few pulls before blowing across the tip. "Anyway. He'll be fine." He pretended to holster his finger. "I never go for the kill shot. I like to see them suffer."

"Lovely." She smirked. "I guess I worried for nothing."

Blaze smiled. No one called Derek on his nonsense faster than Maisy. He could almost see her at their big family dinners, passing an infant to Blaze, taunting Derek and helping his mother harass his father.

"What?" Derek's voice drew Blaze back to the moment. He stared, confused.

"Nothing." Blaze shook off the little fantasy. It was time to get his mind out of the clouds and back on the situation at hand. "Think I can get Maisy out of here without a tail?"

Derek grinned. "Give me a few minutes to talk to the marshals and uniforms." His gaze swept over the cluster of lawmen in the driveway, then narrowed on Blaze's cabin. "Leave your house key, and I'll board up the broken window and deal with the busted doorjambs. Mom will want to handle the mess inside."

Blaze worked the key off his ring and planted it in his brother's hand.

Derek fixed Maisy with a prideful smile. "You did good in there. Protected yourself, my niece or nephew, and my brother. I owe you for that."

"I'm counting on it," she said. "You can start by helping Blaze keep me alive until the trial."

"Already on it," he said, tossing the key into the air, then catching it. He winked before jogging away.

Thirty minutes later, the congestion in the driveway had thinned to Derek and Blaze's trucks, a cruiser and a crime scene SUV. The ambulances had gone, along with most of the lawmen. Derek leaked the story that Blaze and Maisy were headed to a spa outside town until the trial. He'd booked a room for them to help cement the cover, then loaded Blaze's truck with their bags.

A crime scene unit worked methodically through the mess inside Blaze's home, but Derek would stay to see the place secured and cleaned when they finished.

Blaze kept a heavy foot on the gas pedal as they fled town, though he had no plan, and no idea where he was going. A good thing, because if he didn't know the destination, no dirty lawmen could, either.

"We can rent a home from one of those vacation rental websites," Maisy suggested. "Or stay at a bed-and-breakfast under false names."

"False identities are a good idea, and I want to be able to pay in cash. If you feel safe waiting in the car, once we decide where we're going, I can check in alone. Then, anyone stopping by to ask about a couple with a pregnant lady won't find us."

He adjusted his grip on the steering wheel, longing to keep driving until the truck ran out of gas. They could take a cab from there. Stop at the nearest airport, then hop a flight out of the country. Hell, he'd leave the planet if he thought it would keep Maisy and their baby safe. But it wasn't that easy. She needed to see Dr. Nazir in the morning.

A small rusted sign at the next crossroads caught his eye and moved his foot from the gas pedal to the brake. Brandy Falls, just ten miles ahead.

"I have an idea." Blaze hit his turn signal, though there wasn't anyone on the road behind him, and headed up the mountain.

"The ski resort?" she asked. "The season won't open for another month."

"Exactly." Off-season meant an affordable rate, available lodging and no crowds.

Blaze navigated the winding, hilly roads, following signs toward the lodge. He'd never been much of a skier, but he'd been in the area more than a few times. Hiking in warmer weather. Snow tubing in the winter. "The national park butts up against land owned by the resort. There's a lot of rough terrain this far out but some worthwhile views if you manage the trails. The resort has cabin rentals—there won't be any prying eyes for miles this time of year."

"No well-meaning staff or other guests to spot or recognize me from the news," Maisy said.

He smiled, more confident in his decision by the minute. "We're only about fifteen or twenty minutes from the nearest hospital and your doctor," Blaze said. "A quick drive down the mountain to anything you might need if it isn't available at the general store."

In short, the ski resort was a perfect hideout.

MAISY WATCHED THE beauty passing outside her window. She'd always loved the national park but never knew it stretched this far west. She wasn't a skier, so the entire area was new to her. Unfamiliar, but breathtakingly gorgeous this time of year. Any leaves still clinging to the trees were dressed in an array of color from gold to crimson and eggplant. The road was lined in them.

A small mom-and-pop shop appeared around the next bend, and Blaze hit his turn signal. "General store," he announced, veering into the empty, narrow lot out front. "I'm going to run in and buy a few groceries. Do you need anything?"

Signs in the store's window proclaimed it to be "one-stop shopping." Buy groceries. Order a pizza. Pick up the essentials. Even order flowers.

Her gaze caught on a pink flyer with the image of a bouquet and logo for a national florist. Four words printed beneath had her unfastening her seat belt.

Show someone you care.

"Mind if I come with you?" she asked, already opening her door.

Blaze hesitated before apparently realizing the question was rhetorical and releasing a reluctant sigh.

They made a trip around the store's interior perimeter together before splitting up to shop. Maisy made her way to the counter, hands shaking as memories of the safe house shootout raced in her mind. Clara's funeral had been announced on the radio. A local station was organizing a donation fund for her family. Maisy couldn't attend the service or say a proper goodbye, but she could send flowers. Clara's family should know she cared at least that much. If she survived the trial, Maisy would find a way to apologize in person. To let them know how much Clara's loss hurt her, too. And that she'd died the same way she lived, fighting to protect others.

An older man behind the counter smiled when he saw her. He slid a pair of glasses from the shirt pocket of his blue flannel and placed them on his nose. "How can I help you?" he asked brightly, either a true people person or bored from the lack of human interaction on the mountain this time of year.

"I'd like to order flowers," she said, scanning a colored pamphlet on the countertop.

"We can make anything you'd like if you don't see something you want," he said. "I just punch it into the computer and a florist near the delivery site works it all out."

"It's okay," she said, realizing belatedly that she had to pay cash and didn't have much left. "I'll take this one." She chose an embarrassingly small arrangement, then signed the card with her initials.

"No message?" he asked. "Is this for a friend or family?"

"It's for a funeral," she said, the word lodging painfully in her throat. She completed the order form with details on Clara's upcoming memorial service, then passed the man her money and wiped her eyes. "Thank you."

She took her time searching for Blaze, pulling herself together with each step. She found him crouched before the dairy case.

He squatted next to a full shopping basket with one kind of fruit juice in each hand. The basket brimmed with healthy foods, and he looked at the juice labels as if he might soon get an aneurysm.

"What are you doing?" she asked, sniffing back the leftover emotion that ordering flowers had caused.

He looked up, brows furrowed. "Do you need more vitamin C or D? Or is it folic acid?"

She forced a tight smile, and her bottom lip quivered. "What? No doughnuts and pickles?"

"No." He tucked both bottles into his arms and stood with the basket in hand. "Are you okay?"

"I will be," she said.

And she hoped desperately the words were true.

BLAZE PARKED OUTSIDE the lodge at the top of the mountain, then left his gun with Maisy before hurrying inside to rent a cabin. The middle-aged woman behind the counter barely looked at him, attention fixed to a game on her phone. Still, he made a point of telling her he was a Nevada artist, hoping to find his muse in the Kentucky wilderness.

She grunted, took his cash and wished him well.

Cabin Nineteen was roughly the color of moss, blending easily into the surrounding forest, nearly camouflaged by evergreen trees. The driveway was short and directly accessed by a paved looping road. Several other cabins were visible on the trip from the lodge, though there were no indications they were rented. No vehicles in the drives. No smoke rising from the chimneys.

All very good signs.

Blaze carried the last of the luggage inside, leaving the bags in the entryway. The air was stuffy, tinged with bleach and must. Likely unoccupied for months. The walls were paneled. The floors, cabinets and furniture were pine. The look was rustic but clearly fabricated. The front and back doors were visible from the large square space divided into a living room and kitchen, with a small dinette in between.

Maisy appeared from the hallway, her button nose wrinkled. "One bedroom?"

He laughed. "Sorry. I needed to pay cash for a week and have money left over for necessities. Also, I had to keep up the appearance of being alone." He was thankful he'd had so much cash on hand. He'd pulled a large amount from savings months ago, planning to buy a fishing boat, only to change his mind. He hadn't gotten around to putting the money back in the bank, and for once, the procrastination had worked in his favor.

She leaned a hip against the couch, a smile playing on her lips. "All you Nevada artists are the same, with your watercolors and your one-track minds."

Blaze headed into the little kitchen, where he'd left the groceries, then began to unpack. "Don't worry. I'm going to sleep on the couch." He repeated the fact internally a few times, making sure it sank in.

"Oh, I wasn't worried," she said. "But you realize this couch is barely five feet long, right?" She aimed a remote at the television. "You're six-one."

His phone rang, and Maisy tensed. "It's Sergeant Maxwell." He accepted the call and raised the phone to his ear. "Winchester."

"Where are you?" Maxwell asked.

"Safe," Blaze said. "What's going on?"

Maisy circled the couch, one hand on her bump, then lowered onto a cushion. The channels changed as she searched, presumably for the local news.

"I spoke with the judge," Maxwell said. "He won't move the trial, and he isn't interested in receiving testimony by video, but he agreed to discuss a livestream with counsel and get back to us."

Blaze leaned against the counter, both relieved and hopeful. "That's more than I expected, so I'll consider it a win. Maybe we'll get lucky and the attorneys will both agree."

"And maybe pigs will fly," Maxwell said, "but we

won't know until he asks. On that note, I also need to tell you the prosecutor wants to meet with Miss Daniels. He says it's time to review her testimony. He'll prep her for what to expect from the defense and help her hone her responses. Otherwise the defense is guaranteed to poke holes in whatever she says. She can't afford to let them fluster her, sidetrack her or anything else the jury might see as less than convincing. Plan for a couple sessions this week. An hour or so each time. He doesn't want her to feel rushed or pressured, and I'm sure reliving a story like hers will be slow and difficult."

Blaze tightened his jaw. He didn't like the idea of taking Maisy anywhere other than her doctor's office. And the prosecutor's law firm, located inside the local courthouse, seemed especially risky. Any nut trying to kill her before the trial would expect her to show up there eventually. There had to be a better way. "I'll reach out to him."

"Good."

After a few more assurances that Maisy was safe, Maxwell agreed to trust Blaze, and the men disconnected. Blaze grabbed a bottle of water and carried it to Maisy on the couch.

She accepted the offering easily. "Thanks." After a long sip, she set the drink aside and looked to him with worried eyes. "What did your sergeant say?"

"You have to meet with the prosecutor this week and practice your testimony. He'll review everything he plans to ask you, then prep you for the defense's cross-examination. I'll set the appointment tomorrow. For now, let's just take the rest of the day to settle in and breathe."

She nodded, turning blankly to a rerun on the television. A sitcom from Blaze's childhood.

He looped an arm around her shoulders and tugged her against his side. "You want to talk?"

"No." She rested her head on his shoulder. "Natalie loved this show."

He tipped his cheek against her head and held her.

She watched silently until the next commercial break. "I hate that this is my life right now," she said quietly. "I hate that Nat's gone, and that I have to do this without her. I hate that she went back for Mom's book that day when I should've just let the book go or gone after it myself."

"You didn't ask her to do it," he said. "It wasn't your fault." They'd had this conversation before, but he knew she could never hear his response enough. "Natalie went to get the book because it was important to you, and you were important to her. She wanted to help you."

"She didn't want to die for me," Maisy snapped, voice cracking. "But she did."

"Neither of you could have known. No one could have guessed Aaron was in debt to Luciano. Your instincts told you Aaron was shady. Assuming he was seeing someone else makes a lot more sense than thinking he was about to be murdered by a crime boss."

"She called me to tell me about the car in the drive," Maisy said. "She sent me a picture of it. Then she sent me a video of Luciano with his hands around Aaron's throat. I heard the gunshots. I was on the line while she watched Luciano kill Aaron. I heard her scream, listened as she drove away, terrified, describing it all to me. Luciano said Aaron owed him money and made him look foolish, so he wasn't getting any more chances to do the right thing. That's the price for damaging a psychopath's ego, I guess. The same price Natalie paid for being a witness to murder. Luciano choked him and beat him before ending it with three shots. Then he chased my sister down and ran her off the road and into a tree. The coroner thinks she died on impact, but before he found and took her phone, Luciano shot her three times."

"I am so sorry," Blaze said, pressing a kiss against her head and holding her impossibly tighter as her body shook with sobs.

Her hot tears collected on his shirt where her cheek rested.

Her fingers curled into the fabric of his sleeve and held on tightly as the sitcom droned ahead.

And he stayed with her, unmoving, until her grip loosened. And her thin, thready breaths came slow and deep. Until she finally found rest.

Chapter Twelve

Maisy thought of Clara's funeral all night, wishing she could go and hating more than anything that Clara was gone. Attending the service would've given Maisy closure and the chance to say goodbye, but she couldn't imagine her presence making Clara's family feel any better. Maisy had lived, after all. Why had she and not Clara? She pushed the thought away. It didn't matter. Maisy was back on lockdown. Another lunatic out to kill her. She could only hope that no one else would die because of her.

Dr. Nazir popped swiftly into mind. Maisy selfishly hoped the doctor had heard about Clara on the news, because she wasn't sure she could tell that story again. Attending the appointment without her would already be sad enough.

Maisy wandered through her morning routine, barely tasting the tea, fruit or yogurt before her.

Blaze padded into view as she finished her breakfast. He poured a mug of coffee then took the seat across from her. His hair was damp from the shower, and the scent of his soap and shampoo hung around him like a cloud. "You look miserable," he said. "Are you nervous about leaving the cabin this morning?"

"A little," she said, sure that was at least partially true. She didn't feel like mentioning Clara's funeral was today, or how much she wanted to be there, even if Clara's family might not want to see her. Instead, she motioned to the folded blanket and pillow stacked on the cabin's stumpy, utilitarian couch. The furniture piece was sturdy and fine to look at but uncomfortable to sit on. She couldn't imagine sleeping there had been very restful. Which made it seem all the more ridiculous and impractical that she'd been alone in a queen bed while Blaze had suffered all night in the living room. It wasn't as if he hadn't shared her bed before or wouldn't be able to keep his hands off her.

Though she wasn't sure she could be trusted to return the favor. It didn't even matter she was a little in the dumps this morning. Just seeing him made her want to be held by him. Protected. Touched. "Did you get any sleep?" she asked, forcing a change in the direction of her thoughts.

"A little." His lips formed a small, inauthentic smile that didn't reach his eyes.

Her curiosity budded. She'd been beating herself up internally, wondering if her desperation to make Luciano pay for what he'd done to her sister had ultimately led to the deaths of several more people, like Clara.

But what had Blaze looking so conflicted?

She held his gaze when it flickered to her for the dozenth time in half as many minutes. "What's on your mind, Detective?"

He cleared his throat. "Should we talk about what happened yesterday?"

Her lungs itched with immediate memories of the smoke bomb. The sounds of splintering wood as the doors to Blaze's home were kicked in. The feel of the frying pan in her grip as it connected with the intruder's head. A criminal who, until now, she'd barely spared another thought. Was that what was on Blaze's mind? Had she killed the guy? Her stomach roiled at the thought. "Did you hear something more about the home invasion?" she asked. "About the men who were injured?"

Blaze puckered his brows. "No. Before that." He averted his eyes while she considered what he might mean. When he drew his attention back to her, he looked ten years younger and a little like a kid who'd just stolen a cookie from the jar.

The proverbial lightbulb flickered on, and she blushed. "The kiss," she said, realizing now he clearly regretted it. She'd replayed it gratuitously through the night. Recalling each moment vividly, turning in his arms and reaching for his handsome face. Now her nervous stomach rocked for a new reason. Blaze thought kissing her had been a mistake. Why else would he want to talk about it?

She dropped her hands to her lap, embarrassed and scrunching the napkin she'd placed there in her fists. She'd been dreaming of a world where she and her baby were safe and Blaze was in their lives. Maybe even in a forever kind of way. The heat of humiliation flamed hot across her cheeks.

"I enjoyed helping you with the Lamaze class," he said carefully. An obvious attempt to avoid hurting her feelings.

Her mind filled in the rest. He'd enjoyed the class but hadn't expected to be physically attacked afterward.

She imagined changing her name and moving to Bogotá. Anywhere far enough to start over. Leave her world of crime bosses, assassins and handsome, brooding detectives behind.

Unfortunately, she wasn't a runner. She was cursed with a concrete stay-and-fight disposition. So, uncomfortable or not, she'd have to get through this conversation, then suck up the bruised heart and ego. There were bigger problems on her horizon. "You enjoyed the Lamaze class," she repeated back to him when he didn't go on. She raised her chin, hoping to look stronger than she felt. "And you hoped we could do another one after the appointment this morning?"

"I'd like that," he said. "If you're feeling up to it." He wrapped his long fingers around the steamy mug, still looking unforgivably guilty. "I know your world is in complete upheaval right now, and I don't want to make it more complicated."

She pursed her lips as her heart fell. The tiny piece of her that had hoped she was wrong fractured.

"I want to help you," he continued. "However I can."

"Good." She smiled. "Because I hear I'll need a lot of help after the baby's born. At least in those first few days while I recover from delivery."

His expression changed suddenly. Flashes of emotion too brief and fleeting to name swept through his blue-gray eyes then vanished, locked behind the careful cop veneer he'd mastered long before Maisy had met him. "Whatever you need."

She forced herself upright, pushed her chair in and delivered her dirty dishes to the sink. There weren't many things she could control in her life at the moment, but she could still walk out of this awkward, miserable conversation. "Right now, I need a shower. I don't want to be late for Dr. Nazir."

BLAZE KICKED HIMSELF MENTALLY, and repeatedly, as he waited for Maisy to return from the shower. He'd also taken his time getting ready this morning, planning what he wanted to say to her about their kiss. He wanted to know why she'd pulled away from him, and if it was possible that he could find a place in her future. Longer than a few days after her delivery.

Kissing her hadn't been part of the plan when he'd found the Lamaze class online. He'd known the temptation would be there, working so closely with her, preparing for the birth of their child. But he'd firmly resolved to let the moment be about her and their baby. Not his inability to keep his hands off her. Then, the moment she'd set a palm against his cheek, he'd fallen straight into the tender, yearning look in her eyes. He went for it, trying to tell her exactly how he felt with a kiss.

He'd been lost for her the moment their eyes had met last year. Something about her energy and presence had spoken to him. No, it called to him. Their relationship had been deeply intimate and wholly unprofessional from the start. It was consuming. Breathtaking. And everything he could have asked for. He'd often wondered what she thought of him while she was away. The detective who'd taken a grieving woman to bed while hunting for her sister's killer. He had to admit, it didn't look good. Now she was back and carrying his child. This seemed like fate. The perfect opportunity to show her the man he really was, integrity and all. But thirty minutes of holding her and watching her smile through a basic Lamaze class had brought him right back where they'd started.

Even finding the video online had been laced with ulterior motive. He'd wanted to impress her. To prove he'd been thinking of her and that he'd heard her when she said she still needed the classes. He'd wanted to give her something good and peaceful in a time filled with tragedy and noise.

He hadn't meant to make it into anything else.

He was supposed to show her he cared about her deeply and beyond their profound physical connection.

When the whir of the blow-dryer silenced, Blaze considered marching down the short hall and knocking on her door. He wanted to tell her he'd botched their earlier conversation and that he hadn't regretted the kiss, if that was what she'd thought. He'd regretted the timing. He wanted her to know he was a safe place for her. And she could trust him to be whatever she needed, without him making it physical. He wanted to remove her problems, not add himself to the list.

He scraped his palm against his cheek, determined to give her room. He'd double down on the task at hand. Keep her safe until the trial. Then she'd take the stand, give the testimony and begin to rebuild her life. If he played his cards right, she might even let him be part of that.

Maisy reappeared ten minutes before they needed to leave for her doctor's appointment, dressed in black stretchy pants and a soft green sweater. Her sharp hazel eyes looked at everything except him. "We should go," she said. "Better to be early than late."

Blaze grabbed his keys, determined to show her how much she meant, even if he couldn't seem to find the words.

The short drive into town felt like hours as he searched for things to say.

"It's really getting cold this week," he tried. "The

weatherman is predicting snow. Should make for some beautiful views from the cabin."

Maisy trailed her fingertips across the window at her side. "Hopefully the resort maintains the roads off-season. I'm nervous enough about talking to the prosecutor without worrying we'll slide off a mountain trying to get to him."

Blaze smiled, thankful the ice between them was beginning to thaw as Dr. Nazir's office came into view. "I'll get you to the appointments and anywhere else you need to go. Whatever the weather," he promised. "I'll rent a snowmobile if I have to."

She laughed, and his heart warmed.

Blaze parked in the small office lot and smiled through the window. "So, which came first, the obstetrician's office or the bakery right across the street?"

Maisy smiled. "I'm not sure, but the bakery gets my business after every appointment. Today I'm thinking about a loaded hot chocolate and a strawberry-filled croissant."

"Done," he assured her, climbing out of the truck and circling around to meet her. "I don't suppose they serve cheesecake there."

Her eyebrows rose and her head began to nod. "About fifty kinds, and they're all delicious. Trust me. I'm a shameless sampler."

The rapid thunder of an air hammer drew Blaze's attention to a new building going up beside the bakery. Construction workers lined steel girders and peppered the ground level, running every manner of power tool and making an earsplitting racket. A sign near the road announced Coming Soon! Mother Hubbard's Book Cupboard.

"I can't wait for the bookstore to open," Maisy said.

"I want to check it out, and I'm tired of hearing all the racket when I come here."

Blaze followed her into the doctor's office, silently planning a day trip to the finished store. They could choose books for their baby's library and top the day off with desserts from the bakery next door. The construction noises lowered to a dull drone as they approached the reception desk. The eyes of every woman in the waiting room followed them.

"Hello." The woman behind the counter beamed at Maisy, then Blaze, and back. "Dr. Nazir asked me to take you right in when you arrived."

Maisy was weighed, then given a plastic cup with a smile.

Blaze waited under the watchful eyes of nurses and other waiting patients.

When she returned from the restroom, they were taken to an exam room, and Maisy climbed onto the table. Framed images of women at every age lined the muted pink walls. Girls flying kites. Grandmothers on porches. Teens lying on their backs in a field.

"I guess they don't see a lot of men around here," he said after the nurse closed the door. "I feel like I've intruded on the girls' club."

Maisy rolled her eyes and pointed to the wall behind him. "All those women were staring at you because you look like that. Don't pretend you don't know."

He turned to face the wall and started at the sight of himself in a mirror. A slow grin spread across his face.

"Stop," she warned, watching his expression in the reflection.

"You still think I'm handsome," he accused.

Something shuffled outside the room, and Blaze's hand went to his sidearm.

"Do not shoot my doctor," Maisy instructed.

An attractive thirtysomething woman froze in the doorway, eyes wide. The words *Alaya Nazir, MD*, were embroidered in blue on her white lab coat. Her wide whiskey-colored eyes darted from Blaze to Maisy, who nearly threw herself off the table at the woman.

"Maisy." She breathed the word, kicking the door shut behind her as they embraced. "Oh, it's so good to see you. I heard about what happened, and I've been horrified by all of it." She released Maisy, then extended a hand to Blaze. "Thank you so much for bringing her."

"Wouldn't have missed it," he said.

"Sit. Sit." The doctor motioned him to a small plastic chair and Maisy onto the table. She grinned at Maisy. "Now, tell me everything. Start with why your friend wants to shoot me."

Maisy laughed, then made a formal introduction.

Dr. Nazir gave Blaze a long once-over. "So this is *the* Blaze Winchester." A little smile played on her lips. "I see." She wagged perfectly sculpted brows.

A deep blush rose on Maisy's cheeks, and Blaze smiled. "Yep."

Dr. Nazir flashed a mischievous look at Blaze, then turned her full attention to Maisy. "You weren't kidding."

The women laughed, and before long, Maisy was lying back on the little paper-covered table. The doctor pressed a device to her bump, and the baby's heartbeat rang out, strong and true. "That's fast," Maisy said. "Faster than I remember. Is that okay?"

Dr. Nazir smiled warmly. "Yes. Quite. Would you like to know your baby's gender, now that you're both here?"

Blaze looked to Maisy, a thrill rocketing up his spine. She didn't look as sure. "Only if you want to," he said. "You've waited this long. I can wait a few more weeks."

She bit her lip, then looked at her doctor.

"How about this," Dr. Nazir suggested. "I'm going to perform an ultrasound and make sure everything looks good. Can't be too careful after the week you've had, and especially after yesterday. If you decide you want to know the gender while I'm working on that, I can show you. If you decide you want to know later, you can call the office."

Maisy nodded. "Okay."

The ultrasound made Maisy cry, and Blaze wasn't too far from it. Seeing the strange black-and-white image of a baby kicking inside her had been more intense than he'd anticipated. If she allowed him to be present at the birth, he wasn't sure he could stay composed.

When the appointment ended, Dr. Nazir delivered strict instructions to Blaze. "Make sure she rests. The amount of physical and emotional stress she's under is no good for anyone, especially not a woman at this point in her pregnancy. She needs to be still. Feet up. Healthy foods. Plenty of water. And peacefulness. We want to maintain this pregnancy as long as possible. Understand?"

"Yes, ma'am," he answered, remembering all the scary articles he'd read about premature births. "I'll do everything I can."

"Good." The doctor smiled. "I want to see you again in two weeks."

Maisy made the return appointment at the front desk, then took Blaze's hand as they left the building. "Thanks for coming with me."

Construction noise roared to life as they stepped into the parking lot. Blaze had completely blocked the sounds out by the time they'd made it to the exam room. Now, the jackhammer seemed offensively loud. "I wouldn't have missed it. Will we get to see the baby at the next appointment?"

"Maybe," Maisy answered, pressing her free hand to her ear. "Dr. Nazir has been incredibly generous with the number of ultrasounds she's allowed. From what I've read online, most women only get one or two."

Blaze squeezed her hand, his heart full to the brim. "Still in the mood for that loaded hot chocolate?"

"I'm always in the mood for cocoa."

Their strides fell into an easy unison as they reached the crosswalk. *This is how life should have always been*, Blaze thought, folding his fingers with hers.

He almost didn't hear the suddenly revving engine or squealing tires as a black sports car fishtailed out from the alley between buildings and flung itself screaming in their direction.

Chapter Thirteen

Maisy caught sight of the out-of-control car as Blaze jerked her forward. The roar of the engine became the only sound in her world. She wrapped her free arm around her middle as she ran, towed by Blaze toward the sidewalk ahead. Her strides were awkward, her balance hindered thanks to her completely wrecked center of balance. And she knew with a lung-crushing punch that she couldn't clear the car's path in time. A growl of agony ripped from her core. After all she'd been through, a car would be the thing to finish her.

Then Blaze was at her side. No longer dragging her forward. And her feet were off the ground. Swept from beneath her as he pulled her completely into his arms like a child. One swift and fluid motion later, they were nearly airborne as his long legs finished the trip. Blaze launched them to safety, darting between parked cars at the roadside in a wild, adrenaline-fueled leap.

Blaze wrecked his hip on the larger car's grille, setting off the alarm before they landed in a heap on the strip of grass between the curb and sidewalk. He took the brunt of the fall, doing all he could to put himself beneath her. Wind from the racing car whipped over them as it passed, tossing Maisy's hair and blasting road dirt into her eyes.

A split second later, her head cracked against the soggy ground and her vision blurred.

"Is she all right?" a woman yelled, rushing from the bakery to their side.

"Yes," Maisy said weakly. Her voice was thin and warbly to her ears. "I don't know," she amended, a rush of emotion flattening her heart. "The baby." An inexplicable numbness settled over her—shock, she supposed. Confusion. And fear. She'd survived the attacking car, thanks to Blaze, but what about her baby?

Blaze rose to his knees. "Call 911," he said. "Tell them there was an attempted hit-and-run, late-model black sports car. Give them the location." He cupped Maisy's face in his hands, expression conflicted. "I'm going to move you." He scooped her up once more with a curse and jogged back across the street with a limp. "Did you hit your head?" he asked, grimacing with every pace. "Can you move all your limbs? Do you have any specific pains?"

Maisy couldn't answer. She couldn't breathe. If Luciano's henchman had hurt her unborn child, or worse, how could she survive it? He'd already taken Natalie and Clara. Her mind shoved the possibility away.

"We need help," Blaze demanded, shoving the door to her doctor's office open with his shoulder. "She's hurt. She took a hard fall. Hit her head, I think. We need Dr. Nazir. Now!"

Patients gasped. The office staff kicked into gear, rushing to aid them.

Maisy's ears rang, and her world tilted as people fluttered into action around her, hurrying out of their way, opening the door to the hall with exam rooms and asking questions as Blaze barreled forward.

A woman in scrubs led them to an exam room. "Put her on the table."

Blaze obliged, a tortured expression on his handsome face.

"Maisy?" Dr. Nazir arrived on the click-clack of heels, concern drawing lines across her tawny brow. "What happened?"

Blaze recapped as the doctor shined a light into Maisy's eyes and a nurse pulled Maisy's shirt up, then loaded her skin with icy goo.

Blaze moved away, giving the medical professionals room. He gripped the back of his neck with both hands, looking more grief-stricken than anyone she'd ever seen. His shirt and jacket were torn and dirty. A collection of bloody scrapes tore across his cheek and forehead.

"Our baby," she choked, afraid he somehow knew something she didn't.

"I'm looking at your baby now," Dr. Nazir said calmly. She drove the ultrasound wand over Maisy's bump. And there was silence.

"Where's the heartbeat?" Maisy cried.

A nurse slipped a pulse oximeter over the tip of Maisy's finger. "Shh," she soothed. "She's okay. Just busy, dodging the transducer." She pointed to the screen as a small white leg kicked out.

Then, the heartbeat began.

"There we go," Dr. Nazir said. "Your little one is all amped up from the action."

A deep relief rushed from Maisy's chest, and a fresh round of tears began. "Sorry," she sobbed.

The nurse handed her a wad of tissues, smiling sweetly. "See? Everything is going to be okay."

Maisy wiped her eyes. She replayed the previous moments, then looked to Blaze, who'd collapsed into the chair against the wall. "Did you say she?" she asked the nurse. "She's okay?"

The nurse looked to Dr. Nazir, then back to Maisy. "You and your baby," she said.

Maisy let a new possibility form. She took a long, deep breath, then a personal inventory. Intuition tugged, and Maisy gasped. "I'm having a girl."

Blaze peeled himself away from the wall, arms collapsing at his sides. He drifted forward, eyes wide and fixed on Dr. Nazir. "Is that true?"

The doctor looked to Maisy. "Do you want to know?"

"Yes," Maisy said, gaze flicking to Blaze for confirmation.

He dipped his chin.

"Then, yes," Dr. Nazir confirmed. "Congratulations, Mom and Dad. It's a girl."

Blaze nearly bowled the nurse over getting his arms around Maisy. He kissed her lips, nose and forehead. Then cupped her face and stared into her eyes. "We're having a girl." The wonder in his voice, sent shivers over Maisy as a single tear rolled over his scruffy, battered cheeks.

"Okay," Dr. Nazir said. "Let's finish this ultrasound. Strong heartbeats are good, but a thorough exam is better."

Blaze's phone rang, pulling him back. He squeezed Maisy's hand before moving to the edge of the room, unwilling to leave her. His switch from supporting dad to hard-nosed homicide detective was instant and seamless. He recapped the events and the car's description in clipped, authoritative syllables while the doctor and nurse tended to Maisy.

When Dr. Nazir finished, she helped Maisy rise from the table.

"Doctor?" the nurse asked, voice tight and drawing the room's attention.

Blaze lowered the phone and moved in Maisy's direction as she turned in search of an answer. "What is it?"

A small circle of blood stained the crinkled paper where Maisy had been seated.

"What does that mean?" Blaze demanded, shoving the phone into his pocket. "What's wrong?"

"It means we're going to get Maisy back onto the table and have another look," Dr. Nazir explained. "A physical exam this time. You're welcome to stay or leave the room. Whatever the two of you decide, but let's move quickly."

Blaze's phone rang.

Maisy's skin went cold. "Go," she told him. "It's okay to leave. Help the police find whoever did this. Dr. Nazir will take care of me."

"Do you want me here?" Blaze asked, eyes hot and fervent. "Say the word."

"You're going to need to undress and don the gown," Dr. Nazir urged.

Maisy stared, unsure, shocked and terrified. What if the ultrasound had been wrong? What if she lost her baby? *Her daughter.* The air squeezed from her lungs.

"Derek," Blaze growled, phone pressed to his ear once more. "Grab Lucas and get up here. Dr. Nazir's office in Fairmont." He recapped the situation as the nurse helped Maisy out of her pants. Her trembling legs were unwilling to hold her.

"It's okay," Maisy repeated. "You can go. You don't have to stay."

The doctor eased Maisy back and pulled the metal stirrups up to hold Maisy's feet.

Blaze's hand curled over hers a moment later, cell phone tucked away. "I'm not going anywhere until you order me away. Even then, you won't get me farther than the outside of this door."

"Thank you," she whispered.

His jaw locked and determination settled in his cool blue-gray eyes as the doctor began her exam.

Twenty long minutes later, Dr. Nazir gave a reluctant nod. "You're both okay. Everything is as it should be. There's no doubt you have a guardian angel, or nine lives. And you're two centimeters dilated," she said. "Try to stay off your feet and rest." She scooted away from the table and fixed her eyes on Blaze. "I realize you couldn't predict or control what happened out there, but I need you take her someplace safe now. I don't care if it's a pyramid in Egypt, but keep her out of danger for at least the next four to five weeks. She can't continue going on like this without consequences. She's long past lucky. Get her off her feet. Help her relax." She swung her eyes back to Maisy. "Don't do anything more than you have to. Don't lift anything. Don't go for long walks. Feet up. No exceptions. And no more stress." She pressed her lips together and tossed her gloves in the bin with an expression of anguish. "Come back to me next week," she told Maisy. "I want to see you sooner so we can follow up. Go directly to the ER if you have any extreme pain, headaches, blurred vision or dizziness. Call me if the bleeding doesn't stop, or gets heavier, by bedtime." She flipped a business card facedown and scratched a number on it. "That's my personal cell phone. Call it if you need anything. Don't hesitate. Either of you." She looked to

Blaze. "It's okay if you bring her rolled in bubble wrap. Do whatever is necessary."

Blaze frowned. "Yes, ma'am."

Maisy redressed, then returned to Blaze's waiting arms and prayed they wouldn't need to use that number.

BLAZE SPENT THE afternoon on the phone while Maisy took a long, hot shower and an even longer nap. He checked on her frequently, between calls to his sergeant and brothers, eager to see her smile once more. She was having his daughter! His heart leaped with fear and excitement and a host of countless other emotions every time the thought came to mind.

He loaded wood into the fireplace as the sun began to set, then stoked it with care. The latest weather report had confirmed the earlier prediction of plummeting temperatures and incoming flurries. Possibly even a snowstorm by the week's end. Their cabin would likely see the brunt of whatever was coming, thanks to its position atop the mountain. Thankfully, the little rental had everything they needed, at least for several more days.

With nothing left to do but stir, he put a frozen pizza in the oven for dinner, then crept back down the hall toward the bedroom.

Maisy's eyes snapped up to meet his as he peeked through the open door. She'd illuminated the bedside lamp and propped herself up with the pillows since his last visit. "Sorry I slept all day," she said. "I didn't realize how tired I was." The glass of water he'd left on the nightstand was empty.

"How are you feeling?" he asked, taking a seat on the edge of the bed.

"Not great," she admitted. "There's a knot on my head, and I feel like the car might've actually run me over."

Blaze frowned as he reached for her, carefully testing the lump on the back of her head. "Is that why you stayed on your side?"

Maisy laughed. "I sleep on my side because lying flat on my back would probably kill me." She waved her hands around her bump in explanation. "Not to mention I'd never be able to get up."

Blaze smiled. "Are you getting hungry? I put a frozen pizza in the oven."

"That sounds great," she said. "Thank you." She looked him over carefully then, scrutinizing. "What did you learn about the case while I was sleeping? Any word on the car or driver who tried to kill us?"

He did his best not to grimace. Today's attempt on her life had gone largely unnoticed by the community. To his significant dismay, only the waitress who initially came to their aid even saw the car. She couldn't describe it beyond the color, and if Blaze hadn't clipped his hip against a parked vehicle, setting off the alarm, she wouldn't have seen that. "Everyone's working on it," he said instead, hoping to sound positive. "Derek's canvassing area homes and businesses, asking about the car and searching for witnesses. The construction noise masked the engine's sound and your scream, so we haven't had as much response as we'd like."

"No one heard a thing," she said, tone solemn.

She was right. Most folks had no idea anything happened until the police arrived.

"Is Derek having any luck?"

"So far, the people he's spoken with haven't recognized the car's description, but that's not a bad thing," he assured. "It might be a lead. We're thinking the owner isn't from Fairmont. A car like that would stick out in a small town. Someone would have known who it belonged to, or at least remembered seeing it around." It was a long shot to think the new hit man was from the area, but on the off chance the ride was stolen, which could've provided another clue to his identity, it was worth taking the time to ask.

Maisy wound and unwound a loose thread from the comforter around her finger. "No witnesses. That seems about right, given my recent record of awful luck."

"This isn't over yet," Blaze assured. "Lucas is requesting surveillance footage from every business on the street with a camera." Though he hadn't had much luck the last time Blaze spoke to him. Most of the cameras were useless. Dummies meant to dissuade criminals. Or broken and collecting dust. The few feeds of footage Lucas reviewed hadn't provided a clear view of the license plate or driver, but Blaze kept that to himself. Lucas wasn't finished yet.

"And the marshals?" she asked, skin going pale, as it always did at the mention of that branch of law enforcement.

"They're pressing Sergeant Maxwell to have you returned to their protection."

Her jaw sank open. "Are they insane?"

Blaze set a hand over hers, stroking her soft skin and stilling the busy thread on her finger. "Maxwell won't order me to return you. And if he did, you know I wouldn't listen. We've just got to stay here and keep a low profile a few more days. Then the trial will be over, your testimony given, and the worst will be behind us."

She wiggled free from his grip, abandoning the thread and folding her hands with a frown.

"It's not so bad, is it?" he asked, hoping that being stuck alone with him wasn't somehow a worse predicament to her than being hunted by hit men.

"I don't particularly enjoy feeling useless," she said. "But I'm not sure what I can do about it."

Blaze crawled over Maisy's legs and sat beside her at the headboard, crossing his ankles and trying to look at ease. "You're not useless. You're on a very important mission, and your job is to keep your feet up. So far, you're doing great." He nudged her playfully. "Bonus points because I know how much you hate being idle."

"So do you." She sighed. "Now you're stuck on the sidelines, too, because of me."

He turned his head to face her, waiting for her to look his way. "Hey."

Her mouth pulled down at the corners as she brought her warm hazel eyes to his.

"There is nowhere else I'd rather be." He scooped her hand in his, then raised it to his mouth for a gentle kiss. "I say we take advantage of this little time-out we've been given. It's the perfect opportunity for us to catch up. A lot's happened in the last six months, and I want to hear all your stories. We can sleep late and nap in the middle of the day. You can soak in a tub until the water goes cold and your skin turns pruney. How often do adults get to do any of that?"

She smiled. "I suppose it won't be long before I'm wishing I had time to sleep at all."

"Exactly. And you know what we can do right here, for hours, without even leaving this bed?"

Her cheeks darkened and a smile formed. "What?"

Blaze slipped a hand into the pocket of his hooded sweatshirt and produced a deck of cards. "You still like to play poker?"

Maisy barked a laugh, eyes twinkling. "You still like to lose?"

"I never liked to lose," he said, shaking the deck from the box. "I just didn't mind how happy it made you to beat me."

Blaze shuffled, and Maisy dealt.

They played cards and talked until the oven dinged. Then they ate in bed, picnic-style. Poker, pizza and microwave popcorn. Maisy's laughter erased the misery of the day and filled his head with images of a possible future. Long, lazy days with his best friend. He shook the image away, determined not to get ahead of himself. He'd already kissed her once, and she'd been very clear when she said she couldn't.

Blaze was deep into his losing streak when it occurred to him how wrong he'd been about his relationship with Maisy. He'd thought of his behavior in their early days as unprofessional and inappropriate, because he'd focused on the marathon sex and their powerful physical connection. But he and Maisy were much more than that. They'd done everything together in the short time they'd shared. From cooking and shopping to bonfires and laundry. And it had started with an easy and natural friendship that bloomed into something fast and fevered. But the fever didn't lessen their bond—it had strengthened it.

"Do I have sauce on my face?" she asked, grinning mischievously. "Why are you smiling at me like that?"

Blaze shook his head, awed and pleased by his epiphany. "I really missed you," he said. "I missed this. Us."

She bit her lip, and a sweet pink blush rose across her fair skin, backlighting her freckles. "Me, too."

"I don't regret kissing you," he said, surprising them both with the unplanned confession.

"You don't?"

"No." His voice was low and rougher than he'd intended, but he pressed ahead. "You already have enough pressure. I didn't want to add to your problems, or be that guy."

"Who?"

"The handsy detective who is supposed to be protecting you but won't keep his lips to himself." He grinned.

"I like your lips," she said, gaze flicking to his mouth. "And your hands. Besides, I'm the one who kissed you. Not the other way around."

Blaze replayed their kiss for the hundredth time. Maisy might've been the one to lean in, but he'd been the one aching to get his hands on her since the moment she'd arrived. And she'd been the one to stop it. "You also ended it."

"Because I felt guilty," she said. "There I was, enjoying myself when other people were being killed because of me."

"You're allowed to be happy, Maze," he said. "People are being killed because Sam Luciano is a psychopath, and that has nothing to do with you. Your lost loved ones would want you to have these moments. To live loudly and profoundly and fill every second with joy. I'd offer to take you anywhere you want to go and do anything you want to do, if we weren't under orders to stay right here and relax."

The blush returned to her cheeks as she looked up at

him from beneath her long dark lashes. "Since we're here. Would you be interested in helping me relax?"

The moan that poured out of him wasn't intentional, but it was fitting. "Are you sure about that?"

Maisy nodded shyly, and Blaze climbed off the bed. He gathered the remnants of their picnic and card game, piling it all on a chair in the corner. He returned with a broad, Cheshire-cat smile. "Have anything specific in mind?"

Maisy's hands went to the collar on her nightshirt. She dragged a single pink fingernail along the place where the soft fabric met. "I hear skin-to-skin contact is incredibly comforting."

A breath of air escaped him in a hiss as she freed the first tiny button.

He watched intently as she continued the chore. When the material parted, exposing a silky bra and full, beautiful breasts, he climbed back onto the bed, drawn like a bear to honey.

Her thin fingers tugged the hem of his hoodie upward, and Blaze peeled the layers off his torso. He tossed the shirt and hoodie onto the floor, then waited for her next command.

"A massage would be very relaxing," she said. "We could start with that." Her narrow brows rose in question. "I'm not really supposed to exert myself, but kissing also sounds quite nice."

Blaze's rigid body went impossibly tighter with anticipation of all the things he wanted to do to her. Each of which were guaranteed to leave her boneless. And he wouldn't have to remove another stitch of his clothing.

Chapter Fourteen

Maisy soaked in a warm bath before breakfast, her limbs loose and mind in a haze. She hadn't had any additional bleeding after they'd left the doctor, and she'd held Dr. Nazir's assessment close to her heart. She and her baby were okay. The relief and comfort in that knowledge had made her brave. She'd asked Blaze for exactly what she'd wanted, and he'd delivered.

Flashes of the things Blaze had done to her were enough to steam the mirror. His mouth was magic, and he'd used it on every inch of her. Slowly and gratuitously. It was the first time she'd been touched in months, barring their kiss on his cabin floor, and it had felt exactly right, the way it always had with Blaze. She closed her eyes briefly, savoring the memories.

Blaze had been right about them. He and Maisy shared a bond that was bigger than she'd given credit. They'd been instant friends, confidants and allies from the start. The chemistry and physical attraction were the icing, not the cake. All those factors together made them stronger, not weaker, and no outside force would pull them apart.

She smiled as she toweled off and dressed, choosing a soft cream-colored V-neck sweater and a fresh pair of comfy cotton leggings. The cabin was warm and cozy.

Rich scents of freshly brewed coffee and warm buttered toast met her in the hallway, accented by the soft crackle of a fire. Under other circumstances, time alone with Blaze in this cabin would be the stuff fantasies were made of, but the nightmare of their reality kept scratching its way in.

Blaze spotted her immediately, rising from his place at the small dinette, where his laptop sat open. His warm gray eyes and sweet crooked smile belied the fierce protector she also knew him to be. The fact he saved this side of himself for her alone made her dizzy with appreciation and gratitude. He moved toward her on bare feet, then pressed a tender kiss to her forehead. "How are you feeling?"

"Rested," she said. "Peaceful, and trying not to wait for the next shoe to drop."

He pulled out a chair at the table for her. "There hasn't been much news through the night on your case. Who knows? Maybe we'll have a shoe-free day."

"That would be a first," Maisy said. "But a girl can hope."

Blaze made a trip to the counter and returned with a cup of herbal tea and plate with toast and fruit. "Hungry?"

"Yes, and this is perfect," she said. "I promise to make it up to you after we get out of here."

He laughed. "You're doing far more for me right now than I can ever do for you," he assured, smiling at her bump. "So we probably shouldn't keep score."

"You wouldn't say that if you weren't so accustomed to losing to me." Maisy grinned as she raised the mug to her lips. She'd been struggling for months with her complicated life and emotions, but seated there with Blaze looking at her like he was, she knew one thing for absolute certain.

She was deeply, unequivocally in love with him.

Blaze fielded phone calls and worked on his laptop after breakfast while Maisy watched the first snowflakes fall. She read to her bump before lunch, then napped and laughed with Blaze afterward. She had nowhere to go and no one to answer to. And he was right—she loved it.

She curled on the couch in time for the evening news. Blaze arrived with two glasses of ice water and a kiss. He set the drinks on the coffee table, then slid an arm around her shoulders. "You look good."

"I feel good," she answered truthfully. "How's your work going?"

"Derek's at the station, pretending to visit Lucas, but doing his best to pick up on new information. He says the marshals who arrived after my cabin was invaded are meeting with Maxwell. Two suits from the FBI were on their way out as he arrived. No word on what that was about, specifically. I haven't had a chance to speak with the sergeant. Lucas's staying in touch, but there was a rape on campus that's kept him away most of the day, working with the college's security team."

"Do you think the marshals are trying to regain control of my security?" she asked, a shiver rocking down her spine.

Blaze's jaw tightened, and he grimaced. "Yeah, but I'm confident Maxwell will avoid giving me the order to turn you over until his job is threatened. If the marshals get the mayor's ear, and he demands it, Maxwell will have to follow through. Hopefully it won't come to that. He knows I won't comply."

Worry twisted Maisy on the cushion. It was nice that

Blaze and his sergeant were willing to do what they could to protect her, but completely unfair that they could be punished for it. "Will you lose your job?" Her stomach ached at the thought. Blaze loved being a detective, and he was incredibly good at it. "If Luciano can puppeteer all these people to come for me, and intercept a marshal who was sent to transport me, it seems reasonable that he could get the mayor to fold for him, as well."

Blaze shrugged. "Maybe. It won't matter. Protecting you is the right thing to do, regardless of any orders that come down."

"It's not fair." She sighed as the words registered to her ears. "None of this is, I know, but I hate how wide the path of destruction is becoming."

"Don't worry about that," Blaze said. "Maxwell will only give the order if he has to. And I'll understand if he does. He shouldn't lose the thirty years he's worked toward retirement or put a big black mark on his other-wise stellar career over this. Not when he can give the order and know I will ignore it. I'd rather lose my job than put you in danger. I can get another job. I can't get another you."

She leaned her head against his shoulder, sad and help-less. At least the trial was only six days away. "Any idea who's working with Luciano from the inside?"

"Not yet." His head tipped against hers, and he stroked her fingers with his own.

The news covered a local flower show and other com-munity and celebrity puff pieces before turning to the Luciano case. A photo Maisy recognized from a few days before appeared in the bottom corner of the screen. The caption: Gene Franco, Missing US Marshal, Found Dead.

Maisy's stomach rocked as a reporter covered the

story from the scene. A flurry of men and women moved around a field where Franco's body had been found. Shot three times, then abandoned. His government-issued vehicle apparently stolen by one of Sam Luciano's known associates. A man whose body was recently discovered in a similar condition after his image was released by local news channels.

A deep sigh poured from Maisy's chest. So it was true. The marshal sent to transport her was dead. She'd expected as much, but the news felt exceptionally devastating anyway.

Blaze squeezed her hand. "You okay?"

"No. I keep thinking that this started for me when Luciano killed Natalie and Aaron. Then I wouldn't stop pushing until he'd been tracked down and put behind bars, awaiting trial. Now, because we did that, because I wanted justice for those two deaths, he has killed the marshal sent to pick me up, Clara, two other witnesses and the original hit man." Her breath shuddered out of her. "That's five more dead because I wanted justice for two. If he wasn't awaiting trial, there wouldn't be a need for witnesses. And he wouldn't be killing them."

"This isn't your fault," Blaze reminded her. "Luciano is a killer. His body count would be much higher if he was free. And if you weren't willing to testify, to make sure he winds up in a maximum-security prison, his body count would never end."

Maisy knew that was true, but she hated what was happening anyway and feared where the ripple effect would go next. "I'm worried for the prosecutor's safety," she said. "And for Dr. Nazir. What if she loses her life over this, too? Just because she's the unlucky doctor Clara and I picked to monitor my pregnancy." She pushed away from Blaze so she could look into his face. "Whoever tried to run me over yesterday knew she was my doctor."

His sharp gray eyes searched hers until she could nearly see their thoughts aligning. "And the driver knew when you'd be there."

"But you'd just moved that appointment up a day before," she said. "How is that possible?"

"I wondered about that, too," he said. "And I passed the question on to Derek, Maxwell and Isaac. There were a handful of lawmen outside my cabin with me when I called to move the appointment. Any one of them could have overheard me."

"Or…" Maisy's shoulders tensed, and her lips parted. A terrifying new possibility registered. "Is it possible your phone is tapped?" If so, could they use the tap to track them? Were they in danger? Even here on a mountaintop?

Blaze shook his head. "No. I've checked it thoroughly. The phone's not bugged, but someone was listening that day. I called the personal number Nazir gave us while you were sleeping and asked her if there were any new employees at her office. It was a long shot, but I worried Luciano could have gotten an ally hired. She assured me there were no new hires."

Maisy relaxed by a fraction. She'd imagined the planted employee hurting her doctor if Luciano gave the order, and the thought sent shards of ice through her veins. "Good."

"Yes and no," he said. "Honestly, the leak could still have come from the doctor's office. Anyone can be bought for the right price, because everyone has a weak spot. If Luciano or his goon figured out who your doctor

was, he could easily have bribed or blackmailed someone who's worked there for years."

"Everyone's a suspect," she groaned. "I'd be mad, but
I know that once our baby is born, I'd do anything to
protect her."

Blaze pressed a kiss against the back of her hand, still
twined with his. Then another on her bump. "There's also
the possibility no one at Nazir's office is dirty. And none
of the men on site at my place overheard me change the
appointment. There aren't a lot of obstetricians in the
county where your safe house was situated. Some quick
deduction would narrow the options once Luciano's men
saw that you were pregnant. Being as far along as you are,
and knowing you were in the cabin when it was smoke
bombed, maybe the office was simply being staked out."

"Assuming I'd show up for a proper exam," she said.

"Maybe. But regardless of the course of events that
brought us here, we're going to be okay," he promised.
"The trial is less than a week away. Prosecution is alive
and well, as far as I've heard. And we still have two witnesses. So the weight of Luciano's trial isn't completely
on your shoulders. Maxwell or the marshals could still get
one of the men who broke into my house to turn on him.
Our case can only get stronger. All hope isn't lost yet."

His phone dinged with an incoming text message, and
he shifted away from her to grab the device. A second
notification dinged as he released her hand to enter the
password on his lock screen. The sound came a third
time as he frowned at the screen.

Maisy stroked his lean, sinewy forearm while he read,
thankful for his presence and the hope he continually provided. Especially when she was feeling hopeless.

Blaze was right, of course. She wasn't in this alone.

There was still another witness and known associates who might talk in exchange for leniency.

Blaze muttered under his breath as he scrolled. The crease in his brow confirmed the news wasn't good. He typed. Then swore.

"What?" she whispered, unable to wait any longer. If the new killer had found them, she wasn't sure she had enough luck or stamina to survive another attack.

Blaze turned the phone's screen in her direction, revealing the image of a police report apparently photographed then shared with him by text.

"Death report," Maisy said, chest tightening as she scanned the record for details, trying to place the name. "Kelly Hartman?"

"Yeah." Blaze dropped the phone into his lap, then pressed one hand across his forehead. "She was the other witness."

Chapter Fifteen

Maisy's hands began to shake. A tremor beat its way through her as she watched Blaze typing on his laptop at the little table. He'd called his brother, then his sergeant, searching for more information about Kelly Hartman's death. He'd been at the dinette for the better part of an hour, but Maisy couldn't move. Fear had glued her in place.

The other shoe had dropped, and it was a pattern she'd grown to hate. Each time she let herself believe the daily horror and tragedy had reached its end, something like this reminded her the situation would only end one of two ways—with her dead or Luciano in supermax. Maisy was doing all she could to make it the latter.

The thought of her death hollowed her, and she wrapped protective arms around her middle, rejecting the possibility. If she died, her baby died, and Maisy would not allow that.

Blaze's gaze flicked to Maisy as he pushed upright and rubbed his jaw. He tucked his cell phone into the pocket of his hoodie as he returned to her side. "Sorry, that took longer than I expected."

He exhaled long and slow as he lowered onto the cushion beside her. His legs stretched out before him. His shoulders drooped with fatigue, and his eyes were burdened. "It seems that Kelly Hartman was a longtime girlfriend of Luciano," he said. "She was also the mother to two of his children. Someone from her staff found her body this morning inside her Nashville home."

"Shot?" Maisy asked. Three bullets seemed to be the theme.

"No. The initial report listed her cause of death as an overdose. Her blood alcohol level was high, and there were a number of prescription drugs in her system, though none of those had been prescribed to her. The children's au pair claimed Kelly rarely had more than a single glass of wine and didn't take any medications outside the occasional aspirin or antihistamine. But there's speculation that Luciano's imprisonment and upcoming trial had worn on her in ways she hadn't let on outwardly." He scrubbed his jaw again. "The coroner will know more in a few days, but the timing makes it hard for me to think she's dead for any reason other than Luciano ordered it."

Maisy stared, nearly choked with disbelief. "I can't believe he'd kill the mother of his children." Her stomach pitched and turned at the thought. Was Luciano even human?

"He didn't do it with his own hands," Blaze said, "but he most likely pulled the trigger, figuratively speaking."

"How old are the kids?" Maisy asked, not sure she really wanted to know. Knowing would only make the facts harder to process.

"Seven and ten."

"Those poor children," Maisy said, feeling the weight of their loss on her heart. "What happens to them now?

Will they be handed over to Luciano if he gets out of jail? Raised by a murderous monster?"

"I don't know," Blaze said. "Maybe."

"What if he's sent to supermax?"

Blaze considered the question a moment before answering. "The children would be better off in nearly anyone else's care," Blaze said. "So that wouldn't be a bad thing for them. Chances are good that Kelly had family who will want them. Fighting for custody should be easy given Luciano's lengthy criminal record, even if he's set free. Which he won't be. Because we're going to do everything we can to keep that from happening."

Maisy's heart fell impossibly further for the children she'd never met. There wouldn't be a happy ending for them. "I'll bet that if anyone tries to take Luciano's children, he'll unleash the full power of his money and influence to stop it from happening. Assuming he doesn't just kill the potential guardians and be done with it," she said. "In which case, the kids will go through yet another unthinkable loss."

Blaze pursed his lips, presumably in agreement.

"Did you learn anything else?" Maisy forced her mind away from Luciano's children.

"A little." He nodded. "Maxwell said local police responded to a break-in at the Hartman home last week. The family was out, but the security alarm was triggered. The intruder wasn't caught. Nothing appeared missing or disturbed. Could be nothing, but again, timing."

"Last week," Maisy said. "So, the initial breech at Kelly's place came before the attack on my safe house."

"By two days," Blaze said. "Could be that the first hit man struck out in Nashville, so he made his way to Kentucky."

"Making his rounds," she mused, numb and horri-fied. "Picking off witnesses." She dragged her fingers across her collarbone, a series of new questions form-ing in her mind. "Why do you think Kelly was willing to testify against Luciano? Why now? And why wasn't she in witness protection? She, of all people, would know how dangerous he is."

"I asked the lead prosecutor, Jack Hisey, the same thing. He said that when she initially came to him, she thought vanishing into protective custody would tip off Luciano or one of his goons. She didn't have regular con-tact with her ex, but she believed someone was watch-ing her, likely a henchman," Blaze said. "She thought it best to behave as if nothing out of the ordinary was about to happen."

"That had to be awful," Maisy said. "Knowing the father of her children was the kind of man Luciano is, and feeling as if he had someone watching everything she did." She shivered at the thought.

"She was right," Blaze said, "or that's my take, any-way. Hisey said her initial split from Luciano was a mu-tual decision. Then she got comfortable in her new life and went on a date. It was her first and last. Her suitor was in a serious car accident on his way home. He's in a wheelchair now. That was nearly four years after leav-ing Luciano."

Maisy's mouth fell open. She took a minute to let that sink in. Four years of believing he'd let her go. Four years of believing her life was her own. And that was how he'd shown her she was wrong. By trying to kill a man she went on one date with. "I don't know how any-thing shocks me anymore, but I wasn't expecting that."

"Psychopaths like Luciano tend to be territorial,"

Blaze said. "Women and children are pawns to them. Equivalent to property. It's unlikely he even views them as human. They are things to own, sell, trade or dispose of as he sees fit. And there is no expiration date on that claim."

Maisy grimaced. "I don't know how you can make a career of this. Surrounded by the ugliest parts of humanity every day. How do you have any hope left at all?"

"It's not all bad, and not every day," he said, managing a feeble smile. "I see good things happen, too. Like when an abused child or spouse finds their footing after trauma and rises above it. I help put killers behind bars. Find justice for victims and punishment for the criminals. If I've helped even one person in the years I've been doing this, then any amount of frustration or heartache I've endured has been worth it."

A spark of wonder and respect formed in Maisy. If Luciano was the epitome of evil, Blaze was the definition of good. Then, Kelly came back to mind, and the positive feeling stretched to cover her, as well. "Knowing all that he was capable of, she was still willing to testify. That's incredibly brave."

"I agree."

"I can probably answer my own question from before," Maisy said, realizing the thing that had been right in front of her. "Kelly chose to testify against him now and not sooner because this is the first time he's been in jail, with a murder trial coming and three others willing to testify." She knew this was her chance to help put him away for good. She wasn't alone in the fight. "Once he's in the supermax prison, he wouldn't have the same reach or control over her. This was her chance at real freedom for her and her children."

"The odds were definitely in her favor with four of you slated to take the stand," Blaze said.

Maisy longed to scream in frustration at the injustice of it all. "How is this happening?" she asked. "We're less than a week from trial, and the case against him is being completely dismantled one witness at a time. I can't decide if it's ironic or just really on the nose that a murderer is going to get off his murder charges by having the witnesses murdered." She dragged angry hands through her hair, digging deep against her skull and curling her fingers into the soft brown locks. "How can a man behind bars have this kind of impact on the outside world?"

"County lockup isn't exactly Fort Knox. He's allowed phone calls and visitors. The contact is monitored, but permitted nonetheless. And Luciano's smart enough not to say or do anything we can use against him. Which is why we want to see him reassigned to Cumberland, preferably for life."

Maisy considered the phone calls and visitors. "Can you check the jail's logs to see who he's been in contact with, then question them? Maybe one of those people is the hit man, or at least the middleman passing the orders."

"Maxwell's already looking," Blaze said.

She drummed her fingers on her bump. West Liberty's police force was good at what they did. She remembered that from when they'd helped her before, following Natalie's death.

Blaze curved a protective arm around her shoulders and tugged her close. "We're going to get through this," he promised.

"We have to," she said quietly. "All these lost lives can't be for nothing. Kelly's children, and Clara's, all have to grow up without their mother because of him.

There has to be something we can do before he hurts anyone else."

"Not tonight," he said. "Tonight we obey Dr. Nazir and try to relax. I'll keep tabs on the case. You should try to rest. Tomorrow, we'll set an appointment with the prosecutor."

BLAZE OPENED THE door for Derek early the next morning. A gust of icy wind blew him inside, curling Blaze's bare toes against the chilly wooden floorboards.

"Hello, brother," Derek said, another box of doughnuts in hand with a pint of mint chocolate chip ice cream on top. "Clever hideout."

"Thanks." Blaze tucked the ice cream into the freezer, then grabbed a pair of mugs from the dish rack. "No pickles?"

Derek shrugged, helping himself to a mug and the freshly brewed coffee. "I didn't like the selection at the general store. I asked the man behind the counter if he'd seen you. He said he had." He lifted the steaming mug to his lips, one eyebrow pulled high. "He described you both to a tee."

Blaze took a bear claw from the doughnut box, then bit into it to stifle a curse. "I knew we spent too long in there."

"He thought Maisy was a 'lovely young lady.'" Derek formed air quotes around the description.

Blaze felt his jaw lock. He'd been reckless shopping there. He should've gone to a big box store in another county, someplace with a thousand shoppers that no one remembered.

"At least you paid in cash," Derek said. "He remembered that, too. You didn't use a credit card to check in here, did you?"

"Of course not."

"Well, you did shop at the only store on the mountain," Derek challenged. "Register under false identities?"

"Yeah, and I went into the lodge's office alone. I pretended to be an artist, traveling from out of state."

Derek nodded. "That's good. Hopefully Maisy didn't say too much to the guy at the general store."

"She wouldn't." Blaze refilled his mug, then motioned Derek to have a seat with him at the table. "But we should probably set up a false trail. There are only five days left until the trial." He sipped the bitter pick-me-up, ordering his brain to kick in with a plan. Something to misdirect anyone searching for her. "Why don't I send one of my credit cards with you?" he suggested. "You can make a few purchases. Create a false trail for us. You and I look enough alike to fool anyone who doesn't know us." Despite a distinct difference in eye color, anyone not looking too closely could easily make the mistake. "Get cash from ATMs. Pay for gas somewhere. Buy groceries."

"Pickles?" Derek asked, a cocky grin on his face, palm open in acceptance of Blaze's offer.

"Anything you want. Keep the receipts." He smiled. "Why don't you trade me cars when you leave? That'll help sell it if the tracker asks about my vehicle, or gets a look at a surveillance feed." He fished a rarely used card from his wallet and passed it to his brother.

Derek smacked his lips. "You've been after my truck since the day I drove it off the lot."

Blaze laughed. The unexpected sound vibrated through him. "You got me."

Derek pocketed the credit card, looking a lot less

happy about shopping with the card when his truck would be in Blaze's care. "How's Maisy holding up?"

"Better than me, I think," Blaze admitted. "She's always been formidable, but the pregnancy seems to have fortified her. I'd almost feel bad for anyone trying to harm her now."

"Well, there's at least one guy at the county hospital who'd agree," Derek said, a thick smirk in his tone. "The guy she hit with Nana's frying pan is still under observation."

Blaze grinned. "She's only five weeks from delivery, and the sky is falling around her. I have to keep reminding myself I've just got to get her through the next few days, and her life will become incomprehensibly simpler." He tried not to think about how different things would be a week from now. A month. A year. Not yet. Now was the time to concentrate. One thing at a time. First, lie low. Then, the trial. After that, he'd see if she still wanted him the way he'd always wanted her.

Was it possible that she might? Even when she didn't need him anymore? And if so, for how long? It had been his experience that women rarely tolerated sharing him with his job, and being a detective was a 24-7 gig. He was never truly off the clock. And to be honest, he didn't want to be. He needed someone who understood that and supported him in the choice. The same way he would support her on whatever she wanted in return.

"I'm here to help," Derek said. "At your disposal. Don't forget that."

Blaze rubbed his unshaven chin. "I know, and I appreciate it. Maisy's the last witness standing. Luciano's man is going to be working hard to silence her. Her doctor tasked me with keeping her calm and rested. She's concerned about preterm labor." He dropped his hand in a moment of total candor. "I'm a wreck, man."

Derek set his coffee mug aside, eyes narrowing. "I would be, too. There's a lot at stake here."

"Everything is at stake here," Blaze corrected.

Derek kicked back on his chair, arms crossed and jaw clenched. "I hate that the two of you are going through this. I think about you and your situation a lot, and, honestly, I don't know what I'd do in your position."

Blaze rolled his shoulders forward, resting his forearms on the table. He clasped his fingers and counted his breaths, trying to rein back the surge of desperation. "Every time I think we're going to get through this safely, there's another attack or someone else is murdered. I feel like we're in an out-of-control car without seat belts. I'm trying to keep it together for her and the baby, but I can't sleep. Can't eat. Can't concentrate. And none of that is good. Especially not right now."

"Good morning." Maisy's voice snapped Blaze onto his feet.

His neck and ears burned, and he prayed she hadn't heard his confession. He'd tell her all about his fears and feelings of ineptitude someday, when this was behind them, if she wanted. Right now, he needed her to believe she was safe and that he could keep her that way. Partly to manage her stress level, but mostly because as long as Maisy still believed in him, Blaze could keep believing in himself.

"What's going on?" she asked, gaze circling suspiciously from brother to brother.

"Derek brought doughnuts and ice cream." Blaze smiled, then waved an open hand in his brother's direction.

"Yep," he agreed casually, shooting Blaze a pointed

look. He flipped open the lid on the doughnut box, then turned a smile on Maisy. "I hope you like bear claws and cream sticks."

She grinned, already headed toward the table and the open pastry box. "Morning," she said softly to Blaze as she selected a fritter. A tiny smile curved her mouth as she glided past him to an empty chair.

His heart ached with the need to protect her, and with the utter helplessness he felt in the face of an unnamed enemy. At least when Maisy had arrived on his doorstep, she'd seen the safe house shooter. They'd had something to go on, someone to look for. Now, he had no idea who was after her. "Can I make you some tea?" he asked, setting a hand against the small of her back.

"That would be great. Thank you." She took the seat beside Derek, then fixed him with a scrutinizing stare. "You didn't come all the way out here to bring me doughnuts, did you?"

Derek shifted in her direction, slinging an arm across the back of his chair. "I'm also checking up on my little brother and future niece or nephew."

Maisy set a napkin on her bump, then watched Derek as she took a bite of the fritter.

Blaze returned with her tea.

"Do you also come bearing news?" Maisy asked Derek.

"'Fraid not." Derek straightened in his seat, looking genuinely remorseful.

"Making any progress on identifying the leak in law enforcement?" she asked.

Blaze shook his head. Negative.

Maisy refocused on her tea and fritter, looking a little deflated after the brief exchange.

Derek's expression brightened. "Everyone's pointing fingers, though. The cops are blaming the marshals, since the safe house shooter was masquerading as one of them. The marshals think someone at the police department tipped the shooter off about the transport. The guys at the PD have a pool going on which agency has the mole. So far, most of the police force is leaning toward the marshals, but there's growing interest in the warden at county lockup. Everyone has their own reasons and theories. Maxwell keeps demanding they knock it off." He pulled a stick of gum from his pocket, unwrapping it with a grin. "Bets are unprofessional and distracting. I've got my money on the guard. It wasn't an option in the poll, so all I've got to win or lose is pride."

Maisy rolled her eyes. "Good thing you have a little of that to spare."

Blaze laughed, enjoying the easy dynamic.

Derek stuffed the gum into his mouth, then neatly folded the wrapper. "Any chance you might want to move this party closer to the courthouse?"

"Why?" Maisy asked, as Blaze gave a firm "No."

Derek's attention flicked to Blaze. "If not today, then sometime before the trial. The drive to West Liberty from here provides too many opportunities for an ambush, especially the morning of the trial, when you're expected to come out of hiding."

Maisy's ivory skin paled impossibly further. "An ambush?"

Derek lifted a palm, then lowered it to the table. "I'm just trying to troubleshoot."

Blaze reached for Maisy's hand, and she easily turned her palm to his, linking their fingers.

Derek's eyes flashed over the familiar touch, then locked on Blaze. "Have you spoken to the prosecutor?"

"Yeah. A few times since Kelly Hartman's body was found. We're meeting with him tomorrow."

"Opposing counsel rejected the suggestion of a livestream testimony?" Derek guessed.

"They haven't responded," Blaze said. "But now that we're down another witness, Hisey's going to present the possibility to the judge again. Kelly's death was made to appear self-inflicted, but even the possibility her overdose was murder should motivate Judge Wise to accept our request. The prosecution also plans to suggest we enter a video recording of Maisy's testimony as evidence and have it played for the jury instead of any live interaction. Honestly, I prefer that to anything else. The more space I can put between her and this trial, the better."

Derek nodded. "Surely no one can argue that."

"Oh, they can," Blaze assured. "And they will. I'm certain of it. Luciano's legal team won't lie down that easily. They're going to be ready for a fight."

Maisy's thin fingers tightened on Blaze's, and he stroked the back of her hand with his thumb. "I can take the stand," she assured. "I've come this far. I can finish this."

"I know you can," Blaze said, swaddling her hand in his. "And I'm going to keep you safe while you do."

Chapter Sixteen

Maisy was strapped into Blaze's borrowed truck and headed back down the mountain at precisely three o'clock the next day. The truck was enormous, with an extended cab and dual rear wheels. She would've felt invincible inside the beast, but it barely seemed to fit on the winding resort roads and didn't match much better with the suddenly narrow highway lanes.

She fiddled with the chipping paint on her fingernails, unexpectedly nervous. She'd waited for what felt like an eternity to get to this point. Four days left until the trial. The ball was in motion and picking up speed. The reality of it all was nearly overwhelming. The end was finally in sight.

She'd spent an hour choosing an outfit to meet the prosecutor, not that there was much left in her maternity wardrobe that still fit comfortably. Her bump seemed to have doubled in size these last few weeks. She wanted to look as trustworthy and believable as possible if she got the chance to video record her testimony today. A cream tunic top and black leggings had been the winning ensemble. Simple. Presentable. Forgettable. If the recording was seen by a jury, she didn't want them to remember her clothing. She wanted them to remember her words. She'd wrapped a simple black ribbon around her hair like a headband and worn the earrings Natalie had given her at college graduation for luck. Her mother's book, the one that had started it all, was inside her handbag. The Daniels women were all represented today. Right down to the sweet baby girl inside her.

Blaze had dressed casually, in jeans and a gray V-neck sweater, the collar of a white T-shirt barely visible beneath. He'd paired that with his black bomber jacket and leather boots. The overall look was enticing. The intense concentration on his face was borderline lethal. She could only imagine what he was thinking, and she didn't feel brave enough to ask. He'd confirmed the appointment after breakfast, using the attorney's personal email account. Blaze said he couldn't be sure the office phones weren't tapped, so email was better. Silent. And the account was never used for business.

Her baby kicked, and Maisy placed a palm against her abdomen, eager to feel the little movement once more. She rested her head against the seat as she waited, watching snow-dusted trees and rooftops zip past the foggy window.

Blaze's repetitive gaze heated her cheeks, probably working out everything that could go wrong, and how to troubleshoot it.

She turned to offer him a small smile. "Everything okay?"

"I was going to ask you the same thing. More contractions?"

"No." She caressed her bump. "Just a few kicks."

"Okay." His gaze dipped briefly to her lips, and a blast of memory rushed over her.

They'd shared another amazingly intimate and possibly stupid night together. One she'd shamelessly enjoyed every second of and was certain never to forget.

Despite her bulbous shape and the forty pounds she'd gained, Blaze somehow still thought she was beautiful. Sexy, smart and fierce. He told her as much, fervently and often. He claimed he saw sensual curves where she saw added weight. Most importantly, he saw her. Just like he always had.

She swept her gaze away from him, hopeful but unsure. She'd read about men with hero complexes while she'd been stuck at the safe house, wondering if what she and Blaze had shared could've been real. According to her research, some men in professions like his were addicted to the thrill of saving lives, of swooping in and being the big, tough protector. What would happen when she didn't need that anymore?

Did he truly love her? Or was he simply enamored by her constant need for protection?

The truck rocked over a pothole as Blaze made the final turn into town, returning Maisy's attention to the moment. Emergency lights slashed through the sky near the courthouse, and a crowd gathered on the sidewalks outside.

"What's going on?" she asked, straining to identify the cause of the commotion.

Blaze frowned. "I don't know." He powered the window down as they arrived in the thick of the congestion, then stretched an arm outside, motioning to a uniformed officer.

The man's brows rose, and a smile bloomed in recognition. He jogged to a stop outside Blaze's window. "What are you doing here?" he asked. "Everyone's been looking for you."

"I'm not here," Blaze said, pausing to let the point settle in.

The other man's eyes flicked to Maisy, then back. He dipped his chin once in acknowledgment.

"What's going on?" Blaze asked.

The younger cop rocked back on his heels. "Someone took a shot at Judge Wise. He's fine, but the rest of the building's staff is a mess."

Maisy's heart pounded against her ribs. She knew that name.

"He's set to preside over Luciano's trial next week," Blaze said.

"Yeah, and he's ticked." The cop grinned. "Wise said he refuses to be intimidated by a criminal. The trial won't be moved or delayed."

She pressed a palm to her sternum, trying to remain calm. Her gaze drifted carefully over the faces in the crowd. Across nearby buildings, streets and windows, searching for signs of a shooter.

"How'd someone get a gun past security?" Blaze asked.

"Didn't," the cop said. "There was an anonymous tip about a bomb, and they evacuated. The shot came after everyone was outside. I heard it as I got here. Pure chaos. Scared everyone except Wise. It just made him angry."

"Anyone get a look at the gunman?"

"No, and get this." The cop leaned closer, his voice low. "This is the second bomb scare in two days. Luciano's going all out to postpone this trial. Best part is that nothing's working. His time's nearly up, and he knows it."

Maisy started at the blast of a whistle.

The crowd outside began to move back through the courthouse doors.

"Guess I'm done here," the cop said, nodding at Blaze, then tipping his hat to Maisy. "Stay safe. You're almost to the finish line."

Blaze powered up his window, sealing the icy air outside once more.

Maisy tracked the exiting man with her eyes. "How well do you know him?" she asked. What if he was the dirty lawman? He could be on his way to tip off Luciano or the hit man. *He could be the hit man.* "Do you trust him?"

"That's Van," Blaze answered, rolling slowly forward with traffic. "And yes, I do. I trained him when he joined the force last year."

Maisy concentrated on her breathing and tried not to remember her previous talk with Blaze. The one where they'd established that anyone could be bought or blackmailed.

He parked Derek's massive truck in a small lot outside the historic brick building, then ushered Maisy quickly inside.

Staffers and guests filed through security, then scattered on the other side, hurrying across the wide marble floors, down hallways and into offices. Their expressions were wary, the tension palpable.

Maisy waited anxiously as Blaze flashed his badge at a guard with salt-and-pepper hair and deep russet-colored skin. "I hear you've had quite a day," Blaze said.

The guard motioned them through the gate, then split his attention between Blaze and the continued flow of incomers. A silver name badge identified him as Terrance Moreland. "Yesterday folks were afraid there was a bomb," Terrance said. "Today they're worried about a bomb and a shooter. What's tomorrow going to bring?" He trailed a curious gaze over Maisy.

She lifted her fingers in a nervous wave.

"How's Judge Wise doing?" Blaze asked, redirecting Terrance's attention.

He laughed. "Wise is one tough old bird." He motioned the next man through the gate. "He wasn't hit. Says he'll wear a bulletproof vest if he has to, but he won't let a criminal corrupt the justice system. Poor stenographer, though. She was so shaken, she took a medical leave until the trial ends. She was standing with Wise when the shot came. Bullet lodged in the brick, not two feet away."

Maisy watched the thinning crowd, thoughts torn. She liked the idea of a judge unwilling to be bullied by Luciano, but felt equally awful for the woman who'd taken a leave to deal with the threat. Then a new worry formed. "Who will replace the stenographer?" And how could anyone be sure that person wasn't a plant?

Terrance's brows rose. His eyes fixed on Maisy.

She regretted the question immediately. He'd barely noticed her until she'd opened her mouth.

"We'll let you get back to work," Blaze said, offering Terrance his hand for a shake.

He accepted, then turned back to the men and women moving through the gate.

Blaze set a hand against the small of her back, then guided her down the nearest hall. "Everyone who enters the courtroom that day will be thoroughly vetted," he assured quietly. "We all know what's riding on this case, and the lengths Luciano will go to get away with murder."

Maisy shivered. She could only hope the killer wouldn't really blow up the courthouse if that was what it took to stop the trial.

BLAZE ESCORTED MAISY into the prosecutor's office. The waiting room was vacant, the receptionist's expression expectant. "There you are," she said, rising with a warm smile. "Right on time despite the chaos."

"Hi, Karen." He hugged her, then stepped back to introduce Maisy. Karen had been one of his mother's friends for as long as he could remember. "Is Jack ready to see us?"

"I'm sure he is," she said, returning to her seat. "Just give me a minute, and I'll let him know you're here." She pressed a few numbers on her telephone then announced into the speaker that his four o'clock appointment had arrived. "He's been in there preparing all day."

When Hisey's closed door didn't immediately open, Blaze motioned Maisy to a pair of seats in the farthest corner of the room. Seats with clear views of every door and window. "I've been thinking we should request your testimony be recorded, regardless of how the judge and other attorneys respond to our request. Having a taped account on hand is smart. Just in case."

The office phone rang, and Karen answered. Her sudden smile suggested it was a personal call.

"What does that mean?" Maisy whispered, drawing his attention back to her wide hazel eyes. She'd wrapped thin arms around her middle again. "Do you mean, in case I'm dead?"

Blaze blinked. His heart plummeted at the suggestion, and it took him a moment to understand her question. "No!" he hissed, stunned at her interpretation. "Of course not." His whisper cracked like a whip through the nearly silent room. "I meant, in case you can't make it to trial because it becomes too dangerous to be here in person." He rubbed his brow, struggling to make sense of Maisy's reaction.

Her wide eyes narrowed. "If the trial moves forward, I have to be there. Otherwise there was never a purpose for any of this. The chaos. The deaths. The only reason to send a recording in my place is if I can't be there, and I can only think of one reason for that."

Blaze felt his temperature rise, and he locked it down. "I know that's what you want, and I'll do my best to get you there, but Maisy," he said, pausing to search her face, allowing her to search his, "I won't knowingly endanger your life and the life of our baby."

Her lips flattened into a thin white line, and heat flashed across her beautiful face. "Judge Wise isn't letting Luciano keep him from presiding over this trial, and I won't let Luciano stop me from testifying. It's the right thing to do, and I've waited half a year to do it."

"I don't care what Judge Wise does," Blaze said, holding tightly to his calm. "His risks don't matter to me. Yours do. I'm here to protect you."

Her ivory skin turned pink as she leaned in his direction, expression hard. "You don't care what the judge does because his loss doesn't impact your life. Does that mean his life doesn't matter? That it's somehow less valuable than mine?"

"To me," Blaze said, his words rushing out. "Yes."

Maisy's angry expression fell into something strangely blank. She caressed her bump, quieted by his outburst and offering no rebuttal. The fire had gone out of her eyes, replaced by something like shock or confusion.

Silence gonged around them, and a quick look in Karen's direction confirmed she'd heard the exchange. She was still on the call, but her eyes had fixed on Blaze.

He checked his watch, then stretched upright, eager to get their appointment over with and return Maisy to the safety of the cabin. At least there, they could talk about this without fear of another bomb scare or whatever else might happen next at the courthouse.

He strode back to Karen, then waited for her to disconnect her call. They'd already waited ten minutes past Maisy's scheduled time with Hisey. Given her situation, it was hard to believe he hadn't rushed her inside the minute Karen announced her arrival. "What did he say when you told him we were here?" Blaze asked, tipping his head in the direction of the lawyer's closed office door.

She stared from behind large round-framed glasses, her sleek silver bob tucked behind her ears. "Nothing, but I'm sure he'll only be another minute. He's been awaiting Miss Daniels's arrival all day and preparing for it all week. He didn't even leave during the bomb scare this time."

"Oh no." Maisy's whisper reached his ears easily, raising the hairs on his arms to attention. She drifted to his side and reached for his hand.

Blaze squeezed her fingers briefly, hoping to convey reassurance before releasing her in favor of his sidearm. "When was the last time you spoke to him?" he asked Karen.

"This morning. He brought in scones and lattes, then told me to hold his calls and visitors until you arrived. Where are you going?"

Blaze curled his fingers over his weapon's grip as he headed for Hisey's closed door. He rapped his knuckles against the heavy wood. "Hisey?"

"Someone took a shot at the judge during the evacuation today," Maisy said from behind him, much closer than she should be.

"What does that have to do with Jack?" Karen asked.

"Hopefully nothing." Blaze rested a hand on the knob and gave it a slow turn.

"Attorney Hisey wouldn't shoot anyone," Karen said. "This doesn't make any sense."

"That's not what we're suggesting," Maisy said.

Not at all, Blaze thought, pulling his gun and swinging the door wide.

The scream that followed was Karen's.

Jack Hisey was slumped behind his desk, a gunshot wound in his forehead.

Chapter Seventeen

Maisy curled on the couch with her mother's book the next morning. She hadn't slept well after the stress of finding the lead prosecutor's body, but she was slowly making up for the lost z's with naps and easing her nerves with tea. She and Blaze hadn't talked about what he'd said in the attorney's office, that her life meant more to him than the judge's. Instead, Hisey's death had consumed him.

Blaze had worked the rest of the day and into the night, bringing the prosecution's B-team up to speed and coordinating the replacement materials needed for the trial. Whoever had killed Hisey—while the rest of the building's employees had blazed a trail to the sidewalk—had also taken every paper file and scrap of evidence on Luciano. Putting an even larger, albeit temporary dent in the case.

The trial was just three days away, and Maisy had no idea what to expect, or if she'd have the opportunity to prepare. Everyone involved was in a frenzy, scrambling to pick up the torch for Hisey and carry on, but time was slipping away. It was hard not to worry. Judge Wise had refused another postponement, despite the loss of lead counsel. He rightly claimed that these tragedies would continue to happen until Luciano was sentenced, and putting off the trial would only lead to more unnecessary deaths. Whatever Luciano thought could keep him out of supermax.

Blaze and his brother reviewed the case details from the cabin's little kitchen–turned–makeshift war room. Derek had slept over, not that either man appeared to have actually slept. They'd fretted through dinner over the prosecution's mission to find a replacement for Hisey. Someone brave enough to oppose Luciano and tenacious enough to get up to speed in three days, when Hisey had been preparing for half a year. Maisy had called it a night by eleven, emotionally and mentally exhausted beyond measure.

A hoot of victory turned her on the cushion for a peek into the kitchen. Derek had set up a printer on the countertop, and the cabinet doors were covered in papers, maps, photos and sticky notes. Two laptops, empty coffee mugs and takeout containers cluttered the small dinette. "What?" she asked, a bubble of hope forming inside her. It was the first happy sound she'd heard in a long while.

Blaze moved in her direction, latching broad hands over the back of the couch and smiling. "They found a replacement for Hisey. A law professor named Julia Struthers. She hasn't practiced in two years, but her record before moving to the classroom was impeccable. She's at the prosecutor's office now, familiarizing herself with the details of the case. Maxwell's meeting with her in an hour to supply anything she needs from local PD, and she has a similar meeting with the marshals first thing tomorrow."

A smile opened Maisy's mouth, and she felt a weight lifting from her shoulders. "That's fantastic."

He nodded, a small grin spreading across his lips. "It's a good start."

"There's more?" she guessed.

"She's coming here to talk to you today," he said. "There's no time to waste. I'm picking her up in Derek's truck from a café in the next town. She won't be announced publicly as Hisey's replacement until the evening news, so our chances of going unnoticed are good. She'll be home with a security detail before the cat's out of the bag. And you'll be here, safe."

A mix of emotions spun in Maisy's heart and head. "So, you're leaving me here while you get her?" She looked past him to Derek who snorted in the kitchen.

"Derek's staying with you," Blaze said. "I think he's right about us becoming a target on the road, if we were spotted and identified. You're safest here, so that's where we want to keep you. At least for a few more days. Derek can protect you."

She cast another look in Blaze's brother's direction. Derek was a well-respected P.I., sharing a private practice with their cousin. He wasn't an official lawman, but he was undeniably tough, if a little reckless, but smart and fast, too. He would undoubtedly defend her and their baby, probably to the death if needed. There was something about these Winchesters and their need to be heroes. "Okay, but how can you be sure Julia Struthers isn't being bribed or blackmailed to intentionally throw the case? Or to gain access to me and…you know…" She formed a finger gun with one hand, and Blaze quickly covered it with a gentle palm.

"Julia has agreed to a pat down, so I can check for wires and weapons. She'll power off her cell phone to stop digital tracking and allow me to examine it for signs of listening devices. She fully understands what's happening here and why the precautions are necessary. She's eager to see Luciano's reign of terror stopped and would probably agree to anything that made us feel safe."

"Wow." Maisy nodded, a smile forming. "Okay, then."

He laughed. "That was exactly the way I felt when I spoke with her." Blaze leaned over the couch and kissed the top of Maisy's head. "Refresher on your tea?"

"Sure."

"Getting hungry yet?" He accepted the empty mug with tented brows.

"No." Her stomach had been queasy since they'd returned to the cabin yesterday. Anxiety, she supposed, and she was doing her best to emotionally disengage from the trauma, for her baby's sake. High blood pressure wasn't something she could afford to develop this late in her pregnancy.

Blaze watched her carefully, as if trying to read her mind. He thankfully relented without further questions. She didn't want to talk about the nausea, or the Braxton-Hicks contractions that had nearly brought her to tears after breakfast. She could handle those things on her own, by following Dr. Nazir's prescription for rest. Blaze needed to stay focused.

Maisy excused herself to freshen up when Blaze left to meet Julia Struthers.

Derek eyed her suspiciously as she made the announcement, but he only smiled and said he'd be there if she needed anything.

She curled on her bed and fought a budding sense of panic until she fell unexpectedly back to sleep.

Her eyes opened at the sounds of a vehicle outside. The engine was too quiet to be Derek's diesel truck returning, and the sound of a closing car door nearly caused Maisy's heart to seize. Images of the impostor marshal who'd killed Clara flashed through her mind. "Derek?" she called, swinging her feet over the edge of the bed. "Derek?"

His lithe footfalls sounded softly outside her open door. "It's fine, but stay here." He held her gaze a beat longer, then vanished, back toward the living room.

She followed, unable to stop herself. There wasn't a back door near the bedroom. If Derek was taken by a killer, she'd have no means of escape there. The cabin was designed with two points of entry. A front door and a back door. One in the living room. The other in the kitchen. Both were down the hallway where Derek had disappeared.

He stood at the front window, staring at something outside, and glanced her way when she approached. "Blaze warned me that you don't follow instructions well."

She shoved her feet into sneakers as memories of her last harrowing escape grew more vivid and terrifying. Her limbs twitched, ready to run.

"Looks like one of the resort's trucks," Derek said, his attention fixed beyond the glass once more. "Snowplow on the front. Resort logo on the side. The guy got out and started shoveling debris out of the ditch across the road. He's wearing a reflective jacket, coveralls, work boots. Fits the right visual." He lifted his cell phone to the window and snapped a photo.

"Sure," Maisy said flatly. "And the man who came for me at the safe house was wearing a marshal jacket. Driving the real marshal's government-issued vehicle." Her voice quaked with the words. Clara's killer had taken what he needed after murdering the marshal. For all she knew, a resort worker could be dead somewhere now, too.

"Stay here." Derek unlocked the dead bolt and swung his gun behind his back. "I mean it this time."

"What?" Maisy stepped into the kitchen, closer to the opposite door. "What's happening?"

"My truck's back," Derek said. "I'm going to meet my little brother outside."

Maisy's breaths came short and quick as Derek left her in the cabin, pulling the door shut behind him. She accessed her cell phone's dial pad and put 911 on the screen, then hovered her thumb over the green button, ready to send the call.

Outside, a round of husky laughter echoed in the air. She took a small step forward, listening intently.

"All right, man," Blaze said, his voice boisterous and friendly.

Maisy hurried for a look out the window.

Blaze spoke to the man in coveralls, a welcoming smile on his face.

Derek slunk around the large white work truck, taking photos of the license plate and through the window of the cab, then several of the man speaking with Blaze.

Maisy erased 911 from her dial pad and called the resort's lodge instead, eyes fixed on the men outside. She started as the silhouette of someone inside Derek's truck caught her eye. She'd temporarily forgotten the lawyer was coming to talk with her.

"Yes, hello," Maisy said to the woman answering her call. "I just saw a man in one of your trucks lurking along the roadside. Is he allowed to do that?" she asked, making her voice high and working up a deep southern accent. "He isn't some kind of voyeur, is he?"

"No, ma'am," the woman responded. "Our maintenance crew is out clearing ditches today. The rain has washed the storm drains full of leaves and mud, which has caused some minor flooding in a few areas. We wouldn't want those to freeze when the temperature drops again tonight. Ice on these roads can make travel nearly impossible. If you'd like, I can confirm the man's name and description, so you know he's where he should be and doing what he's supposed to be doing. Did you happen to notice the number on the truck?"

Maisy hesitated. As much as she'd like the confirmation, she hated to give away her location. Blaze was supposed to be an artist staying alone. She watched as he and Derek waved goodbye to the man then turned toward the cabin. If they were satisfied, she would be, too. "No, thank you," she said. "I can see it's fine. Goodbye."

The man in coveralls climbed back into his truck and drove away as the cabin door swung open. Derek arrived first. "That guy seemed legit. I took some pictures to check up on him and the truck, but you don't need to worry."

She smiled. "I won't. The lodge confirmed—"

"Hey," Blaze interrupted, crossing the threshold with a willowy brunette. "We're back." His smile was triumphant, and Maisy found her smile widening in response. "Maisy Daniels. I would like you to meet Julia Struthers, the new lead prosecutor. Your second-biggest advocate."

Maisy warmed, knowing Blaze was her first.

Julia extended a hand to Maisy. Her dark hair fell in curtains against her cheeks and jaw, streaked with gray and grazing her shoulders. Her smart green eyes scanned Maisy warmly. A motherly smile curved her petal-pink lips.

"Thank you for doing this," Maisy said. "For taking up the torch. For coming here. It's very courageous of you."

"I'm no more courageous than the woman at this case's center," she said with a wry grin. "I've been following your sister's case from the beginning. Your love and devotion has been evident from the start. Not many people know this, but I left trial law for teaching because I'd become so exhausted by the number of people willing to walk away from justice if the right amount of money was offered."

Maisy tried to imagine taking money in exchange for dropping the charges against Natalie's killer. But she couldn't. How could anyone?

Julia's expression turned sad and knowing. "You've probably noticed no one from your friend Aaron's family plans to testify."

A spark of surprise zipped through her. She hadn't given him much thought in the past few months, but she'd assumed his family was pursuing Luciano as actively as she was. She'd expected to see them at the trial. "They dropped their charges?"

Julia nodded. "They can still be subpoenaed, compelled to provide testimony, but I don't plan to do that. They've made their position clear. They're at peace with the loss they can't change. They aren't comfortable dredging up their most horrible memories. Forcing them to take the stand could wind up hurting our case. It's better to focus on what we have working for us."

"You think Aaron's parents were bribed?" Maisy asked.

"Or threatened," Julia said. "Either way, I won't press the matter. They've been through too much already. Just like you. But if you're still willing to testify, I will stick by you every step of the way."

Maisy pulled in a fortifying breath and released it with a smile. She would do anything to see Luciano never hurt anyone else again. "Let's get started."

Chapter Eighteen

Blaze walked Derek to his truck after a late dinner. They'd made chicken noodle soup from cans and baked rolls in the oven. It wasn't a fancy meal, but it was warm, comforting and cozy, filling the cabin with the rich, buttery scents of home. A perfect ending to a successful day. Maisy had connected with Julia in a real and trusting way during her visit, and Maisy's testimony had been recorded, in case it wasn't safe for her to attend the trial.

Blaze had taken Julia back to the coffee shop where they'd met, then returned in time to help with dinner. Maisy had been in good spirits, though she'd eaten far less than he thought she should. Now, it was time for Derek to go home temporarily. He'd made the same short escape the day before, leaving to care for his horses and get some sleep before returning to keep watch while Blaze tried to rest a few hours before dawn.

"I'll be back by midnight," Derek said, squinting as the snow fell over them.

Blaze rubbed tired eyes and struggled to suppress a yawn. "Take your time. If I haven't told you lately, I appreciate what you've been doing here. So does Maisy."

"What are brothers for?" Derek grinned. He clapped Blaze on the back, then pointed his eyes at the cabin.

"Keep an eye on her tonight. She was sick all day and lied about it."

"You noticed that, too, huh?" Blaze followed his brother's gaze to the flicker of light from the television inside the front window.

"Yep. I'm guessing she doesn't want to worry you."

"Well, it's too late for that," Blaze said. "All I do is worry."

"Three more days," Derek said. "You're almost there. With a little luck, Julia will convince Judge Wise to accept the recording as evidence tonight, or the other attorney will agree to a livestream during the trial."

Blaze forced a smile, but they both knew Maisy's luck wasn't that good. "Maybe," he conceded. "I'm going to give her doctor a call when I go back inside. That should help put some of my anxiety to rest. Maisy will protest, until I say I'm worried about the baby, then she won't fight me on it. There's nothing she won't do for her."

"Her?" Derek's brows tented. "A little girl? Are you sure?"

Blaze beamed, unable to stop himself. "I wanted to let her tell you, but these last few days have been nuts."

"A girl?"

Blaze nodded. "Yeah. She's going to make a great mom."

Derek pulled Blaze into a hug. "And you're going to make a great dad. You already have all those awful jokes."

"Shut up." Blaze shoved him toward the open truck door. "Go home. Drive safely. Come back rested." He shook his head as he climbed the steps to the cabin's small porch, then watched as the truck's taillights faded slowly into the distance.

Every minute that passed without a crisis was a cherished moment closer to the end of the chaos. A moment closer to his new beginning with Maisy.

He stomped snow from his shoes before slipping inside.

Maisy smiled at him from the kitchen. She leaned against the countertop, a glass of water in one hand. Uncertainty colored her cheeks, and as he toed off his boots and drew closer, a line of sweat became evident over her brow. "Everything okay?"

"I was going to ask you the same thing," Blaze said. He pressed the back of his hand to her forehead, then pulled her into a hug. "You aren't fevered, but you're clammy. Does that mean you're trying to hide nausea or contractions?"

She stepped away with a grimace, wrapping both arms around her middle. "I just need to lie down. It's been a big day, and I ate too much at dinner."

"You barely ate anything at dinner," he said. "And you've looked like this since we left the courthouse yesterday. Tell me what's going on."

Maisy pressed her eyes and lips shut briefly before peeling weary hazel eyes open once more. "Fine. I don't feel well. I'm nauseous and tense. My stomach's been upset more often than it hasn't, and my back aches almost nonstop."

Fear flattened Blaze's heart. He struggled to maintain his warm smile while fishing his phone from his pocket. "Come here." Her pulled her against him, rubbing his palm against her back as she snuggled close.

Maisy pressed her cheek to his chest. "I can't shake the nausea. I've been reading online all day about it, and

I think it's normal, especially under stress, but I can't seem to get rid of it. I've tried everything."

Blaze kissed the top of her head. "Why don't I call Dr. Nazir? She'll know if it's anything to worry about, and what we should do either way."

Maisy nodded, releasing him slowly, then let him lead her to the couch.

"Give me just a minute." He scrolled to the doctor's number, saved in his phone, then called, switching on the speaker function so Maisy could listen in and take part.

Dr. Nazir was pleasant, but concerned. She worried about Maisy's hydration, and suggested Blaze get her a sports drink to help the cause. She also recommended a safe, over-the-counter pill for the nausea.

Maisy was visibly relieved when the call disconnected. "I'm going to be okay," she said wistfully.

"Sounds like it," Blaze agreed.

Still, her skin was pale and dewy from a sheen of sweat. "It's the stress," she insisted, dragging a forearm across her brow.

Blaze propped Maisy's feet on a pair of throw pillows, then delivered a cold, wet washcloth for her forehead. "We'll visit Dr. Nazir's office first thing tomorrow morning," he said. "For tonight, rest and hydration." He knelt on the floor before her, concern tightening his limbs and gut. "I'm going to run to the general store before it closes and pick up the medication she recommended for nausea." He checked his watch. "I can make it if I leave now, and bring you back something to help with hydration, too."

He had another thirty minutes before the store closed, but he only needed seven to get there, and five to gather the items on his list. Resort roads would be empty this time of day in the off-season, making it possible to double the posted speed limit.

She reached for him, curling her small hand around his much larger one. "Thank you for taking care of me." A small tear hung in the corner of her eye.

Blaze caught the droplet with the pad of his thumb and brushed her hair away from flushed cheeks. "I will always take care of you."

Her returning smile pinched his heart, and he sent up a silent prayer that she would feel better soon. That she would rest, and that the doctor would tell them she and their baby were perfect after seeing her tomorrow morning.

Blaze had been a soldier, had been shot at in foreign lands and had been endangered regularly since becoming a homicide detective, but he'd never been afraid like he was now. He lifted her hand to his lips and pressed a kiss against her knuckles, then another to her forehead, sneakily checking for signs of a fever. Thankfully, she was cool.

"If you're going to be at the store," she said, looking shyly up at him, "see if they have those little oyster crackers? And more herbal tea? I've gone through most of our stash."

"You've got it," Blaze said. He collected her cell phone from the kitchen counter and placed it on the coffee table in front of her, wishing he had another Taser to offer. "The cabin's locked up tight, but call me if you hear or see anything that makes you uncomfortable. Better to sound a false alarm than miss an opportunity for help." He hesitated, torn between what he knew she needed right now, and the help she might need if he left. The pallor of her skin and faint grimace of discomfort she tried to hide made the former impossible to ignore. "I'll be back as quickly as possible."

He kissed her gently, then dashed outside, carefully locking the door behind him.

The drive down the mountain was fraught with unexpected clusters of actual deer in the headlights, but Blaze made it to the general store in under ten minutes, despite the wildlife roadblocks. He parked near the door in an otherwise empty parking lot, then hustled inside with his mental shopping list.

The aisles were void of people, but well stocked, much like before. And he found everything he needed in minutes. His arms were loaded when he reached the counter. "How much for the flowers?" he asked, righting his purchases on the counter. He swung a finger toward the bouquet of miniature pink, orange and cream roses on display.

The older man behind the register lifted a pair of glasses from his pocket and set them on his nose. "I remember you," he said, passing the bouquet in question to Blaze. "You were here a few days ago with your wife, right?"

"No, sir," Blaze said, hating the fact Derek had been right. This man remembered them, and that could be very dangerous for Maisy and their baby.

"Yes, yes." The man smiled. "Maybe she wasn't your wife. I don't know, but she was lovely. Brown hair, hazel eyes. Pregnant," he reminded Blaze, mimicking the shape of her bump with his hands. "The flowers are on me," he said. "How's she holding up?" He pulled the crackers and sports drinks across the counter to scan them. "I remember these days." He laughed. "My Margaret ate her weight in crackers when she was pregnant with our sons. What are you having? A boy or a girl?"

Blaze pushed the other items closer for the man to ring them up. His mind reeled over how to answer. Was there a way to ask him not to let anyone know they were there, without telling him why it was so important their whereabouts stay concealed? Blaze could show his badge, mention the trial that was on every newscast. But was this man trustworthy?

Would knowing put him in danger?

"Twenty-five twelve," the clerk said, dropping the last item in the bag. "I didn't mean to pry," he apologized, still smiling. "I get a little bored in the off-season. It's lonely. I talk too much."

Exactly what Blaze was afraid of.

"You can let her know her friend's arrangement made it to the funeral on time, just as promised." He shrugged. "Like I said, I've got a lot of extra time, and she looked so heartbroken when she placed the order. I wanted to be sure the flowers made it to their destination safely, so I gave the place a call."

"Funeral?" Blaze asked, passing a pair of twenties across the counter. "She asked you to send flowers to a funeral?"

"Sure." The man tapped the cash register, and the drawer popped open. "We're part of the National Flower Distribution Network." He handed Blaze his change and receipt, then pointed to a pink flyer on the window.

"Can you tell me exactly where those flowers went?" Blaze asked, stuffing the wallet back into his pocket and gathering the bags with Maisy's bouquet. Not that he needed confirmation to know they'd been for Clara. Of course she'd want to send her condolences. Why hadn't he thought to handle this for her? She could've made the selection, and Derek could've handled the delivery. He could only hope she'd been wise enough to pay in cash and not include a card.

The man presented a completed order form. Fake information in the sender section. Good. Delivery details were as expected. Clara's memorial service in North Jackson.

"Did she include a card with the order?" he asked, feeling slightly more comfortable with the situation.

"She didn't specify, so I wrote 'warmest thoughts and prayers.' That's the standard for funeral arrangements."

"Did she pay cash? Or sign the card?"

"Yes to both, though she only signed with her initials."

Blaze's grip tightened on the flowers and packages. That was half of what he'd wanted to hear. "May I see the cards you include in these matters?" He watched raptly as the man fished one from a pile behind him. Blaze begged silently that the small white square be marked with the national chain name only.

"There." He passed a blank card to Blaze with a smile.

Brandy Falls Ski Resort was embossed in golden font across the top.

MAISY SHUFFLED AROUND the living room, nausea pushed aside by a powerful, teeth-gritting contraction. Her nerves were wholly and completely shot, and she was beginning to panic. It was the first time she'd been alone since leaving her safe house behind. Before that, it had been months. Now, the trial was less than seventy-two hours away, people associated with it were dropping like flies and her body was reacting just as extremely as her mind.

Every sound in the forest sent fresh waves of terror down her spine as she puffed through another false contraction. She imagined shooters in the trees, taking aim through the windows. Killers lurking in the shadows along the exterior wall, just out of sight and slowly prying open the cabin windows and doors.

The sound of an engine outside sent her hurrying to the front window, eager to see Blaze's strong, comforting smile.

The big ski resort truck was back, parked along the road's edge again.

She collected her phone from the coffee table and hesitated. Call the lodge to confirm the worker was back? Tending to gutters after dark? Or call Blaze to tell him she was in pain and scaring herself silly?

Her phone rang before she could decide, and Blaze's face appeared on the screen. She smiled in relief. Sometimes she was sure they shared a cosmic connection. At the moment she was intensely thankful for it. "Hello?"

"Maisy?" Blaze's voice was a mashup of tension and fear. "Did you send flowers to Clara's funeral?"

"Yes," she said, attention glued to the man in coveralls climbing out of the truck. "It was impulsive, but I was careful. I was going to tell you right after I did it, but I got distracted. Listen," she rattled on, unable to pause or catch her breath. "The man is back to clean the gutters, and I'm kind of freaking out about it."

Blaze swore. "Check the door locks, and turn the lights out. Just to be safe. I'm in my truck now."

Across the phone line, an engine revved to life.

Maisy hit the light switch, then tucked her feet into sneakers, kept on standby near the rear door. "I didn't sign my name to the card. How'd you find out about it, and why does it matter? Also, please tell me I'm overre-acting about this ditch cleaner."

Blaze's truck engine roared across the line. "You used your initials. And the card was embossed with the ski resort's logo. Go into your room and lock the door. I'll talk to the guy when I get there."

Maisy's gaze darted through the dark cabin. There was nowhere to hide, and a hollow interior door with a cheap knob lock couldn't protect her.

Outside, the man in coveralls headed up her walk, a shovel swung onto his shoulder like a baseball bat. "He's coming," she whispered, stumbling backward against the rear door. Moonlight glinted on the handgun at his hip as he reached the small front porch.

He knocked. Then tried the knob.

There was only one thing left for Maisy to do.

Run.

Chapter Nineteen

Maisy stepped into the biting cold, heart racing and instantly regretful that she hadn't grabbed a coat when she put on her sneakers.

"Are you there?" Blaze barked. "Is he in the house? Are you hidden?"

The sudden crash of their cabin's door bursting open set her feet in motion. She choked back a scream as fear propelled her through the snowy woods. "He's inside. I think he broke down the door. I'm outside. I'm running. Blaze, hurry!"

Icy winds burned her skin, slicing easily through her thin cotton pajamas. She pulled hair from her eyes as she muddled forward, over tree roots and mud. Her steps were uneven, thrown off by her too-high center of gravity. She slid on wet leaves and patches of icy earth, tossing her forward and nearly onto her knees. Her heartbeat pounded in her ears as she raced into the night, desperately adding space between herself and the killer.

"You can't hide!" An angry male voice echoed behind her. "I know you're out here, and you're never going to make it back inside alive."

"He's outside now. He knows I'm out here," Maisy cried into the phone.

"Stay put. I'm two minutes out," Blaze growled.

Maisy couldn't stop, couldn't risk being caught, couldn't risk her baby's life.

She dared a look behind her and felt her rioting heart collapse.

The man had a spotlight.

Her toe clipped something hard and immobile on the forest floor, pitching her forward as she turned her attention back around. She crashed sideways into a large evergreen and involuntarily yipped in pain. Her cell phone popped loose from her grip and collided with the snowy ground. Rough bark tore the tender skin of her arm, aching and stinging as she bit back another cry. Heavy breaths puffed from her lips in smoky white clouds as she edged around the tree, pressing her back to the wood, listening for signs of his nearness.

Maisy's eyes blurred with unshed tears as her footprints came into view on the snowy ground, marking a path to her hiding spot.

Bang! The blast of a gun split the night, ringing her ears and scattering birds from the treetops.

Bang!

Bark burst into bits at her side.

Maisy darted into the thickest part of the forest, praying the limbs of heavy pines and multitude of trunks would disguise her plight.

A third shot rang out, exploding divots of earth over the snow several yards away.

She locked her jaw against another scream, unwilling to disclose her position and knowing the shooter would soon catch her anyway. Her stomach twisted with nausea, and a contraction gripped her middle hard enough to double her over.

"You can't hide," the voice bellowed. "You've left me a path, and you can't run forever in your condition."

Maisy forced her trembling legs to move, forcing her fear into a mental lockbox. She had to live. Had to protect her baby. *And Blaze will be here soon*, she reminded herself.

She just had to stay alive long enough to be rescued.

Maisy ducked beneath the heaviest limbs, crouching as she hurried through a thick blanket of fallen pine needles, making her footsteps invisible.

Something moved in the distance, and Maisy yelped.

A deer ran through the forest, and another gunshot went off.

The little she'd eaten made a reappearance at her feet, spilled freely at the thought of the poor deer's possible fate. Her throat burned, and her teeth began to chatter as she pitched herself forward once more. Carried on wobbly knees and frozen legs across the pine needles, refusing to look back. Unwilling to see if the deer had made it, or if the poor thing had become another casualty in the war she had started.

The cadence of steady footfalls rose through the night, close enough now to be heard. Close enough for the next shot not to miss.

And Maisy had nowhere left to hide. The trees ended a few yards ahead, opening broadly to a large snow-covered field.

She scooted around the massive trunk, then backed herself into a gaping hollow at its core, trying to make herself as small as possible.

The broad beam of her hunter's spotlight flashed into view across the forest floor. Snow crunched under his feet as he stopped only a few feet from the tree.

Maisy's breaths raked loudly through her ears, each exhale a smoke signal to her hiding spot.

The next contraction hit like a sledgehammer, buckling her knees where she stood.

And a trickle of something warm and wet rolled down her thigh.

"Maisy!" Blaze's voice echoed in the trees, bringing a flood of hot tears to her eyes.

Outside her narrow hiding place, the spotlight vanished, and her hunter's footfalls moved away.

She melted into the tree with short-lived relief.

Then the gunshots began.

"Police!" Blaze called between blasts, his voice low and bursting with authority. "You are under arrest. Put down your weapon. Now!"

Another shot sounded, and Maisy's ears rang anew. Choked by fear and a constricting chest, the world began to darken around her.

A steady beating erupted, and the trees began to sway.

The pain of a fresh contraction broke over her, hitting like a punch in the spine and forcing her legs out from under her. She slid down the rotted tree, its frozen bark pulling up the back of her shirt and breaking the skin as she fell. Her numb and frozen hands reached for the ground to soften her landing in the pine needles and snow.

A tortured scream ripped through her as the next contraction followed in the wake of the last. Moist heat warmed her trembling thighs as she rolled onto her back on the frozen ground. Above her, the treetops undulated wildly, and the beating grew impossibly loud.

Her breaths came short and shallow. She pinched her eyes closed against the pain.

"Maisy! Maisy!"

She peeled her eyes open, unsure how long they'd been closed. The unequivocal ache at her core nearly too much to bear.

A blinding light hovered in the sky, and she shut her eyes once more.

"She's here!" Blaze called, then his arms were around her. "Stay with me," he pleaded, but her frozen lips couldn't form a response.

Her body writhed with the next contraction, and she was sure she'd die.

"It's okay," Blaze demanded. "I'm here. We've got you."

Sleet pelted her face as the silhouettes of strangers surrounded her, aiding Blaze as he carried her into the light. Toward the beating sound.

Onto a helicopter and into the air.

Chapter Twenty

Blaze watched helplessly as the medical staff at West Liberty United Hospital rushed Maisy down the hall ahead of him on a gurney. A flood of panic and adrenaline tunneled his vision and rung his ears. Scents of bleach and bandages stung his nose and throat as he jogged the corridor toward the maternity ward.

He owed everything to the chopper pilot and crew who'd landed in the snowy field, charged with the capture and arrest of Luciano's hit man. They'd easily changed missions when they found Blaze with her, unconscious, in his arms. The helicopter had flown Maisy to the hospital in less time than it would've taken Blaze to carry her out of the woods and meet the arriving ambulance. The ambulance would've taken another twenty minutes to drive her off the mountain.

The pilot had radioed ahead to alert the hospital, and the hospital had contacted Dr. Nazir.

Now, Blaze could only hope Maisy and their daughter would be okay.

"What can you tell us about her condition?" an older woman in blue scrubs asked over her shoulder.

"She's been nauseous all day," Blaze said. "She's had

intermittent contractions for much longer. More than a week, at least." The words poured from him, almost faster than he could speak them. "She was in the woods at least thirty minutes without a coat before I found her. She was hiding. I apprehended the shooter," he rambled, "then I couldn't find her. She's been in and out of consciousness."

"Shooter?" a second, younger nurse, helping pilot the gurney, asked.

"She's a witness in a trial this week," Blaze answered, slowing with the group as a broad set of doors marked Obstetrics swung open before them.

The older woman glanced at him once more, expression firm. "This is Maisy Daniels? The woman from the news?"

"Yes, ma'am."

She gave Maisy's slack face a long look, then pushed Maisy's medical chariot into the ward. "How far apart are the contractions now?"

Blaze's mind faltered and scrambled. "I don't know." So much had happened so quickly, he hadn't thought to keep track. He'd only worried that he'd been too late to save her. "Not long. A few minutes."

"Put her in a delivery room," the older woman told the younger one. "I'll perform an exam and call anesthesiology to get someone on standby for an epidural."

"She's not due for five weeks," Blaze said, a bead of fresh panic welling in his heart.

Dr. Nazir had given him one job. He was supposed to keep Maisy safe, rested and relaxed. Because she needed to maintain her pregnancy as long as possible. It'd only been days since he'd promised to do those things no matter what, and he'd failed.

And Maisy would pay the price.

The nurses parted ways at the next intersection of hallways.

Blaze stuck close to the younger woman piloting Maisy's gurney, buzzing past arrows with Labor and Delivery written across their centers, while the older woman jogged toward a massive nurses' station.

Maisy's head rolled over her shoulder, her arms limp at her sides.

She'd been eerily white when Blaze had found her. Her cheeks red and lips blue. Her thin canvas sneakers and cotton pajamas were soaked with melted snow.

The nurse drove Maisy's gurney into room 427 and parked it beside a waiting bed, then clamped the brakes.

The older woman returned, rushing past Blaze where he'd stalled just inside the doorway. "Let's get her out of those wet things and into a gown. I brought a set of heated blankets. Ready?"

Maisy's eyes fluttered open as the nurses changed her, then hauled her onto the bed and covered her. "It's too soon. You have to stop the contractions," she pleaded weakly. "She can't come yet."

The following scream and grimace on her pale, twisted face said differently.

The baby was definitely coming.

The nurses moved in a perfectly choreographed dance. Setting Maisy's IV and connecting her body to a barrage of nearby monitors within minutes.

The older nurse pulled a pair of gloves from a bin on the wall and pressed her hands into them. "I'm going to take a look now and see what's going on. Okay, Maisy?"

Maisy agreed, and the older woman moved to the foot of the bed.

Blaze's limbs seemed to lock in place. "Don't we have to wait for the doctor?"

The nurse started at the sound of his voice, as if she'd just taken notice of him. Her gaze slid pointedly to the badge hanging from the chain around his neck. "You can go now, Detective. We'll take it from here."

"What?" he stammered, confusion clouding his brain. "I can't stay?" he asked, his normally confident voice no more than a hoarse whisper.

The woman's expression swung hard from shock to distaste. "I'm afraid not. There's a chair just outside the door if you need to guard your witness."

"No!" Maisy groaned the word around another contraction.

"She's not my witness," he said, heart aching, feet rooted. She might've started that way, in what felt like another lifetime, but now, he realized, now, she was his life.

Maisy's thin arms clung to her middle, her eyes and jaw clamped tight. "He's the father."

A banner of pride swept through Blaze's chest at the words, and the weight of their significance.

The nurse's eyes widened. "I'm so sorry. I didn't realize. Given the situation…"

"It's fine," he said, moving slowly forward. "But is she okay?"

The nurse nodded to the chair beside the bed. "Come. I'll see if it's time we talk about that epidural."

Blaze moved to the head of Maisy's bed and reached for her hand. Her fingers were cold, and images of the darkened forest rushed back to his mind. He'd nearly been shot by her assailant before eventually shooting him instead. It had taken all of Blaze's restraint, and the knowledge that Maisy was missing, to stop him from emptying his entire clip into the lunatic. Instead, he'd kicked the man's gun away, checked his pulse then cuffed him to a tree as the sirens of emergency vehicles became audible in the distance.

With a little karma, the hit man would wind up on the same cell block as Luciano.

By the time Blaze found Maisy, the cavalry had arrived, thanks to Sergeant Maxwell. He'd identified the leak in their system earlier that morning. Luciano was blackmailing a guard at the jail. His image was visible, reflected in the glass of the police station door he'd left ajar for the intruder who'd attacked Maisy in the ladies' room. Fortunately, the man spilled everything while under interrogation. And he'd agreed to testify in exchange for leniency.

When word made it to Lucas that the shooter was headed to the ski resort, he told Maxwell that Blaze was hiding Maisy there. A team and chopper were dispatched, along with local police.

Unfortunately, Blaze hadn't been there to protect her when she'd needed him most.

Whatever happened to her and their baby now would forever be on him.

Maisy screamed again, thrusting her head and shoulders forward. Pain etched hard lines over her delicate features as her entire body seemed to tighten.

"No time for an epidural," the nurse said brightly. "The baby is coming."

Two DAYS LATER, Maisy kissed her daughter's tiny, perfect fingers while slowly memorizing every feature and contour of her small face. From her dad's gray eyes to her precious rosebud lips, she was more than Maisy had ever dreamed of.

Born more than a month early, Natalie Clara Winchester was a late-term preemie. She might've weighed in at just over five pounds, but she more than earned her name every day. Because just like Natalie and Clara, Maisy's little princess was a fighter.

"I'll be back soon," Maisy promised, raising her daughter's delicate hand to her lips for a kiss. "I wouldn't leave if I didn't have to, but there's something very important I need to do. Until then, the nurses will take good care of you."

Blaze wrapped a strong arm around Maisy's middle and pulled her against him, cool gray eyes fixed on their perfect daughter. "I'm so proud of you both." He kissed Maisy's head, then rested his cheek against the crown of her head for a long moment. "The two toughest ladies I know."

"Yeah? Then why do I feel like crying, or cuffing myself to her bed?" Maisy asked, laughing awkwardly at the ridiculous truth. "I've never been farther than a few doors down the hall from her. It feels like ripping off one of my limbs," she said, emotions clogging her throat at the thought of telling her baby goodbye.

"She'll be fine," Blaze whispered. "She'll rest and grow and dream of her mama until you return."

Maisy smiled, enjoying that thought and hoping it was true. "I love her so much. I didn't know I could love someone so completely," she whispered, gazing at their infant in the NICU, a precautionary move, given her size and precarious beginning.

"I did," Blaze said, lifting her face to his for a chaste kiss.

Maisy's hands rose to his chest, fingertips landing gently on the smooth fabric of his tie. "Thank you for always being so kind and loving and patient with me." He was the embodiment of all her favorite qualities in a human, a partner and a friend. And even after a few short days, she had no doubt he was going to make the world's best father.

Blaze chuckled low in his throat. "Maybe you just bring out the best in me." He kissed her forehead. Her closed eyelids, the tip of her nose. "Are you ready?"

"Not even close," she said, lacing her fingers with his as they walked away from the NICU, casting more than a few backward glances at their little girl.

"You've got this," Blaze promised. "And I've got you." The most comforting words she'd ever heard.

Maisy concentrated on her breathing and the feel of his hand in hers as she followed him out of the hospital.

Then into the courtroom.

Epilogue

Maisy rolled onto her side in bed, instinctively reaching for Blaze. She hadn't slept alone since leaving the hospital two months ago, and she loved having him so near. Her fingertips slid over the cool, rumpled sheets. Her sleepy eyes peeled open when her hands came up empty.

Blaze's side of the bed had clearly been slept in, but he wasn't there.

She rose onto her elbows, searching for signs of him in the dark, but found none.

The baby monitor on the nightstand was silent, unplugged or powered off, and an icy finger of fear slithered up her spine. Unwelcomed memories skittered through her mind. Memories where she and her baby were in danger.

Memories, she reminded herself, *nothing more*. And that wasn't her life any longer.

She climbed out of bed with her chin held high, then wrapped herself in the fuzzy robe on the bedpost. She'd accomplished her goal, as promised. With Blaze's help, she'd been able to give testimony in court against Luciano that helped the jury find him guilty. Now, he would live out his days in Kentucky's supermax prison.

Which meant that Maisy was safe.

Better than safe, she thought, tying the belt on her robe. She was loved and happy, healthy and pampered.

Blaze had invited her and Natalie to stay with him until Maisy could find a job and save enough money to move out. She'd eagerly agreed. Her life at the safe house was over, but her old life, the one from before Luciano, was packed into a storage unit. Her apartment long ago rented to someone else.

Now, she was a single, homeless, unemployed mother of an infant.

Thankfully, Blaze's invitation was open-ended, and he told her daily how much he loved having her and Natalie with him. He asked her not to rush into looking for work, not that she'd worked in forever, and when she had, the jobs were never especially wonderful. She'd put her office administration degree to work with paying bills as her singular goal. Now, Blaze told her not to settle. To only choose something she loved. Until then, he encouraged her to preserve every moment she had with their infant daughter for as long as possible, and he'd vowed to help however he could. True to his words and nature, he did more than his share of everything, from cooking and cleaning to late-night feedings and diaper changes. And he seemed to enjoy it all.

Maisy and Natalie certainly enjoyed him. His humor, love and company. She couldn't imagine leaving, so she tried not to think about it. The notion left her empty and cold.

Natalie deserved to spend every minute she could in her daddy's adoring arms. A lifetime of him looking at her as if she might walk on water, if she could walk at all, should ensure that no man would ever get away with mistreating her.

Outside the bedroom, moonlight streamed through gauzy white curtains, painting silver lines across the wide wooden floorboards. She tiptoed softly toward the little nursery, listening carefully for sounds he was there.

The low tenor of his voice sent gooseflesh down her arms, and she strained to make out the words.

Natalie cooed, and Blaze chuckled.

Maisy smiled, falling deeper in love with the both of them as she drifted closer. Eager for a peek at their late-night fun.

"Knock, knock," she whispered, pushing the door slowly open.

The space that had once been little more than a storage room had become the most enchanting nursery Maisy had ever seen. Blaze had worked on it, day by day, until it was perfect. The walls were a faint pink, with accents in ivory and cream. A flowing white curtain draped over the single window, held back by a long velvet tie. A floppy white elephant, wearing a tutu and tiara, sat on Blaze's mother's rocking chair in the corner, a hot-pink shag rug beneath it. Twinkle lights lined the ceiling, and a massive growth chart, made by Derek from an old barn beam, was anchored to the wall. Natalie's toy box brimmed with things she wouldn't be old enough to play with for a year and stood outside a refinished wardrobe filled with enough dresses to clothe a dozen little girls, and accessories to go with every one.

Natalie's little booties came into view, busy as always, narrow legs kicking away her long pink nightgown. Dainty fists waved above her head. A tiny bundle of energy. Always in motion. Going nowhere, but tickled to death about it.

Maisy's heart leaped and her smile doubled at the sight

of her. "What are you doing?" she asked, slipping into the dimly lit room. Her daughter's perfect cherub face and cool gray eyes turned to look up at her.

She reached for her baby, raising her lovingly to her chest before turning to search the space for Blaze. She stopped short as a glint of light drew her eyes to the mobile of happy clouds dancing above the crib.

A diamond ring dangled from the white satin ribbon tied to a cloud.

Her breath caught at the sight of it.

"Maisy?" Blaze's voice turned her toward the shadows, where he'd apparently slipped away for a surprise appearance.

She snuggled Natalie closer, tears of joy forming in her eyes. "I woke up and you weren't there," she said, trying to sound more calm than she suddenly felt. "I thought I'd find you here."

Blaze moved in closer, eyes dancing with delight. "Natalie and I have some serious heart-to-heart talks this time of night."

Maisy laughed. "Oh yeah?" She commanded herself not to look at the ring. Maybe he didn't know she'd seen it. Maybe she wasn't meant to. "What do you talk about?"

Blaze kissed his daughter on her forehead, then he reached for the ring from the mobile, casting a mischievous look over one shoulder. "Sometimes NASCAR. Sometimes the Nasdaq." His smile widened as he stepped back, ring in hand. "Mostly you, and how much we love you."

"Oh yeah?" Maisy's cheeks heated, and her body warmed with his words. Blaze had never left her wondering how much he cared about her, but the ring was more than she'd dared to hope for. She'd wanted to believe that, someday, if things went well for a year or so, he might want to take another step with her. After she was on her feet again, and they'd dated long enough for him to be sure that she was what he wanted. Forever. The way she'd known the same about him since practically the moment they'd met.

Blaze pinched the classic solitaire's band between his thumb and forefinger. Then he lowered onto his knee and said the most perfect two words she'd ever heard him say. "Marry me?"

And Maisy said, "Yes."

* * * * *

COLTON 911: SOLDIER'S RETURN

KAREN WHIDDON

To my beloved husband and daughter.
I love you both more than I could ever express.

Chapter One

The sun shone bright yellow in a blue sky speckled with fluffy white clouds. Happy clouds, Carly Colton thought. The kind she used to imagine were animals and ships when she was a child. All around her, birds were singing cheerful songs and the still-crisp air carried the promise of warmer temperatures to come. Typical spring in Chicago. One minute, cold enough for snow flurries; the next, warm enough to cause trees to start to bud and flowers to bloom. Finally, nice enough weather to enjoy the outdoors, to take more walks, maybe even visit the lakeshore.

Despite being outside, in the warm sunshine, Carly couldn't stop looking over her shoulder. The beautiful April day did nothing to lessen her unease. For the past six weeks, whether shopping or taking a walk, she'd been certain someone was stalking her, even though she'd never actually been able to catch sight of them.

It was more of a gut feeling, a visceral instinct. She'd be walking along familiar streets and then feel someone's gaze on her with a tingle of nerves in the back of her neck. Who? Terrified, she'd spin wildly, hoping to catch her stalker in the act. But so far, she'd been completely unsuccessful, unable to locate a single person or even a group of people paying her the slightest bit of untoward attention. Nothing, absolutely nothing, out of the ordinary. Enough to make her wonder if her father's and uncle's murders had made her become overly fearful.

These days, she had to make herself venture out of her home, despite craving the fresh air. Her neighborhood had always been perfectly safe, and she loved her street.

Even now, on a perfect spring day, she swore she could feel someone watching her. Unsettled, she managed to force herself to continue on her walk, though every instinct screamed she should run home as fast as she could. As usual, she resisted the urge.

Paranoid? Maybe. But then she had reason to be on edge considering her father and his brother had been murdered a few months ago. The killer had yet to be caught. Even so, she didn't like feeling uneasy outside her own house in her wonderful Hyde Park neighborhood, the one place she should have felt safe. Until a month and a half ago, despite occasional bouts of bad weather, she'd always enjoyed her early-evening strolls around her block, waving at neighbors and enjoying a bit of fresh air.

Now not so much. In fact, she'd begun to realize she might need to consider stopping them altogether. Which would be a shame, since she considered walking her main stress reliever after working as a pediatric nurse in the NICU—Neonatal Intensive Care Unit. She hated to lose that one little bit of joy in what could sometimes be long, and often painful, days.

Determined to persevere, she'd continued her walks, heart often racing, always alert, looking for proof that the eyes she felt watching her were real. If she saw anything, any tangible evidence to confirm her fears, she'd stop immediately.

Her family would be worried if they knew. Ever since the devastating death of her fiancé, Micha, two years ago, they had a tendency to treat her as if they believed she might break. Plus, with everyone still raw after her father's and uncle's murders, she hadn't wanted to worry them.

Same with the man she'd been dating, though she'd decided to tell him that evening over dinner. Since Harry Cartwright was a police officer, she figured he just might take her seriously. Maybe he'd even offer to help.

Someone had to. Because instead of going away, it was getting worse.

Carly picked up her pace. Once she'd made it around this next corner, she'd be able to see her house. The sight of her tidy little brick bungalow never failed to lift her spirits. Though she wasn't a runner, if need be she figured she could always sprint for home.

Again, she scanned her surroundings, unease sitting like a lead balloon in the pit of her stomach. She saw nothing out of the ordinary. A man walked his dog on the other side of the street. A woman holding fast to her child's hand moved at a leisurely pace several houses ahead.

Yet she could not shake the feeling of being watched.

Frustrated, she rounded the corner, still at a brisk walk but on the verge of breaking into a jog. And then she saw him, stepping out into her path from a drive-way, his dark sunglasses and longish, wavy brown hair doing nothing to disguise his achingly familiar—and ruggedly beautiful—face.

It couldn't be. No freaking way.

Shocked, Carly froze. Now she knew she'd officially ventured into the land of needing professional help. Because the man standing less than ten feet in front of her had died two years ago. How could she be looking at a ghost?

He took a step toward her, disturbingly solid. No ap-parition, but muscle and bone and skin. Real.

"Micha?" she heard herself ask, as if from a distance. Because it couldn't be and yet… "Micha Harrison, is that really you?"

Of course, this man, whoever he was, with his strik-ing features and stylishly shaggy hair, would now speak and tell her no, she'd made a terrible mistake. Because people just don't come back from the dead.

"It's me," he said instead, his words and the famil-iar husky voice making her stagger. "Carly, we really need to talk."

She couldn't catch her breath. Heart pounding, she stared.

Talk? She wanted to scream, push past him, but she couldn't seem to make her legs move. How could he be there, this beautiful, rugged, beloved man who'd de-stroyed her by his absence. Which had all apparently been one huge pack of lies.

"Have you been following me?" she asked, still numb, struggling to make sense of how she was supposed to feel. The man she'd loved, whose ring she just stopped wearing on a chain around her neck, had died. She'd never forget the day she'd opened her front door to find a uniformed soldier standing on her porch with the gut-wrenching news that Micha had been killed.

Had that been fake? Clearly, it must have been. But why? Why would the man who'd promised to love her forever do such a thing to her? How dare they? How dare he?

Suddenly furious, she wrenched herself away from him and broke into a run. Despite her lack of expertise, her anger fueled her and she raced down her street and into her driveway.

To her immense relief, Micha didn't chase after her.

Once she'd made it safely inside her house, dead bolt locked, she doubled over. Out of breath, in pain, her rage warring with a stunned sense of disbelief. And the grief, oddly enough, resurrected from the dark place she'd shoved it, as surely as the man she'd had to let go.

Micha wasn't dead. She wasn't sure how to process this. Dimly aware of the tears streaming down her face, she angrily swiped at them with the back of her hand.

A moment later, the sorry bastard had the nerve to knock on her front door.

She froze, then squared her shoulders, took a deep breath and wiped her eyes once more. On the one hand, she wanted to fling open the door and tell him to get the hell off her porch. On the other, she wanted to throw herself into his arms and hold him tight, as she'd dreamed of doing so many times while aching from his loss.

Alive. The love of her life. He'd ruined her for anyone

else. She'd hung on to the memory of him, of their love shining bright and incandescent. She'd *mourned* him, damn it. He hadn't died. Alive. And he didn't bother to show up until two freaking years later.

Pain, fresh and as new as the day she'd learned of his death, slammed into her gut, almost sending her to her knees.

Carly had never been an indecisive person, but she honestly didn't know what to do.

Micha knocked again. "We need to talk," he said, the solid wood door muffling his raspy voice. "Please, Carly. Let me in. I promise you I can explain."

She wanted to. Oh, how much she wanted to. Right now, she warred between a furious need to pummel him with her fists and to haul him up against her and kiss him senseless.

Micha had destroyed her. And now he wanted to tell her how and why.

In the end it was this, curiosity over the explanation, wondering how anyone, anywhere, could possibly rationalize what he'd done, that made her unlock the door and invite him inside.

Stepping back, she said nothing as he moved past her, his shoulders every bit as wide as she remembered. Still silent as she secured the dead bolt and turned to face him in the entryway of the house they'd chosen together. She'd gone ahead and purchased it after his death.

He still wore his sunglasses. The better to hide from her, she supposed, her chest twisting. "Take them off," she demanded, pointing.

He did, revealing his dark brown eyes and something else she hadn't expected. Scars. Numerous ones, a network of them around his forehead and right cheek.

Unable to help herself, she moved closer, reached out and traced her finger over the lines. Her touch made him shudder, which brought her back to reality. Shaking her head, she took a hasty step back.

"What happened to you?" she asked softly, trying to infuse a bit of steel in her voice. "I thought you were dead."

Her question made him swallow hard. She couldn't keep from following the movement in his damn-him-for-still-being-so-sexy throat.

"Could we sit somewhere and talk?" he rasped. "Please?"

Talk. She struggled to process the word. As if this was an ordinary situation, easily solved with a rational conversation. Except right now, she thought viciously, he should be groveling on his hands and knees, full of abject apologies and recrimination over what he'd done. He'd let her believe him dead for two freaking years. She should show him the door, toss him out on his rear.

Except…she really wanted to know what had happened. His reasons. What would make a man destroy the woman he'd supposedly loved. Just like that, the flare of anger dissipated, leaving her weak.

Usually when stressed, Carly talked. Chattered actually. But this time, she didn't feel the need to fill the silence with words. No. Not now. That would have to be Micha's job.

"Sure," she said, leading the way down the hall into the living room. At the last moment, she reconsidered and veered into the kitchen, indicating her red-and-chrome retro dinette set. "Can I get you something to drink?"

Her polite and distant tone made him flinch. She wanted to shrug and tell him to take what he could get. Civility, no matter how remote, was a far better response than giving in to her tangled emotions.

"No, thank you." Dropping into a chair, Micha dragged his hands through his shaggy hair. He'd never worn his hair so long, she thought absently. When they'd been together, he'd kept it closely cropped in a military-type cut, fitting since he'd been a soldier.

Still Micha didn't speak. She waited, but he simply watched her, his achingly familiar features a study in emotion.

Fine. Then she'd start. She had so many questions. She deserved answers.

"You've been stalking me," she said. "Why?"

"I wanted to make sure you were all right," he admitted. "I hadn't planned on letting you see me, but…" He shook his head, letting the words trail off.

"It's been two years, Micha." The anger came roaring back, though she managed to keep her voice steady. "Not only did you let me believe you were dead, but after all this time, you couldn't be bothered to get in touch with me and let me know you were all right. Why now?"

She took a step toward him, still trying to rein in her emotions, not entirely sure she was succeeding. Once, the big man sitting at her kitchen table had known her well enough to see right through to the heart that beat erratically inside her chest. If he still could, then he'd understand the complicated mixture of raw pain and sadness, anger and, oddly, defeat.

Since he hadn't responded, she took a deep breath and continued, as ruthless as she knew she had to be. "I've moved on, Micha. I'm finally getting on with my life. I'm dating a very nice guy, Harry, and—"

Micha pushed to his feet, towering over her. "I know, Carly," he said, his voice rough. "And believe me, I'm well aware I have no right to show up and disrupt your life. I just couldn't stay away." His gaze blazed with heat. "I tried, Carly. Believe me, I tried."

Something—maybe his palpable anguish or the way the heat in his eyes brought back memories of his big hands on her skin—had her taking a half step toward him. Pushing to his feet, he met her halfway, sweeping her up against his broad chest, slanting his mouth over hers in a kiss that was everything it shouldn't have been.

Two years vanished in a flash. For weeks, months, she'd dreamed of this, yearning for him, aching for his loss, so how could she possibly let him go? She might be full of regrets later, but for now she chose to give in and ride this wave of welcome passion. For the first time since learning of his death, Carly Colton came alive.

She denied him nothing. Greedily, she clung to him, allowing herself to touch his muscular, still-familiar body. Despite the velvet warmth of his tongue alongside hers, part of her still couldn't help but wonder if she might wake up to learn that this turned out to be yet just another dream.

But the force of his arousal pressing against her had to be real, her own body heavy and warm in response.

Her skin tingled and she couldn't shed her clothes fast enough. Gaze locked on hers, he did the same.

More scars crisscrossed his chest, his stomach, and wound a horrific path down his arm. She noted these, knew she'd ask about them later, but all she cared about now was the man inside his skin.

Unbearable, this craving. She was weak, yet on fire, her heartbeat throbbing in her ears, ecstasy spiraling with each stroke of his tongue against hers.

Naked finally, skin to skin, her flesh on fire. He called her name, a guttural moan, as his lips seared a path to the hollow of her throat.

She arched her back, giving herself over to him even as she tugged him closer, wanting him inside her. Needing him inside her with the heat of a thousand suns.

"Wait," he managed, grabbing his discarded jeans and removing a condom from his wallet. Watching as he tugged it over his magnificent arousal, her mouth went dry.

Dizzy with desire, she reached for him again the instant he'd finished sheathing himself. His dark eyes smoldered as he swept his gaze over her, even as he murmured her name like it was a prayer.

Somehow, they made it to her bed, falling onto the sheets, their bodies still tangled together.

He took her then, sweeping her beneath him with one simple motion, both familiar and thrillingly new. The engorged tip of him pressed against her. Ready, warm and wet, she opened herself to him. Micha had finally come home.

"I never forgot," she gasped as he entered her, filling

her completely. The feel of his hard body, both familiar and foreign, electrified her, sending her into a kind of pleasure overdrive. Micha. She writhed beneath him, urging him to move, but maddeningly he held himself completely still, tension running through every muscle in his body.

"Hold still," he managed to order. "Please. If you don't, this just might be over before it even begins."

This statement, coming from a man who'd always been able to take his time leisurely bringing her to pleasure, drove her wild. She could scarcely catch her breath, but with her heart pounding, she managed to do as he'd asked and not move. Though she could do nothing to stop the little pulses her body gave at him so deep inside her.

And then he began to move.

Pure and explosive pleasure, sweet agony of the kind she'd never thought she'd experience again. She saw colors, heard music, felt her heart expand even as her body melted. She could no longer control her cries of pleasure, matching his thrusts with wild abandon.

As she gave herself over to her release, she felt him catch his breath as he did the same. This at least hadn't changed.

They held each other as their shuddering subsided, she clinging to him as if he might vanish in the space of the next gulp of air she allowed into her lungs. And he…he held on to her with a similar sort of desperate possessiveness. She traced her fingers over him, exploring while no longer in the throes of passion. His muscular body bore more scars, a tangled web of jagged lines that surely had something to do with his disappearance. She'd hear the story behind them soon, though not now, not yet. She wasn't ready.

Neither spoke. She, because she didn't want to ruin the fragile peace of the moment with reality. He, most likely because if he did he might have to explain. And right now, she really didn't want to hear it.

Her phone chimed, the calendar alert reminding her she'd agreed to meet Harry for dinner in less than an hour. Just like that, her insides twisted into a knot.

"You should go," she told Micha, trying not to look at him in all his naked, masculine splendor. "I have plans tonight."

"With him?" No inflection in his voice, just the question, asked so quietly.

Miserable now, she nodded. "Yes."

With a sinfully languid movement reminiscent of a big cat stretching in the sun, he got up from her bed and sauntered toward her bathroom, detouring into the hall to scoop up his clothes on the way. "I'll be out of your hair in a minute."

Despite everything, she couldn't tear her gaze away from his naked rear. She'd always loved his body, surprisingly graceful despite his sheer size. Now his skin looked like something she was familiar with from her work as a nurse. She'd spent a few of her clinical rotations in the burn unit. She'd seen skin grafts that looked like this, and horrific burns that had eventually healed, leaving their mark behind.

She ached to run her fingers over those scars, to kiss

them to show she still found him beautiful and sexy, and always would.

No. She couldn't even let her thoughts go there. She needed to shower and get ready to meet Harry.

And probably ruin forever what had been a burgeoning relationship.

Micha emerged from her bathroom a moment later, fully dressed. His shaggy hair even appeared to have fallen back into its former artful disarray. He looked, she thought grimly, both the same and completely different.

She followed him down the hall toward the front door. He reached for the knob to let himself out, but at the last moment he turned.

"Don't go to meet Harry tonight," he said, letting her see the naked emotion in his eyes. "Stay here with me and talk. We've got a lot of catching up to do."

Heaven help her, she caught herself swaying toward him. At the last moment, she caught herself and shook her head. "Like I said earlier, I've moved on. I've started over, made a life for myself. His name is Harry," she pointed out. "We bonded over our shared grief. He lost his wife and daughter in a car accident around the same time I lost you. I'm not going to bail on him when he's been there for me all this time."

A flash of something—jealousy, maybe—crossed his face. "Are you planning to tell him about this? About…" He swallowed. "What just happened between us?"

She lifted her chin, letting him see some of the bitterness she felt. "I am. I'm not going to lie to him, Micha. All I can do is admit to my mistake and hope he forgives me."

"Mistake." Expression anguished, he stared at her. Spotting a pad of paper and a pen on the table near the door, he jotted down his number. "Call me if you change your mind or just want to talk."

Slowly, she nodded. Then he let himself out the door without another word.

The instant it closed behind him, she instinctively locked the dead bolt. Devastated, she fought the urge to double over and cry. Refusing to allow herself to think, she spun around and marched toward the shower. She needed to wash every last bit of Micha off her body before she told Harry what she had done.

Somehow, she managed to make herself look presentable by the time Harry arrived to pick her up. When he rang the bell, she let him inside. He wore his usual faded jeans and cotton button-down shirt, with a baseball cap on his head. He looked familiar and comfortable and she didn't know how on earth she could break his heart.

With her own heart hammering, she struggled to make small talk. She knew she should tell him now, instead of in a crowded restaurant, but struggled to find the right words.

"What's wrong?" Harry finally asked, his sharp gray-green gaze missing nothing.

"Micha's alive," she blurted, inwardly wincing as she braced for Harry's reaction. He simply stared at her for a moment, clearly trying to assess the situation.

"Could you, er, elaborate?" he asked in what she'd come to think of as his professional police officer tone.

She nodded. "Maybe you'd better sit down?"

"Sure." With a wry smile, he walked into her living room and took a seat on the couch. "Go ahead," he said, once he'd gotten settled. Gaze watchful, he appeared calm and merely curious. His rock-steadiness had always been one of the things she'd liked about him. Harry would never abandon her and pretend to be dead for two years.

She told him everything, starting with the constant feeling of being watched all the way through ending up in bed with Micha. "He had no explanation for where he's been these past twenty-four months," she finished weakly, even though she guessed that detail wouldn't be what Harry would be focused on.

Instead of the hurt or even anger that she'd expected, Harry continued to regard her soberly. "During the time we've been together, we've talked a lot about the people we've lost," he said. "I know how much you loved Micha and how deeply you grieved his passing."

Confused, she frowned. "Yes, but he wasn't really dead."

Harry pushed to his feet. "You've been given a great gift, Carly. A second chance."

"What are you saying? That you think I should get back together with him?" Which defied comprehension. "After what he did?"

"Yes." Expression fierce, Harry swallowed hard. "Do you know what I'd give if Marie and Emily could walk back in my front door?" Anguish twisted his handsome features. "I'd give anything, forgive everything, if I could have a second chance like the one you've been given. Give Micha a shot."

"But—"

"I wish you nothing but the best, Carly." He kissed her cheek. "I hope the two of you can work things out. You deserve that kind of happiness."

On that note, Harry left, leaving Carly to stare after him, more bewildered than before.

Harry's easy acquiescence, while surprising, told her one thing she hadn't expected. She hadn't lost him. She'd never had him to begin with.

Micha coming back to life might seem like a miracle, but after two years she wasn't the same trusting woman she'd been before. Despite her overwhelming physical reaction to him, she couldn't simply pick up where they'd left off, pretending he hadn't done something so unquestionably horrible. If only he had been able to see her, doubled over with the pain of his loss. How long she had grieved, how changed her life had become. While he'd done what? Gotten the military to deliver a fake death notice? Or had they, too, actually believed him to be deceased, which seemed much more likely?

Either way, clearly Micha hadn't been the ordinary soldier he'd pretended to be.

So how many lies had there been? How could she take back a man she couldn't trust?

Her head began to hurt, almost as much as her heart. While part of what Harry had said rang true, she wasn't sure she could ever get past what Micha had done. Heck, she wasn't even sure she wanted to. Because, honestly, if Micha could do something like that to her, she very much doubted he'd ever loved her. At least, not the way she'd loved him.

But then why had he returned? Why now, when she'd

thought she might finally be able to settle into some sort of normal existence? Sure, Harry hadn't made her feel even one tenth of the joy, pleasure and fulfillment she'd experienced with Micha. Music had seemed sweeter, colors brighter, and even food had tasted better. Life had been vibrant then and she'd honestly thought she'd found that once-in-a-lifetime kind of love. Clearly, she'd been wrong.

Now she just needed to figure out how to deal with Micha's presence back in her life.

Chapter Two

Micha Harrison had made love with his Carly. Still reeling, he tried to process a real-life scenario where his former fiancée not only welcomed him back with open arms but kissed him and touched him as if she'd been as starved for him as he'd been for her. He hadn't let himself think, only feel. And he had to admit, sex with Carly felt better than damn good.

Then, once they'd slaked their passion, she'd done an immediate about-face.

In his military training as intelligence gatherer—aka spy—Micha Harrison had learned how to not react to just about any scenario. He'd developed a hell of a poker face, a skill that had served him well in every single situation he'd found himself in while serving his country. In addition, he'd taught himself to clamp down on his emotions, to never give in to impulse or panic and, most important, not to be swayed by pain. The latter had been what had almost cost him his life. Most men, when captured by the enemy, eventually gave in to the agony of torture. Micha had not. Because of that, they'd almost killed him.

Micha was good, damn good. He could retreat inside himself to an untouchable place, no matter what hell rained down upon him.

Yet despite all of his training, all of his skills, Carly proved to be the exception. *His* Carly.

He hadn't meant to let her see him. Now healed and finally healthy, though scarred, he'd returned to Chicago with the intention of simply checking on her. With all of his heart, he'd hoped to find her happy and well, having fully moved on with her life.

At least that's what he'd told himself. All of that went out the window at the first glimpse of her, which had hit him like a punch in the stomach. Her long blond hair still looked soft as silk and her bright blue eyes were as lovely as ever.

Two years and the loss of him had done little to dim her light. That light had been the first thing he'd noticed about her when he'd met her. Carly freaking *glowed*. He'd never been one to believe in auras or any of that sort of nonsense, but Carly nearly changed his mind. She radiated an appealing mixture of goodness and compassion and humor, qualities a man as broken as him had been unable to resist.

Her sensuous beauty had been a bonus, though she'd never been able to see herself the way he saw her. Larger than life, everything he loved about Chicago exemplified in one person. He hadn't been looking for love, but it had found him. Until meeting her, he'd believed his military career would be his life; that he'd need nothing more.

Growing up on a small dairy farm in rural Ohio, all Micha had dreamed about was escaping an existence of livestock and drudgery. With no money for college—like his brother, Brian, before him—Micha had enlisted in the army right after graduation from high school.

To his surprise, he'd thrived. He'd actually found his niche in the military. He'd always done more than his best, giving it his everything. His higher-ups had noticed, singling him out for specialized training.

And then one day on leave in a city he loved, his life had completely changed for the better. He'd finally, at the ripe age of thirty-one, understood love songs and romantic movies, things he'd semi-scoffed at before. All because of Carly and her love.

Until he'd met her, his life had been the military. In the army, he'd finally found the one thing that had been missing all his life—a sense of belonging. The military had become his family, especially when his older brother had been killed while on tour in Syria. His parents had been devastated, and when Micha had taken leave to go home for the funeral, they'd demanded that he return home and take over the dairy farm since Brian wouldn't be able to now. They'd known Micha had only wanted to escape that life and now they expected him to step into his brother's shoes. Incredulous and grieving himself, he'd refused.

That's when his father, both broken and stern, had declared if he remained in the army he would no longer consider Micha his son. Reeling from a now-double loss, Micha had packed his bags and returned to base without even attending his brother's funeral. From that moment on, he'd been determined to dedicate the rest of his life to the service of his country.

Life had clicked along. Over time, the ache of losing his parents had begun to fade. His mother occasionally secretly wrote him, though she asked him not to write back. He'd given her his cell number, but she'd never called. As years passed, he'd been satisfied with his lot and mostly fulfilled.

When he went stateside on extended leave after the successful conclusion of an extremely dangerous mission, he didn't visit the farm or the family that no longer wanted him. Instead, he'd decided to visit the city that had always fascinated him growing up, the place where he could see himself living one day. Chicago. The Windy City.

And as fate would have it, that was where he met Carly. Being in special ops, he'd known better than to go and fall in love. But some things were inescapable. The instant he'd seen her, something had clicked inside him, as if a puzzle piece that had been long missing had finally been fit into place. They'd started out meeting up for coffee and then had gone on a few dates. They'd both fallen fast and furious. For the first time in his adult life, he'd experienced pure, unadulterated happiness. He'd realized there could be more to life than his military career.

Before he'd allowed himself to consider the repercussions, realizing he wanted to spend the rest of his life with her, he'd proposed. She'd joyfully accepted, and they'd planned a wedding for when he'd wrapped up his latest mission, which happened to coincide with the end of his enlistment. Luckily, he hadn't yet re-upped. Of course, she hadn't the faintest idea what he did for the army. He hadn't been allowed to tell her. But he'd vowed as soon as he completed this mission and his military service came to an end, he'd tell her everything. He'd leave his military career so he and Carly could marry and start a family here in Chicago. He'd figure out a civilian job soon enough.

Except life had something else in store for him: capture and torture, rescue and numerous horrendous injuries that would have ended his career. With burns over 60 percent of his body, the pain had been excruciating. Skin grafts and a medically induced coma had been part of what had saved him, but once he'd finally been allowed to regain consciousness, he'd almost wished he had died, as the army had at first believed. Scarred, disfigured, he'd believed Carly wouldn't want him now. Even if she had, he'd convinced himself he was no longer worthy.

Water under the bridge, or so he'd told himself. So great was his disfigurement and so much time had passed, he'd known he could never return to that happy, perfect time of his life. But he'd never stopped thinking about Carly, missing her with every fiber of his being.

Two years later, finally healed, he'd done a bit of internet searching. Carly appeared to have gotten over his loss and had moved on. She'd even recently changed her social media status to *In a Relationship*. Micha had also been surprised to learn she'd purchased the historic brick bungalow they'd longingly talked about owning once they were married. He'd recognized it from some of the photos she'd posted. Carly had gotten on with her life, as people do, while Micha felt as if he was treading water in the same place. With his military career over, he hadn't found a new direction for his life yet. All of his energy had been used to survive and heal, battling the twin demons of self-doubt and depression while missing Carly.

They should have had a life together, damn it. Instead, he'd lost two entire years. He told himself he just had to see her, one last time, and then maybe he could finally move on. Part of him suspected he'd known that was a lie even before he'd hopped a plane to Chicago.

She hadn't been difficult to find. He'd gone first to the hospital, hoping to see her arrive for work. He'd actually watched her from the parking lot, while sitting in his rental car, feeling like a creeper yet unable to help himself.

The first sight of her, striding across the pavement in her nurse's scrubs, had stolen the breath from his lungs. Carly, his Carly. Seeing her, he felt alive for the first time in two damn years.

He must have told himself a hundred times that he needed to go, get back on that plane and fly to Denver or LA, somewhere far enough that he wouldn't be tempted to disrupt her life. As far as she knew, he'd died in Baghdad two years ago. Maybe it was best to let things stay the way they were.

Except his heart, that traitorous thing that still beat strong and sure inside his chest, wouldn't let him. Somehow, he'd managed to stay away from her for three entire days, revisiting all their old haunts, hoping he'd run into her. To his utter disappointment, he hadn't.

Instead, he'd started watching her house. He told himself he just wanted to be certain she really was happy

and, most important, safe. He'd learned about her father's and uncle's murders—in fact, that had been one
of the major factors in his decision to check on her in
person. If anything happened to Carly, Micha knew he'd
lose his mind.

And then he'd been standing on the sidewalk down
the street from her house, trying to decide whether or
not to knock on her door, and she'd come out, clearly
taking a walk and enjoying the beautiful spring day. Unable to resist, he'd begun trailing after her, taking care
to keep himself hidden.

Until he'd given in to impulse and stepped out of
the shadows and into the sunlight. And if that wasn't
a metaphor for the part she played in his life, he didn't
know what was.

Now, moments after making love, she'd looked him
in the eye and told him she was meeting her boyfriend.
He'd swallowed his pride and asked her not to go, partly
because he had a lot to tell her, but mostly because he
couldn't stand the thought of her with another man.

Whatever he'd expected when he'd found her again,
it hadn't been this. And while he knew he really had no
right to feel betrayed, he did, anyway. The only thing
that tempered those feelings was imagining how Carly
must feel, believing him dead these past two years, only
to find out he wasn't. Talk about hurt and betrayal.

Back at his hotel, he took a shower and got dressed,
trying to decide where to go for dinner. Lou Malnati's
Pizzeria sounded perfect, even though it, too, had been
one of the places he and Carly used to go back in the day.

His cell phone rang just as he got into his car. Carly.

His heart skipped a beat. He'd imagined by now she'd be having a meal with her boyfriend.

"Do you have any time this evening to talk?" she asked, defeat tingeing her voice. "It turns out my date tonight was canceled."

While it might be wrong, Micha allowed himself to feel relieved satisfaction. "Sure," he replied. "In fact, I was just about to drive up to Lou Malnati's. Do you want me to pick you up?"

She went silent while she considered his invitation. In his mind, he could see her, no doubt pacing while she tried to decide if their talk should be in public or not. In the end, the lure of deep-dish won out.

"I haven't been there in forever," she said. "And since I haven't eaten, pizza sounds great."

"I'll be there in fifteen minutes," he told her. He couldn't help but feel optimistic, not only because she was open to sharing a meal with him, but because she was also willing to hear him out.

He pulled up in front of her bungalow and parked. Carly came out before he even had time to kill the engine. Though it had only been a couple of hours since he'd seen her last, just the sight of her had his heart beating faster.

"Hi." She got into his rental car, glancing sideways at him. "I have to say, it still feels really weird to see you."

"Really weird isn't the reaction I'd hoped for," he countered.

Though she smiled faintly at that, she didn't reply. Navigating Chicago's traffic felt comfortable, almost as if he'd never left. Staring out the window, appearing lost in thought, Carly didn't talk for the rest of the drive.

He knew better than to prod her. He'd let her go at her own pace.

She waited until they'd mostly demolished a large pie before sitting back and crossing her arms. "Explain," she demanded. "All of it, especially how you could allow me to believe you were dead."

Taking a deep breath, he nodded. "In the military, I worked in special ops. My job was to gather intelligence."

"Like a spy?"

"Sort of." He tried to keep his voice expressionless, to recount the story as if it had happened to someone else. "When I left you to go on that last mission, I was captured by a terrorist cell. They imprisoned me for six months." He decided not to mention the torture. Even now, he could hardly stand to even *think* about the things they'd done to him.

"Six months." She winced. "That's a long time. Did you escape or were you rescued?"

"They sent in a team to get me out, at the risk of their own lives." If he closed his eyes, he could still hear the gunfire, smell the smoke, hear the urgency in the man's voice who'd cut him free. There'd been shouting and smoke, ducking and dodging, as he'd tried to run on legs that could barely stand.

With his rescuer's help, they'd made it to the waiting chopper, which took off the second he'd been shoved inside.

They began to climb, amid heavy gunfire. Micha was

in bad shape. He already knew that, but the expressions on the faces of the medics who began tending to him told him it might be worse than he'd thought.

And then they were hit.

Somehow, the chopper pilot had kept them aloft, taking them out of enemy territory. When they'd finally gone down, initial reports had indicated no survivors.

"I was badly burned and my back was broken. Some locals found me, unconscious, and got me to a hospital. I didn't have my dog tags and couldn't speak, so no one notified my commanding officer." He met her gaze, his own unflinching. "That's why you were notified of my death. I'd listed you as kin along with my parents."

Expression troubled, she nodded. The compassion in her bright blue eyes warmed his heart. "How long were you in that hospital before you were able to tell someone that you were an American?"

"I'm not sure. Months, I know. I was in and out of consciousness, they said. They did surgery and tried to patch me up as best they could, but no one believed I'd ever walk again."

Carly reached across the table and covered his hand with hers. "But you proved them wrong."

"I did. But not until I'd recovered enough to insist they notify the US base that I was there." In all this dark retelling, he could now offer the one bright spot in those terrible times. "Turns out I wasn't the only survivor of that chopper crash," he said. "Andy Shackleford, one of the team who'd rescued me, made it, though he lost his leg. And the medic who'd been taking care of me was also found alive. He had burns, too, and some broken bones, but all in all, he was in much better shape. Of course, he hadn't been held captive for six months, either."

Across from him, he could see Carly struggling to come to terms with what for her seemed like a complete rewrite of history. He ached to take her in his arms and hold her, not just to comfort her, but for himself, as well. He rarely spoke about what had happened to him, mainly because doing so brought it all back. The pain, the frustration, the urgent need to get back to the life he'd had before.

"Once the army finally got me stateside, I had multiple surgeries. I still wasn't given very optimistic odds as to whether I'd walk again, but I was determined." He took a deep breath and locked his gaze on hers. "Because of you, Carly."

Those words had her stiffening, her gaze gone cold as she removed her hand from over his. "You didn't even try to contact me, Micha. Not even once. You let me continue to think you were dead." She shook her head, the sheen of unshed tears in her eyes. "I grieved. Every single day. For weeks, for months, for *years*. Why, once you were able, didn't you reach out and let me know you were still alive?"

He considered his next words carefully, not sure he could explain properly. But he knew he had to try and, hopefully, by sharing honestly, he could gain her understanding. One thing these two years had given him was the ability to look back objectively.

"This was a low point in my life," he said haltingly. "I couldn't see past the darkness." Ashamed, he admitted the truth, something he'd never said out loud. "For a really awful period, I honestly considered taking my own life. My career—to which I dedicated everything—was over. I had scars, both physically and mentally. I didn't think you'd want me. I wasn't the same man at all."

"But you didn't even give me a choice." Carly pushed to her feet, refusing to meet his gaze. "I'd like you to take me home now," she said. "Thank you for explaining. Clearly I have a lot to think about."

Try as he might, he couldn't detect any lingering bit of sympathy in her expression. He'd given her nothing but the truth, so he'd done all he could.

He left enough cash on the table to pay the bill plus a tip, and did as she asked. When he pulled up in front of her house, she turned to eye him.

"You gave me quite a scare," she said. "Following me around these past six weeks." She got out of the car and he followed her.

"Six weeks?" Confused, he shook his head. "I've only been back a week. What are you talking about?"

She stared at him, her eyes wide. "I've had the sense that someone has been watching me for the last month and a half," she said slowly. "It had gotten to the point where I'd decided I might have to stop taking walks."

Immediately, he thought of her father's and uncle's murders. "Have you told someone? Your family? The police? Isn't your boyfriend Chicago PD?"

"Former boyfriend," she corrected. "And no, I haven't said anything about this to anyone. I'd planned to mention it to Harry tonight."

This time, he didn't even allow himself to react to

the other man's name. "I've got some friends who can do some checking for me," he said. "Contacts in both the military special ops and the FBI. We'll see what they can dig up."

"Knock yourself out," Carly said, turning and walking back into her house.

Micha sat in his rental car until she'd made it inside and closed the front door. He'd start making phone calls immediately once he got back to his hotel room. And he'd be back to see her again tomorrow, and the day after that, every day for as long as she'd let him.

Just like before, being around Carly made him toss all his careful plans out the window. Except this time, finished with the military, he actually could follow through and do what he should have done before—court Carly properly and finally make her his wife.

But first, he needed to concentrate on keeping her safe.

UNSETTLED, CARLY HAD felt like a jittery mess all through dinner. Despite being a big fan of Lou Malnati's, she'd had to force herself to eat. The deep-dish was delicious, as always, but it would have been far too easy to allow herself to fall back into what had once been a comfortable sort of old habit with Micha.

Except two long years had gone by. She didn't know this man anymore. And he didn't know her. She was no longer the same wide-eyed innocent she'd been before. After losing Micha, she'd resigned herself to living a life without finding the same kind of passionate love. Harry had confided in her that he felt the same, and if this easy companionable friendship they shared was the best they could do, so be it.

In retrospect, she understood why he had found it so easy to let her go.

Micha was another story. When she got out of his rental car, it had taken every ounce of self-restraint she possessed to keep from inviting him inside. Too easily, she could imagine what would happen if she let him kiss her again. What she *wanted*, she admitted. But she kept her spine straight and marched up her sidewalk, letting herself into her house and locking him out.

When Micha had informed her that he'd only been in town a week, her first reaction had been a shiver of fear snaking up her spine. How could that be, when the feeling of being watched had started over a month ago?

Then, as usual, she began to question herself. Maybe she'd only imagined it. Perhaps it had been paranoia, brought on by her father's and uncle's murders.

As if Micha knew her thoughts, her phone rang and his number came up on caller ID. Her heart began to pound as she answered. "Are you calling from out front?" she asked, her resolve rapidly weakening. If he was, she suspected she'd go open the front door and invite him in.

"No, I'm driving back to the hotel," he responded. "But I have a few more questions if you don't mind."

She closed her eyes, full of both thankfulness and regret. "Go ahead. What do you need to know?"

"Do the police have any leads on your father's killer?"

"No," she answered. "And I doubt one has anything to do with the other. I wasn't involved in my father and uncle's business. They were shot outside their offices. My cousin January is engaged to one of the police detectives, named Sean Stafford. He'd tell us if there'd been any new leads."

"Good to know. I'll touch base with him, too. Since I'm going to be around awhile, I might as well do some digging."

Surprised, she gripped the phone tightly. "Are you? Going to be around awhile, that is?"

"Yes, I am."

"Why?" She couldn't resist asking. If he had expectations, she might as well level with him.

"You know why." The slow smile in his voice lit a simmer deep inside her. "But I'll spell it out, anyway. We were meant to be together, Carly Colton. I won't be going anywhere again. Not this time."

"Slow your roll," she replied. "It seems to me like you're taking a lot for granted." She held up her ringless hand, even though he couldn't see the gesture. "We're no longer engaged." She saw no need to tell him his ring no longer hung on a chain nestled between her breasts, close to her heart. In fact, she'd only made the decision to take it off last week.

"I understand," he said softly. "But I'd like to ask you to give me another chance."

"I'll have to think about that," she said. "Do you have any other questions?"

"Not right now," he said, sounding far too cheerful. "I'll talk to you later." And he ended the call.

Putting her phone down, she strode into her kitchen,

her hands shaking as she fumbled to get a drink out of the fridge.

So much had happened in the span of one day. Her head ached nearly as much as her heart.

Micha was alive. She'd always believed she'd buried most of her heart with him. Now he, instead of Harry, would be looking into the possibility that she might have a stalker.

It felt good, she acknowledged, giving over some of her fear to someone else. Normally, such a thing would make an independent woman like her bristle. But ever since her father and his twin had been brutally murdered, she and the rest of her family had been on edge. Being a Colton meant their family was well known and easily identified. Like any prominent family, they had enemies as well as friends.

Since she had to work an early shift tomorrow, she knew she'd need to turn in early. But with everything that had happened, she was way too keyed up to go to sleep any time soon.

In just one day, her reality had completely changed. Everything she'd believed to be true for the last two years had been completely upended. The weirdest part of discovering that Micha hadn't died was that the discovery did nothing to dispel that small knot of grief she carried around with her. Now, instead of mourning his loss, she supposed she grieved what might have been.

Seeing him had been a shock. In fact, she still hadn't processed or sorted through all the tangled emotions that his resurrection had caused. Making love with him had been a huge mistake, a kind of knee-jerk reaction to the shocking sight and touch and feel of him. Her visceral reaction had come without thought, without reason. Now, after the fact, she understood it had been something she should never have allowed to happen. She'd need to make sure it didn't occur again. Because she knew if she let it, she'd be risking her heart.

She'd finally gotten over losing him. Not completely—she'd begun to see such a thing only faded in small doses, with waves of grief overwhelming her unexpectedly. She'd gone from a period of being unable to function, to attending grief counseling. There, she'd learned how to claw her way out of the dark pit of despair and begun making plans to be able to face her new reality.

Now her new reality had been blown to rubble. She wasn't sure she was emotionally equipped to deal with that kind of fallout again.

Micha seemed to think they could pick up right where they'd left off. As if he hadn't broken her heart. She wasn't certain she could risk feeling that way again. She didn't think she'd survive.

Sitting at her kitchen table sipping on her drink, she tried to adjust to her new reality. It sure wasn't easy.

A rattle and a thud outside made her go still. It seemed to have come from her backyard. Was someone trying to break into her house?

Heart pounding, she hurried into the kitchen. She double-checked the dead bolt, making sure it was locked. Staying away from the window, she stood still and listened, praying the sound didn't come again. She'd been meaning to get a lock for that back gate and now she seriously wished she had.

Outside, the wind had picked up. Maybe that had caused the noise. She'd left her phone in the living room. She ran back and grabbed it, trying to decide whether to call 911 or Micha.

Micha? Thoroughly annoyed with herself, she had to admit having him around made her feel safe.

Another thud, louder this time. Deciding not to mess around, she dialed 911. Feeling slightly foolish, she told the dispatcher she thought someone might be trying to break into her house. They promised to send someone as soon as they could. Carly hung up, nerves still on edge. She had to fight the urge to call Micha, which annoyed her to no end. The man had barely been back in her life for half a day. She'd survived on her own for the last two years. She'd managed by herself, thank you very much. And she'd continue to do so now.

A squad car pulled up fifteen minutes later. Carly stayed inside, nervously waiting to see if they found anything. She could hear them moving around in her backyard and saw their flashlights.

Finally, they knocked on her back door. She opened it to find two of Chicago PD's finest standing on her back stoop.

"We did a complete search of the premises, ma'am," one of the officers said. "No intruder turned up, but we think we located the source of the noises you were hearing. We found a stray dog trying to get under your storage shed. She's pretty emaciated. Since Animal Control is closed, we'll send them around to pick her up in the morning, if that's okay."

"A stray dog?" Lately, she'd been thinking a lot about getting a dog. She'd intended to go up to the pound and pick out an older pup but wasn't sure if her occasional twelve-hour shifts were conducive to having a pet. "Is she friendly?"

"She is," the other officer chimed in, grinning. "I had a sandwich I'd picked up for lunch and didn't get a chance to eat. She gulped that thing down. Maybe put some water out for her?"

"Can I see her?" Carly asked instead. Maybe this dog, a homeless stray, was meant to be hers.

"There." The second guy pointed with his flashlight. "She's standing right there, watching us."

Peering into the darkness, Carly spotted a thin, black dog watching them intently, her eyes gleaming in the flashlight beam. Crouching down, acting on instinct, Carly spoke softly, attempting to call the animal over. "Come here, pretty girl," she crooned. "Would you like to come inside out of the cold?"

To her surprise, the dog inched closer.

"I don't have any dog food." Distressed, Carly continued to crouch in what she hoped was a nonthreatening way. "Is it okay if I give her chicken or beef?" As the dog slunk closer, Carly could see all of the canine's ribs and backbone. "It looks like it's been a really long time since she had a good meal."

"Sure. Anything healthy will help fill up her belly. Are you planning on keeping her?"

Startled, Carly look up. "I… I've been thinking about getting a dog, so I guess I am. Would that be allowed?"

"You'll need to have her scanned for a microchip," Officer One said. "You can do that at any veterinary office or you can bring her by the shelter when it opens. If there's no chip, talk to the shelter about them letting her serve out her stray hold with you instead of there."

"Stray hold?"

Officer Two shrugged. "Just in case someone might be looking for her. You never know."

That made sense.

"I want to do everything by the book," Carly said. "Thank you so much for checking everything out for me."

"No problem." Officer One touched his hat. "We were all sorry to hear about your father and uncle."

Carly murmured a thank-you. Even to this day, she often found herself startled by how many people had known the two elder Coltons.

"We'll close the gate behind us," Officer One said. "It was open, which is how the dog got in."

She thanked them again, standing on her back stoop while they walked away. The dog, she noticed, turned her head to watch them go, but made no move to follow. Carly crouched down again. "Come here, baby girl," she crooned. "Let's get you inside where it's warm. I'll find something you can eat, I promise."

To her shock, the dog slunk closer, posture wary, but nonthreatening. As the skeletal creature climbed the back-stoop steps, Carly almost cried. Taking care not to make any sudden moves, Carly opened the back door and stepped inside, still calling the dog to her. A full tummy and a warm bath might go wonders to helping the poor animal feel better.

Chapter Three

Micha checked the time to make sure it wasn't too late, and then called the cell phone number of one of his former combat buddies, Charlie Crenshaw, now working stateside for the Chicago PD.

"Hey, man," Charlie said once Micha identified himself. "It's great to hear from you. Last I heard, you were laid up in the hospital over at Walter Reed. Are you all better now?"

"I am. Actually, I'm back in Chicago." He took a deep breath. "As a matter of fact, I wanted to check and see what kind of progress has been made on the Colton murders. Since you're the only Chicago cop I know, I figured you'd be a good place to start."

"Why?" Charlie asked, sounding more confused than suspicious.

"I used to be engaged to Ernest Colton's daughter, Carly. She's had the feeling that someone's been following her for the past six weeks and is worried it might be related to the murder."

"Okay, I get it." Charlie cleared his throat. "I trust

you, Micha, so what I'm about to tell you can't go any further. All right?"

"Agreed," Micha responded immediately. "I'll keep my mouth shut until you give me the go-ahead."

"Good, because the chief wants to talk to the Colton family before the news gets out to the general public. There's been a second set of killings, with the same MO as the twin Colton men, though they weren't twins. Right now, the theory is serial killers, and the FBI has been called in to help investigate."

"Damn." Micha whistled. "Now I'm even more worried about Carly being followed."

"Give her my number and tell her to call me tomorrow. Once I've received an official complaint from her, I can request a protective detail."

Relieved, Micha thanked him. "I'll pass the info along to her. Is it okay if I let her know about the new murders?"

"We'd prefer to notify the family first, but if you think she can keep it to herself, go for it. Just remember, you didn't hear it from me."

"Got it," Micha replied. "Thanks again, man."

"No problem. Let me know when you want to grab a beer and catch up. I work days, so I'm off most nights."

Micha promised to touch base again soon and ended the call. He sat for a moment, staring at his phone, and ultimately decided to wait until the morning to talk to Carly. He didn't want to worry her and possibly cause her to lose sleep.

He wondered if she had to work tomorrow. Since he had no idea of her schedule and hadn't thought to ask, he figured he'd simply show up at her house with coffee in the morning. They could talk and he'd tell her what he'd learned from his friend. Then, if she was open to it, they could make plans to meet up later.

That night, he slept better than he had in years. He'd come back to the vibrant place his soul had always recognized was his true home, and the woman he'd known from the moment he met her was meant to be his.

He was up bright and early the next morning. On his way to her place, he stopped at her favorite coffee shop and got them both lattes, hers with extra whip. He texted her as soon as he got into his car, letting her know he had coffee and asking if it was okay if he gave it to her personally.

A few seconds later, she texted back. Sure, but I have to leave for work in fifteen minutes. I don't have a lot of time.

He made it to her house in five and rang her doorbell with his elbow, a coffee in each hand. She answered a moment later, her blond hair up in a ponytail and wearing pale blue scrubs.

"Good morning," he said, handing her the coffee and drinking her in with his eyes.

Accepting it with a half smile, she thanked him.

"How about I drive you to work this morning?" he asked, going on impulse. "That would give us more time to talk."

She regarded him silently. "But then I wouldn't have a way to get home when my shift is over."

The fact that she didn't decline outright gave him hope.

"I'll pick you up," he offered. "Maybe we can go get a bite to eat or something."

"I can't. I have to come home and take a stray dog to the vet. I'm having her scanned for a microchip, and if she doesn't have one, I'm having her checked out."

A dog. His heart squeezed. Back when they were engaged, he'd hoped to get a dog together as soon as they were married, though he'd never brought it up. "Can I meet her?" he asked, a little too much emotion in his voice.

Carly glanced at her watch. "I don't have time. I've got her a spot all fixed up in my kitchen."

He nodded. "Okay. Maybe later. Now how about that ride to work?"

"I don't know." She regarded him dubiously. "There's been a lot of water under the bridge in two years, Micha. We can't simply pick up where we left off before."

Trying to hide his disappointment, he nodded. "That makes sense. How about we start out as friends instead?"

"Friends?"

Her skeptical tone made him grin. "Sure. And as your friend, how about I drive you to work and pick you up later? I'd love to meet your new dog."

"As long as you understand that what happened between us yesterday can't happen again."

Though this took him by surprise, he realized it wasn't entirely unexpected. If Carly wanted to take things slow, then that's what they'd do. "I understand," he told her. "Now if you're ready, let's go. I have something important I want to tell you."

"Give me just a minute." Turning, she let herself back

into her house, leaving him standing on the front porch. He sipped his coffee while he waited, wondering how he could still feel so strongly for her while she apparently did not feel the same way. It figured, because time had basically stood still for him. He'd been completely disconnected from the regular world for a long time, both while being held captive and then while in the hospital recovering. Despite the aching certainty that he'd finally landed right back where he belonged, he knew he'd need to give Carly time.

She reappeared a moment later, letting herself out and locking the door behind her. "I'm a little worried about Bridget," she mused as she walked with him to his rental car. "She's been a stray for a while and I'm guessing she's not housebroken. I made an area near the back door with newspaper, so I'm hoping she'll use that. If not, then I'll just clean it up."

"How long are you working today?" he asked.

"Unless something happens, I'm only working eight to five," she replied, getting into his car. "The vet is open until six, so I have to rush home and get Bridget." She eyed him. "I don't have a collar or leash or even proper dog bowls. Oh, and I need dog food. Would you mind picking some up for me and I'll reimburse you?"

"Of course I don't mind. What about a dog bed? What size dog is she?"

"Maybe forty or fifty pounds, I'm guessing." Swallowing, she buckled herself in. "Thank you. I really appreciate your help."

He noticed the way she glanced around her neighborhood, an unmistakable hint of apprehension in the stiff set of her shoulders.

"Are you okay?" he asked.

Her sideways glance and rueful smile told him she wasn't sure. "I don't know," she admitted. "It's been so weird lately. I'm actually glad you offered to take me to work."

"Do you see anything out of the ordinary?" Curious, he started the engine and pulled away.

"No, not really. I just can't shake the feeling that someone is watching me."

"Then they would have seen me on your front porch," he pointed out. "Maybe if they realize I'm going to be showing up a lot, they'll move on to something else and leave you alone."

She sighed, but didn't argue with his statement, which he found encouraging.

"I called one of my buddies who works for Chicago PD," he said. "I wanted to know if they'd had any leads in your father's and uncle's murders."

This made her sit up straighter. "Oh, yeah? What did he say?"

"Well, Chicago PD wants to notify your family first. I think they're planning on doing that today." He shrugged. "I feel you should be told because this might have some bearing on your own safety, especially since you've been feeling as if someone is watching you."

He took a deep breath. "Are you okay with knowing before but not saying anything until your mother and aunt are told? Because my friend will have my head on a platter if it gets out that he told me."

"Yes, I am. I have to work, anyway. Why so much secrecy?"

"There's been another double murder, done in a similar manner to your dad and uncle. Now they're thinking serial killer, and they've called in the FBI to assist."

She stared at him, her mouth slightly open. "A serial killer?" she asked. "For real?"

"That's the working theory right now."

"What's the common thread?" Arms crossed, she eyed him. "Don't serial killers usually have a type they kill? Is it because my dad and uncle Alfred were twins?"

"I don't know. My contact didn't elaborate. I'm guessing you'll find out more info once the police department informs your family."

Slowly, she shook her head. "They're going to flip. I hope they tell Heath first, so he can break the news to my mother and aunt."

"There's more. I told my friend how you felt someone might be following you." He handed her a slip of paper with Charlie's number. "He needs you to call him and make an official report. Once they have that, they can start protecting you."

Accepting the paper, she frowned. "What do you mean by that? Are you talking about a bodyguard or something?"

"No. You have me for that." He smiled. "More like they can send a patrol car around your neighborhood more often. Maybe have someone parked out in front of your house to keep an eye on things. I doubt they have the resources to do that 24/7, but because of your connection to the murders, it's better to be safe than sorry."

He saw the moment she realized. "You think the killer might be targeting me." A statement rather than a question, but he knew to tread carefully.

"I think we don't need to take any chances." A reasonable response. "No need to panic, but just continue to be careful."

They pulled up to the hospital. He parked at the curb to let her out. "I'll pick you up here at five."

Gaze locked on his, she slowly nodded. "Okay. If I can get off earlier, I'll text you. I really need to check Bridget for a microchip."

He watched her walk away, her sweet round behind swaying in her scrubs. Unsurprisingly, he had to push away a surge of raw lust. Though he regretted the way things had gotten out of hand between them the day before, if anything the way they'd combusted so quickly told him he still had a chance of making things right with her. He'd just need to be careful to take it slow. The last thing he wanted was for Carly to cut and run.

Now he just needed to find out if someone was stalking her and why. He hoped it had no ties whatsoever to her father's murder and the two latest killings, but no way in hell was he taking a chance. Not when Carly's life might depend on it.

CARLY CALLED MICHA'S police friend as soon as she got inside. She knew if she waited until she started her shift, she probably wouldn't have a chance.

The officer picked up on the second ring. "Charlie Crenshaw."

As soon as she identified herself, his casual tone became more professional. When she told him she'd had the feeling someone had been watching her for the last six weeks, he asked her several pointed questions.

"No, I haven't actually seen anyone. No, no one has sent me weird emails or written messages. No vandalism or anything like that." She thought of last night, calling 911 because of the strange noises she'd heard, but figured that would already be on record. And after all, the sound had turned out to be a stray dog.

Listening to herself, even she began to have doubts.

To his credit, when she'd started to feel like she might have been imagining the feeling of being watched, Officer Crenshaw promised to file a report.

"What does that mean?" she asked. "Where do we go from here?"

"We'll start by having officers patrol your street more often," he replied. "More frequent drive-bys might help."

"Thank you." Relieved that he hadn't said she'd be put under constant surveillance, she ended the call. Since she wasn't even positive about being watched, she would have been extremely uncomfortable losing that much privacy. Hearing about the two new murders gave her pause, though. She wondered who would be notifying her and when. Most likely, her eldest brother, Heath, would be tasked with that chore. As president of Colton Connections, he'd become unofficial head of the family with the two eldest Coltons' deaths.

Expecting his call, she debated whether or not to give

him the news about Micha over the phone. It might be easier to do that in person.

Instead of a call, Heath sent her a text. Sunday, cookout in Oak Park at one. Can you make it?

Since she was always off Sundays unless she switched shifts with someone, she texted back in the affirmative. Apparently, Heath wanted to give his news in person, as well.

Things were pretty quiet in the NICU, relatively speaking. Carly loved working with infants and had a soft spot for the vulnerable preemies. She was grateful for days like this, when she could take care of her charges without rushing from one incident to another. She even had time to chat with a few of the parents, many of whom she'd gotten to know well.

When her lunchtime arrived, she smiled at the nurse who'd come to relieve her so she could eat. They all knew better than to comment on the calm day—to do so practically guaranteed it would end.

She headed down to the cafeteria, planning to grab a salad and her personal weakness, a diet ginger ale. The cafeteria always made sure to keep some in stock for her. As she rounded the corner, she stopped short, stunned at the sight of Micha sitting on a bench just outside the cafeteria entrance.

After the first initial rush of seeing him, she frowned. "Now I'm really beginning to feel like you're stalking me," she said. "What are you doing here?"

He stood. "I thought you might want to have lunch." He held up a bag. Fontano's Subs. Her favorite.

"You remembered." Touched, despite herself, she let her gaze search his face.

"Yep. Homemade meatball with red sauce." He grinned. "And corned beef for me."

For just an instant, the force of his smile took her back. Micha had used to meet her for lunch all the time when they'd first gotten engaged. Sometimes he'd bring her a treat, sometimes they'd eat cafeteria food. What had been important was spending the time together. She'd missed their lunches a lot once he'd gone back to active duty.

Now, though, two years had passed. She'd grown used to eating her lunch alone. She wasn't sure her heart could withstand taking a giant step back into the past.

Noticing her hesitation, his warm smile dimmed. "I can go," he said. "If you want me to."

Eyeing the paper sack, she relented. "I'm sorry. You can stay. You just caught me off guard. Let me go get us a couple of drinks and we'll grab a table."

"In the courtyard?" He nodded toward the outside eating area. With the warm weather, a lot of people took advantage of the chance to get out.

She shrugged. "Sure, if you can find a table. If not, inside's fine."

Inside, she grabbed her diet ginger ale and a cola for him. After paying, she made her way outside, spotting Micha at a two-seat table under a small umbrella.

"Wow," she commented, handing him his drink and taking a seat. "You really lucked out."

Smiling again, he opened the paper bag. She inhaled deeply, her mouth beginning to water at the wonderful scents that escaped. Around them, she saw a couple of her coworkers giving her curious looks, but she ignored them.

As soon as he handed her the meatball sub, she unwrapped it and took a huge bite. The flavor had her humming low in her throat with pleasure. She looked up to find him staring at her, his warm gaze making her face heat.

"I haven't had one of these in a long time," she said, going for a second bite. "So good." She rolled her eyes.

Laughing, he unwrapped his own sub. "I love your gusto," he murmured, before digging into his corned beef.

Love. She pretended not to notice his choice of words. "I talked to Officer Crenshaw," she told him. "He's promised to make sure there are extra patrols on my street."

He nodded. "Any word from your family? I'm assuming by now someone will have notified them about the new set of murders."

"Heath has called a family meeting on Sunday," she replied. "I'm guessing he wants to let us know in person."

"Are you going to tell them about me?" he asked softly.

She finished her sandwich, wadding up the wrapper, and then took a deep sip of her ginger ale. "Yes. That's another thing best done face-to-face, I think. I'll tell them Sunday."

Now that they'd both finished eating, she checked her watch. "I don't want to hog this table," she said, pushing to her feet. "I've only got a few minutes before I need to get back to work. Thank you for bringing me lunch."

"You're welcome." He followed her back into the hall. "When's your next day off?"

"Sunday."

"May I see you?" he asked.

"I'm going up to Oak Park, remember?" she replied.

"After? How about dinner?"

Shaking her head, she considered. "I'll let you know."

"Fair enough," he replied. "I'll pick you up after you get off." And then he walked away without a backward glance.

She watched him go, her emotions conflicted. Once, he would have kissed her goodbye. Though she certainly knew she couldn't return to that past, to that place in time, she missed that kiss with a sudden aching yearning.

The rest of her shift passed uneventfully, a blessing and a respite in a nurse's day. Carly had chosen pediatric nursing early in her career, though she had to do a required stint as an ER nurse before moving to the children's floor. She'd gravitated toward the NICU, where the most seriously ill or premature babies were cared for.

She loved her job, despite getting her heart broken on those awful days when they lost a patient. She always cried, as did most of the other nurses and doctors on her team.

Shaking her head to clear away those dark thoughts, Carly finished up her charts and got ready to hand everything over to the night nurse who'd be arriving soon. She had to admit the thought of seeing Micha again made her heart beat a little faster. Though she knew it might be foolish, she couldn't contain the quick rush of joy she felt seeing him pull up in front of the hospital entrance and wave to her.

Getting in the car also brought back an odd combination of nostalgia and uncertainty. To cover, she checked her watch. "We've got to hurry. I don't want to be late for the vet appointment."

"Okay. All your supplies are in bags in the back seat."

She turned to look. "Thank you. I'll write you a check later." Locating the collar and leash, she removed the price tags. "I'm going to need these."

Once they reached her house, she jumped out of the car. "I'll be right back." As she unlocked her door, she wondered how much damage the stray dog might have done. She'd barricaded her in the kitchen with an old comforter to sleep on, food and water in old plastic bowls, and she'd also laid out newspaper near the back door in case of accidents.

When she stepped inside, her house seemed quiet. A bit apprehensive, she walked back to the kitchen, moving away the old baby gate she'd pulled from the garage.

Bridget sat on the old comforter where she'd made a nest. She eyed Carly warily, though her ears remained up and her tail wagged. She'd eaten all the boiled chicken, but as far as Carly could tell, there'd been no potty accidents.

Moving slowly, Carly crouched down and reached to put on the collar. To her surprise, the dog lowered her head and allowed this. Since Carly had already attached the leash, she stood and gave a little tug to see if Bridget would follow her.

The dog slowly got to her feet and did.

Carly led her outside, locking the door behind her. Signaling to Micha to wait, she took Bridget to the side grass, waiting while the dog relieved herself.

"How about cars, girl?" Carly asked, leading the dog over to the back door. When she opened it, Bridget promptly jumped inside.

"She's been someone's pet," Carly mused, climbing into the front passenger seat. "She's clearly used to walking on a leash and riding in cars. I don't know how long she's been on her own or why, but if someone is missing her, I hope we can find them."

"Hopefully, she's chipped," Micha said. "If not, you can check with shelters. Plus there are usually lost-dog groups on social media."

Though Carly nodded, she couldn't help but feel a twinge of disappointment. Truly, she felt as if Bridget was meant to be her dog. She guessed she'd just have to wait and see.

Inside the vet clinic, despite two other clients and their dogs waiting, Bridget stayed close to Carly, sitting with her side pressed against Carly's leg and her head down. She ignored Micha and the other two dogs.

Once they were taken back to an examination room, Carly explained how she'd come to be there with Bridget. The vet tech, a young woman with purple hair and a broad smile, went and got a microchip scanner and waved it over the dog's neck and shoulder areas. The device beeped.

"We have a chip," the tech announced. "We'll contact the chip company and get information on the dog's owner."

Heaven help her, Carly thought she might cry. She managed to nod, all the while continuing to stroke Bridget's soft fur. "Thank you," she said. Micha squeezed her shoulder, as if he understood her inner turmoil.

"There's no sense in doing any vaccinations or exam yet," the young woman continued. "You should wait until we hear back from the dog's owner. There's no charge for today."

"Okay." Deflated, Carly took Bridget's leash and headed outside, blinking back tears. Silently, she loaded the dog into the back seat of Micha's rental car, before climbing in the front and buckling herself in.

"It's going to be all right," Micha said as he got in on the driver's side. "You did a good thing. Gave the dog shelter and now she's on her way to being reunited with her owner."

Carly nodded, keeping her face averted while she struggled to get her emotions under control.

"You really wanted to keep her, didn't you?" Micha asked, touching her lightly on the arm.

"I did." Squaring her shoulders, Carly turned to eye Bridget, now curled up on the back seat. "But I'm glad she has a home. With me."

Back when they'd been together, they'd never discussed having or not having a pet. They'd talked about dreams and values and how many children they'd like to have, but not about cats versus dogs versus pet-free. In fact, until recently, the closest thing Carly had to a pet had been a squirrel that lived in the large oak tree outside her kitchen window.

Curious, she eyed Micha. "What about you? Do you have any pets?"

He shook his head. "No. Up until now, it's been military and then hospitals. But I grew up with dogs." Glancing at Bridget in the back seat, he smiled. "I like yours."

"Thanks," she replied. "I like her, too."

As they pulled up in front of her house, Micha didn't say anything but she could tell from the hopeful look in his eyes that he wanted her to ask him in.

"I appreciate the ride," she said instead. "It was good to see you. But it's been a long day and I want to give Bridget a bath and feed her, plus start taking her out on the leash to see how she does."

He nodded. "Okay." Hesitating, he glanced up and down the street. "Stay safe."

"You, too."

Puttering around her house, Carly found herself constantly reaching to pet her dog. Bridget seemed reluctant to leave her side. She suffered through her bath with a kind of quiet dignity, ate her bowl of kibble with gusto and curled up on the couch with her head resting on Carly's lap while they watched TV. After, Carly took Bridget outside on the leash to relieve herself. Once she had, they came inside and Carly gave her a treat as a reward.

"Ready to go to bed, girl?" Carly asked. Bridget immediately began wagging her tail as if she understood. Heart lighter than it had been in days, Carly led the way back to her bedroom.

Carly had placed the brand-new dog bed on the floor

near her nightstand and when the time came to turn in for the night, she showed Bridget where she should sleep. To her surprise, the pup seemed to understand immediately and curled up there with a soft grunt. Closing her eyes, she promptly went to sleep.

After taking a couple of pictures with her phone, Carly resisted the urge to text them to Micha. Instead, she washed her face, brushed her teeth and got into bed. Turning out the light, she drifted off to sleep.

The vet clinic called early the next morning. "I'm afraid I have some bad news on the owner of the stray dog you found," the caller said. "We've located the previous owner and learned he is deceased. His daughter stated she does not want the dog."

Somehow, Carly managed to restrain herself. "I'm sorry to hear that," she said. "That means I can keep her, right?"

"Yes, you can. Or you can drop her off at the shelter if you prefer."

Glancing at Bridget, sleeping in a stray patch of sunlight, Carly grinned. "That's not happening. She's mine now. I guess I need to make another appointment to get her vetting done."

They settled on a date and time and Carly ended the call. She walked over to her new dog and bent down, crooning softly as she reached out to pet her. "You're not going anywhere, baby girl."

Bridget eyed her, yawned and then went back to sleep.

Carly got up and started dancing around her kitchen. While she found it sad that Bridget's owner had died and unbelievable that his daughter hadn't wanted the dog, Carly couldn't help but rejoice in the knowledge that she got to keep her.

Impulsively, Carly grabbed her phone and punched in Micha's number. He answered immediately, his kind, husky-voiced greeting generating a warmth deep inside her. Talking quickly, she told him the news. "So now I really have a dog," she concluded. "I made another vet appointment to get her checked out."

"Congratulations. I wish I was there to celebrate with you."

She caught her breath, her heart skipping, any words she might have said caught in her throat.

"Too fast?" he asked.

"Kind of. Yes."

Quickly, he changed the subject. "Are we still on for dinner Sunday night?"

Again, she hesitated. "I'll probably be eating a huge meal over at the cookout, so I doubt I'll be hungry."

"I get that. Maybe we can just grab a cup of coffee."

"Micha…"

She could picture him steeling himself. "Yes?"

"I know we agreed we'd try to be friends for now, but I think maybe this is moving way too fast."

"Hey, it's just coffee." His quiet laugh sounded forced. "Actually, I just want to see you."

His words and the husky tone to his voice had warmth unfurling inside her. Was she really that weak?

While resistant, she considered the idea. "We really should give each other a few days' space," she replied.

"Please. We can do whatever you want. Even if you

just want to sit outside in your backyard and watch your dog play."

The quiet plea in his husky voice made her relent. Once, she'd never been able to deny him anything. "Look, I've got to head in to work. I'll call you when I'm on my way home from Oak Park tomorrow," she said. "We can figure out something."

Murmuring assent, he ended the call. Staring at her phone, Carly wondered how it was possible to miss someone so badly when her emotions were all over the place. Losing him had shattered her. She wasn't sure she wanted to set herself up to be destroyed again.

Chapter Four

After ending the call, Micha rejoiced—just a little—at the fact that Carly had actually relented and decided to see him Sunday after her family get-together. Even talking to her on the phone affected him. Listening to the unabashed joy and excitement in Carly's voice as she'd told him about her new dog, his heart had squeezed. He ached for her. Hearing her sweet, sexy voice over the phone wasn't enough. He wanted to be there to share in her happiness, to take her in his arms and dance around her kitchen the way she always did when she was happy. He could see it as clearly as if he was there.

Beautiful, sexy, sweet and smart Carly. The back of his throat stung with emotion. Whatever emotion she experienced, she did with gusto. Her joy was infectious, infusing him with hope for a brighter world. He had no idea how she did it, but merely by her existence, Carly made him want to be a better person. Worthy of someone as special as her.

At this very moment, there were two things Micha craved in this world. The first was to keep Carly safe.

After that, the second would be for her to finally understand that they were truly meant to be together.

She belonged with him and he belonged with her. No terrorists or helicopter crash, burns or long convalescence could take that away from them. He felt it deep in his soul. Once, Carly had felt it, too. Their connection had been instant and deep, searing them forever.

Two years and a huge miscommunication had separated them, driven a wedge in between them. Yet when he'd first seen her, every emotion had come rushing back, filling him with love and desire. And Carly had felt the same things, too. They'd devoured each other, fallen into each other's arms as if no time had passed since they'd been apart.

Imprisonment, horrific injuries and learning she'd been wrongfully notified of his death had conspired to keep them apart. He'd almost let those things and two years apart change him, letting himself believe that he could continue in life without her. Until he'd actually caught sight of her once more and realized how wrong he'd been.

Micha had never been a poetic man. He considered himself a realist, pragmatic and grounded. Except when it came to her. Carly changed everything. He had no doubt that they were each half of the same soul, destined to be together for as long as they drew breath.

He knew she would realize this eventually, he just didn't know when. He knew he had to go slowly, cautiously, so he didn't scare her away. She held the pain and grief she'd been through wrapped around her like a shield. Regaining her trust would only be accomplished slowly. He knew he'd have to resist every impulse to rush things.

As for keeping her safe, at least Chicago PD had gotten involved. While a start, that wasn't nearly enough, so Micha had decided he would become her personal bodyguard and do his best to keep her safe. Considering that he didn't want to freak her out, he planned to do much of that as quietly as possible in the background.

Since he knew he'd be staying in Chicago, he needed to look for a place to rent. His only real criteria would be the location—he wanted to live near Carly. In Hyde Park, if possible.

He figured he'd ask her if she'd mind going with him to look. After all, she'd lived in the city and knew all the good areas as well as places to avoid. He'd bring that up Sunday night when he saw her.

Saturday had a completely different traffic pattern than the days of the week.

With little to do while Carly was at work, Micha drove by her house, with the idea of searching the neighborhood looking for For Rent signs.

He slowed as he approached her place. A white, windowless van was parked at the curb in front. Other than that, the neighborhood appeared quiet.

Telling himself a vehicle like this was nothing out of the ordinary, nevertheless he reduced speed even more. That was when he saw the guy coming out from Carly's backyard. He wore a dark hoodie, too warm for such a nice day, black jeans and a baseball cap pulled low. His furtive movements combined with his odd attire set off all sorts of alarm bells.

Was this the guy who had been stalking Carly? Did he have something to do with the murders of Carly's father and uncle?

Pulling up behind the van, Micha jumped out. He intercepted the intruder halfway between the fence and the sidewalk. "Can I help you?" he asked, as if he actually owned the place.

The guy looked up, clearly startled. Micha caught a glimpse of a short, reddish brown beard.

Instead of responding, the man took off running. Not for the van, but down the sidewalk. Micha ran after him, wondering if he might actually be one of Carly's neighbors. That would definitely explain her feeling of being watched for a good while.

But no, instead of dashing into one of the other houses, the guy kept running. Micha heard the sound of a vehicle starting. He glanced over his shoulder, realizing too late that there had been someone else at the wheel inside the parked vehicle. The runner had an accomplice, who was driving the white van.

And it was headed directly toward Micha.

Turning, Micha faced the van and waited. If it swerved up onto the sidewalk, he planned to jump left, behind the wide trunk of an old oak tree.

Instead, it barreled past him, screeching to a halt long enough for the man Micha had been pursuing to jump in. Once he had, it roared off, running a stop sign before disappearing around the corner.

"Damn." Micha grabbed his phone and called Charlie Crenshaw. His friend picked up immediately. Once

Micha relayed what had happened, Charlie promised to send two officers to Carly's house right away.

Jogging back down the street, Micha waited by his rental car. He dialed Carly's number, aware she probably couldn't take the call while working. As he'd suspected, his call went directly to voice mail. Not wanting to unduly alarm her, he simply left a message asking her to call him.

Dragging his hand through his hair, Micha couldn't shake the feeling that he'd failed. He should have tackled that guy, taken him down and held him until the police arrived.

A moment later, a squad car pulled up. Micha told the officers everything he knew. "No, I didn't think to get the license plate number," he said. "Everything happened really fast."

"All right," one of the uniformed men said. "Please wait here while we check out the house."

Micha nodded. Another thing he should have done, except he hadn't wanted to take the chance of missing the police when they pulled up, or worse, being taken for an intruder.

Debating whether or not to follow them, he stopped when his phone rang. "Carly," he said. "I'm at your house with the police." Explaining what he'd witnessed, he finished with letting her know the police were making sure she hadn't been broken into.

"Bridget's in the kitchen," she said, her voice shaky. "I have to make sure she's all right and didn't get out. Can you please check on her for me?"

"Of course." He spotted the two policemen returning. "Let me call you back."

Moving to meet the officers, Micha tried to get a quick read from their expressions but couldn't.

"Everything looks fine," the first one told him. "No broken windows, back door is still locked. No idea what the guy might have been doing, but it doesn't appear he gained entry into the house."

"Well, the dog barking inside might have scared him away," the second one said. "Listen, we've got this street on our daily patrol. We'll keep a close eye on things."

Thanking them, Micha stood by his car and watched as they drove away.

What had the intruder been doing in Carly's backyard? If he hadn't been trying to break in, and clearly he hadn't since he'd emerged before Micha had a chance to confront him, then why had he been back there?"

Immediately, Micha wondered if he'd installed a camera or some sort of listening device. It would have to be hidden, and protected from the weather, but still have a good view of the house. Again, though, he had to ask himself why.

Either way, he needed to check it out.

Letting himself in through the gate, which the policemen had left open, he made a mental note to ask Carly to get a lock. Double-checking everything, he made sure the back door was still secure. The instant he checked the knob, Carly's new dog began to bark. Micha grinned. At least he could tell Carly that Bridget was all right.

Next he moved on to the windows. They all were secure, locked up tight. The back shed door sat slightly ajar. Inside, Micha found an ancient push lawn mower and some old paint cans. He realized the small pile of leaves had likely been where Carly's new dog had made her bed. Nothing appeared to have been disturbed, so Micha went back outside. He stood in front of the shed, facing the house, trying to ascertain where someone might place a hidden camera so they could keep an eye on things 24/7.

He searched every place that made sense and some that didn't, finding nothing. Maybe he was being too paranoid. After all, a camera out here would only have an extremely limited view of Carly when she came outside.

But what if… What if the man had placed something up against a window with the intent of capturing activity inside the house? Unless Carly kept her back blinds or curtains closed, a camera like that would do an excellent job of monitoring her every movement.

Trying to remember the home's layout, he checked the master bedroom's windows first. Nothing. Moving on to the back door, he found that also clear. The last window was in the kitchen, over the sink. And that's where he located the tiny camera, aimed inside. Which made sense, because Carly left those blinds raised a few inches so her plants could get light.

Micha debated, but left the camera in place for now. He also debated calling the police back out but decided to notify Carly instead. It would be her decision how to proceed from there.

Once he'd made his way back to his rental car, he

called Carly. "First up, Bridget is fine," he told her. "I can hear her inside the house, barking."

"Thank goodness." Carly sounded so relieved. "What about my house?"

"No break-in or damage. All the windows and doors are intact. The police checked everything out and left."

"Really?" With an audible exhale, Carly sighed. Micha could picture her at that very moment, rolling her shoulders and practicing deep breathing exercises to try to get rid of her tension. "Then what was that guy doing in my backyard?" she asked. "Or do you suppose you surprised him before he could do anything?"

"He was leaving when I pulled up," Micha reminded her. "After the police left, I went in your backyard to take another look. I found something. A tiny video camera installed on your kitchen window, looking inside."

Carly went quiet before letting out a murmured curse word. "Did you call the police back out?"

"No, not yet. I wanted you to see it for yourself first. You've got to pretend like you don't know it's there until the police can check it out. They might have a way to trace the feed all the way back to the source," he said.

"Which would mean we could catch the guy," Carly finished. "Okay, that makes sense. But I've got to tell you, it seriously creeps me out."

"Understandable."

She made a sound, somewhere between a strangled laugh and an exasperated cry. "I guess they can watch videos of Bridget for the rest of the day. Talk about an invasion of privacy."

"I'm sorry," he said.

"I have a favor to ask you. Would you mind being there when I get home from work? I really don't want to deal with that alone."

With that, his day became a hundred times better. "Of course I'll be here. What time do you get off?"

"I'm working a short shift today. I'll be home around three."

After ending the call, he got into his car, his heart lighter. Carly needed him, which made his heart sing. Meanwhile, he could get the ball rolling with Chicago PD.

He called his buddy Charlie again, detailing what he'd seen. "But I want Carly to see it before you send anyone to check it out. She'll be home sometime around three."

"Sounds good. We'll probably ask the FBI to help on this one. They can probably trace it. Though I might just stop by and take a look at it myself tonight, along with whatever agent the Bureau assigns. I won't have an ETA until I speak with them, but I'll let you know."

"I'll be there tonight with Carly for a bit," Micha said. "Keep me posted."

MORE SHAKEN THAN she'd let on when talking to Micha, Carly struggled to get through the rest of her shift. With her focus off, she found herself double-checking everything she did. She felt so *violated*. Not only had a stranger been in her private backyard, but he had attached a video camera to her window. She supposed she should consider herself lucky that he hadn't broken in, but right now she didn't feel that way.

Finally, the hands on the huge wall clock at the

nurses' station inched toward two-thirty. Hugely relieved as she completed the last of her charts and handed them off to the nurse coming on, Carly grabbed her purse and headed outside.

As usual, she kept a keen eye on her surroundings, but she was so flustered by the idea of having a video camera watching her every move that she couldn't reach inside and access that gut instinct or sixth sense.

Pulling up into her drive, she could have cried with relief as she caught sight of Micha sitting on her front porch stoop. He stood as soon as she opened her car door, meeting her halfway and wrapping his muscular arms around her. She held on tight, breathing in his familiar scent, wondering again how she'd made it two entire years without him.

That thought right there had her stepping back, out of his reassuring embrace. For a second, she couldn't meet his gaze as she struggled to gather herself back into a cohesive whole instead of scattered pieces. Her defenses had crumbled, however briefly. She'd managed to build them back up, but until then, she'd need to be careful.

"Show me the camera," she ordered.

"Sure. Let's go around back. That way whoever is monitoring it won't know we've seen it. My friend Charlie and someone from the FBI will be here shortly."

Surprised, she glanced at him. "That's fast."

His grin made her melt, damn it. "It helps when you have connections. Come on."

She followed him around the side of her house and threw open the gate. "Maybe I should get a lock for this," she said, closing it behind her.

"Definitely," Micha agreed, glancing back over his shoulder at her. He stopped at her kitchen window, pointing at a tiny metal square situated in the bottom right corner of the window. "That's it. I'm thinking they positioned it there since you leave the bottom of your blinds up a few inches for your plants."

Staring at the miniscule camera, she swallowed hard, willing away a flash of anger. "It's kind of interesting, though. If I moved one of the plants, it would totally block their view. I guess they were counting on everything staying where it is."

"True." He hesitated. "I think if you'd moved a plant, they'd have sent someone out to move the camera."

Frustrated, she turned to face him. "I don't understand. Why would someone do this? My life isn't that interesting, I promise you. And if they're hoping to see me naked, I'd think they'd have tried my bedroom rather than the kitchen."

"If you have a stalker—" he began, interrupted by a noise out front.

"Hello?" a male voice called. "Chicago PD and FBI."

"We're back here," Micha replied. A moment later, two men came around the side of the house. They both were dressed casually, though one wore a police badge on his belt and the other had on a jacket with FBI emblazoned across the back.

"Hi," the shorter man said, offering Carly a handshake. "I'm Detective Charlie Crenshaw with Chicago PD." He glanced at Micha and grinned. "And this here's Special Agent Brad Howard with the FBI."

After handshakes were exchanged all around, Brad

asked to see the camera. Micha pointed it out and the two men talked quietly while they studied it.

Inside, Bridget barked several times. Carly jumped, feeling like the worst dog parent ever. "Oh. Excuse me. I need to let my dog out."

She went around to the front door, not wanting to take a chance of Bridget bolting out the back if she went in that way.

Letting herself into her house, she couldn't help but feel a sense of foreboding. Walking down the hallway to her kitchen, she carefully kept her gaze away from the window and the camera, though it seriously creeped her out that someone might be watching her right this very instant.

Catching sight of Carly, Bridget jumped to her feet, wiggling her entire body in joy. The sight of this made Carly laugh and forget momentarily about the camera. "Hey, baby girl," Carly crooned, climbing over the baby gate and crouching on the floor. Bridget rushed over, licking and wagging her tail and contorting her little black body in all kinds of expressive and happy moves.

After a moment or two of cuddling, Carly stood, grabbed a leash and clipped it to Bridget's collar. "Ready to go outside and go potty?" she asked, grinning to herself at the way she talked to her dog as if she were human and understood every word.

Bridget barked, just once, almost as if responding "Yes!"

Still smiling, Carly led her to the back door. She was curious to see Bridget's reaction to the three men in the backyard.

As soon as they stepped outside, Bridget froze. She let out a low woof, the hair rising on her back.

"It's okay," Carly said, petting her gently. "They're friends."

Bridget glanced up at her, as if seeking reassurance.

Which Carly gave her. "It's all right. Come on, let's go over here and go potty." She led the dog over to the back corner of her yard, near the shed where Bridget had been living before. Once Bridget had taken care of business, Carly walked her back over to the others.

"Hey, girl, remember me?" Micha crouched down, holding out his hand. To Carly's surprise, Bridget sniffed him and immediately wagged her tail.

"Look at that, she knows me!" Clearly delighted, Micha grinned up at Carly.

"Smart dog," Charlie the detective said. At the sound of his voice, Bridget froze. She looked from him to the FBI agent, then to Micha and Carly.

"Too many new people," Micha commented. Moving slowly, he got to his feet and backed away from the clearly terrified dog.

"She's shaking." Carly's heart broke. "Bridget, it's okay. I'm right here."

Despite the reassuring tone and words, Bridget wasn't having it. She pressed her too-thin body against Carly's leg as if she wished she could disappear behind it.

"Ms. Colton?" Brad Howard asked. "We're about to get out of your hair for now. We'd like to ask you to leave this camera in place and try to pretend like you don't know it exists. I'm going to ask for one of our best IT specialists and see if he can trace it. But it's got to be transmitting for him to do that. Will that be all right with you?"

"How long will it have to be there?" Eyeing the tiny camera, she shuddered at the thought of someone watching her while she went about her everyday life.

"I'm thinking a day or two," the FBI agent responded. "Maybe three at the most. It all depends on how long it takes to get the video feed tracked."

Slowly, Carly nodded, all the while absently stroking her new dog's head.

The two men thanked her and let themselves out of her backyard. Once they were gone, Bridget relaxed.

"That was weird," Carly told Micha. "I'd hoped they would just take the video camera with them."

"What the FBI agent said makes sense. It's got to be transmitting to be tracked. If they'd pulled it, whoever is monitoring the thing would have just shut it down. That's why it's important that you pretend it's not there."

She grimaced. "Easier said than done, but I'll try."

With the other men gone, Bridget had finally gotten brave enough to venture a few feet away from Carly so she could sniff the grass. Once the dog had finished, she tugged on the leash as if letting Carly know she was ready to go inside.

Carly glanced at Micha, standing several feet away with his hands in his pockets. "Would you like to come in?" she invited. "I really don't want to be alone with that camera just yet. It's going to take me a little bit to get used to the idea."

"I'd love to," he replied, the warmth of his smile going

straight to her core. She had to take a deep breath to gather her suddenly scattered thoughts.

Letting them in the back door, Carly did her best not to glance in the direction of the camera. This proved more difficult than she'd imagined. She bent over, released Bridget from the leash and busied herself pouring dog kibble in a bowl.

"Are you hungry, girl?" she asked, setting the bowl on the floor. Bridget immediately began chowing down.

Carly smiled, though she still felt unsettled. As if he sensed this, Micha came up behind her and gently pulled her into his arms from behind. Mouth against her ear, he nuzzled her neck. "If they're watching right now, I want them to understand that you're mine," he murmured.

She should have protested that statement. She wasn't his, not any longer, but her brain appeared to have short-circuited. Instead of moving away, she allowed herself to go limp in his arms and relax into his embrace.

Bridget briefly glanced up at them but continued eating.

Carly turned. He kissed her then. A slow, leisurely exploration of his lips on hers, his tongue inside her. Despite her every resolve to the contrary, she kissed him back, a slow burn unfurling through her cells and making her knees go weak.

Just when she thought she'd collapse in a puddle of desire on the floor, he broke away, kissing first the tip of her nose before moving on to her shoulders and neck.

"I need your help with something," he asked, still nibbling on her ears, which sent little shivers of lightning through her. At that very moment, she doubted she could deny him anything, so she nodded. He traced the hollow of her throat with his lips, making her again weak with longing. She knew she could move away, tell him to stop, but she didn't want to. No one had ever been able to make her feel the things Micha did, not before him or after him, and she'd missed this.

"What?" she finally asked, breathless.

"After I turn in the rental car, I'll need a ride to the dealership so I can buy something of my own. After that, I want to look for a place to live. Living in a motel is getting old and expensive."

Somehow, he managed to make even that sound sexy. "Mmm-hmm."

"And I need your expertise," he continued. "You know the area. Will you go with me?"

"I will." Taking a half step back, she finally managed to put some air between the two of them so she could think. "Are you looking to rent or buy?"

"Rent," he replied, the heat in his gaze almost as intoxicating as his kisses had been. "I'd like to find something low maintenance, like maybe a condo or a town house."

"I have a Realtor friend I can check with," she managed, taking another step back when all she really wanted to do was lose herself in his arms.

Bridget, apparently having had enough of being ignored, chose that moment to give a single, loud bark. Eyeing Carly mournfully, she managed to make herself look both pitiful and expectant.

Both Carly and Micha laughed.

"I'm sorry, girl." Carly dropped to the floor and beckoned the dog over. "Come here and I'll love on you, too."

Micha went still at her words, but Bridget immediately sidled over, tail wagging ninety to nothing. Carly began petting her.

"Is that what you were doing?" Micha asked quietly. "Loving on me?"

Unable to meet his gaze, she concentrated on her dog and tried for a flippant response. "Right now, Bridget is the only one around here who gets loved on."

Then, feeling guilty, she glanced up just in time to see the hurt flash across Micha's expression. "I'm sorry," she said quietly. "I'm not trying to be mean, just real."

"Real?" He shook his head. "Real is returning my kisses. That connection we have between us is real. I don't understand how you can pretend it doesn't exist."

"I'm not," she replied. "But, Micha, everything with you is intense. Too quick, too fast and too deep. You need to slow your roll."

"I'm trying." Still, he smiled at her choice of words, which relieved her much more than it should have. "You know how you affect me."

She ducked her head, unwilling to respond. He didn't need to know the inner battle raging inside her. She craved his touch, his kisses, his body inside her, while also aware she had to protect her heart. She wasn't sure she could have both.

Chapter Five

Micha's initial intention had been to show the sick bastard who was spying on Carly that she was his and no one else's. Frustrated, he'd struggled to come up with a way to convey the fact that he'd lay down his life to defend her, but other than speaking directly to the camera and giving everything away, he couldn't conceive of one.

Instead, he'd done what he'd been aching to do from the moment she'd arrived home. He kissed her.

Like always, the passion simmering just beneath the surface had erupted. He'd struggled against the urge to take that kiss a step further, aware she wanted him to as well, which was the most powerful aphrodisiac possible.

Yet he hadn't. One, because he didn't want the voyeur to see this over the video camera, and two, because Carly had told him it couldn't happen again. She'd practically made him promise and the one thing he couldn't go back on with her was his word.

"Did you want me to go get something to eat?" he asked, aware he'd need the time to get his composure back.

Glancing up at him, he saw a flash of panic in her

eyes at the thought of being alone. He hated the fact that she now felt that way in her own home.

"How about I order us some Chinese takeout?" she said instead. "Do you still like sweet and sour chicken?"

"Sweet and Sour Saturday." He grinned. "I haven't had it in years, but yes." Once, they'd not only done Taco Tuesday, but Sweet and Sour Saturday, and even the occasional Meatball Monday. Though the first time they'd had Chinese takeout together would always be special. He wondered if she remembered and then wondered how she could forget. Was her food choice for tonight intentional, some sort of hint, or was she simply in the mood for sweet and sour chicken? Briefly, he considered asking her, but decided to do so would be unwise.

Though her tentative smile dimmed at his unintentional reminder of the time they'd spent apart, she nodded. "Let me call it in. They usually can get it here in thirty minutes or less."

While she placed the order, he got up and wandered over to the kitchen window—and the camera—pretending to study her plants. One of them, a good-size aloe vera plant, jogged his memory.

"I gave you this," he said, once she'd finished with her phone call.

"You did," she agreed, coming to stand beside him. "It was a lot smaller. I've transplanted it twice since then."

They both eyed the plant, neither glancing at the camera. He wondered if she also struggled with the urge to slide the plant over to block the camera's view. Of course they couldn't.

What they could do was move out of the area the video camera could see.

"How about we go catch up on the evening news while we wait for our food?" he asked her, casually holding out his hand.

After a moment's hesitation, she took it, her slim fingers intertwined with his. "Come on, Bridget," she called. "Let's go snuggle on the couch."

Though he knew he had to stop reacting to her every word choice, *snuggle on the couch* had him aching to do exactly that. But she'd been speaking to her dog, and the instant she sat down, she patted the seat cushion next to her as a signal to Bridget to jump up.

Ignoring Micha completely, Bridget did, curling into Carly's side and effectively preventing Micha from getting close. Which probably had been Carly's plan all along, Micha thought with a wry grimace.

Carly got out her phone and typed a text. A second later, his phone pinged.

Can the camera still hear us? she'd asked.

I don't know, he texted back. "It's unlikely since it's having to record through the window." He spoke those words out loud. "Relax. Since the guy who planted it didn't get into the house, it's unlikely there are listening devices or other cameras in here. Unless..."

"Unless what?"

"Have you had any break-ins?" he asked. "Recently, that is."

"No," she replied. Bridget placed her head on Carly's leg, nudging her for attention. When Carly resumed rubbing the dog's tummy, Bridget groaned with happiness. For the first time in his life, Micha found himself envying a dog.

"No one's come inside to do any kind of repairs or installations?"

She frowned. "No."

Relieved, he nodded. "If no one's been inside, then you should be safe from any internal monitoring devices."

"Good." Carly used the remote and turned on the television. "I DVR the evening news," she said. "That way I don't miss any of it."

For the next few minutes they caught up on the headlines of the day.

The doorbell rang, signaling the arrival of their food. Micha jumped up, motioning to Carly to stay seated, and went to get it. He gave the delivery driver a ten-dollar tip and brought the bags back into the living room.

"Let's eat in front of the TV," Carly suggested, sending an aggrieved glance toward her kitchen. "That used to be my favorite room in this house."

"It will be soon again," he reassured her. "Hopefully, that camera won't be there too much longer."

Clearing off the coffee table, she nodded. "We'll just spread everything out here."

Bridget, who had been eyeing the bag of food, licked her lips.

"I think your dog will like that," he teased.

Carly cracked a smile at that, then reached into the bag and began unloading the containers. "Here you go," she said. "I forgot how much they give you."

He hadn't. Everything about the first time they'd had this meal would forever remain etched in his soul.

The first bite—sweet and sour chicken, delicately breaded and seasoned with something that tasted like flowers—brought back so many memories that he stopped chewing and allowed himself to let the flavor wash over him. For the rest of his life, he knew he'd always associate mind-blowing, passionate sex with this meal.

"Do you remember…?" they both asked at the same time. Carly's color seemed high, her breathing jagged.

"The very first time we made love," she said softly.

He managed to nod, reaching for a second bite. After a moment, she did the same. They continued to eat in a kind of supercharged silence, he unable to help but wonder if she'd invite him to her bed after the meal.

"I didn't do this on purpose," she finally muttered, clearly able to discern his thoughts. "I just thought Chinese food sounded good. It wasn't until I placed the order that I realized I might be sending you the wrong message."

Struggling to conceal his disappointment, he simply nodded and cracked open his fortune cookie. The message inside made him laugh. "'Better times are ahead,'" he said, reading it out loud. "Good to know." Taking a bite of the cookie, he eyed her. "I can't wait to see yours."

She pushed her container away and reached for her cookie. When she read the little slip of paper inside, she shook her head, the tiniest hint of a smile tugging at one corner of her mouth. "Here," she said, passing it over to him.

Reading it, he grinned. "'Passion awaits you.' That's perfect."

"Is it?" She leaned back in her chair, her expression once again serious. "If I'd invited you to dinner with the intention of luring you into my bed with sweet and sour chicken, it would be. But since we've already settled on the fact that's not going to happen, it almost feels like…" She shrugged.

"Like I got the restaurant to put that particular message into your cookie?" Still grinning, he shook his head. "You know I didn't."

"I know," she groused, her color still high. "But you have to admit it's an odd fortune to receive. Why couldn't it have said something like 'You'll win an all-expenses-paid trip to Cancun'?"

"I'd be happy to take you to Cancun." The words slipped out before he'd had time to consider them. "If you really want to go, that is."

"Figure of speech, Micha. That's all." Getting to her feet, she started to gather up the empty containers. "I can't believe we managed to eat all that."

He got up and helped her. Together, they took everything to her kitchen trash can. Both studiously avoided glancing at the camera. Bridget, having abandoned her sleeping place on the couch, followed them, nose twitching as she sniffed the floor.

"I didn't drop anything, girl," Carly said, ruffling the dog's fur. "Chinese food wouldn't be good for you, anyway."

Micha couldn't help but find the way she spoke to Bridget as if she was human charming. He checked his watch. "I guess I'd better be going."

Again, that brief flare of panic in her eyes. But this time, she simply nodded. "I'll walk you to the door."

Until the actual moment he stepped out onto her front stoop, he'd harbored a wild and fervent hope that she'd change her mind, kiss him and invite him into her bed. Instead, she put on a brave smile that broke his heart and waved goodbye.

Halfway down the sidewalk, he pivoted, about to tell her he couldn't stand to leave her alone with that camera mounted in her kitchen window. But she'd already quietly closed her front door, so he got in his car and drove back to his lonely hotel room, where he knew he'd spend the rest of the night dreaming about her.

LEANING AGAINST THE back side of her front door, Carly listened until Micha started up his car and drove off. The awful sense of loss she felt at his absence both stunned and worried her. The video camera on her kitchen window freaked her out, and she wasn't sure she'd manage to sleep a wink tonight.

Bridget slipped up next to her, nudging Carly's hand with her wet nose. "You'd alert me if anyone tried to break in, wouldn't you?" she asked. Though she knew the dog most likely didn't understand her question, having her there made Carly feel slightly more secure.

"I've got a big day tomorrow," she said, continuing her habit of speaking to Bridget as if she was a person. "I'd take you with me, but I'm not sure how my family would react. So you'll have to stay here. At least I won't be gone as long as I am when I work all day."

She took Bridget out once more before getting ready for bed, glad of the way the back porch light illuminated most of her backyard.

As soon as she got into her bed, Bridget came and sat by her side, looking up at her as if asking for permission. "Come on up, girl." Carly patted the comforter.

Bridget needed no second invitation. Gracefully, she leaped up, turned two full circles and settled into her place next to Carly's leg. Carly fell asleep with the comforting weight of her new dog pressed against her.

In the morning, she had her usual cup of coffee in the living room rather than at the kitchen table. Today, she'd have to break the startling news of Micha being alive to her entire family. Knowing how much they'd all loved him, she felt pretty certain they'd be ecstatic, but she didn't want to have to share her own conflicted emotions. She loved her family, but her personal life needed to stay just that—personal.

She tried to make the drive out to Oak Park on a regular basis, more often these days after losing her father and uncle. Her brothers, Heath and Jones, did the same. Since the two families lived next door to each other, they'd begun having combined dinners on a regular basis, attended by all the cousins. They used to have those all the time growing up, so everyone felt a faint hint of nostalgia, which made them miss the two elder Colton men even more. Their loss created a huge hole in all of their lives.

After spending the morning puttering around her

house, enjoying her dog and avoiding the kitchen, that afternoon Carly got in her car to make the trek north-west to the suburb. Though no one knew yet that Micha was alive, she had still debated inviting him, but knew doing so would make more of a statement than she was prepared to handle right now, so she went alone. She couldn't decide whether to break the news before Heath dropped his bombshell about the new murders or after. She guessed she'd just play it by ear.

Since the day was unseasonably warm for April, they'd decided to move the get-together outside and have a backyard cookout in their shared backyard. Grandma Jones had been positively gleeful at the prospect. She'd assigned everyone a different dish to bring, but every-one knew they'd all be purchasing theirs from Tatum's restaurant True.

Since Carly had brought Harry to the last family din-ner, she knew everyone would question his absence. That would be as good a time as any to tell them Micha wasn't dead, after all, though she dreaded the assump-tions that were sure to follow.

Carly's brothers, Heath and Jones, were in charge of manning the massive stainless-steel grill. Two other men, Sean Stafford and Cruz Medina, stood with them, shooting the breeze. Carly's three cousins—Simone, Tatum and January—were already outside, chatting with Heath's fiancée, Kylie.

As Carly walked over, she noticed that January couldn't seem to tear her gaze away from her fiancé, Sean. Ditto for Tatum, who was making googly eyes at her new man, Cruz. Since Tatum was a renowned chef who owned True, a restaurant downtown, she was in charge of the food. Everyone just purchased whatever sides they'd been assigned from her, which basically meant she was catering the luncheon, right down to providing seasoned and marinated cuts of meat for the guys to grill.

None of the cousins had inherited Tatum's cooking skills. Simone worked as a professor at the University of Chicago, January was a social worker as well as a busy volunteer, and Carly a nurse; they all preferred to eat Tatum's wonderful cooking over their own. Grandma Jones often chided them, but she, too, dug in with gusto to whatever Tatum brought, so Carly knew she didn't really mind.

Until the double murder, they'd been a loud, boisterous, close and joyful family. Over time, and slowly, Carly hoped they'd all manage to make their way back to where they'd once been.

Walking into the spacious backyard, Carly immediately headed over to her mother, who sat in a brightly painted Adirondack chair next to her aunt. Both women, identical twins who took great pains to wear their hair differently, looked up at her approach.

"Carly!" Aunt Farrah stood, somehow managing to look both warm and regal at the same time. She enveloped Carly in a perfumed hug, before releasing her and sitting back down.

Carly's mother, Fallon, also pushed to her feet. She crushed Carly to her, holding on so tightly that Carly struggled to breathe. When Fallon finally released her, Carly stepped back and studied her mom. Fallon's short, curly hair looked as stylish as ever, and she'd clearly taken pains with her makeup, outfit and jewelry. This had to be a good sign, Carly thought.

"What's new, sweetheart?" her mother asked, her intent gaze sweeping over Carly. Ever since losing her husband, the older woman had become subdued, her former vibrant personality dimmed. While Aunt Farrah Colton had always been loud, in an outgoing, charming way, Fallon had always been more reserved, yet warm and caring. Carly actually missed her aunt's occasional yelling. At least she had her twin, Fallon, living next door to grieve with. Since both women had lost their husbands at the same time, they leaned heavily on each other.

They all mourned differently, Carly reflected. Carly had thrown herself into her work, picking up extra shifts and keeping as busy as possible so she didn't have time to think. Of course, ever since losing Micha, she'd been a bit of a workaholic. The loss of her father had just intensified those tendencies again.

"I got a dog," Carly said, figuring she'd start with that and work up to the really big news. After all, at some point Heath had to make his announcement about the new double murder. No doubt he planned to wait until after they'd all eaten, so the news wouldn't put a huge damper on everyone's mood.

"You what?" Fallon's perfectly arched brows rose. "I wouldn't think you have time to deal with a puppy."

"Bridget isn't a puppy, Mom. I rescued a dog. The vet says she's about two years old and has likely had at least one litter of puppies. She's got an appointment tomorrow to get spayed."

The twin sisters shared a glance. "What kind of dog, dear?" Aunt Farrah asked.

"The vet thinks she's a lab mix." Carly pulled out her phone, ready to show pictures. She certainly had a lot of them.

Her trio of cousins ambled over, clearly curious. Everyone dutifully oohed over Bridget's pictures.

"She's really thin," January said, expression concerned. She'd always been tenderhearted, which was part of the reason she'd gone into social work and did so much volunteer work. "Are you feeding her several small meals a day?"

"I am," Carly replied, which made her cousin beam.

"Where's Harry?" Simone asked, glancing around as if she expected him to appear at any second.

"We're taking a break," Carly replied, bracing herself for the comments that were sure to follow. Her cousins exchanged quick glances. Simone frowned, while January appeared confused. Since she'd been the one to set Harry and Carly up, Carly knew she owed her an explanation. "He's a great guy and I appreciate you introducing us. We just weren't right for each other. He's good with it, though, much more so than I thought he'd be. Maybe you can work your magic and fix him up with someone else."

Still frowning slightly, January nodded.

Tatum hugged her. "I'm sorry. Are you okay?"

"Mostly," Carly allowed. She figured she might as well get this over with now, though she wanted her brothers to hear, too. "Heath, Jones. Do you have a minute?"

Since they hadn't actually started cooking anything, they came over.

Jones slung a casual arm across her shoulders. "Looking good, Carly." She smiled up at him, while inside she couldn't help but wonder how they all were going to take her news.

"What's up?" Heath asked, his shaggy dark blond hair blowing in the slight breeze.

"Micha is alive," she blurted, inwardly wincing at her bluntness. "He showed up at my house a couple of days ago."

Everyone started talking at once, asking questions. Heath cleared his throat loudly and held up his hand. "Quiet," he ordered. "Let Carly explain."

Carly told them everything, all except the part where she'd fallen into bed with Micha. When she finished relaying Micha's story, Simone shook her head. "That explains Harry's absence."

Which meant that Carly had to tell them Harry's reaction. Part of her still couldn't digest the fact that he'd let her go so easily.

"Proof he wasn't the right guy for you," Jones drawled supportively, hugging her again. "I hope you're not losing any sleep over him."

"I'm not," she said, surprised to realize the only thing stung had been her pride. Looking up, she realized both her mother and aunt had tears in their eyes.

Carly eyed January. "Thank you for fixing me and Harry up. He's a great guy. I promise you, I never wanted to hurt him in any way."

"It sounds like you didn't," January admitted. "He'll

be okay. But poor Micha," she said, sighing. "It sounds like he's been through so much."

Carly nodded, not sure how to react to that. While Micha had suffered a horrible ordeal, that didn't excuse the fact he hadn't reached out to her in two damn years. "All this time," she said out loud, "I thought he was dead."

"I'm so happy for you," Fallon said, sniffing. "You get to have a second chance. I wish your father could have been here to see that. He always was fond of Micha."

Carly's stomach twisted. She didn't have the heart to tell her mother that she wasn't sure she wanted a second chance with Micha. Especially not now, when she knew her mother would have given anything to have her husband back. As would Aunt Farrah.

"When's the wedding taking place?" Simone asked softly. "Or haven't you had time to start planning it yet?"

"I want to cater it," Tatum interjected. "Or maybe you could just have the reception at True."

Overwhelmed, all Carly could do was slowly shake her head.

Standing across from her, Heath narrowed his eyes, something in the tightness of his expression letting her know he understood at least some of the tangled emotions inside her.

"Give Carly a break," he ordered. "I imagine all of this came as quite the shock."

"It did," Carly managed. She checked her watch. "Shouldn't you two start grilling? I'm hungry."

Grinning, Jones touched his finger to his forehead in a mock salute. "We'll get right on that. Come on, Heath."

Carly exhaled as her two brothers sauntered away. For a moment there, she'd seen a flash of anger in Heath's steely gaze. She'd been really glad he wouldn't be confronting Micha yet. She had a lot of her own upset feelings to deal with first without her older brother bringing his own into the mix.

"Why didn't you bring Micha today?" Tatum asked, one brow raised. "It would have been great to see him after all this time."

"I agree," Simone said. "I always liked him."

Carly shrugged. "Can we change the subject, please?"

All three of her cousins laughed. January hugged her this time. "Sure we can."

A quick glance at her mother revealed she and her sister were in a deep, whispered conversation. Which was fine. Carly knew the two women could use a distraction. Since she didn't want to worry anyone, Carly decided not to mention her feeling of being watched for the last six weeks. At least not yet. The police knew, Micha knew, and that would have to be enough for now.

Once the meat—tender, delectable cuts of beef, chicken and pork that Tatum had marinated, seasoned and prepared—had been grilled, all the sides were carried out and placed on a long table. It would be a feast. Carly, unable to keep from wondering what Micha would make of it, hung back a little while the others lined up to fill their plates.

Heath joined her, his expression troubled. Since she'd promised she wouldn't, she couldn't reveal that she already knew about the recent double murders. No doubt her older brother was worrying about how to tell the family without causing a mass panic.

Meanwhile, Heath apparently took her preoccupation for worry about Micha. "It's going to be all right, Carly." He patted her shoulder. "Right now it must feel overwhelming, but things will sort themselves out."

She managed to summon a smile. "I know they will," she replied, even though she knew no such thing. "Life sure can be complicated."

"It can," he agreed. "If you need to talk through anything, or just feel like some company, you know you can contact me or Jones anytime."

"That's right," Jones chimed in, balancing a very full plate as he passed them on his way toward a seat. "Or if you want to come by the brewery and drown your sorrows, I'm up for that, too." He winked. "I brought some of our newest beer for everyone to sample today if they want."

Once everyone had gotten their food and sat down to eat, Carly allowed herself to simply be in the moment, pushing her worries away for later. A delicious meal with her family, lots of laughter, bright sunshine and spring warmth would lighten anyone's mood.

Heath and Jones went back for seconds. Carly almost followed their lead, but Tatum reminded everyone to leave room for dessert. Since whatever Tatum had chosen to concoct was bound to be spectacular, Carly stayed in her seat.

Grinning, Heath returned to his chair with a second heaping plate. Jones did the same. "I'll always have room for any of your delicious desserts," Heath said, before digging in.

Tatum waited until both men had cleaned their plates before getting up and disappearing inside the house to retrieve her concoction. Everyone took wild guesses on what she might have made since she'd refused to say, claiming she wanted it to be a surprise.

"I'm hoping cheesecake." Carly sighed. "Or cobbler."

"Or tiramisu," January interjected. Simone nodded her agreement. "Tatum makes the best tiramisu."

"I vote chocolate," Jones chimed in.

A moment later, Tatum reappeared. She carried a large covered metal pan. "Something new," she said with a mysterious smile. "Bourbon bread pudding."

Everyone collectively sighed.

"My mouth is already watering," Heath said.

Rapt, everyone watched while Tatum dished up portions into bowls. Next to them, she'd placed a carton of French vanilla ice cream with a metal scoop on top. "Come and get it," she announced, stepping back. "Mom and Aunt Fallon first."

Simone stood, fetching the two older women's portions before grabbing her own. One by one, the rest of them got their dessert.

As usual with anything Tatum made, it tasted amazing, managing to be both light and filling, the flavors both simple and complex. Carly ate it slowly, so she could savor every bite.

By the time everyone had finished, a contented silence fell over the group. Carly glanced at her big brother, figuring now would be the time he broke his bit of news.

Heath looked around and then slowly stood. He took a deep breath before tapping his spoon on the side of his water glass to get their attention. "Everyone, I'm afraid I have a bit of bad news," he said. "Chicago PD has notified me that there was another double murder, with a similar MO to Dad and Uncle Alfred. The FBI has been called in. They're thinking we might have a serial killer on our hands."

After a moment of stunned silence, everyone started talking at once. Carly stayed quiet and listened while everyone expressed worry, shock and concern.

Heath let them go on for a moment or two before raising his hand and clearing his throat. "The police have promised to keep us posted. They've asked everyone to be careful and let them know if you see or hear anything unusual. If it is a serial killer, they aren't sure what attracts him to his victims."

"How do you know it's a male?" Fallon asked.

"Most serial killers are."

"Were the victims also twins?" Jones asked, shooting his brother a dark look, no doubt upset that Heath hadn't filled him in first.

"No." Heath looked from one family member to the other. "Despite that, or maybe because of it, I'm still worried. I want you all to promise me you'll report anything unusual."

Everyone murmured their assent. Carly kept her mouth closed, though she figured she'd probably better tell her brothers about her stalker. But if she did, she knew Heath would sweep in and take over, like he always did. Being the head of the family and the family business had given him more than enough responsibilities and things to worry about. She decided to keep it quiet for now. After all, Chicago PD and the FBI were already involved. And she had Micha to help keep her safe.

Chapter Six

Since Micha had no way of knowing what time Carly would return from her family get-together out in Oak Park, he spent the afternoon looking at For Rent listings online. He found several that looked promising and bookmarked them to revisit later with Carly. Once he'd finished with that, he started studying sales prices of vehicles he liked. He figured out a strategy, decided how much he was willing to spend in cash and then he drove north to a Jeep, Chrysler and Dodge dealer and took a look at the new Jeep Wranglers. The dealership was closed on Sunday, so Micha parked outside the gate and walked around the lot looking at vehicles.

He found a fully loaded black one he liked, jotted down the information and resolved to come back Monday when the sales office was open.

On the way back to his hotel, he realized he needed fresh air, so he took a detour and drove to Burnham Park, where he could walk along the lakeshore and see the water. Everyone, it seemed, had come out on such a beautiful spring afternoon. The tennis courts were full, the path crowded with joggers, cyclists and people out for a walk.

Here, in the midst of nature, with Lake Michigan glittering in the sunlight, he missed Carly so much he ached. To him, she represented everything he loved about his city of choice. Walking in this beautiful green space might be nice, but he needed Carly with him to fully experience it.

He found an empty bench and sat. Once, he and Carly had huddled together in this very spot, bundled in their winter coats, hats, scarves and gloves. They'd been giddy with love, braving the icy chill of winter to marvel at the beauty of the frozen lake. He wondered if she'd ever come here by herself, after his supposed death. Maybe she'd sat on this same bench, mourning him.

It couldn't have been easy for her. If the situation had been reversed, and he'd lost her, the devastation would have surely taken him under. Instead, he'd spent a good chunk of time unconscious, even more in physical therapy relearning basic skills, all the while yearning for someone his fuzzy brain couldn't remember. Then when he'd clawed his way to some sort of normalcy and realized what he'd lost, so much time had passed that he'd understood he could never have her back.

Still, unable to let her go, he'd traveled to his favorite city to see her one last time. As if. He'd hashed the scenario out over and over, unable to rationalize simply letting her go.

And now he knew he never could. If she sent him away, he'd end up living the rest of his life as half a person.

His phone rang. When Carly's name flashed up on the screen, his heart skipped a beat. *Here's to second chances*, he thought, and answered.

"I'm on my way back to the house," she said. "If you want to come over in about thirty minutes, that'd be great."

"I'm at Burnham Park," he told her. "So not far from your place at all. Maybe we could take Bridget for a walk here sometime."

"She'd love that," she promptly said. "But not until I've made sure she's up to date on her vaccines first."

"You're already an awesome pet parent," he said. "I'll see you in a half hour."

After ending the call, he remained on the park bench a few more minutes, soaking up the atmosphere and feeling like the luckiest man alive.

Then he got up and made his way to his rental car to make the short drive over to Carly's house.

Despite taking his time, he still arrived before her. He parked at the curb in front of her house and went to sit on her front porch steps. When she pulled into her driveway a few minutes later, he got up and went to meet her. Bridget, apparently recognizing the sound of Carly's car, began barking inside the house.

The sound made Carly grin. "I love having a dog," she said.

"It sounds like she's glad you're home." He slung a casual arm across her shoulders. Though she tensed at first, she actually allowed herself to lean into him a little. When she reached her front door, she stepped away from him and unlocked it. She barely had it open wide enough for her to step through when a blur of black fur came barreling at her, barking in what Micha could only describe as a happy sound. Happy, hell. The dog sounded ecstatic.

Carly crouched down, grinning broadly while her new pet welcomed her home. "Come on, girl," she finally said, getting to her feet. "Let's get you outside."

Micha waited in her kitchen while she took her dog out back. Ever conscious of the camera, he avoided glancing at the window at all.

A moment later, Carly and Bridget returned. "It's gone," Carly announced, slightly breathless. "The video camera is no longer attached to my window. I even checked the ground below, just in case it fell. There's no sign of it anywhere."

Naturally, he had to go look for himself. As she'd said, the camera had disappeared as if it had never been there.

"What does that mean?" Carly asked, frowning.

"I'm not sure," he admitted. "It's possible whoever installed it figured out we were on to them."

"Do you think maybe the FBI took it?" she asked, turning to grab the dog food bowl so she could feed Bridget.

"Let me see if I can find out." He sent a quick text to Charlie's cell phone. A moment later, Charlie called him.

"What do you mean the camera is gone?" Charlie asked, getting directly to the point. "The FBI hasn't had a chance to get their analyst out to look at it. They're having to fly someone out from New York. I think he's arriving here tomorrow."

"He'll be too late."

Charlie cursed.

"I'm just glad it's gone," Micha admitted. "But for the record, both Carly and myself were careful not to do anything to alert anyone that we knew the camera was there."

"I'd better notify the Bureau." Charlie sounded resigned. "There's no reason for them to send their specialist out here now."

"Thanks, man. I'll let you know if anything changes." After ending the call, Micha turned to find Carly watching him.

"I take it he didn't remove it?" she asked.

"Nope. The FBI didn't, either." He decided to try for a little humor. "Maybe the guy realized he had the wrong house."

Though this earned him a smile from her, she shook her head. She put the dog bowl full of food down, where Bridget immediately began devouring it.

Watching the shadows in her eyes as she gazed at her dog, Micha fiercely wished he could protect her always. He vowed he would, no matter the cost.

"You have an awfully intent look on your face," she commented. "What are you thinking about?"

Not wanting to worry her even more, he shrugged. "Nothing in particular. How'd your family get-together go?"

Her smile told him she didn't believe him. "It went well. I told them about you being alive. And here in Chicago."

"How'd they take it?"

"Well. You know how much they liked you. Several people asked why I didn't bring you with me."

"What did you say?" he asked, needing to know.

She sighed. "I changed the subject. Honestly, Micha. I'm still not sure how I feel about all this. Having you back and here with me is wonderful, but it's also scary as hell."

"Scary?" Her choice of words made him consider. "How so?"

Now she wouldn't look at him. "Losing you hurt, Micha. It took me a long time to pick myself up and climb out of that deep, dark place."

The pain in his heart made him rub his chest. "Would you rather I hadn't come back? Would you..." He had to swallow hard to keep his voice from breaking. "Would you rather you still thought I was dead?"

"Of course not."

Her instant denial made him feel slightly better. "I'm glad," he began.

She shook her head and held up her hand, interrupting him. "I'm still struggling with the fact that you waited two entire years before even attempting to contact me. I know you have your reasons, you've been pretty clear on that. But what you don't seem to understand is this. I can't go through that again. I wouldn't survive losing you a second time."

So much pain. And yet, so much love. He could fix this, he thought, given enough time. For now, all he could do was simply show her he wouldn't be leaving her again.

Needing that skin-to-skin contact, he gently tugged

her close and brushed his mouth across hers. "I'm sorry," he murmured. Though he immediately released her, his body stirred. Wide-eyed, she stared at him, her lips slightly parted, almost as if she wanted him to kiss her again.

Instead, he turned away. "I found a few places I might be interested in looking at renting," he told her, grabbing his laptop. "If you don't mind, I'd like you to tell me what you think."

"You've got to stop doing that," she said, though she smiled as she spoke.

"Kissing you?"

"Stopping," she replied, laughing a little. The naked vulnerability in her eyes told him how much it had cost her to say that.

With his laptop forgotten, he crossed the space between them. She met him halfway. This time, he kissed her properly.

Bridget barked, running back and forth from the kitchen to the front door. Carly immediately stepped back, her color high. "Is someone out there?" she asked her dog. "What is it, girl?"

Though his arousal made it difficult to walk, Micha headed for the entry. Carly followed close behind. "Let me grab Bridget," she said. "She seems pretty upset. I don't want her running out."

Waiting until she had her dog's collar, he opened the front door. Outside, the late-afternoon sunshine seemed mellow. A car or two drove by and he could hear kids down the street playing. Just a typical spring afternoon in Chicago.

A squirrel dashed across the front lawn. Watching it climb up a tree, he wondered if Bridget had somehow sensed its presence. He'd bet she'd chased a few squirrels for food when she'd been living on the streets.

Returning to Carly, he shrugged. "No idea what she might have been barking at. I saw a squirrel, but nothing out of the ordinary."

"Okay, good," she replied, clearly relieved. She let Bridget go, and the dog heaved a huge sigh before making a beeline to her dog bed. Turning several circles, she finally settled down and closed her eyes.

Since the previous mood had been destroyed, he went to get his laptop so he could show her the places he thought he liked.

"Wait," she said. "Did you write down the addresses?"

"I actually printed out the info sheet on each. I brought my top five."

His comment made her grin. "Wow, you're organized."

He smiled back. "I kind of have to be. It's not easy living out of a hotel room."

"How about we take a drive and look at a couple of those properties?" she asked. "While we'll only be able to check out the outside, at least you can get a feel for the neighborhood. That way, you'll know if you want to make an appointment to see the interior."

Surprised and gratified, he looked at her and nodded. "I'd like that," he said. "Do you want to do that now?"

"Sure, why not? We can bring Bridget with us since she enjoys car rides."

"Sounds good. Let's take the rental car since I'm hoping to turn it in tomorrow. I went and looked at cars today, too, even though the dealerships are closed."

Finally, after taking Bridget out back once more, she asked if he was ready to go.

"Sure. I'll drive." He waited while she put the leash on her dog. They went out the front since he'd parked at the curb.

Since the rental car had remote start, he decided he might as well use it at least once, so he pressed the button on the key fob. Instead of instantly starting, he heard a familiar catch in the ignition. Acting on instinct, he spun and launched himself at Carly, knocking her to the ground just as the car exploded.

EARS RINGING, HEAD THROBBING, Carly tried to process what had just happened. Her elbow hurt, knee, too, and she was pretty sure she'd torn her jeans in the fall. Micha lay on top of her, so still she worried he'd been seriously injured, and she couldn't see her dog anywhere.

"Micha?" she croaked. "Bridget?"

Instead of responding, Micha groaned.

Meanwhile, she could hear the roar of the fire consuming his rental car. Squirming, she tried to move him. Her futile efforts appeared to rouse him. He groaned again, and pushed himself off her, rolling away before collapsing on his back on the front lawn.

"We've called 911," someone said.

Her neighbor, she realized. Without Micha's weight crushing her, Carly managed to rise up on her knees. A small group of people had begun to gather near her yard. "My dog," she said. "Have you seen my dog?"

No one responded. She blinked and decided she wanted to stand. Her pounding head thought otherwise, but she had to make sure Micha was all right and also find Bridget.

Sirens sounded in the distance. Fire truck and ambulance, most likely.

"Are you okay?" Micha asked, his deep voice full of gravel and rasp. He'd managed to sit up. A cut on his arms dripped blood onto his jeans.

"I think so," she replied. "How about you?" Without waiting for him to answer, she slowly got to her feet. Shaky, but standing. "What the hell just happened?"

"Someone set up the car to blow." He shook his head, then winced. "If I hadn't used the remote start, we would have been in that car."

With dawning horror, the truth of his words hit her. They wouldn't have had a chance for escape since the bomb had detonated the instant the engine started. They would have been killed. Even her dog.

Her dog.

"Bridget is missing," she said. "The explosion must have terrified her."

"I don't blame her." Moving with deliberate caution, Micha got up. Other than a tear in the shoulder of his T-shirt, he appeared all right. The cut on his arm appeared to be superficial and the bleeding had slowed to a trickle. "My ears are still ringing," he commented.

"Mine, too."

The sirens got louder. A moment later a fire truck and an ambulance turned onto her street, lights flashing. The small crowd of neighbors clustered closer together as the emergency vehicles pulled up and parked.

Micha swayed, looking for a moment as if he might lose his balance. Carly went to him, slipping her shoulder under his arm to offer support. Shooting her a grateful look, he allowed himself to lean on her.

While the fire department began working on getting the car fire put out, the EMTs came over to check on Carly and Micha. Though Micha tried to wave them away, it was clear he'd been hurt. Carly thought she was okay, even her ears weren't ringing as badly, but also agreed to an exam. The EMTs led both of them over to their ambulance. By now the police had arrived and two uniformed officers were taking statements from neighbors.

"I need to find my dog," Carly announced. "She was with us when the car exploded. I've got to make sure she's okay."

"In a minute, ma'am," the EMT said. "Let me make sure you're all right."

Nodding, she allowed him to check her out, taking her temperature, shining a light into her eyes and asking numerous questions. No, she had no joint pain. No, she didn't think any bones were broken. Thanks to Micha shielding her with his body, she had no cuts or burns, other than the scrapes on her elbows and knees. Yes, she knew she was lucky, but she really had to go look for her dog. It killed her to think Bridget was hiding somewhere terrified and alone.

"We'd like to take you to the hospital for observation," the other EMT told Micha.

"No." His emphatic reply left no doubt. "I'm fine. I've been banged up far worse in Afghanistan. I'm not leaving Carly alone."

Though they argued, he refused to be swayed. And since they couldn't force him to go to the hospital, they finally ended up passing him over to the police detective who'd arrived to take his statement.

Carly managed to slip away, determined to find Bridget. She went into her backyard, fairly certain she had a good idea where Bridget would have run to hide.

She found her dog exactly where she'd expected, in the shed, cowering in the corner. Immediately, Carly crouched down, speaking in a soothing low voice, determined to remain there as long as she had to until Bridget was willing to approach her.

To her surprise, once Carly started talking, Bridget crawled over to her, low to the ground, almost on her belly. She was panting heavily, but her long tail wagged as if to say she had hope that Carly could help her. Since her leash was still attached to her collar, Carly simply gathered it up, still crooning reassuring words. To her surprise, Bridget pressed right up against her legs, allowing Carly to touch her.

"You must have been terrified, weren't you, girl?" Carly asked, gathering the dog close and holding her tight. "I was, too. Come on, let's get you inside the house."

Once she'd coaxed the still-shivering animal into the kitchen, Carly took a deep breath and hobbled back out front to check on Micha. A police officer, catching sight of her coming down the steps, hurried over to intercept her.

"Ma'am? We've been looking for you," he said, his tone brisk. "Your husband has finished giving his statement and we need yours."

Too exhausted to correct him, she simply nodded. "Lead the way."

As he walked her over toward a small group of police officers, she spotted Micha's friend Charlie. He caught sight of her at the same moment and hurried over.

"There you are," he said, taking her arm. "I've got this, Trevor."

Charlie waited until the other officer had walked away before leaning in close. "We're waiting on the FBI," he said, pitching his voice low. "We suspect a definite tie to whoever placed and removed the camera."

She nodded. "I thought the same thing."

"What we don't know is who the explosive device was targeting. Since it was in Micha's rental car, it most likely was him. But on the other hand…"

"Whoever did it might have hoped I'd go somewhere with him," she finished.

"Yes. But they couldn't have known for certain."

Micha walked up, still moving carefully, but looking much better than he had before. "Hey," he said, putting his arm around her shoulders. "Did you find Bridget?"

"I did." She shifted her weight, aware he probably needed to lean on her for balance. "She'd run into the shed and was hiding there. I've moved her into the house. She doesn't appear to have been hurt."

"Good." He let his gaze sweep over her. "What about you? Everything okay?"

She nodded. Before she could speak, one of the policemen came over with some questions.

By the time EMTs, the fire department and law enforcement left, most of the neighborhood spectators had wandered back home. Dusk had arrived and it would soon be dark. Micha had finally sat down on her bottom porch step, clearly too tired or hurt to stand any longer. Carly could definitely relate. She felt weird—a mixture of amped-up restlessness and exhaustion.

"Let's go inside," she told Micha, putting her hand out for him to use to help him get up.

He managed a grateful smile and allowed her to pull him to his feet.

They made it inside with him leaning heavily on her. She helped him to the couch, where he lowered himself with a grunt. Bridget came running up, sniffing his legs, though she didn't jump up on the couch near him.

"Where are you hurt?" Carly asked. "Maybe you should have let them take you to the hospital for tests."

Shaking his head, he eyed her. "No way am I leaving you alone after someone just tried to kill us. No way in hell."

Touched, she wanted to hug him but knew better. "Us? Do you think they targeted your rental car hoping I'd get in it with you?"

"No." He grimaced. "Both Chicago PD and the FBI believe I was the target this time. They can't rule out it was somehow tied to the video camera, and the fact that it happened in front of your house is suspicious to me, but they feel strongly you would have just been collateral damage."

"Collateral damage," she repeated. The coldness of the term made her shiver. "But why, Micha? Why would anyone want you dead?"

"That's just it. I don't know."

"It's just too much of a coincidence," she said. "I've been feeling as if someone's been watching me for weeks, which is even more frightening since someone murdered my father and uncle. You magically reappear, back from the dead." She sighed. "After that, someone puts a video camera on my kitchen window, I learn there's been another murder with a similar MO to my father's, and then someone blows up the car you and I were about to get into. Does that about cover it?"

"Come here." He patted the couch next to him. "We're alive, and unhurt for the most part. Sit. Try to relax. We'll deal with the rest later."

But she felt too jumpy to just sit. Restless and conflicted, an almost sexual energy buzzed through her. She had no idea how to deal with herself except to try to keep busy as a distraction.

Meanwhile, Micha watched her, almost as if he knew the way she felt. She eyed him back, wondering how badly he'd been hurt. Since she needed some way to occupy herself, checking him out would be a start.

"Let me take a look at you," she ordered. "Let's get your shirt off."

This made him laugh, though he immediately winced in pain. "This definitely isn't how I pictured you asking me to take off my clothes."

"Off with it." She refused to rise to his baiting. "I'm sure the EMTs checked you out thoroughly, but I want to see for myself. I take it you don't have any broken bones?"

"No, ma'am," he drawled, struggling to get his torn T-shirt off.

Moving carefully, she helped him, pretending her fingers weren't trembling. Once the shirt came off, she gasped at the huge, angry purple bruise on his shoulder. He had another, even larger one lower on his rib cage. There were a few scratches and scrapes, but overall it didn't appear he'd been seriously injured.

Thank goodness. But her relief did nothing to ease her tension. She needed something else. She needed…him.

Impulsively, she placed a gentle kiss on his shoulder. "I'm glad you're all right," she said.

"Me, too." His gaze had darkened, but he kept still, clearly letting her make her own choice.

"Thank you for protecting me." She kissed him again. A low thrum of desire had settled low in her belly. They'd survived a horrible attack—together—and she felt an almost overwhelming need to reaffirm their survival.

"How much do you hurt?" she asked softly, wanting to be sure.

Turning his head, he met her mouth with his own. "Not that badly," he murmured, kissing her deeply.

She kept her gaze on him as she removed her torn clothing, piece by piece, matter-of-factly with no attempt to shield herself from his heated gaze. Though he struggled, he watched her while he did the same, leaving on only his boxers. She straddled him, closing her eyes as she allowed the desire coursing through her veins to overtake her.

Pushing down his boxers, she freed him, allowing herself to marvel at the sheer force of his erection before she lowered herself over him, taking him deep inside her.

He made a sound, arching his back and driving himself into her. Laughing and wild, she pushed him down, pushing away her inhibitions, her worries and fears, everything but her desire for him.

Letting go. And holding on. As her climax slammed into her, she called his name. An instant later, he joined her. It wasn't until she'd collapsed on top of him that she started to cry.

He held her while she let the tears fall, asking no questions, saying nothing. She wasn't sure exactly of the reason for the waterworks, but her life had changed with her father's and uncle's murders and had continued to change up until this very moment.

Finally, she'd cried herself out. Sniffing, she wiped at her eyes with the back of her hand and sat back. "Sorry about that," she said.

"No need to apologize." Reaching up, he used his fingers to tuck a wayward strand of her hair behind her ear. "That was intense. I get it."

"Intense." She tested out the word. Not terrifying, or even frightening, but intense. "You're right," she said. "It was. All of it."

"I didn't use protection," he murmured, his gaze locked on hers. "But I can assure you I haven't been with anyone else and I was tested for everything before I left the hospital."

She nodded. The last thing she wanted to do was bring up another man right now. "I've made sure I was always protected, as well," she said, hoping that would suffice. "And I take birth control pills, too."

Before he could respond, she got up and grabbed her discarded clothing, hurrying to the bathroom to get cleaned up.

Inside, she eyed her wild-haired, flushed self in the mirror, refusing to allow even the tiniest bit of regret. She stepped into the shower, rinsing herself off.

"Mind if I join you?" Micha's voice, just outside the door.

Startled, she found herself grinning. "Come on in," she said. "I'll wash your back if you'll wash mine."

"Agreed," he replied.

The intimacy of soaping each other off, wet bodies pressed so close together, aroused her again, to her stunned disbelief. When she felt Micha's arousal pressing against her, she laughed out loud. "Again?" she asked, breathless with anticipation.

"Again," he replied, his hands silky on her slick body.

They made love under the warm spray of water, this time taking their time, lingering over exploring each other, which drove Carly over the edge more quickly than she would have liked. Micha immediately followed, giving a primal cry of release.

Later, clean and dry and feeling human again, Carly opened a bottle of red wine she'd been saving for a special occasion. She figured being alive after narrowly missing being blown up in a car explosion qualified. Micha ordered a pizza, her favorite comfort food. Though she shouldn't have been hungry, considering how much she'd eaten earlier, she managed to devour three slices. "I guess I worked up an appetite," she said, smiling. Bridget lay curled at her feet, staring longingly at the remains of the pizza.

"Me, too." Micha got up, moving restlessly around the room. He appeared distracted and unsettled, the opposite of a man who'd just made love to her twice.

"What's wrong?" Carly finally asked, slipping Bridget a small bit of crust.

Micha stopped moving long enough to meet her gaze. "I'm worried that by trying to protect you, I've put you in danger. The more I think about it, the more likely that car explosion was meant for me. You could have been killed. Because of me."

"I get that," she replied. "But since we don't know who might have been the target, it's pointless to blame yourself. Besides that, do you have any enemies? Someone who hates you enough to want to kill you?"

"Not that I know of." Voice as grim as his gaze, Micha shook his head. "But I'm thinking whoever rigged that car to blow had to be handy with explosives. I knew people like that over in Afghanistan. For whatever reason, I was the intended victim."

"But what about that video camera?" she asked, genuinely perplexed.

"Maybe someone was watching you hoping I'd show up," he told her. "No more secrets, Carly. What happened in the war seriously messed up people. While I was rescued, others lost their lives. I need to do some checking with some of my military contacts."

Moving closer, he put his hands lightly on her shoulders. "I'll keep watch over you, I promise. If there is someone after you, I'll keep you safe. If there's someone after me..." He paused. "I'll deal with them. We need to be extra vigilant."

Carly scratched Bridget's head, right behind the ears. "I wonder if she was trying to warn us when she barked earlier," she said. "We looked outside, but no one was there."

"She probably was," he replied. "Whoever rigged that car worked quickly and efficiently, which means highly skilled."

She shuddered. "What if they do that to my car while I'm at work? I'm not sure what to do."

"Let me use your car tomorrow," he told her. "I'll drop you at work and park it. I'll stand guard. Maybe we can catch this person red-handed."

Though his plan sounded dangerous, she agreed. She could see no other choice.

Chapter Seven

Either way, Micha figured he had a good chance of catching the person who'd blown up his rental car. If the bomber was actually after Carly, Micha would watch out for her no matter what. He'd give his life for her if need be. And if Micha himself was the target, well, he'd already been to hell and back. Somehow, he'd survived. After that, nothing shook him. He'd actually welcome putting a rapid end to this craziness. Bring it on.

In the meantime, if any bright spot emerged from all of this, it was that the near-death experience had clearly caused Carly to push away her lingering misgivings about Micha. To his delight, for the first time since his return into her life, she invited him to spend the night with her, in her bed. His heart had leaped at the warmth in her bright blue eyes when she'd asked him to stay.

Not wanting to appear overly eager, he'd pretended to have to consider her offer, when in fact he could hardly contain his joy. For once, she wasn't pushing him away. He hated that it had taken such a horrible event to cause this, but he also understood she'd made a choice. Instead of turning away, she'd leaned in. He'd take it. Hell, when it came to Carly, he'd take whatever she was willing to give. Somehow, he suspected she knew this.

That night he'd held her close while she slept. His heart was full.

In the morning, they made love again, this time with the comfortable ease of longtime lovers. Micha took his time pleasuring her, holding off on his own release until she'd had hers. After, she clung to him without talking, almost drifting off to sleep until her dog's soft whine reminded Carly she had to get up and take care of Bridget.

As Carly stirred, Micha propped himself up on his elbow to watch her. He wasn't sure what to expect—would she have regrets? To his relief, she glanced at him and grinned, her gaze bright and unabashed. "I've got to let Bridget out and feed her. Don't you dare try to leave while I'm gone," she said.

Astounded, he shook his head. "Carly, you know better. I'd never treat you—treat *us*—as a one-night stand. I'm not going anywhere except to take a quick shower."

"Good," she replied, calling her dog. "There are spare towels in the bathroom cabinet. Make yourself at home."

Make yourself at home. Her choice of words humbled him. Profoundly grateful for his good fortune in the midst of this turmoil, Micha had a quick shower while Carly took care of Bridget. Then, while she showered, he puttered around her small kitchen, deciding to surprise her with breakfast.

By the time she emerged, hair still damp, he'd put together a skillet of scrambled eggs, made toast and fried up some turkey bacon.

"Wow!" she exclaimed, taking a seat as he poured her

a glass of orange juice. "This all looks awesome. When did you learn to cook?"

Pleased, he lifted one shoulder. "I picked it up a little bit here and there over time."

Making little sounds of pleasure, she devoured her breakfast, her dog lying under the table, gazing up at her hopefully. Micha ate quickly, too, unable to keep from watching her eat, wondering if she knew there was something sensual in the unabashed pleasure she took from the food.

When she finally pushed away her plate, he eyed her. More than anything he wanted to take her back to her bed and coax a response from her body. He couldn't believe he was once again turned on, even after making love this morning and the night before.

She picked up on the heat in his gaze and shook her head. "I know what you're thinking and I can't. I've got to be on time for work."

He didn't try to hide his regret. "Too bad. Is there any way you can take a day off?"

"Just so we can go back to bed?" She laughed. "I'm flattered, but…"

"More than that." He spread his hands, still hopeful. "I'm hoping to buy a new Jeep today, plus I've got to get to the car rental place and file an insurance claim. All of that would be a lot more enjoyable if you came with me."

"A new Jeep?" she asked. "Let me guess. Jeep Wrangler?"

Her response made him grin. "Yep. How'd you know?"

Now her expression stilled. Her gaze skittered away

before she raised her chin and looked at him again. "When I used to dream about our life together once we were married, I always pictured you driving a Jeep Wrangler. Silly, I know. But it just seemed to suit you."

Touched, he nodded, unsure if he should try to force words past the lump in his throat.

Luckily, Carly didn't seem to notice. "Anyway, I'd love to take a day off," she told him, drinking the last of her juice. "But I can't. I'd have to find someone to cover my shift and it's too short of a notice. Working with the littles in the NICU, it's imperative to have enough nurses on the floor."

Though disappointed, her response made him love her even more, if such a thing was possible. Carly had been born to be a pediatric nurse. Her caring, nurturing nature guaranteed she'd been good at it. "I understand. Is it all right if I use your car to take care of everything?"

"Ahh, now we get to the real reason you wanted me to take off." Her teasing tone let him know she didn't mean it. "But yes, you can use my car. Just don't let it—and you—get blown up." Though she smiled as she spoke, he could tell she was serious.

"I won't take my eyes off it," he promised. "I'll run my errands after I stand guard outside the hospital for a bit."

"Guard outside?"

"Yes. I want to see if anyone tries to mess with your car. If so, I can catch them red-handed."

With a sigh, she grimaced. "Be careful, okay?"

Touched by her concern, he promised he would.

He had her drive to work while he sat in the passenger seat, making no effort to hide. She parked in the covered parking garage. After turning off the ignition, she sat for a moment. "Now what?" she asked, checking her watch. "I can't be late."

He leaned over and kissed her cheek, inhaling the lightly floral scent of her. "Give me the keys. Then we'll both go inside."

"You will? I thought you were going to watch my car. How are you planning to do that?"

"Because after I go inside with you, I'll stand just inside the entrance. If someone is watching with the idea of planting another bomb, I'll see them."

She shivered. "I don't like that," she said, dropping the keys into his hands. "Do you really think that same person will do that again?"

"You never know," he replied. "It depends on how determined they are to get their target. Either me or you. You should be safe inside at work. And if anyone tries to mess with your vehicle, I'll catch them red-handed. I'll give it a few minutes. If nothing happens, I'll go talk to the police and the car rental agency, and maybe swing by the dealership. I'll be back in time to pick you up when your shift is over. Just don't go outside until I come get you."

Though she agreed, she grimaced, her expression troubled. "I don't like not feeling safe," she said. "And I hate having to worry about you, too."

He kissed her again, this time a gentle press of his lips on hers. "We'll all be fine," he promised with an assurance he didn't have to fake. "We've got Chicago PD, the

FBI and my friends in special forces working on this. It won't be long until this guy is caught."

Appearing unconvinced, she nodded and then got out of the car. "I've got to go. I don't want to be late."

He walked just inside the automatic doors with her, watching until she entered an elevator. From inside here, he had a clear view of her car and anyone who went near it.

Though he watched and waited for thirty minutes, nothing happened. Finally, he walked back outside and got into her vehicle. He couldn't help but brace himself as he started the ignition, half expecting to hear that familiar click before being blown to bits.

Instead, the engine started just fine. Glancing around him, he saw nothing out of the ordinary so he backed out of the parking spot and headed toward the car dealership he'd visited yesterday when they'd been closed.

Once he arrived, he parked and walked inside, pretending to inspect the vehicles on display in the showroom. Immediately, several salesmen appeared, talking quietly among themselves, their suits nearly identical in color and style. Finally, one man detached himself from the group and strolled over, smiling broadly. "Can I help you?" he asked. "I'm Johnnie."

"As a matter of fact, you can," Micha replied. "I'm interested in a Jeep Wrangler out on the lot." He led the man over to the one he'd chosen.

"Would you like to take it for a test drive?" Johnnie asked.

Micha declined. "I've driven them before." Instead, he asked the man to name his best price without doing the usual talk-to-my-manager dance. At first, Johnnie looked a bit startled, but then he grinned. "Give me a minute," he said, jotting down the inventory number and motioning to Micha to come inside with him.

Two hours later, Micha found himself the proud owner of the sweet black Wrangler. Johnnie told him he'd have it cleaned up and ready to go by Tuesday morning, but Micha insisted he needed it now and was willing to wait. He planned to leave Carly's car parked at the dealership until he could pick up Carly from work and swing back to get it. The lot had numerous cameras, so Micha figured that would be the safest option. And he'd be driving a vehicle that no one would associate with him.

"Now, huh?" Johnnie asked.

"Please." Micha grimaced. "I really need it immediately. Or as soon as you can get it to me."

With a shrug, Johnnie pointed toward the waiting area. "I'll put a rush on it. Might be an hour or two. There's coffee and snacks in there."

Micha sat down to wait. He figured he could use this time to handle the car rental agency and the insurance. Just after he got a cup of coffee and took a seat, his cell phone rang. After glancing at it, he went ahead and answered, even though he didn't recognize the number.

"This is Special Agent Brad Howard," the caller said. "Is this Micha Harrison?"

After Micha replied in the affirmative, Brad got down to the reason for his call. "We have more information on the car explosion. It was a highly sophisticated setup, usually practiced by those with military experience. Rigged to detonate the instant the engine came on."

"I suspected as much," Micha said. "I saw a lot of similar bombings when I was stationed in Afghanistan."

"Interesting background," Brad allowed. "Which, of course, we looked into. I'm sure you guessed we'd be checking on you."

"I'd have been disappointed if you hadn't."

"Could you provide us with a list of people who might hold a grudge against you?" Brad asked. "Even if some of the names seem improbable, they might be worth looking into."

Micha thought back to his time in special ops. "Any enemies I made were terrorists or people working against the USA. None of them would have had reason enough to hunt me down two years later. If someone had wanted to take me out, their best bet would have been during my extended hospital stay. I was in a coma for a long time."

"We'd still like you to compile a list," the special agent requested. "It never hurts to check all angles."

"I'll get you something by the end of the day," Micha promised. "Any news on the double homicide? The one that seemed similar to the elder Coltons' murders?"

After a moment of hesitation, Brad replied. "The victims were older males, both shot in the head. We believe their murders were the work of two gunmen with rifles. I've been tasked with investigating a serial killer possibility. So far, I'm still working on that."

Which meant he either had nothing, or he didn't want to tell Micha. Understandable.

"I'll save your number in my phone," Micha said. "Is it okay with you if I text the list? It's probably going to be really short, anyway."

"No problem. Let me know if you think of anything else."

After ending the call, Micha spent a few minutes trying to come up with names of anyone stateside who could hate him enough to want to kill him. He couldn't think of anyone. Maybe that guy Carly had been dating until Micha showed up again? But no, Carly had said her former boyfriend had willingly let her go. Which meant he clearly hadn't cared deeply for her.

Since he wasn't getting anywhere, Micha decided he might as well call the car rental agency and let them know what had happened to their car. The police had promised to email a police report, and since Micha had taken out insurance, he'd need to file a claim.

Dealing with all of that took a little more than an hour. After hanging up, Micha eyed the clock on the waiting room wall and decided to go search for Johnnie to see if he had an estimated wait time.

Just as he approached the salesman, Johnnie looked up and grinned. "We're all set," he proclaimed. "They're bringing around your new vehicle now."

Walking out front with Johnnie, Micha waited patiently while Johnnie went over all of his new vehicle's features. Finally, he accepted the keys and drove off in the Jeep, feeling confident that whoever had blown up the rental car wouldn't recognize him.

For now, he considered himself essentially invisible.

TROUBLED AND RESTLESS, Carly got busy immediately after signing on to her shift. For over a month now, she'd gone through her days with a vague sense of unease, starting after her father and uncle had been murdered. At first, she'd attributed all of that to grief. Then, when she'd begun to suspect someone was stalking her, she'd wondered if she'd gotten paranoid. The discovery of a video camera on her kitchen window and a car bomb blowing up Micha's rental car had definitely proved she wasn't, as well as upped the stakes. Another set of double murders, a possible serial killer on the loose in Chicago and the sudden return of a man she'd believed dead was enough to cause anyone to stumble.

Now that Micha had come back into her life, she not only feared for herself, but she also had him to worry about. Not to mention Bridget, her already well-loved dog, who could be hurt simply by being around Carly and Micha.

While she wasn't entirely sure, she'd venture a guess that since the bomb had been placed in his rental vehicle, Micha had been the target. Why, he seemed to have no idea, or so he claimed. Of course, considering the fact he'd kept so many secrets from her, she wouldn't put it past him to have more that he hadn't revealed yet. As in the reason he might have an enemy who wanted him dead.

Micha, handsome, strong Micha. A single look from

his velvety brown eyes still made her weak in the knees. Having him return to her life felt like a blessing—and a curse.

She hated not being able to trust him. And while she'd actually never stopped loving him, she wasn't sure they could ever have a future together without that. That thought made her heart hurt, so she shoved it aside and concentrated on the seriously ill children who needed her help.

By the time she neared the end of her shift, she sat and did the required charting. She texted Micha, letting him know she'd be out in a minute. He responded immediately, letting her know he was waiting by the side entrance, in a black Jeep Wrangler with the engine running.

Grinning despite herself, she hurried down. Outside, she spied Micha, waving from behind the wheel of the shiny new vehicle. Getting in, she breathed in that new-car smell and checked out the red leather interior. "Nice," she told him. "But where's my car?"

"I left it at the dealership," he explained. "They have security and all that. So we need to go collect it. I hope that's okay."

"Sure." Buckling her seat belt, she glanced at him, her heart quickening. "Did you get everything resolved with the car rental place?"

"I gave them all the information I had. Luckily, I took out their insurance policy, so it's fully covered. Someone from there is supposed to contact me soon."

Nodding, she allowed her eyes to drift closed as he drove, letting the cadence of the wheels on the pave-

ment soothe her. For a few minutes, she allowed herself
to pretend they were simply a regular couple who lived
a normal, quiet life without danger of violence.

Somehow, she must have fallen asleep because the
next thing she knew Micha had his hand on her shoulder, gently shaking her awake, and calling her name in
a soft voice.

Blinking, she sat up straight, looking around with
bleary eyes. "Oh," she said, realizing they were at the
Jeep dealership. "I need to get out, stretch my legs and
maybe down a cup of that notoriously awful auto dealership coffee before I get behind the wheel."

He followed her into the showroom, pointing her in
the direction of the waiting room. She made herself a cup
of coffee so thick she thought of it as sludge, managed
to choke down three sips before deciding she was ready.

"I'll follow you home," he said.

Relieved, she nodded. Even though she had her new
dog to alert her to any intruders, she really wasn't ready
to be alone just yet.

As she pulled into the driveway, she noticed Micha
had parked his new vehicle at the curb two houses down.
Waiting for him as he walked toward her, she admired
his athletic build and tried to decide if that was a wise
move or foolish.

"I know," he said as he reached her. "I had to weigh
the possibility of it being broken into versus the chance
of whoever attempted to blow us up wanting to try again.
I chose the lesser of two evils. At least if it's parked down
there, no one will know it's mine."

She eyed him. "Your logic makes sense, even if I

don't like it. This is one of those times that I really need to clean out that old garage behind my house. Maybe I can move some of the stuff that's in there into the storage shed."

He slung a casual arm across her shoulders. "I can help you with that," he said as they walked up the front porch.

As she turned her key in the front lock, Bridget barked a greeting. The instant she had the door open, the dog leaped on her, tail and behind wiggling with joy. Laughing, Carly got down on the floor with Bridget and gathered her close, petting her. When she finally climbed back to her feet, she brushed off the dog hair and grabbed the leash.

"I'll be right back," she told Micha, lurching forward as Bridget pulled her toward the back door.

When they returned, Carly headed straight for the kitchen with Bridget trotting along behind her. "Are you hungry, cutie pie?" she crooned. "Mama will get you your food."

Looking up, she realized Micha had taken a seat at the kitchen table and was grinning at her. With a shrug, she grinned back and filled the dog bowl with kibble. Once she'd placed it on the floor next to the water bowl, she eyed Micha. Damn, he looked good. Even at the end of a long, hard day. Or maybe *especially* at the end of the day.

"You might as well stay here," she said, crossing her arms and striving for casual.

Micha eyed her, his handsome face devoid of expression. "For tonight? Or…"

Amazingly, she felt her entire body heat. Flustered,

she shook her head. It wasn't like she'd just invited him to her bed, though she wouldn't deny that was in the back of her mind, too. "How about we play it by ear? At least until you find your own place. I don't see a reason why you should continue paying for the hotel room."

"I see." Gaze warm, he regarded her. "So long-term, then. Why, Carly?"

"I... I don't want to be alone," she admitted. "Plus, I am enjoying your company."

When he didn't respond, for one terrifying moment she thought he might say no. "I enjoy your company, too," he said softly, appearing to be considering his next words.

A loud knock on her door cut him off. They both went still, though Bridget immediately started barking. Carly muted the TV and looked at Micha.

"Should I answer it?" Carly asked, her voice trembling. She absolutely hated that she now felt unsafe in her own home.

"Do you have a peephole?" Micha asked, making his way toward the front entrance ahead of her. Since she did indeed have a peephole, he looked through it.

"Well?" she demanded when Micha simply continued to stare outside silently. "Who is it?"

"I think it might be your brother," he told her, stepping back. "It's been a while since I've seen him, but that guy really looks like Jones."

"Let me see." She took a quick look through her peephole, before unlocking the dead bolt. "Jones! What are you doing here?" She stepped aside, ushering him into the house, locking the door behind him. "Come on in."

After pulling her in for a quick hug, her brother grinned, his bright blue eyes full of mischief. "I came to make sure you're all right."

Had he heard about the car bomb? She eyed Jones, with his short dark hair and athletic build, deciding to stay quiet about that for now. The last thing she wanted to do was alarm her family.

"I'm fine," she said firmly.

"Good." Eyeing Micha, Jones held out his hand. "And I'm not going to lie. I wanted to see Micha. It's been two years, after all."

Jones had always liked Micha, and vice versa.

The two men shook. "It's been too long," Micha said.

"Yep. We've got a lot of catching up to do, for sure."

Carly motioned them toward the den. "Jones, can I get you something to drink?"

Her brother laughed and lifted up a paper bag. "I brought a few bottles of our newest beer for you both to try. Micha, I remember how much you enjoyed a good IPA."

"Your newest beer?" Micha asked. "What do you mean?"

Straightening, Jones beamed. "I own Lone Wolf Brewery. It's in West Loop. We only serve beer and a few quick bar snacks."

"It's really nice," Carly agreed. "Though the last time I was there, Jones was still working on getting it ready to open. Lots of space, and I'm guessing he's got it all fixed up now."

"I do." Jones beamed. "I purposely kept it small and intimate. We can hold around twenty people at the bar, and thirty more at tables in the general area. So far, it's exceeding my early expectations," Jones said with modest pride. He dropped down onto the couch and gestured at Micha to join him.

"I'd love to see it." Sitting, Micha accepted the beer Jones handed him. "Tell me about how you got started."

Watching the two men banter, Carly felt a warm glow of pleasure. She kept her distance, wanting to give them time to catch up. But Jones glanced up and shook his head. "Don't try to vanish into the kitchen. Come sit with us. Put up your feet and try my newest beer."

Slightly sheepish, Carly did as he asked. Instead of joining them on the couch, she took the armchair. Jones tilted his head but didn't comment as he handed her a can of beer.

Immediately, she jumped back to her feet. "Does anyone else want a glass?" When both men shook their heads, she practically dashed into the kitchen, beer can in hand.

"Do you think she's avoiding us?" she heard Jones ask.

"She's had a horrible few days," Micha replied. And then, to her horror, he told her brother all about the car explosion.

Stomach in knots, Carly poured her beer into a glass, squared her shoulders and made herself march back into her living room.

Jones's eyes narrowed. "Were you going to tell me about this at all, Carly?"

"Eventually." She glanced at Micha. "Now I don't have to."

Glancing from one to the other, Micha frowned. "Why am I getting the feeling I should have kept my mouth shut?"

Carly snorted.

"You shouldn't have," Jones said. "Clearly, someone has to look out for Carly."

"Ouch." Carly clenched her teeth. "Jones, you just got here. I planned to tell you eventually. I just want to ask you not to mention this to Heath or any of the rest of the family."

"You've got to be kidding me." Taking a long drink of his beer, Jones didn't bother to stifle his disbelief. "Carly, everyone has to be told. This is a clear danger. You never know who in the family might be next."

"Except we aren't sure who was the target," Micha pointed out. "The device was installed on my rental car, not Carly's vehicle. That would seem to make it likely that I was the intended victim, not her."

"Is that what the authorities think?" Jones asked.

"I believe so. The FBI asked me to provide a list of any known enemies."

Surprised, Carly eyed him. Again, he'd kept something important hidden from her. "Why didn't you tell me that?" she asked, carefully keeping her tone neutral. She couldn't help but wonder if he'd kept silent because he'd thought she might not need him to stay with her.

Micha shook his head. "I'd planned to get around to it tonight. We'd just started talking when Jones got here."

"Give the guy a break," Jones interjected in typical younger brother fashion. As the middle child in the family, Carly had often been stuck between Heath's firstborn bossiness and youngest Jones's teasing. "Come on, sis. Lighten up."

As Jones had known it would, his admonishment annoyed her. Refusing to give him the satisfaction of reacting, Carly shook her head and sent a jab of her own. "You act more and more like Heath every day."

Instead of being infuriated, Jones laughed. "Touché," he said. He looked from Carly to Micha and back again. "I'm having a little family get-together at the Lone Wolf on Friday at eight and I wanted to personally invite you both."

Carly's first instinct was to balk. She still wasn't sure she was ready to bring Micha around her family. Mostly because she knew when she did, her female cousins would immediately start planning the wedding.

Instead of responding, Carly took a sip of her beer. The light, slightly citrusy flavor made her smile. She drank again. "Jones, this is really good."

"Thanks." Expression serious, her brother glanced between her and Micha. "So are you both going to come?"

Micha simply watched her. She appreciated the way he allowed her to decide, rather than jumping in and agreeing to go.

"You know how pushy the cousins are," Carly said. "They already started as soon as I told them Micha was alive." She met Micha's gaze. "Are you prepared to deal with them acting as if we're having a wedding sometime soon?"

"Are *you*?" Micha shot back. "Prepared to deal with them, I mean? They're your family. I've never had a problem holding my own with them."

"Is that a challenge?" Jones teased. "Because it sure sounded like one to me."

"I can deal with them," Carly responded, again refusing to let her brother get under her skin. "What do you think, Micha? Would you like to go?"

Though it wasn't super obvious, the way Micha exhaled told her he'd released tension. "That sounds like fun."

She nodded, facing her brother. "That settles it. So yes, we'll be there."

About to push to his feet, Jones knocked a coaster on the floor. Both he and Micha reached for it at the same time, just as the front window shattered.

"Gunshots!" Micha said. "Everyone down on the floor."

Petrified, at first Carly didn't move.

"Now!" ordered Micha.

Immediately, Carly dropped to the rug. "What's happening?" she asked, shocked to realize Micha had a pistol.

"Someone shot out your front window," Jones muttered. His eyes widened as he caught sight of Micha, crouched low and moving toward the front door with his weapon drawn. "Damn, Micha. What the hell are you doing?"

Micha barely glanced at him. "I'm betting this was a drive-by. But I want to get outside in case the shooter comes back again. I'll take cover behind that huge tree out front."

Carly's first impulse was to argue, to try to dissuade him. But her brother reached out and squeezed her shoulder. "Don't," he murmured. "I have a feeling Micha knows what he's doing."

Reluctantly, she swallowed back her words, stomach clenched and chest hurting as she watched Micha open the front door and dash outside.

"Don't get up just yet," Jones warned. "If Micha is right, and there's a second drive-by, they'll go for anything that moves."

"But why?" Her anguished question didn't really require an answer.

Jones gave her one, anyway. "I don't know. Maybe whoever blew up the car is trying again. Micha is here, after all." He hugged her. "Carly, I don't like this. I don't think you should stay here any longer. I have room at my place."

Wide-eyed, she couldn't respond. Heck, she couldn't even think. As a matter of fact, delayed reaction had set in and she'd started to shake.

Seeing this, Jones scooted over and put his arm around her shoulders. "It's going to be all right," he said.

The sound of a motor revving had them both tensing up.

"It's coming back," Carly moaned, out of her mind with worry for Micha.

"That's not a car. It's a motorcycle." Still, Jones kept her down with his arm. "Stay still. Micha clearly knows how to defend himself. He was a soldier, for Pete's sake."

"Special forces," she corrected, almost automatically.

"Well, there you go."

They both listened, bracing themselves for more gunshots. The motorcycle revved again, getting louder as it approached.

Again, the sharp crack of gunfire. A few more, as Micha must have responded. The rest of her front window caved inward, glass shards flying.

Then the motorcycle was gone, roaring off down the street.

In the silence, Carly could barely breathe. Eyes glued to her front door, she counted to three, waiting for Micha to reappear.

When he didn't, she pushed to her feet, shrugging away from her brother.

Jones got up, too, his expression shaken. "What are you doing?" he demanded.

"I've got to find Micha and make sure he's all right." She couldn't lose him again, she just couldn't. In that moment, frozen in terror, how much she cared for him slammed into her.

"You're not going to lose him," Jones replied, making her realize she must have spoken out loud. Grabbing her arm, Jones put his face level with hers. "I'll go," he said. "Mom would never forgive me if I allowed you to get hurt."

Dizzy, all Carly could do was nod. "I can't lose you, either," she said. "Please, Jones. Stay safe."

As her brother started for the foyer, she sank back down to the floor, barely registering the spray of glass all over her carpet and furniture. Bridget whined from somewhere in the kitchen and Carly began to crawl toward her, needing to make sure her pet hadn't been hurt.

Just then the front door opened, and Micha stepped inside. His grim expression revealed nothing. "Call 911," he told Carly.

Chapter Eight

Carly froze, all the blood draining from her face as she stared at him. Concerned, Micha started for her. "Are you hurt?" he rasped, his chest tight at the thought of something, anything, having happened to her.

"N-n-no," she stammered, her wide-eyed gaze sweeping over him. "I'm okay. What about you? That looks like blood on your arm."

Glancing at himself, Micha cursed as he realized she was right. Of course, the instant he noticed it, the damn thing started hurting. "Must be a flesh wound," he said. "Do you have a clean rag or something I can use to stop the bleeding?"

Jones rushed into the kitchen, glass crunching underfoot, and returned with a dish towel. "Here you go," he said, handing it to Micha. "I hope you don't mind," he told Carly. "It's all I could find."

Though it wasn't long enough to tie a proper tourniquet, Micha tried to make due. His arm now throbbed like hell and he at least needed to stop the bleeding.

Seeing the problem, Carly hurried into her linen closet, removed an old but clean sheet and tried to tear it. Failing that, she grabbed a pair of scissors and cut a long and wide strip, which she folded over to make it thicker. "Let me," she said, wrapping it around his arm. "Leave the dish towel in place, but this should work until we can get your arm checked out."

"It's just a flesh wound," he started to protest, but then he noticed how her hands shook and held his tongue.

The instant she'd finished, she swayed and stumbled as if she might fall. Instinctively, he reached for her, wincing as he tried to use his injured arm. Jones noticed and rushed over and helped his sister to the sofa. "Sit," he ordered. "Are you all right? You look awfully pale."

She stared up at him and grimaced. "I don't know," she replied. "I feel really weird." Her gaze became unfocused, though she remained conscious and sitting up. Micha dropped down on the couch next to her and put his arm around her while exchanging a worried glance with her brother.

"I think you might be in shock," Jones said. "Let me get you some water."

More glass crunched underfoot as he got a glass of water and brought it to her. Murmuring a thank-you, she accepted it and took a sip. Keeping one arm around her shoulders, Micha reached in his pocket for his phone, but it wasn't there. Which meant it must have fallen out at some point, likely when he'd been crawling toward the door. Damn it. He needed to find it, but not right now. Carly was his main concern.

"We need to call 911," he said. "Chicago PD is supposed to be doing increased patrols, but they clearly missed this. I want to have Carly looked at."

She opened her eyes. "You need to have your arm checked out first," she said, squirming out from under his arm. "I'm fine. Why don't you go ahead and call them?"

"I need to find my phone first." Micha pushed to his feet and started to search. "It has to be somewhere between here and that big oak tree," he said. "I didn't go anywhere else."

Jones began to help him. "Did you get a glimpse of the shooter?" he asked.

"No. He was wearing a helmet. I squeezed off a couple of shots, but he went by really fast and I wasn't entirely prepared. I'm not sure if I hit him or not."

"I'm calling the police now," Carly said. Though still appearing dazed, she dialed 911 and told the dispatcher what had happened. When she ended the call, she informed them in a shaky voice that the woman promised to send a squad car out immediately. Some of the color had returned to her face and she seemed to be breathing better.

Nodding, Micha continued his search for his phone.

"Here it is," Jones said, pulling it out from under a decorative table near the front door. "It must have fallen from your pocket during all that insanity earlier."

Thanking the other man, Micha did a quick inspection to make sure there'd been no damage. Once he'd ascertained everything was fine, he slid the phone back into his pocket.

In the distance, they could all hear the sirens, which meant the police would be here soon.

"Well," Jones said, dusting his hands off on his

jeans. "I guess we still can't really tell who the shooter was after."

"He shot up *my* house," Carly protested.

"But Micha was inside," Jones replied. "So he could have been after either one of you."

"What about you?" Carly took another long sip of her water. "Is it possible someone might be after our entire family?"

Jones shrugged, appearing unconcerned. "Anything is possible," he conceded. "But since I haven't had any threats or anything, I think we can rule that out." Eyeing Carly, he frowned. "Speaking of that, I need to call Heath and fill him in."

Outside, the sirens cut off, though the flash of blue and red lights announced the arrival of the police. A sharp knock on the front door had Micha hurrying to answer it.

Bridget barked twice, then took off for the bedroom, tail tucked between her legs, presumably to take shelter under Carly's bed.

Micha opened the door. There were two patrol cars and four officers. Two of them used flashlights to check the outside. The other two came in and inspected the damage, shaking their heads at the broken glass.

"You're the guy whose car exploded, right?" one of the policemen asked. "I wasn't on duty then, but I sure heard about it. That would have been a hell of a way to die."

Thinking back to some of the things he'd seen in Afghanistan, Micha agreed.

Carly, Micha and Jones all gave their statements,

which were duly recorded. Once Jones had made certain nothing else was needed from him, he slipped out to his vehicle to call Heath.

After making sure her dog was safe in her bedroom, Carly closed that door to keep her in there and then got out a broom and began sweeping up the broken glass. "I'm glad Bridget didn't cut her feet," she said to no one in particular.

The two outside officers returned, apparently having finished up. "We're going to speak with your neighbors in case anyone had a video camera. If we learn anything, someone will keep you posted."

Micha crossed his arms. "Just like someone was supposed to beef up patrols on this street after the car bomb?"

The older officer stared him down, though the younger one blinked. "We can check into that, if you'd like. Hyde Park patrols are usually pretty routine, so I'm thinking they would be able to swing by here once or twice per shift."

"What about your arm?" Carly asked, pointing to his makeshift bandage. "He needs to have that checked out."

"Were you shot?" Getting out his radio, one of the cops appeared ready to call for an EMT.

"It's okay." Micha held up his hand to forestall him. "A bullet just grazed my arm. No need to call anyone. Once I clean and bandage it, I'll be fine. It's just a matter of getting the proper supplies."

The youngest officer appeared unconvinced. He blinked and pushed his wire-rimmed glasses higher up his nose. "Maybe we should have someone look at it, just in case."

"No need," Micha insisted. "I had much worse injuries over in Afghanistan. I'm good."

"Oh, you're a veteran. Well, then I guess you'd know." Reluctantly, the cop nodded.

Micha glanced over at Carly, half expecting her to protest, but she didn't. Her gaze had once again gone hazy and unfocused and she appeared lost in her own thoughts. He ached to go to her and hold her, to chase away the shadows in her expression. She didn't deserve this, no one did, but especially not Carly. How anyone could target such a beautiful, gentle soul was beyond him.

Which made the idea of him being the target here instead of her much more plausible. Which meant he needed to seriously try to figure out a short list of his enemies. But he honestly couldn't think of anyone who hated him enough to want him dead.

Once the police had gone, Carly stirred. "I need to clean up this mess," she said. "I don't want Bridget cutting her feet." Moving slowly and stiffly, she retrieved a broom and a dustpan from her laundry room.

Micha took the broom from her as she walked by him. She didn't resist at all, and he considered asking her to sit back down and leave the cleanup to him but figured keeping her busy might help more.

"Let me clear this out," he said, using the broom handle to bust out the remaining pieces of glass from the window frame. Then he swept and she held the dustpan. Working as a team, she dumped the shards into the kitchen trash can. Once they'd finished the floor, she got out her vacuum and went over the entire area to make sure she hadn't missed any. She turned it off and methodically rewound the cord. "I wouldn't want to take the chance of Bridget cutting her feet," she said, repeating herself, her voice devoid of inflection.

"Are you all right?" he asked, concerned.

She looked up, focusing on him, and grimaced. "You know what? I'm not. Not really. I'm trying really hard to get there, though."

Taking the vacuum from her, Micha urged her to sit, either in the armchair or at the kitchen table. The fact that she nodded and shuffled off to do as he'd asked alarmed him. He'd speak to Jones and see if they could get her to agree to get checked out at the hospital.

Quickly, he used the hose to do the couch. He knew for certain more than a few glass shards had made it there. Then he went to check on Carly. Jones still hadn't returned from his outside phone call. He'd been gone so long that Micha began to wonder if the younger man had left.

Micha debated going in search of Jones, but Carly mattered more. He found her sitting at the kitchen table, staring straight ahead, both hands wrapped around her water glass. She glanced up when he entered, her lips parted. "Hey," she said, greeting him softly.

His chest squeezed. "Hey," he responded in kind, going to her and carefully wrapping his arms around her from behind. "It's going to be all right," he promised, breathing in the slightly floral scent of her hair.

"Is it?" she asked, leaning back into him. "I just don't

understand how someone can do such horrible things. Or why."

"Agreed." He lightly kissed her cheek, allowing himself to linger. "We have to believe that sooner or later whoever is doing this will make a mistake and be caught."

"Carly?" Jones's voice as he came through the back door into the kitchen, still on his phone. He glanced curiously from one to the other. "Carly, Heath wants to talk to you."

Carly barely managed to stifle a groan. Micha released her and Jones handed her the phone. She took a deep breath, pressed the speaker button and placed the phone on the table in front of her.

"Heath, the last thing I need right now is a lecture," Carly said, apparently having decided to go on attack first. "It's been a crazy few days. I'm exhausted and terrified. And none of this is my fault." She took a deep breath.

"I get all of that," Heath responded, his voice surprisingly gentle. "None of this is your fault, it is crazy and I can imagine how awful you must feel. But I'm your older brother. It's my job to be worried about you. I'm glad Jones was there."

"And Micha," she pointed out, her gaze sliding over to him. While he felt kind of awkward, listening in to the conversation, Carly clearly wanted him to hear. "By the way, I've got you on speaker."

After a second or two of completely awkward silence, Heath cleared his throat. "Why?"

"Because I'm tired," Carly replied. "And I know you

have good intentions, but in this situation, there's absolutely nothing you can do to help."

"I can call Chicago PD and demand more patrols."

"Micha's already done that," Carly shot back.

"What about the FBI? I have contacts there since I've been dealing with the agents who are investigating the possible serial killings." Before Carly could respond, Heath sighed. "Let me guess. Micha's already done that."

Micha decided to speak up. "Hey, Heath. How's it going?"

Instead of responding in kind, Heath went quiet again. "Micha, I need to know something. How much of all this is happening due to you hanging around my sister?"

"I don't know." All Micha could do was give Heath the truth. "We still haven't figured out if I'm the target or if it's Carly."

"Maybe you two should consider splitting up for safety's sake." The hard edge to Heath's voice told Micha that he meant business. But the notion—even thinking about going away and not seeing Carly for a protracted period of time—felt like a knife in the gut. Plus, who would protect her if he was gone?

But still, he hesitated. Possibly Heath was right. Perhaps being around Carly wasn't the best thing right now for her safety. Except…what if he left her alone and she turned out to be the actual target? He needed to stay with her, if only to protect her. While he knew Heath wouldn't understand in a million years, Micha wouldn't even want to live anymore if something happened to Carly.

To Micha's relief, Carly shook her head. "No splitting

up. That's not going to happen," she said, her tone firm. "I just got him back, almost from the dead. I can't send him away so soon. Plus, I feel safer with Micha around."

Her words had him going to her and slipping his arm around her shoulders. He could feel her tension as she waited for Heath to argue. Jones wisely stayed out of it, leaning on the door frame silently in the background watching, while sipping on another one of his beers.

"Well, I guess that's your choice," Heath finally said, which made Carly glance up at Micha, her surprise plain on her face. "But, Carly, I wanted to offer you another choice. Come stay with me. Or even Jones. Clearly someone has targeted your home. You can't tell me you believe you could be safe there any longer, not until this person or people are caught."

Jones finally spoke up. "He's right, Carly. You've got to stay somewhere else for a little bit." He eyed Micha. "How about Micha's place?"

"No, that won't work," Carly answered. Micha silently thanked her for not telling her brothers that he'd been living in a hotel. "I have a dog now. And I don't like the idea of someone driving me out of my own home."

"I don't like the idea of someone killing you, either," Heath said, his tone dry.

Micha decided he'd heard enough. "Look, I understand your concern. I'm right there with you. But if Carly wants to stay in her own home, she should. I'll be here with her. I have a gun and I know how to use it. I give you my word that I'll protect her, no matter what. Even with my own life, if it comes to that."

Carly gasped. "Don't talk like that," she admonished

Micha before turning her attention back to the phone. "Heath, I'm twenty-nine years old and a responsible adult. I promise you that I'll be careful. I won't go anywhere alone. When I'm not at work, I'll be with Micha."

"Plus, the police are on it," Micha interjected. "And the FBI is also involved. They should catch this guy soon."

"I still don't like it," Heath grumbled. "Though I can see I don't have a choice."

"You don't." Carly spoke firmly. "I'll see you Friday at Lone Wolf, okay?"

"Fine. I assume you're bringing Micha?"

"Of course," she answered.

Of course. Micha allowed himself a second to bask in that phrase.

"Good." An undercurrent of warning colored Heath's voice. "Micha, you and I will talk then." And he ended the call.

"That sounded like a threat," Jones said, strolling into the room. "Proof positive how rattled big brother is."

"I'm rattled, too," Carly said, her tone sharp. "Aren't you?"

"Yes, I am." Jones shook his head. "We need to get some plywood and cover this window. Carly, do you have any?"

"Plywood?" She shrugged. "I doubt it. But who knows? The previous owner never emptied the storage shed, so there might be some there. And my garage is full, too. I've never gotten around to cleaning it out, though I definitely plan to before winter gets here."

"Let's go take a look," Jones suggested.

Carly grabbed her flashlight. "Let me check on Bridget," she said. Despite Carly calling her, Bridget refused to leave the bedroom, clearly still terrified. Micha suspected Carly would have to do quite a bit of coddling before she could coax the dog out.

Finally, with Carly leading the way, all three of them went outside to look for plywood or something they could use to board up the window temporarily.

Inside the shed, they found several full sheets of plywood, though most of them were either warped or had split. Micha and Jones chose the best one out of the stack. "This will be large enough to entirely cover that window," Micha said.

"Agreed." Jones looked at Carly. "Do you have a hammer and some nails?"

"Yes. They're in the garage," she replied.

With the two men carrying the plywood between them, they headed back toward the house. They made a quick pit stop at the garage, where the sheer amount of stuff Carly had crammed in there made Micha wince.

Carly turned on the light, rummaged around for a moment, and then emerged with a hammer and a box of nails. "I knew I had some," she said.

Working together, Micha and Jones made short work of nailing the plywood over the broken window. "That should work until you can call the glass repair company in the morning," Jones said.

"Thanks." Carly sighed. "I'm also going to contact an alarm company. Besides an alarm, I might look into having cameras installed on the outside of the house."

Jones hugged her. "I think that's an excellent idea. I'm

going home now." He glanced at Micha. "Micha, would you mind walking out with me? I'd like to have a word."

When Carly made as if she intended to follow, Jones shook his head. "In private," he said. "Why don't you go work on seeing if you can get your dog to come out? Poor thing is going to need some heavy reassurance."

Carly frowned. "Jones, is this really necessary? Heath has already said enough. I really don't need you to make things worse."

"Please. I'm not Heath," Jones replied, his tone mildly offended. "I have no intention of chewing Micha out. I just want to have a private word with him."

Considering, Carly finally nodded. She turned away without another word, apparently heading toward her bedroom to check on Bridget.

Jones and Micha headed outside. The neighborhood had fallen peaceful once more, everyone tucked safely inside their houses.

When they reached Jones's vehicle, Jones turned. "Do you love my sister?" he asked.

Micha didn't hesitate. "Yes. Of course I do."

As if he'd expected that answer, Jones nodded. "Then I strongly suggest you do what you can to get her to go somewhere safe until this is over. With or without you." Then Jones got into his car and started it, driving away without waiting for Micha's response.

AFTER STOPPING BY the kitchen to grab a handful of dog treats, Carly walked quietly into her bedroom. She could see the shine of Bridget's eyes from her spot under the bed. Carly sat down on the floor, making no move toward the still-terrified animal, and simply began to speak softly to her. She repeated the same words and phrases, even though the dog most likely didn't understand them, telling her over and over again that she was safe, she was loved and everything would be all right.

She placed a dog treat in the space between her and the bed, where Bridget could see it, and continued talking. Eventually, as Carly had expected she might, the dog inched closer, her nose twitching.

Careful not to make any sudden moves, Carly placed another dog treat on the floor, closer to her this time. After Bridget scarfed down the first one, she came all the way out from under the bed, got the second and crawled into Carly's lap.

Carly gathered her close, still crooning, and stroked her silky fur. At first, the dog trembled, but eventually even that stopped.

The front door opened, which meant Micha had returned from his chat with her younger brother. At the sound, Bridget stiffened and raised her head. "It's just Micha," Carly told her, hoping her new pet understood. When the dog gave a quick thump of her tail, Carly thought she might.

When Micha appeared in the doorway, Bridget let out a low woof. More of a greeting than a warning. Micha got down on his haunches and Bridget wiggled her way over to him on her belly. "Such a good girl," he said, scratching Bridget behind the ears. He glanced at Carly over the dog's head. "Still okay?"

She nodded. "Still okay."

"Do you need help getting up?"

"No, I'm good." Though she felt stiff, Carly climbed to her feet. "Is everything all right with you and Jones?"

"Sure." Micha rose, too, beckoning her to follow. "He didn't read me the riot act, if that's what you're asking. He just asked me to try to talk you into staying somewhere else until this mess is figured out. Which you have to admit does make sense."

They'd reached the kitchen. Bridget went immediately for her water bowl. Carly eyed Micha, trying to think. "Both the car exploding and having my house shot at are terrifying," she admitted. "But I hate to let some crazy person drive me out of my own home. Plus, where would I go? I don't want to stay with Heath or Jones. You live in a hotel. And my dog needs an outdoor space like I have here."

"I could rent a place," he offered, dragging his hands through his longish, wavy brown hair. Two years ago, he'd worn it short, in a military cut. She liked it better this way, she thought. The longer cut made him look sexy, almost roguish. More like a pirate than a soldier. Though bad boys had never been her type, Micha made her want to change her mind.

Mouth dry, she tried to force her thoughts back on track. "Rent a place?"

"One of the ones we were going to go look at," he continued. "That way you'd still be close to work."

Leaning against her kitchen counter, she crossed her arms. "And then what happens if this crazy person finds us again? If he's staking out my job, all he has to do is follow us. Once he knows about your new Jeep, that could be a target, too. We'd have to keep moving, which isn't possible right now. I have a job I love, my first dog and family here. This is our home. We can't keep living our lives on the run."

She caught her breath as she realized she'd said *us* and *we* and *our* rather than simply herself. She'd included him in her future, as if she already decided he'd be there. The realization made her stomach do a somersault.

If Micha noticed he gave no sign. "That's a valid point," he agreed. "Still, until they catch this guy, there's got to be something we can do."

"Precautionary measures?" She was good at those, mostly because she had to be as a nurse. "I've already started on some. As I said, I'm planning on hiring an alarm company to put in a monitored alarm with outside video cameras. Tomorrow I'll call a glass company and get that window replaced. And I'll get that garage cleaned out on my next day off, so we can park our vehicles inside."

Gaze serious, he studied her. Her heart skipped a beat at the heat in his eyes. "Are you sure you want me hanging around? What if this person is after me instead of you? My presence here will only endanger your life."

All this back and forth exhausted her. He needed to take a stance and stick with it. "I'll leave that up to you," she finally told him. "If you don't want to face this as a team, I get it. If you go, I can handle it." She lifted her chin. "I'm used to being on my own."

"Ouch." He winced. "I'd never forgive myself if something happened to you because of me."

"Then you have quite the conundrum," she drawled, refusing to give in to the sudden, sharp urge to beg him to stay. Never again, not after he'd disappeared and allowed her to believe him dead. She still couldn't wrap her head around his decision not to make contact. If the situation had been reversed, she would have moved heaven and earth to make her way back to his side.

That was what hurt more than anything.

Some of her thoughts must have shown in her face. He crossed to her, placing his hand gently under her chin. "I'm not leaving you," he declared, right before he kissed her.

More relieved than she cared to admit, even to herself, she kissed him back. By the time they broke apart, she could hardly think straight.

"Come," he said, taking her hand and leading her into the bedroom.

Carly only got up once for the rest of the night—to take Bridget out. She finally fell asleep, wrapped in Micha's strong arms, feeling safe and extremely well loved.

Carly's cousin Simone called early the next morning as Carly had just gotten her first cup of coffee and filled Bridget's bowl with kibble. Taking a deep breath before she answered, Carly wondered if Heath had already notified the entire family about what had been going on with her and Micha. But if Simone knew, she didn't bring it up. Instead, she wanted to talk about finding their fathers' killers.

"Since classes are out for the summer, I'm planning to dedicate all of my time to this," Simone declared. "January is too busy with work, so I thought I'd ask you if you wanted to help."

"Help with what?" Carly asked, resisting the urge

to mention that she also had a full-time job. While she might have today off, she always had a lot to do in her limited leisure time. Especially today.

"Well," Simone said. "Clearly the police aren't making the case their top priority. Now that we know it's likely the work of serial killers—"

"The FBI is taking the lead," Carly interrupted. "At least, that's what I've been told."

"Either way, no one but family has as deep of an interest in catching the murderer," Simone continued, unfazed. "I've been doing a lot of research on serial killers. It's a fascinating subject. I had no idea."

Carly made a noncommittal sound, aware Simone didn't really require a response. Among family, Simone had always been the one who loved to research whatever happened to be her interest at the moment. Right now, that appeared to be serial killers.

"Do you want to meet up for coffee in an hour and talk more about it?" Simone asked. How she knew Carly had the day off, Carly wasn't sure.

Glancing at the clock, Carly sighed. "I can't. I have a ton to do today. In fact, I need to let you go so I can finish getting ready."

Micha walked into the kitchen just then, barefoot and shirtless, with his faded jeans riding low on his hips. Carly completely lost her train of thought. Apparently oblivious, Micha strolled over and kissed her cheek. "Good morning," he murmured, his raspy before-coffee voice sexy as hell as he moved past her.

"Who's that?" Simone chirped. "Is that Micha? Did he spend the night at your place?"

"Yes," Carly replied. "Sorry, Simone. I've got to run." Heart pounding, she quickly ended the call.

Admiring Micha's backside while he made himself a cup of coffee, she knew she needed to finish her morning preparations, but she couldn't make her legs move. Usually, she preferred to start her days off enjoying a leisurely coffee on her back patio but all she could think of at this moment was how to lure Micha back to bed.

"Who was that?" Micha asked, turning to face her, holding his mug with both hands. As he raised it to his mouth to take a sip, she caught her breath, unable to tear her gaze away.

"That was Simone," she replied, pushing the words out past her suddenly parched throat. To cover, she drank some of her coffee and picked up Bridget's now-empty food bowl.

"Ah. I'm guessing Heath has already told everyone about the explosion and the gunshots?"

"That's what's so weird," she said. "Simone didn't mention any of that. Instead, she wanted to talk about investigating our fathers' murders. She's really into research and she's been learning about serial killers and what makes them tick."

Bridget scratched at the back door, whining to indicate she needed to go out. Glad of the distraction, Carly took her dog out, bringing her coffee with her. Once outside, she breathed in the fresh morning air while she watched Bridget explore the backyard. She hadn't known she'd love her dog so deeply or so quickly.

How the hell Micha could still affect her so strongly, especially since they'd spent the night wrapped in each other's arms, she didn't understand. She wasn't sure she even wanted to.

The back door squeaked, alerting her to the fact that he'd joined her outside. "Nice morning," he said, sounding a bit more normal now that he'd had a few sips of coffee.

"It is." She tried hard to sound normal, too, as if her heart wasn't racing and her skin prickling with the awareness of him.

"I'm thinking of giving up my hotel room today," he said. "Assuming you still want me to stay here with you."

"I do," she replied, even though living together was a huge step. Deciding to qualify that, she turned to face him. "At least until the danger is over."

Micha kissed her cheek. "At least until then," he agreed. "Would you mind giving me my own key?"

She hid her smile. "Of course I don't mind. Roomie." Because she was determined that was all they'd ever be—roommates. She couldn't risk having her heart broken by him ever again.

Chapter Nine

Micha dressed carefully for the Colton get-together at Lone Wolf Brewery. He figured Carly's entire family would be scrutinizing his every move. Even though she'd tried to play off her asking him to move in with her as strictly a safety thing, they both knew better. She might try to pass him off as just a roommate, but he knew none of the Coltons would look at it that way. He remembered how they'd scrutinized him when he and Carly had gotten engaged. He was pretty sure Heath had even run a background check on him. Actually, Micha couldn't really blame them. Carly was pretty damn special. It made perfect sense they'd want to make sure the person she chose to share her life with was on the up-and-up.

After the two-year absence, despite what had happened to him, he imagined the scrutiny would be even more intense. Eager to prove to them he would be there for her from now on, he was ready for whatever they dished out. He welcomed it even.

Even Jones, who'd always seemed low-key to Micha, had delivered a brotherly warning. Micha expected no less from the rest of the Colton clan.

Beyond that, he really was looking forward to touring the Lone Wolf Brewery. The idea of crafting and distributing beer interested him. He had to give props to Jones for following his passion.

"What do you think?" Carly asked, emerging from the bathroom wearing a formfitting black dress and sky-high heels. She wore her long blond hair down, a silky curtain swirling around her shoulders.

Stunned, he could only stare for a moment, his entire body zinging with desire. "You take my breath away," he told her. "Now all I can think about is how badly I want to get that dress off you."

She grinned, her bright blue eyes dancing. "Thanks. You don't look too bad yourself. I like your jeans. And that button-down shirt looks great on you."

Ridiculously relieved, he thanked her. Though he'd met and interacted with her entire family numerous times in the past, he felt as if he were meeting them for the first time again.

They took his new Jeep to West Loop. To Micha's surprise, Lone Wolf Brewery was housed in quite a large building with ample parking. A large sign proclaimed the establishment was closed that evening for a private party. "Wow," Micha commented. "This is not at all what I expected."

Carly gave him a curious glance. "What did you expect exactly?"

"I don't know. Something smaller. More on the scale of a first-time brew pub owner."

This made her laugh. "Right. We're Coltons. We don't do anything halfway."

She had a point. The family business—Colton Connections—was well-known in the entire Chicago area. It made sense that when any of the Colton offspring decided to start their own ventures, they'd be done with finesse and flair.

As they walked toward the entrance from the parking lot, Heath came out the back door and intercepted them. "Glad I caught you," he said, sparing Micha a single hard glance. "Carly, I haven't said anything to the family about the car bomb or the shooting. Jones hasn't, either. Let's keep that quiet for now. I don't want to worry Mom, okay?"

"Sure." Carly nodded. She squeezed Micha's hand. "She's got enough to stress about, so that's perfectly fine with me."

"Good." Opening the door, Heath motioned them to go past him.

"Where's Kylie?" Carly asked.

For a moment, Heath's hard gaze softened. "She'll be joining us later. She had a few things she wanted to do at work first."

"Kylie is Heath's fiancée," Carly told Micha. "They met at Colton Connections. She's one of the VPs working for Heath." She flashed a mischievous grin. "It was a workplace romance."

Heath rolled his eyes and strode away without responding.

Watching him go, Carly tugged on Micha's arm. "Just ignore him. I'm guessing he's got something else on his mind."

Micha nodded. Inside, he took his time and looked

around, pleasantly surprised again. The decor, while rustic, also managed to look hip. There was lots of dark wood and metal, with numerous large beer tanks located behind the bar. On the wall, a large sign hung with the Lone Wolf label—a gray, smiling wolf's head on a bright red background.

"Nice," Micha said, turning a slow circle to take it all in. Not huge, but not overly small, either. And he spotted a red exit sign, indicating the emergency exit, and made a mental note. Always good to know.

"Thanks." Jones appeared, smiling from ear to ear. "Come. Let me give you both a private tour of the place. We'll be doing a beer sampling later and then I have a big announcement for us all to celebrate."

His enthusiasm had Carly grinning, too. "Sounds perfect," she said. "I really like what you've done with the decor."

"I had help with that," Jones replied. "Tatum did most of it. You know how well she's done with her restaurant. She took one look around and knew exactly how to decorate this place."

"You remember my cousin Tatum, don't you?" Carly asked Micha. "She owns a wildly successful restaurant called True. Not only that, but she's also the chef."

"We'll have to go there sometime," Micha said.

"You bet we will." Carly glanced around. "Where's the rest of the family? We ran into Heath on the way in but haven't seen anyone else."

Jones shrugged. "Heath has been running in and out. You know how he is. And everyone else hasn't arrived yet. You are a bit early, aren't you?"

"You said seven, right?" Carly checked her watch. "It's five after."

"Actually, I said eight." Jones smiled to take the sting from his words. "But that's okay. You two can be the first to have a private tour. I've got my waitstaff setting things up in the kitchen, so let me show you where the main magic happens."

"Main magic?" Carly frowned. "What do you mean?"

"Where we make the beer!" Jones practically jumped up and down with excitement. "It's a detailed process, so I'll have to explain every step of it to you."

"Maybe you should wait for everyone else so you only have to go over it once," Carly pointed out. Though Jones appeared surprised by the notion, Micha had to admit it made sense. Even if he secretly wanted to see it all right now.

Plus, a tour with everyone would definitely keep the rest of the Coltons from focusing so much on him.

"What about you?" Jones asked Micha, clearly disappointed. "Would you like a quick look around before everyone else arrives?"

Micha shrugged. "Sure, why not. I'd really like to. We'll see it again with the others, too."

The door opened just as Jones was about to lead them off. Carly's mom and her aunt strolled in arm in arm. "I see we're not the only early ones," Fallon trilled. Meanwhile, Carly's mom had stopped short, her gaze locking on Micha.

"So it *is* true," Farrah said. "You *are* alive."

"Yes, ma'am." Micha flashed her a smile. "Luckily so."

She moved closer, a still-beautiful woman who carried herself as if she knew it. She walked right up to Micha, ignoring her daughter. "Where were you?" she demanded. "Two whole years went by with Carly thinking you were dead. If you only knew how much she suffered."

"Not now, Mom," Carly protested. "We can have this discussion later."

"It's all right," Micha reassured her. "I don't mind." Speaking quietly, he explained about being taken prisoner, the rescue mission six months later that had gone wrong, the crash, the injuries, the coma, all of it. By the time he'd finished Farrah Colton had tears in her eyes.

"Oh, you poor man," Farrah said, hugging him. "I'm so sorry all that happened to you. Carly did mention it, but she must have glossed over the details. It sounds much more horrible coming from you."

Not sure how to respond to that, Micha simply nodded. Carly squeezed his arm, commiserating silently with him.

The door opened again. "Everyone must have decided to come early," Carly murmured. January and a man walked in holding hands, with Tatum and another man right behind. "The one with January is Sean," Carly said. "And Tatum's beau is Cruz. The two men have a lot in common since they both work for the Chicago Police Department. Sean is in Homicide and Cruz is in Narcotics."

This info had Micha eyeing the two newcomers with renewed interest. "I wonder if they know my buddy Charlie."

"I guess you can ask them. Though Chicago has a huge police force, you never know."

"Are they working on the murder investigation with the FBI?" he asked.

"I'm not sure," Carly responded. "Heath is the point person on all of that. He just passes the info on to the rest of us. Though now that Simone has gotten obsessed with the case, she probably knows more than even Heath."

"Simone..." Micha tried to remember. "Isn't she the college professor?"

"Yep. Psychology. When she decides to investigate something, she really dives into her research."

Micha looked around, trying to see if he could spot her.

"She's not here yet," Carly said. "She's always punctual, so she should be here closer to eight."

Rolling his shoulders, Micha gave himself a mental order to relax. Before being taken prisoner, he'd enjoyed social gatherings. He'd considered himself outgoing and got along easily with all types of people.

Since then, that part of him had changed. Though he knew he didn't have to, the second he entered a room he made a mental note to locate the exit, as he'd done here. He constantly checked over his shoulder, tried not to let anyone come up unexpectedly behind him and held a lot more of himself in reserve.

Jones moved among his family, pointing out a fantastic spread of appetizers and samples of beer that had been arranged on the bar.

The door opened and a woman who had to be Carly's cousin Simone arrived. Slim, with chin-length brown hair and the same piercing blue eyes as the rest of the Coltons, she carried herself with a kind of quiet dignity.

Her face lit up when she spied Carly and Micha and she made a beeline for them.

Bestowing a quick hug on Micha, she stepped back and studied him. "I'm so sorry for everything you went through," she said quietly. "I'm so glad you found your way back to us."

"Thank you." He could hardly talk past the sudden ache in his throat. "I really appreciate that."

Smiling, she dipped her chin before turning to Carly. "I heard Heath is planning to update us on the investigation into our fathers' murders. I've tried my best to find out what he knows, but he isn't telling." She dug in her oversize tote bag and removed an old-fashioned spiral notebook. "I've made a lot of notes."

Carly nodded. "Maybe we can look at them later," she said. "Right now we all need to focus our attention on Jones and his wonderful establishment."

"Of course." Simone slid her notebook back into her bag. "I'll touch base with you later." And she headed off to greet the rest of the family.

"I just dodged a bullet," Carly murmured. "There's no way I care to learn everything she's discovered about serial killers. Especially not the gory details of their methods."

"I don't know," Micha teased. "It sounds interesting. You might like it."

Shaking her head, she elbowed him in the side. He grinned at her and took another drink of his beer.

Everyone stood around, beers in hand, chatting and

sampling the appetizers that Jones had put out. Though Heath moved confidently among the little groups of his family members, Micha noticed Heath spent an inordinate amount of time watching the front door.

When a slender, dark-haired woman walked through, Heath's expression lit up. She'd barely taken a few steps inside when Heath met her halfway, sweeping her up into his arms and kissing her as if he hadn't seen her in days.

"PDA, ugh," Carly commented, though she was smiling. "I've never seen my older brother so happy. It's amazing."

Micha put his arm around her shoulders and drew her close. "Hopefully, they'll be saying the same thing about you," he said, waiting for her to stiffen.

Instead, she relaxed against him. "I know I should say something sarcastic right now," she murmured. "But you know what? I hope so, too."

ADMITTING HER INNER hope to Micha had been a lot less scary than she'd thought it might be. Bless him, he hadn't pressed for more. Instead, he'd simply kissed the top of her head and continued to hold her close. She liked the way she felt, sheltered against his muscular body.

Though she caught a few stray curious glances directed her way, most of her family seemed accepting. Now that everyone had arrived, Jones started his behind-the-scenes tour. Carly half listened as he described the process of making beer. Malted barley, mash, boil, cooling, fermentation, straining—it all sounded like a lot of work. Judging by the animation in both his voice and expression, Jones clearly loved every step of it.

As he led them back into the main bar area, he beckoned to Tatum to join him at the front of the room. "And now for the big announcement!" he said. "Tatum is going to be serving Lone Wolf Brewery beer at True. It's going to be wonderful exposure for us, especially since her restaurant is packed every single night."

"Not *every* night," Tatum chimed in, grinning. "But pretty darn close!" She and Cruz locked gazes and she blushed, going doe-eyed. Carly looked on, happy for her cousin.

"Everyone, feel free to sample any of our craft beers," Jones announced. "And let me know if you have any questions."

Everyone clapped and began congratulating Jones.

As people began circulating, January and her fiancé, Sean, made their way over. Carly introduced Micha. The instant the other man heard the name, he frowned. "I swear I heard about you the other night while at the precinct. Aren't you the guy who had someone put an explosive device inside your car?"

Unfortunately, Sean's question rang out just as one of those occasional odd silences fell over the room. Carly tensed up as just about everyone's heads swiveled around to stare.

Micha nodded, making a face. "We're trying to keep that quiet," he murmured. "Can we talk about something else?"

Too late. Now January looked from Micha to Carly, clearly horrified. "When was this? Were you there when that happened, Carly?" she demanded.

Sean, noticing how everyone had stopped talking to

listen in, rapidly tried to change the subject, but January wasn't having it. "Were you?" she persisted.

"Maybe," Carly muttered, wishing she were somewhere else, anywhere else.

"Good grief. Was anyone hurt?" Clearly oblivious to everyone else's interest, January grabbed Carly's arm. "When did this happen? Why didn't you tell any of us?"

The entire family murmured agreement and moved closer, circling Carly and Micha.

"Chicago PD and the FBI are working on it," Carly said. "It's over, no one was hurt, so let's talk about something else, please."

Heath, clearly catching on to Carly's need for a distraction, cleared his throat and tapped his beer glass with a knife. He waited until everyone's heads had swiveled around to face him. "The police have assured me that they are actively working the investigation. They're not sure if Carly was the target or Micha, though I believe they're leaning toward Micha."

He took a deep breath, waiting until everyone had a few seconds to digest his words. "Now, I'd like to talk a little about the serial killer investigation," he said. "Since Sean here works in the homicide division, I've asked him to give us an update."

Though Sean appeared nonplussed for a second, he quickly regained his composure and strode to the front of the room. Meanwhile, January sidled over to Carly and tugged on her arm. "You're not getting out of this so easily," she whispered. "I think everyone is going to want to hear about this."

"Probably," Carly whispered back. "Now hush so I can hear what your fiancé has to say."

Unfortunately, Sean informed them that the investigation had very little new information. He reiterated that Chicago PD was working jointly with the FBI, touched on the recent murders, but was unable to contribute any new information.

"This is very disappointing," Simone said, once Sean had finished speaking. "I've been doing a lot of research on serial killers and I'd be happy to share what I've learned with anyone who is working the case."

"Thank you," Sean replied. "But since the FBI is very knowledgeable in that area, I figure they have already brought in more than one expert. I'll give them your name, just in case."

Simone nodded.

"Now tell us about this car explosion that Micha was involved in," January chimed up, giving Carly a pointed glance. "I want to know if Carly was there. And I want to hear exactly what happened."

Both Farrah and Fallon nodded. Tatum narrowed her eyes and she and Cruz began murmuring to each other. Simone, who until that moment had been lost in reading something she'd written in her notebook, blinked and raised her head. Heath grimaced, one arm still around Kylie. He mouthed, *I tried*, in Carly's general direction.

Now everyone stared at Micha and Carly, even Jones, clearly waiting.

"Sorry," Micha whispered to Carly, though he kept his arm around her shoulders. Keeping his tone level, he relayed the chain of events, ending with the gunshots destroying Carly's window. She noted he left Jones out of it, which was kind of him, though she figured the family would learn about her brother's presence during the shooting sooner or later.

By the time Micha wound down, you could have heard a pin drop in the room. Carly's mother and aunt clung to each other, wearing identical horrified expressions.

"You need to come home," Fallon declared. "Right away. I won't have you staying at that house if you're in danger."

Carly refused to argue with her mother in front of the entire family. "Let's talk about this later," she said. "Right now, we're here to celebrate Jones and his fantastic beer. Let's try to focus on that."

"Agreed." Jones jumped in to save her. Though Fallon's expression made it clear she didn't like it, she dropped the topic, at least temporarily.

Once everyone had started talking again, Carly tugged on Micha's arm. "I'm seriously thinking about trying to sneak out before my mom can get to me."

"You know she'll just catch up to you later." He kissed her neck, making her shiver. "You might as well just go over and talk to her. She's worried, that's all."

"You make sense," Carly grumbled. "Wait here. I'll be right back."

Fallon and Farrah had taken a seat at a little round table in the corner, from where they had a view of the entire room. Jones had made sure they had a platter of assorted appetizers, and since neither women were big on drinking beer, he'd poured them both a glass of wine.

Fallon nodded as Carly approached. "Sit," she ordered. "You and I need to talk."

Stifling a sigh, Carly sat. "Mom, I know you're worried. I am, too. But there's no way I can drive to work from Oak Park every day. It'd be a ridiculous commute, especially with traffic."

Fallon reached across the table and covered Carly's hand with hers. "I can't bear the thought of something happening to you. How about you go stay with one of your brothers?"

"We've talked about that," Carly replied. "But ultimately, I decided against it. I have a dog now plus I refuse to live my life on the run. Especially since I still have no idea who might want to harm me."

Farrah leaned forward. "Do you think they might be after Micha?"

"It's possible." Carly shrugged. "But the police don't seem to think it's connected to the person or people who killed Dad and Uncle Alfred."

"Tell me, what are you doing to stay safe?" Fallon asked.

Now Carly wished Micha had accompanied her. "Micha isn't working right now," she began, and then as she realized how that sounded, she winced. "He's just getting settled back here in Chicago. But since he was in the special forces, he has lots of contacts. Between them and the police, I honestly feel we should be safe."

Her mother and aunt exchanged glances. Carly found herself holding her breath as she waited.

"Well, you are an adult," Fallon finally conceded.

"I don't like this at all, but I'm going to trust you to do what's best."

"Though it would have been fun to have a dog in the house," Aunt Farrah interjected, smiling. "Even if we're not going to be there much after next month, hopefully."

Carly sat up straighter. "What? Where are you going?"

"We've been trying to get back into our old routines," her mother said. "We've resumed running Gemini Interiors, though they managed to continue on just fine without us apparently."

"And we're considering taking a trip together," Farrah added. "Right now we haven't decided anything firm, but we've been looking at going to Dubai."

Pleased, Carly nodded. Before the murders, traveling had been one of her parents' passions. Often, both couples went somewhere together. In fact, right before the two men had been killed, Carly was pretty sure the foursome was planning a trip to Scotland.

"Or do you think it's too soon?" Farrah asked, the anxiety in her voice reflected in her gaze. "To be honest, the grief has been overwhelming and neither of us has felt like doing much of anything."

"But there's only so long one can mope around the house," Fallon interjected. "That's why we're going back to work. Baby steps, you know."

"I do know." Carly glanced back over her shoulder at Micha, who was talking to Sean. "When they told me that Micha had died, I couldn't get out of bed for days. And we had only been together for a fraction of the time you two were married."

"That doesn't make the pain any less," Farrah wisely said. "You were at a different place in your relationship than we were. You were just starting out, full of hopes and dreams and making plans. We were settled, having raised our children and paid our dues." She wiped away a stray tear. "We had so much living yet to do. It hurts to have that ripped away."

Fallon reached over and gave her sister a firm hug. "We're getting through this," she said, her voice fierce. "One day at a time."

"Yes, we will." Sniffing, Farrah hugged her back. "And knowing our children have found their happiness in life really helps. Whether with their dream careers or finding the love of their life—or both—it warms the heart to see you all turned out so well."

Carly nodded. "Thanks. Now if you don't mind, I'd better get back to Micha."

"No need." Fallon grinned. "He's headed this way right now."

Despite herself, Carly's heart skipped a beat. She glanced up, straight into Micha's warm brown eyes. Awareness shivered through her.

"Evening, ladies." Smiling at the two older women, Micha planted a quick kiss on Carly's head. "Do you mind if I join you?"

"Of course not." Farrah waved her hand at the empty chair. "Sit. We have some questions we want to ask you."

Hearing this, Carly stifled a groan. She shot Micha a look of warning as he lowered himself into a chair. She knew her mother and her aunt. Micha didn't know it, but he was about to be subjected to an intense grilling by the matriarchs of the Colton family.

The questions started off casually. They asked him about his time in the army and thanked him for his service. Carly watched him relax at her mother's and aunt's friendly tones. Though she knew he could take care of himself, she fought the urge to warn him. Instead, she sipped her beer and listened as Farrah took the lead, switching from wanting to know about the past to pointed questions about the future.

"Once you're married to my daughter, how do you intend to make a living?"

Whoa, Nelly. Carly shook her head and held up her hand to forestall Micha's response. "Mom," she chastised. "No one has said anything about us getting married. Please don't make that kind of assumption."

Eyes widening, Farrah looked from her daughter to Micha and then back to her sister. "But why not?" she drawled. "It seems you two have picked up right back where you left off."

Despite feeling her face color, Carly stared right back. "Mother..."

"It's all good, Mrs. Colton," Micha interrupted, smiling. "We're still working through a few things, though."

"What things?" Farrah asked.

"We need to figure them out on our own," Micha said smoothly, his raspy voice firm.

Carly exhaled, smiling gratefully.

The two older women took the hint. "All right, dear," Farrah said, patting the back of Micha's hand. "You can't blame me for being concerned for my daughter's welfare."

"I can't blame you at all," Micha agreed.

Carly's heart squeezed. She blinked when Micha stood and held out his hand to help her up. "Are you ready to go?" he asked.

Grateful, she slipped her hand in his and got to her feet. Keeping her fingers intertwined with his, she leaned over and kissed first her mother's cheek, then her aunt Fallon's. "We'll talk later," she murmured. "Have a nice night."

Holding hands still, they went in search of Jones so they could tell him goodbye. Carly felt the gazes of every single family member they passed and realized she didn't care if they saw her and Micha holding hands. Though she knew they'd speculate endlessly, let them gossip. Maybe, just maybe, she might have started to believe she and Micha could actually have a future together.

Chapter Ten

Back at Carly's house, Micha excused himself and went to the guest bedroom that Carly had given him to use, even though he'd yet to spend a night in that particular bed.

Visiting Jones Colton's brewery had lit a fire inside him. In Carly's family, so many of them had found and pursued their passion. Carly becoming a pediatric nurse, Tatum with her restaurant and Jones opening his own brewery had made Micha realize he needed to give serious consideration to his own future occupation. As had Carly's mother with her questions about what he intended to do for a living. He wanted to do more than simply earn a paycheck.

Besides Carly and the military, Micha had one other passion. Most might consider this a hobby and for a while Micha had, too. Now he thought he might be able to make it become more.

While being held captive in Afghanistan, he'd begun to carve wooden figures, toys, just to pass the time. To his surprise, he'd gotten quite good at it. His captors had taunted and mocked him, but they'd taken the toys home to their children. And they'd begun asking for more. He'd learned to trade his little wood carvings for extra food or more time in the sun. Sometimes, he'd thought his toys had helped keep him alive.

Later, after coming out of the medically induced coma in the burn unit, he'd been unable to get his fingers to work well enough to hold a knife. This had fueled a new determination inside of him. Having received an honorable discharge, he was no longer a soldier, and after two years away he knew he wouldn't be Carly's husband, but damned if he would give up his ability to make the simple wooden toys.

By the time he'd completed his physical therapy, his fingers no longer fumbled with the knife and the wood. He figured he'd regained nearly 90 percent of his previous skill and he vowed to keep on practicing until he had it back 100 percent. The little carvings brought him great joy, especially when he saw the delight shining from the eyes of a child who'd received one.

In the back of his mind, he'd known he wanted to do something with that, but until he'd seen Jones's enthusiasm for his brewery, he hadn't given serious thought to starting his own business.

Now, full of enthusiasm, he pulled out the plastic tub full of carvings that he'd brought with him from the hotel. He'd spent many nights alone in his hotel room, turning pieces of wood into animals and elves, cowboys and dragons. He'd been meaning to take this latest batch down to a women's shelter, as he'd done before coming to Chicago, but hadn't made the time to locate one yet.

Now he thought he might wait. He'd need some inventory, prototypes if you will.

Since he'd managed to save quite a bit of money during his time in the military, he figured he wouldn't even need a loan. He'd just need to do research on how to best market the toys, which he could begin with on the internet, and whether or not he'd have much competition.

Practically dancing around the room, he couldn't wait to show Carly and hear her thoughts. As a matter of fact, he'd even started working on a carving of her dog, Bridget. Fishing it out of the tub, he guessed he had maybe another hour left of work until it was completed. He figured he'd finish that before discussing any of this with her.

He could begin his research and see if his passion might be commercially viable. Would there be an actual market for his simple, carved toys? He closed the plastic container and slid it back under the bed. He'd finish the carving of Bridget when Carly was at work and present it to her as a gift.

For now, he guessed they'd watch a little television before going to bed. The simple cozy domestic things like that made him happy. The knowledge they'd be sharing a bed again ignited the simmering arousal that being in Carly's presence always brought.

Despite his best intentions, he couldn't manage to contain his glee from Carly. She picked up on his inner excitement the instant he walked into the kitchen.

"What's going on?" she asked, her gaze sweeping his face. "Do you have news?"

He realized she thought he'd heard something about

the case. "No, nothing like that. Sorry. Your mother's questions made me think a lot about what I was going to do for work. All my adult life, I've been military. It's difficult trying to see myself outside of that box."

"Does that mean you've thought of something?" she asked.

"Yes."

"Let me guess." Arms crossed, she eyed him. "Stop me when I get close. Security guard. Army recruiter. Police officer. Private detective."

He shook his head to all of those, though he had to give her credit. Every single occupation she'd listed was a logical follow-through for a man recently discharged from the military. If in fact his idea didn't work out, then he'd likely consider one of them.

No *if*, he reminded himself. He needed to think positive.

"Then what is it?" she pressed.

"I'm not ready to discuss it yet. I need to do more research to make sure it's a viable option."

Her frown deepened. "Why are you being so secretive? You know me. I'll tell you the truth. What is it?"

Feeling oddly vulnerable, he asked her to wait there, promising he'd be right back. Returning to his room, he retrieved his plastic container from under the bed. Other than his physical therapists and the people who'd accepted the donations at the women's shelter, he'd shown them to no one stateside. Carly would be the first.

Heart racing, he carried the container in his hand carefully to the kitchen, where Carly waited.

"I carve simple, primitive toys for children. And anyone else who wants one," he elaborated. "I started when I was a captive in Afghanistan and was able to use them to bargain with the guards for food or privileges."

Her eyes widened. "And you're wondering if there might be a market for them here in the US."

"Exactly."

"Colton Connections might be able to help with that," she said. "Let me see them."

He hadn't thought of that. Colton Connections developed patents for innovative inventions. He guessed it wouldn't be all that different from starting up his own toy company.

Slowly, he opened the box. Reaching in, he pulled out one of his favorites, a sitting dragon with wings spread that he'd perfected after carving over a hundred of them.

"That's beautiful," Carly breathed, taking it from him and cradling it in the palm of her hand. "I wouldn't call that a toy. It's more like art."

Art. "I was thinking the first thing I'd have to do would be to figure out a way to mass-produce them. Kids seem to love them. My captors took them home to their children and, once word spread, I had a valuable sort of currency to exchange." He shrugged. "I continued to carve them as part of my physical therapy, though I had to relearn to use my scarred and swollen fingers."

He set the box down. "I make a little of everything. These days, I carve them because I enjoy carving."

"May I?" she asked, gesturing toward his collection.

Slowly he nodded, wondering why he felt so raw, so exposed. He supposed he'd better get used to it if he truly intended to market his work. Still, he anxiously watched as Carly sifted through his carvings, taking out one and then another, running her fingers gently over the silky-smooth wood.

"They're amazing," she told him, the wonder in her voice proving she meant it. "Clean lines, no jagged pieces, though I'm guessing they'd have to be targeted for older children, who won't try to chew on them."

Grinning, he let his relief show. "Exactly. From what I understand, a lot of the preteen age group might want to collect them."

"I love them." Gently setting them back in his container, she crossed to him and planted a big kiss on his mouth. "I'm amazed at the things your talented fingers can do."

The suggestive comment sent a ripple of heat through him. As she kissed him again, her body moving suggestively against his, he forgot all about his carvings.

They barely made it to her bedroom, shedding clothes as they went. Falling onto the bed and each other, they made love with the kind of intense familiarity that felt both comfortable yet passionately heated. As she'd been doing, she ran her fingertips gently over the ridged outlines of his scars and kissed them. Having her do such a thing reminded him of how he'd truly believed he'd been damaged too much to have a woman like her.

Clearly, Carly didn't think so. She made it plain she accepted him as he was, scars and all.

Damn he loved this woman. He forced himself to go slow, to keep his raging arousal under control, until he'd helped her reach her own release twice. Only then did he unleash himself, pounding into her with the kind of mindless abandon that sent them both over the edge at the same time.

After, they cuddled. Eventually, Carly's breathing deepened as she drifted off to sleep. Micha held her, allowing his gaze to memorize every beautiful detail of her, from the stubborn tilt of her chin to her high cheekbones. The feel of her lush body, pressed trustingly into his, was a freaking miracle he'd never take for granted. How he'd managed to get so lucky twice, he didn't know. Despite all that he'd put her through, she'd given him a second chance. Briefly closing his eyes, he thanked the powers that be for allowing him to find her again. He couldn't lose her. Not now, not ever.

Too fired up to sleep, Micha slipped out from under her arm and padded to the bathroom. When he emerged, he scooped up his clothes on the way and pulled on his boxer briefs before heading to the kitchen.

Once there, he poured himself a glass of water, pulled out his knife and the wooden dog he'd started for Carly, and got to work finishing it.

WITH SUNLIGHT WARMING her face, Carly stretched, her body aching pleasantly. She let her eyes drift open, rolling to her side to look at Micha. He still slept, turned on his side facing her, his unruly hair and morning shadow making him look sexy as hell, even in slumber.

They'd made love, slept and made love once more, before going back to sleep. Now birdsong outside announced the arrival of morning and she somehow, impossibly, wanted him again. How that could be, she didn't want to overanalyze, so she made herself throw back the covers and make her way to the bathroom. After a quick shower and brushing of her teeth, she towel-dried her hair and pulled on a pair of panties and oversize T-shirt before padding to the kitchen to make coffee and, later, breakfast. Bridget followed her, eager to get outside and then have her kibble.

Flicking on the kitchen light, she let her dog out, waiting while Bridget took care of business. As soon as she was done, Bridget galloped back inside, eager for her breakfast.

Pouring a bowl of dog food and setting it on the floor, Carly went to make herself coffee. The sight of the wooden carving on the kitchen counter made her stop short. Micha had carved Bridget, capturing not only the boundless joy with which the dog faced each day, but the adoration that shone from her big brown eyes.

Reverently, Carly reached out and picked up the piece. She smoothed her fingers over the highly polished wood. Her throat stung and tears pricked at her eyes. Micha might believe his carving to be only a hobby, but the soul of an artist came through. Older children might collect these pieces, but she'd bet adults would, too.

Carrying the figurine with her, she made her coffee and took it and Bridget outside to the backyard. Though she had to be at work in a few hours, she'd gotten up early enough that she had a little bit of time before she had to get ready.

Micha joined her before she'd made it halfway through her first cup. The back-door hinges squeaked as he slipped up behind her, putting his arms around her and holding her close. As always when he touched her, her entire body melted.

"Thanks for the figurine. It's beautiful," she said.

"My pleasure."

She fought the urge to turn around and convince him to go back to bed with her. Instead, she decided to finally ask about one of the things that had been bothering her since he'd showed up alive rather than dead. From what he'd told her in the past, she knew it would be a sore subject. Maybe that, too, had changed during the time he'd been in the hospital. Nearly dying had a way of changing perspective sometimes.

"Do your parents know?" she asked softly. "That you're alive and in Chicago?"

He stiffened, though he didn't move away. "I don't know," he finally replied. "I didn't contact them, if that's what you mean. My father made it very clear that he no longer considers me his son."

While Carly had never met Micha's parents, she had to assume that they, too, had grieved greatly upon being informed of his death. Suffering and grief had a way of changing things, especially words said in anger.

But she wouldn't push, not now, not yet. She'd give Micha time to consider on his own.

So instead of responding, she slowly turned around and gave him a deep, lingering kiss. As she'd known it would, heat instantly erupted between them. Wrapped in each other's arms, they made out as if they'd been apart for days instead of just having climbed out of the same bed that morning.

Finally, Carly came up for air. She glanced around

her backyard and went still. Something was wrong. Her yard appeared empty.

"Where's Bridget?" she asked, trying to quell the rising panic. "Bridget!" she called, adding a whistle. "Bridget, come."

But her dog didn't reappear. A lightning bolt of sheer terror stabbed Carly in the heart. Somehow, Bridget had escaped the yard. She was gone.

For a second, Carly froze, unable to think or move. Then she ran down the steps, refusing to believe what her own eyes told her. Bridget had to be here somewhere, maybe hiding near the shed again.

With Micha right behind her, Carly combed every square foot of her yard. She looked behind bushes, even those that were logically far too small for Bridget to hide behind. They both checked and the gate was still closed. Together, she and Micha searched the shed, even though she'd blocked it off. Bridget wasn't there.

Refusing to give in to her rising panic, Carly sprinted over to the garage and yanked open the door. Even though she knew there was no way the dog could have gotten inside, Carly looked, anyway, calling Bridget's name.

"I don't understand," she said, her voice shaking as she blinked back tears. "There's no way she could have gotten out of the yard. I checked the fence and there aren't any holes. The gate is still closed."

"That's weird. Are you sure you didn't leave it open?" Micha asked, frowning.

"Yes." Puzzled, she eyed him. "Why? Do you think

someone opened it and deliberately let Bridget out while we were standing just a few feet away?"

He didn't have to respond verbally. His thoughts were written all over his face.

"You think someone took her?" Heart pounding, knees weak, she stared at him, silently begging him to contradict her.

"How else would she have gotten out?" he asked instead.

"But why? Why would anyone want my dog?" But the instant she spoke, her heart sank and she knew. "The same person who blew up your rental car and shot out my front window."

Micha didn't say anything. Instead, he reached for her, no doubt intending to offer comfort. Suddenly furious, she dodged him. "Why? Why would anyone want to harm an innocent dog?"

"Carly, first off we don't know for sure that's what happened to Bridget," he cautioned. "Let's recheck the fence again. Maybe she found a hole somewhere and simply got out."

Though worry made her feel queasy, she took a deep breath to calm herself down and nodded. "That makes sense."

"Good." He pointed. "You start on that side and I'll start over here. Check every square inch, even behind bushes."

This time, instead of being in a frantic rush, she went slowly. In the overgrown areas, she got down on all fours and checked behind the shrubs, looking for any gap in her fence.

"I found something," Micha called. "Come see."

Heart in her throat, she hurried over. Micha crouched down, and pushed aside a leaved shrub. "Look."

The entire bottom of three boards was missing, leaving a jagged hole big enough for a dog to squeeze through.

Relief and worry flooded her. "This means she's somewhere in the neighborhood," she said. "Better that than having someone grab her. But we need to find her."

Micha nodded. "Grab some treats and her leash. We'll find her."

The confidence in his gravelly voice made her feel slightly better. She ran into the house with renewed purpose, grabbed a handful of Bridget's favorite treats and met Micha in the front yard.

"Here." She handed him a couple of the treats. "You go that way and I'll go the other."

"We're staying together," he said. "No way we're splitting up without knowing if…" He didn't have to finish the sentence.

She nodded. "Okay. Bridget," she called. "Here, girl."

They walked up one side of the street, all the way to the stop sign. Carly could only hope Bridget hadn't gone too far. The thought of her getting hit by a car was heart-stopping.

"Don't give up." Micha squeezed her shoulder. "She might be scared and hiding. Let's go back toward your house and stay on this side of the street before we cross over."

Two houses from hers, Carly spotted movement in a neighbor's bushes. Catching her breath, she grabbed

Micha's arm. "There," she said. She'd barely gotten the word out when Bridget came trotting out, tail wagging furiously, clearly unaware she'd done anything wrong.

With a cry of relief, Carly dropped to her knees and gathered her dog to her. She hadn't cried so far but damned if her eyes hadn't filled with tears.

"I can't lose you," she told Bridget. "I just can't."

The three of them made their way back to the house. Carly took Bridget inside while Micha went to repair the hole in the fence. He promised to double-check for any others and fix them, too.

Legs shaky, Carly dropped into a chair while Bridget got water and then curled up in her dog bed to nap. Glancing at her hands, Carly realized she was still shaking. The severity of her panic when she'd thought she'd lost Bridget stunned her.

Micha let himself in quietly. Bridget gave a quiet thump of her tail but didn't lift her head. Micha bent down and scratched her behind the ears, which made Bridget give a doggie moan of pleasure. This had Carly smiling, even though her eyes were still streaming tears. Angrily, she wiped them away, not even sure why she was crying.

"Carly?" Micha asked, crossing the room toward her. "Are you okay?"

She started to nod and then ended up shaking her head no. "I thought that psychopath had taken my dog," she said, her voice shaky. "You know things have gotten absolutely crazy when that's the first thought that comes to mind."

"I know." He gathered her in his arms and held her.

She allowed herself to relax into him, inhaling his masculine scent and loving the way his strong, muscular body made her feel safe. "Carly, you really should consider staying with one of your brothers. At least temporarily, until all this blows over."

"No," she replied, without moving. "We've already discussed this. I'm not being run out of my own home."

He stroked her back, his big hand gentle. "It won't be forever. Just until we catch this guy."

Inside, she knew he had a point. Today had proved that. If something happened to Bridget because Carly continued to cling to her stubborn pride, she'd never forgive herself. "I'll think about it," she heard herself say. "But don't say anything to Jones or Heath, okay? I haven't decided anything yet, and if I do agree to go stay with one of them, I'll tell them myself."

His voice a raspy deep rumble against her ear, Micha agreed.

Now that she'd calmed down, Carly knew she needed to get ready for work. Extricating herself from Micha's arms, she glanced at the clock and gasped. "I've got to get a move on," she said. "I can't be late. I never have and I don't want to start now." She rushed off toward her bedroom, determined to get ready as quickly as she could. Being punctual had become a point of pride with her over the years. Not only did she excel at patient care, but her charting was precise and she never, ever had been late for a shift. Nor would she be today.

Somehow, she managed to pull herself together in order to leave at her usual time. As she blew into the kitchen, Micha waited by the back door.

"I'm ready," she told him. "Usual routine?"

"Of course." He gave her a quick kiss. "And please, really think about possibly staying with one of your brothers."

She nodded, even though her mind had already gone ahead to the sick children waiting for her on her floor. She gave Bridget a quick pet and then straightened. "Let's do this," she told him, grabbing her purse and keys. "Time to start another day."

Micha reached out as she swung past, pulling her in for one more tingle-all-the-way-to-her-feet kiss. When they broke apart, they were both breathing heavily.

"Now *that's* the way to start a day," Micha said. "Give me a minute or two before you leave."

She nodded, internally shaking her head at their new routine. Watching as Micha let himself out the back door, she locked it behind him. Then, eye on the clock, she waited.

Chapter Eleven

As he'd done every morning that week, Micha left Carly's out the back door. He hopped the chain-link fence into the neighboring yard, and from there walked down the street to where he'd parked his Jeep. As far as he could tell, none of the vehicles parked on her street were occupied. If no one sat in a vehicle watching the house, unless they'd mounted a camera again somewhere outside, she wasn't under surveillance. Just to be safe, the night before he'd checked the numerous trees closest to her house and found nothing.

Finally, he got in his vehicle, started the engine and drove closer to Carly's house. He waited until he saw her pull out of her driveway. He then put his Jeep in Drive and followed her, allowing another car to pull in between them just for show.

When they reached the hospital, she pulled into the employee-only parking lot and Micha found a place in the parking garage, close enough that he could watch her walk in. They'd kept to this same routine every day, and he'd seen nothing out of the ordinary.

So far, so good. But Micha wasn't willing to take

any chances. He'd do this for as long as he had to, until whoever was after them had been caught. No way was he letting Carly put herself in danger. That's why he really hoped she'd agree to go spend a week or two with one of her brothers. He'd breathe a lot easier once he felt she was safe.

Carly walked briskly up the sidewalk, her long blond hair up in a messy bun, her scrubs marking her as a health-care worker. Some mornings, one or two of her coworkers walked in with her. Others, like today, she made her way alone.

Micha decided to wait until Carly entered the hospital building.

And then Micha saw the man step out from behind a delivery van, clearly intent on Carly. Everything about him screamed of menace, from the too-tight line of his posture to the way he appeared to focus on her to the exclusion of everything else.

Heart pounding, Micha got out of his Jeep with a jump. He sprinted toward the door, worried the guy would take out a gun and shoot her. Instead, the man spun around at the sound of Micha's approach.

Shock and hatred mingled in the man's suddenly familiar face as he and Micha locked eyes.

Clearly unaware, Carly continued forward and slipped inside the doors, which closed behind her. The intruder ignored her, now completely focused on Micha. Something about him... Then Micha remembered.

"About time you got here," the other man drawled. "I'd hate to have to hurt that pretty little lady of yours just to get back at you."

Micha skidded to a halt, still twenty feet away. He ignored the blatant baiting. "I know you," he said. "Lieutenant Andy Shackleford. What the hell is wrong with you? Why are you here?"

"Why? You really have to ask that, after you ruined my life? You deserve to pay for what you did to me."

Pay? Micha had heard enough. "Bring it," he said, settling into a fighting stance, even though he wasn't sure if the other man might have a gun. "Let's settle this like men. No more bombs or bullets. You and me, right now."

"Not yet." Lips lifted in a snarl, Andy spun around and took off running. He raced away. Though Micha sprinted after him, the other man had enough of a head start plus a leaner build to outpace him. How did he run so fast on a prosthetic leg? Micha wondered. Andy jumped on a low-slung motorcycle, kicked it to life and roared away. Knowing there was no way on earth he'd catch him, Micha stood and watched until the bike disappeared.

What the...? Micha hadn't seen Andy for years. He hadn't even *thought* of the man since getting out of the hospital, even when the FBI had asked him if he had any enemies. They'd gone their separate ways and Micha hadn't honestly thought he'd ever see Andy Shackleford again.

Back then, Andy had hated him. Hell, he'd made no secret of that. Lieutenant Andy Shackleford had been part of the team sent in to rescue Micha in Afghanistan. He'd been on the helicopter when it crashed. Like Micha, he'd also been badly injured. Where Micha had suffered burns and a broken back, Andy had lost his leg. Though that accident had cost both men their military careers, Andy blamed Micha, since he was the one who'd needed rescuing. Micha had assumed Andy would eventually get past that. Clearly, he had not. In the time since, that hatred must have festered inside Andy, rotting away at his insides. Now Andy apparently hated Micha enough to wish him dead.

Of course Andy had been the one who'd set up the car bomb. Again, that made sense. Andy had been an ammunitions specialist in the army. His duties had including receiving, storing and issuing conventional ammunition, guided missiles and explosives. If anyone would know how to rig a car bomb, Andy would.

Micha dug out his phone. Though he hadn't yet provided the FBI with a list of his enemies, now he had something concrete to tell them.

Special Agent Brad Howard answered on the third ring. He listened while Micha described what had just happened. After asking a series of pointed questions, he agreed with Micha's assessment of the situation.

"Did you happen to get the license plate number on the motorcycle?" Agent Howard asked.

"No, I didn't," Micha replied, mentally kicking himself. "Everything happened too fast."

"We'll start looking into it. His military records should be easy to access and we'll go from there. Don't hesitate to call if you think of anything else or if you see him again."

After agreeing, Micha ended the call. The only reason he could come up with for Andy staking out the hospital would be in hopes of seeing Micha with Carly. He must have tracked down Carly and possibly had been the one who'd been stalking her before Micha arrived.

But how had he known? A lot of time had passed since the helicopter crash, and their time at Walter Reed. Micha remembered that they'd both been in a lot of pain, and the long flight back from overseas. Micha remembered crying out for Carly. That was about all he remembered, though. Maybe Andy had pieced together something, or it was even possible Micha had said more than he knew.

A shudder ran through him. What if he hadn't come to Chicago to check on Carly? What would Shackleford have done then? Would he have enacted some sort of painful revenge against the woman he knew Micha loved?

With resolve stiffening his spine, Micha strode back to his Jeep. While he knew the FBI would be searching for his enemy, he didn't have the patience to wait too long. Especially since Andy knew he'd been made. He'd increase his efforts to take Micha down, which could also endanger Carly.

No. Micha knew he could not allow that to happen. He'd have to figure out a way to draw the other man out, preferably somewhere far from Carly, and then take him down on his own.

With no real plan other than the vague knowledge of what he needed to do, Micha decided not to go back to Carly's house just yet. He wondered if Andy had been watching the place. No doubt he had.

Which meant Micha would just have to make sure to be seen. If he could get Andy to follow him somewhere far away from Hyde Park and from Carly, he'd take him down or die trying. He just needed to figure out a way. Until then, Micha would need to stay far away from Carly, while managing to also keep her safe.

Quickly, he dialed Jones. Without going into too much detail, he explained what he needed. "Just stay with her, please. I've got a very real lead on who's been behind all this and I need to pursue it. I absolutely need to know Carly is safe."

Once Jones agreed, Micha cut him off before he could ask any more questions. "Tell her I'll be in touch," he said, and ended the call.

Then he began thinking of ways to trap Lieutenant Andy Shackleford. Micha definitely had the advantage here, since that had been one of the things he excelled in while in special ops.

The hunter was about to become the hunted. No matter what he had to do, no matter how long it took, Micha would end the threat once and for all.

Micha discarded any idea he had for drawing Andy out that would even remotely involve Carly. He had to figure out a way to let the guy know where to find him that didn't involve being near Carly's house.

Parking in a doughnut shop parking lot, Micha started making calls. He needed to locate someone who might know how to contact Shackleford, maybe even get ahold of his cell phone number.

But none of the people he reached had seen or heard from the guy in years. For all intents and purposes, Shackleford had become a ghost.

Micha refused to give up. But call after call, even

reaching out to people who'd had extremely limited contact with him or Andy, yielded no results.

Frustrating. Gritting his teeth, Micha tried to think. He hadn't known Andy well, even though they'd shared physical therapy sessions. Each man had been focused on his own healing, as he should be. But at one point, Micha thought Andy had mentioned having a girlfriend or fiancée, maybe even a wife. If Micha could locate her, he might be able to shed more light on Andy's current location.

It was a long shot, but at the moment the only one he had.

Unfortunately, even that turned out to be a dead end.

Now what? Micha didn't want to go back to Carly's house, not yet. Now that he knew the name of his enemy, he also knew how dangerous Andy could be, especially if he escalated. From explosion to shooting, what would be next?

He worried Andy might decide to target Carly just to spite Micha. So he called Jones and, without giving a lot of details, asked him not to let Carly be alone. Jones agreed but wanted to know why. Micha had remained vague, promising to fill the other man in as soon as he knew more, and ended the call.

Now with one less thing to worry about, Micha needed to figure out a way to draw Andy out. Unfortunately, no matter which angle he used to approach the problem, they all pointed back to Carly's house.

Which meant he'd have to get her out of the house. At least for a few days.

But would Carly go? She was stubborn, a trait he usually admired in her, but not if it got her hurt. He decided he'd need to level with her. He'd slip by later tonight and let himself in after most of the rest of the world had gone to sleep. Once he explained, he felt quite certain Carly would understand what she needed to do to keep her and Bridget safe. Once Micha no longer had to worry about her, he could set a better trap for taking down his enemy.

CARLY WALKED OUT of the hospital after her shift and instinctively looked around for Micha's black Jeep. While part of her thought his actions might be a tad bit overprotective, mostly she liked that he was willing to go through so much effort just to keep her safe. The police had also beefed up their patrols and it had become common to see them driving by two or three times a night.

Odd. She checked her watch. Micha must be running late.

"Carly!" Her brother Jones emerged from the parking garage, startling her. "Wait up."

A quick frisson of fear went through her. But Jones was smiling, so that meant Micha had to be all right.

"What's going on?" she asked, once Jones had caught up with her.

"Micha sent me," he explained. "He asked me to stay with you this afternoon. He said he'll call as soon as he can to explain."

"Does that mean he got a lead?"

Jones shrugged. "He didn't say. He made me promise to stay with you the rest of the day. I'm thinking he'll be back before dark, because he knows I have to head over to the brewery."

"Okay. Are you following me in your truck, then?"

Now Jones shuffled his feet, appearing slightly uncomfortable. "Micha told me to ask you to leave your vehicle here at the hospital and ride with me. I hope that's okay with you."

Intrigued despite herself, she nodded. "Sure. I'm guessing he figures it'll be safer in the employee parking lot where there are cameras. I've got to get home and let Bridget out, so let's get going."

Side by side, they walked to Jones's truck. He kept up a steady stream of conversation all the way to her house, though he fell silent as they pulled into her driveway.

"Just wait a second." Jones touched her arm. "With all that's going on, we need to be extra cautious. Look around. Does everything look normal to you?"

Curbing her impatience, she did as he asked. While she wasn't sure exactly what he wanted her to look for, she eyed the back door and the windows, which all appeared to be closed. "Everything's fine," she said. "Now I really need to let Bridget out, if that's okay with you."

Jones laughed, a short humorless sound. "Sure. Just so you know, I still have nightmares about the night your front window got shot out." He pointed to the sheet of plywood still covering it. "What if you'd been standing near there? You would have been killed."

Already out of the truck, Carly turned to look at him. "I've been trying not to think about it," she admitted. "And I've been too busy to remember to call a glass company. I need to set something up for a time either I or Micha will be here."

Jones gave her a disgruntled look. "Yes, you do."

"Now that we've got that out of the way, are you coming?" she asked, starting forward.

Once Jones had caught up with her, he walked with her to the door, waiting while she used her key to unlock it. Inside, Bridget immediately began barking a greeting, which made Carly grin. "I love hearing that," she said.

As soon as she had the door unlocked, she motioned Jones to wait and opened it, crouching low so Bridget could launch herself at her. Laughing, Carly indulged her pet's frenzied greeting while Jones looked on.

"Okay, girl." Carly got to her feet. "Let's get you outside to go potty."

Jones stayed right on her heels as she let her dog outside.

Carly shook her head, keeping an eye on Bridget. "What's going on, Jones? I'm sensing that you're not telling me everything. Why are you acting so overprotective?"

Her brother had the grace to look ashamed. "Sorry," he said. "But I promise I'm not keeping any secrets from you. Micha didn't have a lot to say, really. He just stated it was imperative that I not let you out of my sight."

"What are you going to do when you have to go into the Lone Wolf?" she asked, gesturing for Bridget to come inside. Since the dog knew her dinner would be next, she happily complied.

Inside the kitchen, Jones took a seat at the table while Carly measured out Bridget's kibble. Since he hadn't answered her question, she repeated it.

"I don't know," Jones admitted. "I guess you can come with me if Micha's not home by then."

Carly shook her head. "I just worked a full shift. I'm tired and all I want to do is get off my feet and hang out with my dog. I'm not going with you."

"But you'll be left here without your vehicle."

She grimaced. "Then I guess you'd best take me back to the hospital to retrieve it."

"Micha better come home soon, then," Jones muttered.

"He will," Carly replied, certain.

But Micha didn't come home. The sun sank lower and lower. Jones began to pace, frequently checking his watch. She knew he liked to be at the Lone Wolf before the evening rush started.

"Go ahead and go," she urged him.

"Not until Micha shows up," he responded grimly. "Or at least calls to let us know what's going on."

Carly agreed. Waiting for Micha to call, she put off trying to reach him. "I'm afraid I might interrupt whatever he's working on," she explained.

Jones agreed. "I need to let my people know I'm running late." He sat down on the couch and spoke quietly into his phone. When he'd finished, he looked up at Carly and smiled. "They've got everything under control, at least for now." He checked his watch. "Where the heck is Micha?"

"Good question." Giving in to her growing concern, Carly relented and dialed his number. She listened as it rang several times and then the call went to voice mail. She left a message asking Micha to call her and then eyed her brother. "Seriously, you can leave," she said.

"I'm sure Micha will be here shortly. He must have gotten caught up in whatever he's doing."

Jones hesitated. "What if he doesn't show up?"

Though the thought of that happening made her stomach twist, she kept that hidden from Jones. "He will. And if he's delayed for whatever reason, I'll be fine."

"I don't like this…" Jones began.

"Go." She made a shooing motion with her hands. "I have Bridget and I have my cell phone. I'll make sure everything is locked up tight."

"What about your car? Micha really didn't want it parked here for some reason."

Carly considered and then made a split-second decision. "I'll be fine without it for now. I'm sure Micha had a good reason for wanting me to leave it at the hospital."

Still her brother didn't move. "Carly, if Micha doesn't make it back tonight, I don't want to leave you without any way to go to work in the morning."

He had a valid point. But Micha would show up eventually, wouldn't he? Unless something awful had happened to him and then… Whoa. She put the brakes on that line of thought.

"Take me to get my car," she decided. "I can run through a fast-food drive-through on the way home. I'm too tired to even think about cooking anything."

With a loud sigh, Jones gave in. "Come on," he said. "Make sure you lock up tight."

They drove to the hospital with Jones unusually quiet. As he pulled up near the gate that led to the employee-only parking lot, he turned to face her. "I don't like this, Carly. Something's going on and I don't think it's good.

The fact that Micha is completely out of touch under-scores that."

She thought for a moment and then nodded. "I agree. But what else can we do? We can't wait here in limbo until Micha shows up. You've got a job to go to, as do I. And I refuse to be run out of my own house."

Leaning over, she kissed her brother's cheek before sliding out of his truck. Jones sat and watched her while she got into her vehicle and started the engine. He didn't drive away until after she'd pulled out of the employee parking lot.

After a quick fast-food run and heading back home, she found herself watching her rearview mirror to make sure no one followed her. She didn't think anyone was, but to be sure she took a detour and drove down by the university and then took a circuitous route home.

Traffic ebbed and flowed, but she couldn't spot an-other vehicle making the exact same number of turns as she. Satisfied, she finally turned onto her street, alert to any headlights behind her.

As usual, there were numerous vehicles parked in the street. Slowing, she tried to look inside each of them without being too obvious, but in the end, she felt fool-ish and simply went home.

After parking, she walked up to the front door amid the wonderful sound of her dog barking a joyous greet-ing. She let herself in, immediately locking the door be-hind her, before dropping down on her haunches to let Bridget greet her as if she'd been away for hours rather than a few minutes.

The house felt strangely empty and quiet. Too quiet.

Carly hadn't realized how much she'd gotten used to having Micha around.

She turned on the television, found an old movie and let it play for background noise. Though she didn't want to be one of *those* kind of girlfriends, she texted Micha. Where are you? Is everything okay?

No response. No doubt he was busy. But still, how long would it take for him to text back a simple yes? She hated feeling this vulnerable, and not because she was frightened to be alone in her own home, but due to worrying about Micha's safety.

She loved him. She'd always loved him, even when she'd believed that he'd departed this earth. Love didn't die due to the absence of a physical body. And yes, she'd been furious and hurt that he'd allowed her to believe him dead for so long, but she could also understand his reasoning. Much of that time he'd been a prisoner, then unconscious, only to wake covered in horrific burns that to him must have seemed disfiguring. In fact, she actually found those scars beautiful. A testament to Micha's resilience and, in the end, his ultimate survival.

She also understood that whoever was after him— or them, but she'd come to believe it was him—wanted Micha dead. A car bomb wasn't exactly playing around. That, and the shots through her front window, had only proved the assailant didn't care if Carly was collateral damage.

Micha hadn't wanted her to be alone. Then why wasn't he here with her?

Her sense of unease growing, she checked her texts.

Nothing. No missed calls, no messages. Trying not to panic, she took a deep breath and dialed his number.

The call went straight to voice mail. With her stomach in knots, she left a simple message. "Call me, please."

Something was definitely wrong. Acting on impulse, she called her brother. Jones picked up immediately, sounding apprehensive. "Is everything all right?" he asked. "Are you safe?"

"I'm fine," she responded. "I'm just wondering if you've heard anything from Micha."

"No, I haven't. He isn't home yet?"

"He's not. And I haven't been able to reach him." Striving to sound calm, she took a deep breath. "Did he happen to mention to you where he was going or what he planned to do?"

"No, he didn't." Jones cleared his throat. "You know what? I'm getting bad vibes about this. Why don't you come down to the Lone Wolf and let me keep you company until you hear from him?"

She glanced at Bridget, still snoozing in her dog bed. "I'd rather wait here."

"You can bring your dog," Jones said, almost as if he'd read her mind.

Momentarily, she wavered. Maybe she should go hang out at the brewery. A distraction would be wonderful right now, stop her from imagining the worst-case scenario.

But ultimately, she decided she wanted to be there when Micha walked through the door. Which she had no doubt he would. She simply needed to stop worrying.

"Thanks, but I'll be okay," she told her brother. "With

all that's been going on, I can't help but worry about him. I'm sure he'll be fine."

"I agree. If anyone can take care of himself, Micha can." In the background, someone called Jones's name. "Carly, I've got to go. Call me if you need anything."

After ending the call, Carly wandered around her house. She still found it difficult to go anywhere near the front window. In her mind's eye she could still see it shattering, shards of glass raining down to the sound of gunfire.

Shaking her head, she wandered into the kitchen. Sometimes, when she found herself stressed, it helped to bake something. Plus, she'd bet Micha would enjoy some homemade cookies or bread when he returned.

Feeling a bit better, she hummed under her breath as she got out the ingredients for chocolate chip cookies, Micha's favorite. She could just picture how his handsome face would light up as he walked in the door to the smell of freshly made cookies.

Lost in a happy reverie of measuring and mixing, she put the first batch in the oven and poured herself a glass of wine.

Two hours later, heartsick, she tried Micha's phone again. No answer, straight to voice mail. She sent a text just as a last-ditch effort, and then she took Bridget out and decided she might as well get ready for bed.

But after thirty minutes in bed, she still couldn't sleep, so she abandoned the attempt and got up. Where was Micha? She had to believe he was safe. He had to be. She couldn't lose him again.

Because he'd said she could, she called Jones, knowing he'd be at the Lone Wolf until closing time. He answered immediately. "Still all right, I hope?" he said, an undercurrent of worry behind his light tone.

"Micha hasn't come home. And he's not answering his phone calls or texts." To her absolute horror, she nearly broke down in tears. Taking a deep breath, she managed to pull herself together before she spoke again. "I need you to tell me if he told you anything about where he might have gone."

"He did not," Jones replied. "I give you my word. And, Carly, it's after one o'clock in the morning. It's not safe for you to go out looking for him at this hour."

"I know." Then she said the thing that had been lurking in the back of her mind, almost too ashamed to speak it out loud. "What if he took off, Jones?"

"Took off?" Her brother seemed puzzled. "What do you mean?"

"Disappeared." Though she knew he couldn't see her, she waved her hand in the air. "I really think he might have figured out someone was after him and leaving was the only way he felt he could keep me safe." The thought almost had her double over in pain, but if anything, these last two years had made her stronger.

"He wouldn't do that," Jones finally responded. But he didn't seem convinced. "That man is head over heels in love with you." He paused a moment again. "Though I can tell he'd do anything to keep you safe. Even disappearing if he had to."

"I can't go through this again," she said, her heart cracking. "Honestly, I won't survive."

"He'll come back as soon as he either figures out or

stops the threat." Jones tried to reassure her. "I have to approve."

"Stops the threat," she repeated. "That sounds so dangerous."

"Micha knows what he's doing and he'll be careful. You know he got tons of training while he served in special forces."

"True, but there's still no reason he couldn't have told me what was going on," she argued, heartsick and beginning to feel angry. "A call, a text or even a damn handwritten note left on my table. Something, just so I know he's safe."

"You do have a point," Jones agreed. "Come up here. Being around people will make you feel better."

"No." She swiped at her eyes. "Because despite it all, I want to be here just in case he comes back."

"Just in case?" Jones sounded shocked. "Carly, snap out of it. Now I'm really worried about you. As soon as I get this place closed, I'll be over. Don't go anywhere. Promise."

Wearily, she agreed. After ending the call, she sat at her kitchen table, mindlessly scrolling through social media on her phone. Finally, she put the phone down. How could Micha not understand how disappearing, even for a night, would affect her? She'd been candid with him, sharing her devastation when she'd thought she'd lost him. Why would he do this to her again?

She had to believe he wouldn't. Which meant Micha very well could be in danger.

Chapter Twelve

Taking every precaution, Micha drove around, making sure to circle Carly's street at least once every twenty minutes. He only passed a Chicago PD cruiser once, about to turn onto Carly's street, which he supposed was better than nothing. Still, he'd be making another phone call and asking again for beefed-up patrols.

As he approached Carly's house, he slowed, carefully checking out the surrounding area. As usual, there were numerous vehicles parked in the street, but it was impossible to tell if anyone sat inside them. Until he made it inside the house, he'd have to assume someone might be.

Her lights were on. Ever since she'd gotten her front window shot out, she'd been antsy about being in her living room. She'd even told him she'd actually felt safer with the plywood there. He understood that. Tonight, he fully intended talking her into staying with Jones or Heath. He couldn't do what he needed while worrying about her safety. If he wanted to use Carly's house to trap Andy, she simply had to be somewhere safe.

As usual, he parked down the street from her house and got out of his Jeep, looking left to right and spotting no one. Crickets chirped and even the usual traffic sound seemed muted.

Though the fresh night air relaxed him somewhat, he still checked behind him and kept an eye on the periphery. So far, so good. The cars remained parked at the curb, and no motorcycle or gunshots disturbed the quiet. As he walked up the sidewalk, he got out his phone to call her, wanting to let her know he had arrived so he didn't startle her. He'd send her a quick text instead, so he started to type.

Looking down at his phone, he only caught the movement on the edge of his peripheral vision, spinning around to face it.

A large body slammed into him, knocking him onto the sidewalk.

"What the…?" Micha swung, landing a right hook on the other man's jaw. The streetlight revealed little, a man wearing a hoodie, but Micha figured it had to be Andy Shackleford. He must have been hidden behind Carly's large tree. For all his plans to draw him out, somehow Micha had managed to be caught unaware.

"Damn you," he cursed, twisting and blocking, all the while trying to get his pistol. But Andy beat him to it, pulling his own gun and stepping back, all the while keeping it trained on him.

"Don't move or I'll blow your head off," Andy snarled. "I mean it." He glanced sideways toward Carly's house. "How about we go inside, and you let me mess up that pretty lady of yours?"

"How about we don't," Micha responded. He couldn't let the other man know how desperate he was to keep him away from Carly. In fact, he knew talking wouldn't serve any purpose. Instead, he rushed toward Andy, ramming him in the chest with his lowered head. Somehow, Andy managed to hold on to the pistol, swinging it around and slamming it into Micha's head.

Micha went down, dropping hard and struggling to stay conscious. At least they were still two houses down from Carly's place. He could not let this madman anywhere near her, no matter what he had to do.

Somehow, he managed to push back to his feet. Lurching forward, his vision still blurry, he swung. And connected, though just barely.

Andy laughed. "Want to try that again? Come on, tough guy. You can take me. I only have one leg."

Blinking, Micha tried to focus on the other man. Not only did his head hurt like hell, but he saw double—two Andy Schacklefords when he knew there was only one. Licking his lip, he tasted blood. "Why are you doing this, man?"

"Seriously?" Disbelief rang in the other man's voice. "You know I'm entitled. After what you did to me, you *owe* me. Enough of this BS. You're coming with me."

Micha never saw the second blow coming. He slid into unconsciousness as the pavement rose up to greet him.

When he opened his eyes next, head pounding like mortar shells had detonated inside of it, he realized his hands and feet had been bound. A rag had also been stuffed inside his mouth. He was inside the back of a van or SUV, and the motion made his injured head hurt even more. Flashes of light from passing under the occasional streetlights felt like swords into his brain.

Since he couldn't speak, he closed his eyes. Battling nausea, he felt himself slip once more into darkness.

He came to again as Andy was dragging him out of the vehicle. "Get up. Walk," Andy ordered, prodding him with some sort of stick. A cane or a baseball bat, Micha thought, struggling to clear the fog from his brain. Next, Micha fully expected to be beaten with whatever the stick was. It felt eerily familiar, as if Andy had taken a page from the playbook when the Afghanistan terrorists had taken Micha prisoner.

He suppressed a shudder. He'd barely survived then. He needed to get the upper hand now. Carly. He had to make it back to Carly. At least this bastard hadn't touched her.

Andy herded him inside a metal structure. Not a residence, Micha noted. But some sort of warehouse or storage facility. Though the darkness made getting his bearings even more difficult, Micha tried to look for landmarks. Anything to help tell him where he might be.

Prodding him again, Andy gave Micha one final shove before sliding the door closed. Despite the complete and total darkness, Micha immediately tried to work his hands free. He dropped to the floor—also metal—and realized what the absence of windows likely meant. Andy had stuck him inside of a shipping container or storage unit. No one would hear Micha if he called for help at least until morning.

Whether he was at the Port of Chicago or a trucking yard—either way there would be workers at some point, there to load the containers onto a truck or ship. Though he figured Andy would be back long before sunrise to finish enacting his revenge.

There were two things Micha had to his advantage. One, most shipping yards or storage facilities had cameras, and two, as far as Micha could tell, Andy had forgotten to strip him of his cell phone. He was pretty sure he could still feel it in his pocket. If he could manage to get his hands free, he should be able to call for help. He needed to do something before he either ran out of air or Andy came back to finish him off.

Luckily for him, he'd been in this exact same situation numerous times, both in training and in real life. It took a bit of time, some pain and maybe even blood, but he managed to get his hands free.

Finally. Flexing his fingers to try to regain some circulation, Micha untied his feet. It took a few attempts, but he finally got back enough feeling to be able to stand and move. Next, he went to where he knew the door should be. "Damn it." He remembered reading something about this. Shipping containers weren't equipped to be opened from the inside. Of course they weren't. They'd never been intended to hold people, only goods.

Since he had no idea how long the air would last in here, he tried to conserve his movements. Luckily, he'd overcome any bouts of panic-inducing claustrophobia he'd had back in Afghanistan, out of sheer necessity. They'd kept him in a hole in the ground, maybe eight by six at the most.

The space here also felt small, though not as tiny; which meant most likely he'd been locked in the smaller size of the standard shipping containers, which he believed was twenty by eight.

Okay, so no way out on his own. However, if Andy Shackleford opened that door, Micha would be ready. He shoved his hand in his pocket, but instead of locating his phone, he came up with nothing.

Damn it. Micha figured Andy would be back sooner or later.

Either way, Micha knew he had to be prepared for when the other man returned. That likely would be his one chance to get out of this alive and back to Carly. He couldn't leave her again.

Carly. What if the reason Andy had left Micha here was because he'd gone back to do something to Carly? If he'd had even the slightest idea how much she meant to Micha, Andy would immediately figure out the best way to make Micha suffer was to hurt her.

No. Micha refused to allow his thoughts to go there. First he'd need to figure out a way out of here. Then he could get to Carly and make sure she was safe. He thanked his lucky stars that he'd asked Jones to stay with her. If Andy went there, he wouldn't be expecting her to have company.

Just in case he'd missed something, Micha once again felt his way along all sides of his prison. Nothing. No opening, nothing he could use as a tool to try to force his way out. He was well and truly stuck.

He knew he could rant and rave, pound on the metal walls until his knuckles were raw, use up every ounce of his energy and a great deal of oxygen, all for nothing.

A younger Micha might have done this once, but since then he'd learned a thing or two.

Sinking to the floor with his back against the wall, he settled in to wait. He'd conserve his strength and his air, and when the right opportunity came, he'd take it.

Time passed slowly, the way it always did when monitored. At first, he checked his watch too often, and at some point he fell into an uncomfortable doze.

A sound startled him awake. He got to his feet, not entirely certain he hadn't been dreaming, and listened.

Outside he heard voices and laughter. Teens, from the sound of them. They must be sneaking around the container yard looking for mischief.

Micha waited until they got closer. "Help," he called out. "Please help me. I accidentally locked myself in this shipping container."

The teens went silent. Micha could only hope they didn't take off running. "Please," he called out again, banging on the metal side for emphasis. "I'm afraid I'm going to run out of air in here."

"Let's go," one of the boys urged. "This could be some sort of trick."

"It's not," Micha hollered. "Who the hell would lock themselves in a small metal box and then sit around waiting for someone to show up as a trick?"

"He has a point," another young male voice said. Then, a bit louder: "Where are you, man?"

"In here." Micha banged again, a steady cadence of tapping to let them know his location. "It's dark and hot and I have no idea where the door is."

They began talking among themselves, their voices

too low for him to hear. Heart pounding, he tried to remain still, to wait out their decision.

"Bang again," the same male voice ordered. "There are, like, hundreds of these metal containers here. It's hard to tell where your voice is coming from."

He began tapping again, more softly this time, but loud enough that they should be able to find him.

A second later, he heard the sound of the door bolt sliding back and the door opened. Though it was still nightfall, there were numerous lampposts that gave off enough light to momentarily blind him.

Still, he managed to propel himself forward, stumbling out and nearly falling. Luckily, one of the kids caught him.

"Whoa." The teen stared. "You look awful. What happened to you to mess you up like that?"

Micha glanced down at his shirt and for the first time realized he was covered in blood. He reached his hand for his still-throbbing head and his fingers came back bloody from where Andy had clobbered him with the gun.

"Do any of you have a car?" he asked. "Because whoever did this to me is likely on his way to hurt my girlfriend. I need a lift to Hyde Park."

Most of the kids—teen boys, all of them—began backing away and shaking their heads. "We don't want no trouble," one said. "We're not even supposed to be here."

But one kid stood his ground, eyeing Micha thoughtfully. "You're in real trouble, aren't you?"

Slowly, Micha nodded. "I don't want him to hurt my

lady. You don't even have to take me to her house, just drop me off down the street. I promise, you won't see me again."

While the teen considered him, Micha held his breath.

"Come on," the kid finally said, motioning with his hand. "Since it's my dad's SUV, I get to decide. The only thing is, you can't get blood on the seats, 'kay?"

"I won't," Micha agreed. "My head is the only thing bleeding and I'll keep it away from the seat."

Apparently satisfied, the teen led the way through the maze of containers. They finally emerged in a fenced-off parking lot, skirted the gate and went around to a back street. A large, dark-colored Suburban was the only vehicle in sight.

"You sit up front with me," the kid told Micha. "The rest of you can all fit in the back two seats."

Micha did as he was told. So did the others, who apparently looked up to their leader. "When you got here, did you happen to notice any other vehicles parked around? Specifically, some sort of van?"

"No." The boy started the car. "But I'm thinking maybe you should go ahead and call the police."

"I've got to check on my girlfriend first." The urgency in Micha's tone made all the teenagers go silent. "Please. We need to hurry." He thought again, and then decided. "I do have a friend in the Chicago PD. I'm going to call him and let him know what's happening."

Nodding, the boy passed Micha his phone. Micha dialed Charlie Crenshaw's number from memory, unsurprised when the call went straight to voice mail. He went ahead and left a message, detailing what had happened to him and that he was on the way to Carly's house and the time. "If you get this before morning, meet me there," he said, and ended the call. All he could do now was hope he got there in time.

BRIDGET BARKED, STARTLING Carly awake. She must have dozed off at the kitchen table with her head pillowed on her arms. Blinking, she pushed groggily to her feet and eyed her dog. Now Bridget faced the front door, her tail wagging furiously.

A moment later, her phone chimed, signaling a text from Jones. I'm here, it read. And then almost immediately he knocked.

Padding toward the door on bare feet, she went ahead and checked the peephole before unlocking the dead bolt. Behind her, Bridget stood furiously wagging her tail.

As soon as Jones stepped inside, Carly closed and locked the door, her racing heart settling down into its usual steady beat.

"Hey, girl," Jones said, crouching down to pet her dog. Bridget leaned into him with a groan of pleasure, her eyes half-closed while he scratched behind her ears. Straightening, he held out a cell phone to Carly. "I found this on the sidewalk in front of your house. Did you drop your phone?"

"No." Heart in her throat, she took it from him. "I think that's Micha's," she said, turning it over in her hands. "In fact, I'm positive it is."

Jones cursed. Carly raised her gaze to his. "This means Micha is in danger."

"We don't know that," Jones argued. "Do you know

his passcode to unlock his phone? We might find some more info there."

"I don't," she said thoughtfully. "But I bet I can guess." She typed in 0922, which had been the date she and Micha were originally supposed to get married. The screen vibrated but the phone didn't open. "That wasn't it." Considering, she tried Micha's birthday. "Nope."

Jones watched her with a mixture of concern and amusement. "Not as easy as you thought, I take it?"

"I'll figure it out," she replied. "Clearly, guys think differently than women. How did you decide on your passcode?"

Jones shrugged. "Do you remember the date you and Micha first met?"

"Of course." Without waiting, she typed that in. And just like that, the phone unlocked. "I'm in. Good job, Jones. But how did you know?"

"Just a lucky guess." Jones grinned. "What's open on the screen?"

"It looks like Micha was in the middle of texting me," she said. "He'd typed, About to be… About to be where? Or what?" She frowned. "What did he mean?"

"Maybe, about to be home?" Jones suggested. "Since it looks like he was texting you on the way toward your front door."

"Which means he was grabbed?" Heart beginning to pound, she stared at her brother in horror. "Should I call the police?"

"Not yet." Jones held out his hand for Micha's phone. "Let me take a look and see if I can find any other clues."

She stood close, watching as he scrolled through the

list of recent calls. "He's been busy," Jones commented. "He made several calls this evening. Several of them out of state. Let's check his web browser."

Though doing all this felt like a huge invasion of Micha's privacy, Carly nodded. She didn't see where they had any other choice.

"There are a couple of websites still open. Look." Jones showed her. "A few army ones, and he did a search for someone named Andy Shackleford. Does that name ring a bell with you?"

Carly shook her head. "No. Micha never mentioned him."

"What I think we should do next is call some of the numbers that Micha did. Maybe a few of those people might have some insight as to where he's gone or what he was doing."

Again, Carly had to quash back her uneasiness. "Do you want to call them or should I?" Glancing at the clock, she winced. "You realize we'll be waking all of these people up."

Jones patted her shoulder. "It's for a good cause. I'll do it. I don't mind."

She thanked him. "Do you want something to drink? Water, tea?"

"Do you have any coffee?" he asked. "I know it's after two in the morning, but I just got off work. I'll be up for a long time yet."

"Sure. I can make you a cup."

He followed her into the kitchen, still scrolling on Micha's phone. "He made all of these phone calls much earlier today. There hasn't been any activity since around ten-thirty."

Eyeing him while the coffee brewed, she shook her head. "Maybe we should let the police handle this. I doubt any of those people had anything to do with Micha disappearing."

Watching her, Jones slowly nodded. "You're probably right. Let's call January's fiancé, Sean, since he works in Homicide, alongside Detective Joe Parker, who is also on the case. I'd rather deal with someone we know rather than Dispatch and then whichever officers happen to be on duty."

"I agree." She took a deep breath, calling on her nurse's training to remain calm. "I've been dealing with a police officer named Charlie Crenshaw. He's one of Micha's friends. I'm going to speak to him while you're talking with Sean."

"Sounds like a plan." Jones gave her a brotherly hug. "It's all going to be okay. If there's anyone who knows how to take care of himself, it's Micha."

Though she nodded, she couldn't help but think of the car explosion and the person who'd shot out her front window. Whoever had Micha meant him serious harm. She could only hope Micha would survive this. She couldn't lose him again.

"I love him," she said out loud, shaking her head. "I really, really love him."

Jones stared at her. "Well, duh. Why do you sound so surprised? The entire family knows how much you and Micha love each other. Just like January loves Sean and Heath loves Kylie." He shook his head. "Now let me make my call and you make yours. The sooner we get law enforcement working on this, the sooner we can find Micha and get him back home safe."

"I agree." Turning her back to Jones, she located the number Charlie Crenshaw had given her and called it. As she'd suspected it would, due to the lateness of the hour, the call went straight to voice mail. Carly left her name and number and a quick description of what they thought might have happened to Micha. Right before she was about to end the call, she remembered to add the name Andy Shackleford.

When she'd finished, she turned around to find her brother clearly doing the same thing and leaving his own message.

"No one wants to take a call at this time of the night," he said, shrugging. "But at least the messages will be there whenever they check."

Bridget growled, the hair on her back rising. She rose from her dog bed, eyeing the front door.

"What's wrong, girl?" Carly asked.

Jones grabbed her arm. "Come on," he said. "Out the back door right now."

"I'm not leaving my dog." Quickly, Carly clipped a leash on Bridget's collar. Then, with Jones urging her along, they all rushed out the back door, down the steps and into the yard.

"I want you to hide in the storage building," Jones told her, giving her a gentle push.

But Carly refused to budge. "Not without you. Come with us."

"I'm going to double around and see who's out front,"

he told her. "Please, Carly. Micha would never forgive me if I let something happen to you."

Reluctantly, she ducked into the storage shed, bringing Bridget with her. "Be careful," she told her brother. "Because I won't be able to live with myself if anything happens to you, understand?"

Jones nodded once, and then slipped off into the darkness on the side of her house. Heart pounding, feeling like the worst kind of coward, Carly crouched in the darkness, petting her dog, hoping to keep her from barking.

But although Bridget appeared restless, on edge, she kept quiet. Other than occasionally growling low in her throat. She crouched low, allowing Carly to hold her, though she never took her gaze off the exit.

After what felt like forever, Jones finally appeared. "It's okay to come out," he said, slightly out of breath. "False alarm. I checked all sides of the house and up and down the street. Didn't see another person. Let's get back inside."

Carly exhaled. "I'm beginning to think Micha might have a valid point about me going to stay with you or Heath," she said, her voice shakier than she would have liked. "I can't live like this."

"I can't tell you how relieved I am to hear you say that. But come on." Jones took her arm. "I'll feel safer once we're all behind locked doors."

Agreeing, Carly ran for the back door, Bridget keeping low to the ground but not leaving her side. Jones made up the rear.

Inside the brightly lit kitchen, Carly turned the dead bolt. "There," she said, slightly out of breath. "We're safe."

Still on the leash, Bridget snarled, baring her teeth as she faced the hallway. The back of Carly's neck prickled as she followed her dog's gaze. A man wearing military fatigues and body armor stepped into the kitchen. He had a huge military type of gun pointed directly at her.

"Nobody move," he ordered. "Lady, keep your dog under control or I'll kill it."

Nodding, heart pounding so hard the blood roared in her ears, Carly kept a tight grip on the leash. Bridget continued to snarl, struggling to lunge toward the stranger. "Bridget!" Carly ordered. "No."

To her surprise and relief, the dog instantly quieted, though she never took her intent gaze from the man with the gun. Carly suspected Bridget would bite him if she got the chance, but Carly couldn't take the chance of allowing her dog to be hurt or worse.

Eyeing the man, Carly recognized the pain behind the anger in his eyes. She'd seen it too many times before in the NICU, in both men and women as they tried to deal with the cruel blow dealt to them by fate as their newborns struggled to live.

"Did you know Micha over there in Afghanistan?" Carly asked, hazarding a guess. "Are you Andy Shackleford?"

Surprise flickered across the other man's face, though he quickly buried it. Emotionless, he stared at her, keeping his weapon pointed in her direction. "Shut up. Both of you, back against the wall."

Ignoring him, Jones stepped in front of Carly, his

body language making it plain the man would have to go through him to get to her. "What do you want?" he asked. "Micha's not here."

Andy Shackleford—if that's who he was—bared his teeth in a semblance of a smile. "I know he's not here," he said, the twisted grimace on his face making him appear to be in a weird combination of pain and glee. "Because I have him locked up. I'll deal with him after I make him watch me slowly kill the woman he loves."

Carly gasped. She pushed around her brother so she could see the other man. "Why? Whatever Micha did to make you hate him, killing me won't change anything. You have to know this."

Eyes narrowing, he shrugged. "Maybe not. But at least I'll get to make him pay for what he did to me."

"You are Andy Shackleford, aren't you?"

"I am." His response came without inflection. "Have you heard of me?"

Behind her, Jones grabbed her arm and squeezed, his way of warning her to be careful. While she understood his concern, she figured their only chance right now would be to keep this guy talking. At some point, Sean or Charlie would have to listen to their messages. Hopefully before morning.

She lifted her chin, deciding to respond without really answering his question. "Tell me what he did to you, Andy Shackleford. I at least deserve to know the reason you want to hurt me."

Unblinking, he considered. "I'm sure he's told you the story. He thought he was some big hotshot spy, but he got captured. I was part of the rescue mission to get him out."

"And the chopper crashed." Eyeing him, she put two and two together. "You were also injured in the crash."

"I was." He gave a jerky sort of nod. "Lost my leg. Nearly died. And that was the end of my military career. I was going places and it was over, just like that. Because of Micha. Now the time has come to make him pay."

Chapter Thirteen

The kids dropped Micha off at the end of the block, per his request. He thanked them, dug out a twenty and handed it to the driver. "For gas," he said. He stayed put, watching them as they drove off, wondering if he'd made a mistake by not calling 911. For all he knew, Charlie Crenshaw might be on vacation.

Too late now. Second-guessing himself would only make him less effective.

When he reached Carly's house, he was relieved to notice Jones's vehicle parked out front. Good. At least Jones had stayed with her, so she wasn't alone. Between her brother and her vigilant dog, she'd have plenty of protection. And who knew, maybe Micha was wrong by trying to guess what Shackleford would do next.

As a precaution, Micha swung around to the back. As he'd suspected, yellow light from the kitchen spilled into the backyard. Moving as quietly as possible, Micha noticed the back door hadn't been closed all the way. He'd just reached for the handle when he heard voices.

"Because of Micha. Now the time has come to make him pay." Andy Shackleford. Crossing to the window where the video camera had been placed, Micha peered into the kitchen. Jones and Carly faced the window, luckily. Shackleford should know better, Micha thought, standing with his back to the door like that. He must have gotten overconfident, complacent. Which again would work in Micha's favor.

Then he saw the gun. He recognized it immediately. It appeared to be a Ruger SR-556, an AR-15-style semi-automatic rifle. Overkill for something like this, but he remembered Andy Shackleford had never been subtle.

Damn. Judging from the way the other man held the weapon, Micha figured Andy's finger hovered right over the trigger. If Micha went with his original plan and rushed him, Andy could easily squeeze off multiple shots and hurt or kill both Carly and Jones.

Not acceptable odds.

He'd have to come up with another plan.

Inside, a cell phone started ringing. Judging by the ring tone, Micha figured it was his. No one answered. Micha could only hope Charlie Crenshaw had gotten his message and was now trying to call him back.

That gave Micha an idea. He slipped back around to the front and rang the doorbell, then dashed around to the back door. Bridget started barking and Carly's voice sounded frantic as she tried to calm her pet. Jones added his voice to hers, which led Micha to believe Andy must have threatened to hurt the dog.

Andy cursed. And cursed again. "Who is it?" he demanded. "Who the hell comes to visit after two o'clock in the morning?"

"I don't know." Carly kept her tone calm. "If we don't answer, they'll probably go away."

"Good." Andy turned and motioned toward the back door. "We'll give them a few minutes to leave and then we're going."

"Going where?" Carly asked.

"To reunite you with your beloved," Andy said. "We three have a lot of catching up to do."

Looking toward the window where Micha crouched, Jones must have caught sight of him. His eyes widened, but that was the only reaction he showed. He turned away, stepping in between Carly and Andy. "You're not taking her anywhere without me," he said, arms crossed.

"Such devotion," Andy mocked. "And all for nothing. Are you really willing to die for your girlfriend, knowing she's messing around with another man?"

"She's my sister," Jones replied. "And you'll have to go through me if you intend to try hurting her."

Andy laughed. "Brave words from an unarmed man. You're lucky, though. I still haven't decided what to do with you." With his back to Micha, he motioned to Jones. "Kill you or bring you along with me, that's the question."

The single, staccato whoop of a police siren sounded out front, making even Micha jump. A second later, someone pounded on the front door.

"Chicago Police. Open up."

"Out the back door, now." Motioning wildly with his rifle, Andy herded Carly and Jones toward the exit. Micha knew if he was going to get a chance to take Andy down, this would be it. Andy appeared to be barely able to hang on to the edge of his shredded self-control.

The back door flew open. First Carly, then Jones, ran out; Carly took off left, Jones right. While Andy tried to track them, Micha jumped him.

Andy went down, rifle flying. Jones scrambled for it as Andy rolled, swinging wildly to dislodge Micha. His elbow connected with Micha's jaw, snapping Micha's head back. Before Andy could take another punch, Micha hit him, hard. Once, twice and a third time. He forced Andy's hands behind his back and sat on him, figuring it wouldn't be long until law enforcement showed up.

"Chicago PD." Two armed officers burst through the back door, weapons out. One focused on Jones, who held the rifle loosely. "Drop the gun."

Jones immediately complied, slowly lowering the weapon to the ground before raising his hands up in the air. Carly emerged from the direction of the storage shed, also with one hand up and the other holding tight to Bridget's collar. She walked the dog over toward the house, putting her inside. Then, both hands raised, she sat down on the back porch.

Though Andy continued to try to struggle, Micha had a good grip. He glanced up to see his friend Charlie Crenshaw grinning at him. "Looks like you just about had everything under control," Charlie said.

Micha shook his head. "Could I get a little help here, please? Some handcuffs would be nice."

A moment later, with Andy cuffed and scowling, Charlie helped Micha up off the grass. Carly rushed over, wrapping her arms around Micha's waist so tightly he could barely breathe, and held on. Micha hugged her back.

"We'll need to get statements," Charlie said. "And I'm assuming you want to press charges against this guy?"

"Yes," Carly answered. "And not just for breaking and entering, but kidnapping. He had Micha locked up somewhere."

"In a shipping container," both Micha and Charlie said simultaneously.

"He left me a detailed message," Charlie clarified. "I take it this is Lieutenant Andy Shackleford?"

"Yes." Still holding Carly close, Micha regarded his enemy grimly. "He not only set the bomb that blew up my rental car, but he's the one who shot out Carly's front window."

"Attempted murder, too?" Crenshaw sounded almost gleeful.

"Chicago PD!" another voice shouted, and Sean Stafford ran into the backyard. He'd clearly come here straight from bed, as he looked as if he'd just gotten up. Right behind him came Carly's cousin January.

"Carly! Are you all right?" She rushed over, wrapping up Carly's other side in a partial hug.

"She was supposed to wait in the car," Sean said sheepishly. "I'm just glad you guys took care of everything before we got here." He glanced at Charlie. "I called it in, though. There should be a few more guys here shortly."

They all filed inside, filling up Carly's small living room. Cuffed with his hands behind his back, Andy glared at everyone sullenly. His face had started to swell, the bruises purple where Micha had hit him.

Carly gasped when she got a good look at Micha. "Your head," she said, her eyes wide and worried. "The back of your head is all bloody."

Grim-faced, Charlie eyed him. "I'm going to radio for a couple of EMTs."

"No need," Micha started to say. But Crenshaw shook his head and ignored him.

Carly put her small hand up along his cheek. "That needs to get looked at. At least let the EMTs clean it and see if it needs a few stitches. What did he hit you with?"

"I'm not sure, but I'm thinking the butt of the rifle." Though he felt a little bit foolish, Micha had to admit his head hurt like hell.

She winced. "There's an awful lot of blood. I can start getting it cleaned up and take a look at it."

"Since you're a nurse, I'd rather do that," he agreed.

Her stern look coaxed a smile from him. "I still want the EMTs to look at it. Promise me you'll let them."

Since he could deny her nothing, he agreed.

Two more uniformed officers arrived after everyone had gone inside, ringing the front doorbell. Carly let them in and they took custody of a still-sullen Andy, escorting him to their squad car.

"He'll be held downtown," Sean told Micha.

"Locked up, right?" Carly asked. January had finally pried Carly off Micha and stood with her arm around her cousin's shoulders, clearly trying to comfort her.

The EMTs walked right in, making Carly realize the

front door sat wide open. Shaking her head, she went to close it, then led the paramedics over to Micha.

"There's better light in the kitchen," she told them. "Follow me."

They had Micha sit at the kitchen table. With a gentle kind of competence, one of the men got to work checking out his wound while the other took his blood pressure. He almost protested that, but one glance at Carly's steely gaze had him holding his tongue. She went and got a bowl of warm water and a clean washcloth and began carefully cleaning up his head wound.

"Are you sure you don't want to let us take him to the hospital so they can do that?" the EMT asked.

"I'm a nurse," Carly replied. "And I know he won't go."

"He might need antibiotics," the man continued. "And as you know, only a doctor can prescribe those."

"We'll be all right," Carly said, smiling. "I work at the hospital, so I can get him in to see a doctor if necessary."

The man nodded. He shone a small light into Micha's eyes. "You probably have a concussion," he said, getting to his feet. "But if you're absolutely against letting us run you to the ER, I think you're in good hands here."

Micha mumbled his thanks. Carly got up to let the two men out, and they spoke quietly for a moment at the door. He let his gaze follow her as she made her way through the still-crowded living room, the pounding in his head making him ache to close his eyes. He resisted, partly because he seemed to remember something about not going to sleep with a concussion, but mostly because he didn't want to look away from Carly.

"Are you in pain?" Carly asked when she reached him. "Don't even answer that. Let me get you something."

She left again, returning to hand him a couple of pills and a bottle of water. "Nothing prescription," she said. "But they should still help with the pain."

The steady hum of voices from the other room made him long for quiet. As if she understood, Bridget scooted over under the table and rested her head on his leg. Micha stroked her head, glad to have her company.

More than anything, Micha wanted everyone to finish their business and leave so he could be alone with Carly. Soon, he told himself. Despite his aching head, he wanted to hold her and kiss her and show her exactly how much she meant to him. Catching him watching her, the heat in her gaze told him she wanted the exact same thing.

Charlie had Jones in the hallway, taking notes while Jones finished giving his statement. Judging from his exhausted expression, Carly's brother couldn't wait to get out of there and go home.

"Carly, I'm ready for you next," Charlie said, motioning her over. She nodded but went to Jones first and gave him a huge hug. He hugged her back, his gaze meeting Micha's over the top of her head. Once she released him and walked over to talk to Charlie, Jones dragged his hand through his hair and headed toward the front door. Micha pushed to his feet to join him.

"Thank you," Micha told him, walking him out.

"For what?"

"For keeping Carly safe. I don't know what Andy would have done to her if he'd caught her here alone."

Jones shuddered. "That guy is seriously unhinged."

"Yeah." Micha considered his next words. "Some of what happened over there really messed with a lot of the guys' heads. I didn't know Andy all that well, but from what I was told, before the crash he was career military. They said he put all of his focus on an upward track. The chopper crash kind of ended that for him."

"I understand being bitter about that," Jones said. "But why blame you? Why not blame the pilot?"

"The pilot was killed," Micha replied, his voice quiet. Even now, remembering the crash brought back a lot of pain. "And I guess Andy needed someone to pin his anger on, so he chose me. After all, if I hadn't been captured, there wouldn't have been a rescue mission at all."

"That's flawed thinking." Jones shook his head and unlocked his truck. "I'm going to head home now. I've got a lot of unwinding to do before I can even think about going to bed."

"Thanks again, man," Micha said.

"You take care of yourself and my sister," Jones said, giving a two-fingered wave before getting in his vehicle and driving off.

Micha watched him go and then turned around to head back inside. He made it as far as the front porch steps before he slid to the ground as everything went gray and then black.

ANSWERING ALL OF Officer Crenshaw's questions, Carly kept one eye on the door waiting for Micha to return.

Even though the danger appeared to be past, he had a beast of a head wound. She'd even begun to rethink making him go to the hospital. In fact, once the questions were over, she thought she'd just go ahead and drive him to the ER herself.

When ten minutes had passed and still Micha didn't return, part of her wondered if he might still be talking with Jones. But she'd seen how tired her brother appeared to be and knew how badly he'd wanted to go home. In addition, Micha could barely stand. There was no way he was still out there chatting it up with Jones.

Something was wrong.

Cutting off Charlie mid-question, she took off for the front door, motioning for him to follow.

When she caught sight of Micha slumped on her porch, she let out a low keening cry of worry and rushed to him.

"Do you want me to call for an ambulance?" Charlie asked.

"If we can get him into a squad car, I think it'd be faster to take him that way," she said. "If we could run lights and sirens, that is."

Charlie eyed her doubtfully. "Micha's a big man. I don't know if I can lift him."

"My cousin's fiancé is still here. He's a homicide detective with Chicago PD. If we enlist his help, I'm pretty sure we can get him into a car."

Without waiting for an answer, she ran back inside.

Working together, Sean and Charlie managed to get Micha into Carly's vehicle. Then, with Charlie escorting her, police lights flashing, they headed to the hospital. Sean and January followed close behind.

Once there, Charlie ran inside and alerted the charge nurse. Two orderlies were sent out with a wheelchair, though Carly informed them they'd need to come back with a stretcher instead. Meanwhile, Carly checked Micha's pulse, which was steady, not weak. She wished she had the equipment to check his vital signs. The fact that he'd passed out after a blow on the head had her extremely worried.

After what felt like an eternity, the orderlies returned with two more. All four of them managed to get Micha on the stretcher and inside to triage.

Once inside, Carly was allowed to go back and wait with Micha until the doctor ordered tests, which would be an X-ray and an MRI. "The X-ray will show the bone," the doctor explained. "While the MRI will show the bone as well a soft tissue, so I can take a look at the brain."

Carly nodded. Though she already knew this, she appreciated the doctor taking the time to explain.

While Micha was off having his scans, she returned to the waiting area to let January and Sean know. "Charlie had to go," Sean said. "He wanted me to tell you he'd touch base with you later today."

The small waiting room had free coffee, though Carly knew from experience that it tasted pretty foul. She checked her watch and guessed she really didn't need to ingest caffeine at this hour of the morning. She wasn't scheduled to work today, so she might get some sleep at some point.

Right now, she felt too antsy to sit, so she settled for pacing the waiting room and hallway.

"Did Micha ever wake up?" January asked on her way to get a cup of coffee.

Carly thought about warning her, and then decided her cousin was old enough to make her own choices. "Not that I know of," she said.

Half an hour dragged on by. Carly knew all too well how long things could take in busy hospital ERs, though the near-empty waiting room gave her hope.

"Carly..." January called her name, inclining her head to where the doctor in his white coat had entered, carrying a clipboard.

Heart skipping a beat, Carly hurried over. January and Sean gathered behind her, offering their physical support.

"Mr. Harrison has a linear skull fracture," the doctor said, smiling slightly.

Carly breathed a sigh of relief. "Those are the most common," she told January. "All that's required is usually an anti-inflammatory and rest."

The doctor eyed her approvingly. "That's correct. We feel quite confident that this will heal itself. How did you know?"

"She's a nurse," January answered for her.

"I work in the NICU next door," Carly elaborated.

"Nice to meet you." The doctor smiled again. "He's back in the room, though he was still sleeping so I haven't been able to give him the report. Let us keep an eye on him for a little bit longer, and then we can discharge him to go home with you. I'm thinking another hour or so. Will that work for you?"

"Of course." Carly sagged with relief. Seeing, January put her arm around Carly's shoulders, letting her know without words that she'd help hold her up.

"May we go see him?" Carly asked.

"Certainly." The doctor waved his hand in the general direction of the room. "I'll fill out the paperwork and pre-sign the discharge papers, though I'll make sure the nurse knows he can't leave for at least thirty to forty-five minutes."

Which in hospital-speak meant an hour or more. Carly thanked him.

Once the doctor had left, Carly led January and Sean down the hall to Micha's small room. Micha appeared to still be sleeping, though numerous machines beeped while taking his vital signs. She allowed herself to drop into the hard plastic chair next to the bed. January came over and began to rub Carly's shoulders. "It's going to be all right," she murmured.

Carly's phone, which she'd silenced, began to vibrate, indicating an incoming call. Since it was still way too early for most people to even begin stirring, she figured it might be Jones, calling to check on things. When she saw Heath's number on the caller ID, she shook her head. She might as well go ahead and answer, since Heath wouldn't give up until she did.

"Hi, Heath." She let every bit of her exhaustion show in her voice. "What's up?"

"I just talked to Jones," Heath said. "And as soon as

he told me what had happened, I went by your house, but no one was there. Are you okay? Where are you?"

"At the hospital, but wait," she interrupted him before he could speak. "Micha was injured. He has a skull fracture, but luckily it's not anything requiring surgery. The doctor was just here and said Micha will be discharged soon."

"Do you want me to come up, anyway?" Heath asked, as she'd known he would. "I can be there in thirty minutes."

"No need." Carly didn't bother to suppress her yawn. "We're all exhausted. January and Sean are with me, but as soon as we get to take Micha home, all I want to do is sleep."

"That's understandable." Heath's tone softened. "Are you all right, Carly? Is there anything I can do to help you?"

Carly had never loved her oldest brother more. "Thanks, Heath. Nothing right now, but if I need anything, I know I can count on you."

"Promise me you'll call me."

"I will."

Ending the call, Carly raised her head to find Micha had opened his eyes and was watching her.

"Hey, there," she said, leaning in closer. "How are you feeling?"

Slowly he reached up and felt the bandage on his head. He winced. "What the heck happened?"

"You took a dive on the front porch," she said, leaning in to take his hand in hers. "Turns out when Andy hit you, he fractured your skull."

His eyes went wide. "What?"

"It's okay." Squeezing his hand, she carefully kissed his cheek. "They expect it to heal on its own. The doctor was just in and he's discharging you today. You'll have to take it easy for a while."

"Andy's still in custody, right?"

She nodded. "It's over, Micha. It's finally over."

"At least that part of it is," Micha agreed. "Now they just need to find your father's and uncle's killer."

Touched that he'd thought of her family in the middle of his own crisis, she started to tell him not to worry about that right now but Sean pushed forward.

"We've got multiple people and agencies working on that," Sean said. "Sooner or later, the murderer will make a mistake. They always do. And then we'll have them. Right now it's a matter of trying to make sure no one else gets killed. There's always a fine line in cases like this."

"Thanks," Micha replied, his eyes drifting closed.

Carly turned to her cousin and her fiancé. "I'm a little concerned about Simone," she said, keeping her voice low. "She seems obsessed with finding our fathers' killer. I'm worried she might get herself in trouble."

"I agree." January grimaced, her expression troubled. "When Simone fixates on something, she doesn't give up until she's resolved whatever it is."

"I'll talk to her," Sean promised. "I'll try to make her understand there are numerous professionals working around the clock to solve this case. Hopefully, once she gets that reassurance, she'll stand down."

Privately, Carly doubted that. January caught her gaze

and gave a tiny shake of her head, letting Carly know she felt the same way. After all, she knew her sister.

"Thanks for coming," Carly told them, motioning toward the door. "Since we're just waiting to be discharged, why don't you two go on home and get some rest."

"Are you sure?" January asked, appearing unconvinced.

"I am." Carly shooed them away. "I'll be fine. I really appreciate you both coming."

Exchanging glances, January and Sean quietly said their goodbyes and left.

Alone in the room, Carly sat by Micha's side and watched him sleep. She couldn't believe how close she'd come to actually losing him a second time.

He was her person. The one who understood her, loved her and had her back. Despite two years apart, they still got each other's jokes, understood when certain occasions called for what kind of food.

And the chemistry… One glance from his brown eyes was enough to send her pulse into overtime.

Once, she'd thought they needed to take things slow, to get to know one another again. Now she understood all too well how fleeting and fickle time could be. And she and Micha had always been on the same wavelength. None of that had changed. Neither time nor distance had been able to take that from them.

Micha had opened his eyes again by the time a nurse appeared with his discharge papers. Carly hunted down his clothes, which had been placed in a plastic bag under the bed, and helped him get dressed. The nurse brought a wheelchair, waving off Micha's protests that he could walk. "Standard procedure," she and Carly said at the same time.

"I'll go get the car." Carly took off, almost running.

She pulled around and opened the front passenger door, watching as Micha stood and gingerly got in.

All the way home, Carly drove slowly and carefully, not wanting to jostle him in any way. Once they reached the house, she parked and went around to help him get out. "You can lean on me," she offered.

"I can walk," he insisted, though he let her slip her arm around him with her shoulder under his arm.

Inside the house, Bridget wiggled and wagged, clearly glad to see them. "Just a minute, girl," Carly told the dog. "Let me get Micha settled and then I'll take you out."

In the bedroom, Micha sat gratefully on the edge of her bed and allowed Carly to help undress him. Clad only in his boxers, he climbed in between the sheets. Carly brought him a glass of water and went to take care of her pet.

Once she'd returned, Carly allowed exhaustion to claim her. She downed a glass of water, double-checked all the door locks, turned out the lights and went back to her bedroom with Bridget following at her heels. Bridget got settled in her dog bed, heaving a contented sigh that made Carly smile.

Grabbing her oldest, softest oversize T-shirt, she climbed into bed next to the man she loved. Moving carefully so she wouldn't wake him, she debated on whether or not to spoon him. In the end, she decided just to let part of her arm rest against his back, touching him, yet not enough to disturb him.

"Come here," Micha rasped, rolling onto his side to face her. "You know I can't sleep unless I'm holding you."

This made her happier than it should have. This, with him spooning her from behind, was how she wanted to sleep for the rest of her life. She'd tell Micha that in the morning.

Chapter Fourteen

Micha awoke sometime in the morning with a curvy, soft woman in his arms and a raging hard-on. He also had a killer headache, which should have been enough to destroy any amorous thoughts.

But his body apparently had other ideas.

He tried to ease away, to roll over so Carly wouldn't notice the proof of his desire pressed so heavily against her.

Instead, Carly tightened her arms around him and burrowed deeper into the covers. Her even breathing indicated she was still asleep.

Closing his eyes, Micha tried to clear his mind, to focus on something else, anything else but the aching need to bury himself inside her. The throbbing in his head finally outweighed everything else, and he slipped off to sleep.

When he woke again, he was alone in the bed and sunlight streamed through the window. His headache had gone. Stretching, he stood. He thought he almost felt normal. Though the clock on the nightstand showed it was after ten in the morning, he could hear Carly moving around in the other room, long after she should have been at work. A twinge of unease had him pushing to his feet.

"Carly?" he called out. "What's going on?"

Carly appeared in the bedroom doorway, her expression troubled. "I'm glad you're awake. You got a phone call while you were asleep. I probably shouldn't have answered it, but I didn't want to disturb you, so I did." She took a deep breath. "It was your mother, Micha. Your father is in the hospital. She didn't go into too many details. She asked for you to call her back. It sounds like she wants you to come home."

Micha froze. He started to shake his head, but a jab of pain stopped him, reminding him of his head injury. He hadn't spoken to his mother in person since his brother's death, though he'd kept every letter she'd sent him. He'd supposed the military had notified her of his supposed death, the same way they'd told Carly.

Since his father had already declared Micha dead to him long before the helicopter crash, Micha hadn't seen any need to inform his parents of his ultimate survival. He figured his actual death might have finally given them both peace.

"My mother called?" he repeated, still trying to process Carly's words. "How is that even possible? Where would she get my number?"

"Since clearly she knows you're alive, it seems likely someone in the military gave it to her." Carly came closer, putting her arm around him gently. "And she wants you and your father to patch things up while there's still a chance."

Micha sat back down on the edge of the bed. Carly dropped down next to him. She silently handed him his phone. Feeling hollow, he accepted it, turning it over and over in his hand. "I'm not sure what to think," he began.

"Don't think, feel." Carly laid her hand on his arm. "We've been given a second chance, you and I. Maybe your parents deserve one, too."

Pushing to her feet, she left him there, alone with his thoughts and his phone.

Micha thought of the last time he'd seen his father, of the anguish that had darkened the older man's brown eyes as he'd prepared to bury his firstborn. He'd been so proud of his two boys, serving their country. He'd already been struggling to keep the farm going, pinning everything on Brian's promise to take over when he'd completed his military service.

All of that had been gone in a flash.

Micha had been just as stunned and hurt as his parents, maybe even more since he'd idolized his older brother. The ruin of his parents' hopes and dreams had hit them hard, but after losing Brian, Micha had actually begun to question the wisdom of copying his brother's life choices. At least as far as joining the military.

In the midst of all this grief and uncertainty, Micha's parents had asked him to give up all his dreams and essentially become Brian.

The things his father had said to him when he refused were the kinds of words that could never be taken back. And to this day, so many years later, Micha had not forgotten them.

But there were other times Micha could remember. The county fair, prize calves and the carnival rides after. Every year without fail, his father had taken his boys and let them ride every ride, eat as much cotton candy and as many hot dogs as they wanted, until they'd gotten so tired they'd fallen asleep in the truck on the way back home to the farm.

When Micha had gone on his first date with pretty Sally Fromm from town, his father had sat Micha down and had *the talk* with him. He'd slung his work-roughened hand around Micha's shoulders and they'd talked and laughed and Micha had gone away feeling good about what it meant to be a Harrison man.

Memories came rushing back, one after the other, and to his surprise Micha felt tears pricking at the back of his eyelids.

The events of the last two years—being captured, the helicopter crash, the burns, almost dying and the long slow climb back to recovery. He hadn't dared to even hope for Carly's forgiveness, or to once again have her love. And yes, he'd also missed his parents, his family. He'd even missed that damned dairy farm.

In fact, he'd made a carving of his parents, standing with their arms around each other, and with their family dog at their feet. He thought of that now and went to get it, running his thumb over the smooth and polished wood.

Hands shaking, he pulled up the recent call list and hit Redial to call back the same number he remembered from his childhood, the landline that his parents had clearly hung on to.

His mother answered, sounding so much older he caught his breath and could barely get out the word "Hello."

"Micha," she said, recognizing his voice. She started to cry. "I'm so glad you called."

"It's good to hear from you, Mom," he said cautiously. "What's going on with Dad?"

She told him about his father and the stubborn man's refusal to go to a doctor for regular checkups. As a result, she'd walked into the kitchen one morning and found him nonresponsive. He'd had a stroke. Only her panicked phone call to 911 and their quick response had saved his life. He'd spent ten days in the hospital and had just been moved to a rehabilitation facility. She'd spent much of that time trying to track Micha down.

"Is he going to be all right?" Micha asked, stunned.

"He's got a long road ahead of him," she replied. "He's relearning how to walk, and his speech was also affected. The doctors have been cautiously optimistic about his recovery, but he won't ever be the same man he was before."

Micha wasn't sure how to respond. He was still trying to process the unexpected swell of emotion he'd felt upon hearing the news. His father had always seemed larger than life, invincible.

"Will you come visit?" his mother asked. "Please. I know he'd love to see you, as would I."

Though his first instinct was to hold on to his pride and refuse, the trials he'd been through had made him rethink many things. Holding grudges served no purpose other than to deepen the hurt and bitterness. "Would he want me there?" he asked, even though he wasn't sure he was ready for the answer.

Though she could have lied, Micha's mother gave him the truth. "Though I'd like to think he would, I'm not sure. He has no clue that I called you. But know this, ever since he said what he did at Brian's funeral, he's regretted those words. He deserves a second chance. We both do."

"I'll come," he said, making an instant decision. "But I'll be bringing someone with me. I'd really like you to meet her."

"I'd love that," she said instantly. "I figured there was someone special when she answered the phone. In fact, I'd be honored to meet her. Please tell me about her, where you met and how long you two have been together."

Micha took a deep breath. He allowed the love he felt to show in his voice as he spoke about Carly. He went back to the beginning, to his initial proposal, their plans to marry and then what had happened to him in Afghanistan.

She gasped when he told her about being captured and then went quiet when he talked about his burns, the scars, and the years of physical therapy and recovery.

"We learned when they told us you were alive that you'd been hurt," she said softly. "We just didn't know the extent of it. I called, but because you hadn't put me on the list of people authorized to receive information, they wouldn't tell me anything."

"Wait," he interrupted. "They *told* you that I was alive?"

"Yes, of course. They'd sent two men in uniform to announce your death. Those same two came back to let us know there'd been a terrible mistake."

Stunned, he shook his head. "They didn't correct the misinformation with Carly," he said, bemused. "All this time, she truly believed I was dead. She was furious with me for not reaching out and letting her know."

"I can't say I blame her," she agreed, a hint of reproach in her voice. "That must have been very painful. I know it was for me."

He swallowed back the urge to remind her that she'd stood by his father when they'd said Micha was dead to him. Even now, that hurt. He'd had lots of time to reflect on those words, both while captive and while in the hospital and rehab. He'd finally thought he'd managed to forgive, but he'd known he'd never forget.

"I made a mistake. Shutting Carly out of my life was the worst one."

"I made a mistake, too," his mother said softly. "I can only hope you'll forgive me the same way Carly clearly forgave you."

Those words…she was right. He turned the carving over in his hand, thinking how much he'd like to give it to her. To them.

From the corner of his eye, he saw Carly slip into the room. She sat down next to him and put her hand on his shoulder, offering her physical support. Turning slightly, he placed a kiss on the back of her hand.

"We all make mistakes," his mother continued. "And

we all have regrets. If she had known, would you have let her visit you in the hospital?"

Even now, he wasn't sure. He'd been in a lot of pain, had been told he was disfigured for life, and severe depression had taken hold.

"I didn't want anyone to know what had happened to me," he said, his voice breaking. "Not even Carly. And she's the love of my life."

Next to him, he registered Carly's swift intake of breath. Glancing at her, he mouthed, *As if you didn't know.*

When his mother spoke again, he could hear the tears in her voice. "When can you be here?"

Though he wanted to say they'd leave immediately, he knew he had to check with Carly about her work schedule. It wasn't even a bad drive, right around five hours. "I'll have to let you know. Oh, and Carly's dog will be coming with us. I hope you don't mind."

"Of course not. But please, hurry."

"I'll call you when we're on our way," he said. After ending the call, he dropped the phone on the bed and turned to Carly, taking both her hands in his. "My father had another stroke. It's not looking good," he told her. "My mother wants me to come see him, and her. I agreed." Swallowing, he looked deep into her eyes. "Carly, I'd like you—and Bridget, if that's okay—to go with me. It's time for me to mend old fences and I want you to meet my mom. I know you have to work, but—"

Leaning forward, she kissed him, effectively cutting him off. "Let's go. I already asked for four personal days off due to your head injury. Since I never use my time off, it was granted. So let's get packed and head out."

"I need to shower," he began.

"Fine, just don't let that bandage on your head get wet. Maybe take a sponge bath instead for now." She pushed to her feet, and then turned around and kissed him one more time for good measure.

"Bossy," he muttered, smiling against her lips.

"You betcha." Smiling back, she tossed her head. "By the way, I'm driving. No way I'm letting you near the driver's seat with that skull fracture." She shot him a sideways glance. "I'm looking forward to driving that new Jeep. A road trip is just what it needs to break it in."

As she swept from the room, he found himself grinning. Carly paused at the doorway and wagged her finger at him. "Now shower and pack," she ordered. "I bet we can be ready to go in less than an hour."

Impressed, he nodded and took himself off for the bathroom. Deciding to do as Carly had directed, he took a sponge bath, careful to keep his head and bandage dry. He got dressed, trying to imagine seeing his parents and the farm again after being away for so long and couldn't. Since he'd told his mother he'd let her know when they were on the way, he gave her a quick call before grabbing his rolling duffel bag and beginning to pack.

Carly waited for him in the kitchen when he towed his bag in there twenty minutes later. She'd just finished packing dog food and her own bag sat by the front door. "I've let both my brothers know where I'll be," she told him. "And I was going to make sandwiches for lunch, but now I'm thinking we can just get fast food along the way."

She'd left her long blond hair down and the sunlight streaming through the kitchen window lit her up in a golden glow. Her bright blue eyes and serious expression only made him ache for her. He always had and figured he always would.

As if she knew his thoughts, she met his gaze. A slow smile blossomed across her face, lighting her up from within.

He went to her and took her into his arms. Holding her close, he breathed in the light floral scent of her, marveling at what a lucky man he was to have her.

"You're the love of my life, too," she said softly. "I want you to know that, Micha. I'm glad you came back to me."

Then, just as he was debating kissing her, maybe even try to convince her to go back to the bed for a bit, she stepped away and heaved a sigh. "Mushy stuff over," she said with mock severity. "We need to get on the road," she said, her voice brisk. "I'll carry everything out and get it loaded in your Jeep."

Bemused, he managed a nod, though damned if he was going to sit around and watch her do all the work. He'd injured his head, not his arms. As she went out the door, he grabbed his bag and followed her.

Though she raised her brows when she saw him, she only shook her head and held out her hand for his keys.

GRIPPING THE STEERING WHEEL, Carly warred between nerves and exhilaration. Bridget had settled down in the back seat and quickly fallen asleep. "How are you feeling?" she asked Micha, driving 90 South toward Indiana.

He shrugged, trying for nonchalance, but she could see the tension in the way he held his shoulders. "I'm not sure. My father is dying. I haven't seen either of my parents for years. So much wasted time, all because of my father's stubborn pride. And now I'm going to see him when it's too late to try for any kind of meaningful relationship." He swallowed hard. "I'm not going to lie. It hurts. Like hell."

The sorrow in his voice had her aching for him. He'd been through so much and somehow managed to emerge from everything with more strength and compassion than any man she'd ever known, with the exception of her brothers and her late father and uncle.

"You'll get through this," she promised. "*We'll* get through this."

Micha nodded but didn't comment. He'd put the address into the Jeep's navigation system for her and turned his head to look out the window. About an hour into the trip, Carly could tell by his even breathing that he'd fallen asleep. She figured this had to be a good thing. That way, he'd at least be well rested, which would hopefully give him strength to deal with what lay ahead.

Alternating between watching the road and checking on Micha, she realized there was something very important she needed to do before meeting Micha's mother. The thought made her feel as if drunken squirrels had taken up residence in her stomach. But the longer she drove, the more she came to understand this was the right thing to do. She just wasn't sure when. Since she had no actual plan, she figured she'd simply have to play it by ear. As long as Micha continued to sleep, she didn't have to worry about it, so she pushed it to the back of her mind.

A little over two hours from when they'd left Chicago, she took the exit toward a town called Goshen, Indiana, simply because she liked the name. Cruising down Main Street, she eyed the refinished storefronts, enjoying the warm, welcoming feel of the small town. She pulled into the parking lot of a place called Hopper's Pike Street Grill, and parked under the shade of a huge oak tree.

When she did, Micha blinked and sat up. "Where are we?" he rasped.

"Goshen, Indiana. This seemed like a good time to stop for lunch. A lot of the downtown places appear to only open for dinner, but this one looks like they have lunch."

He nodded, covering a yawn with his hand. "I've been asleep the whole time, haven't I?"

"You have. I'm thinking you must really need the rest." *Now? Should she ask him now?* Her heart started to race and she took a deep breath to calm herself. Maybe after lunch.

"Do you mind getting something to go?" Micha asked. "I'm not sure I'm up for going in to eat right now."

"I understand." Reaching over, she squeezed his shoulder. "That was actually my plan. But I also need to stretch my legs and visit the ladies' room, plus let Bridget out. Are you sure you don't want to get out and walk around, too?"

Micha considered, finally giving a small nod. "That might not be a bad idea."

After taking Bridget on a leash to relieve herself, Carly poured some bottled water into a plastic bowl she'd brought so her dog could get a drink. "Though it's not really hot, I'm not comfortable leaving Bridget in the Jeep," she said. "You go ahead in and when you come back out I'll take a turn."

Micha touched the bandage on his head. "Do you think they'd believe it if we said she was my service dog?"

Considering, Carly shrugged. "It's worth a shot, even though we don't have a vest on her or anything. Some restaurants let dogs eat out on the patio. Maybe they have one out back."

With Bridget at her side, Carly and Micha walked into the restaurant together. Immediately, the delicious smell of fried chicken made Carly's mouth water. "I'll meet you back here at the entrance," she told Micha. "Then I'll see if I can place a to-go order."

Turning, Micha frowned. "I've changed my mind. Let's sit down and take a few minutes to eat. The break will be nice. That is, if they let my service dog stay." He spoke loudly enough so that the hostess looked up, eyed him and Bridget, and gave a quick nod.

Since the lunch rush had clearly already happened and the restaurant seemed mostly empty, this no doubt influenced the hostess's decision. Carly held the dog while Micha went to the men's room and he did the same when her turn came.

When they were all together again, the hostess found

them a booth in the back of the room near the window
and brought them menus. Bridget settled quietly under
the table. "She's the perfect dog," Carly told Micha.

The waitress came and took their drink orders, asking
them if they knew what they wanted or if they needed
time to look at the menu.

Checking out the lunch specials on the back page,
Carly ordered the fried chicken. Micha did the same.
To her relief, Micha's gaze appeared to be a lot more
focused than it had been earlier.

"Are you feeling better?" she asked, trying to push
back her nervousness so she could put out there what
needed to be asked. Was now the right time? Her stomach churned, making her realize she couldn't do this and
eat, so once again she decided to wait.

"I am." He studied her intently. "But are you? You
seem worried or upset."

Though she knew he'd see through her fake smile, she
smiled, anyway. "I'm fine. Maybe a bit nervous about
meeting your mother." Which was the truth, just not
all of it.

Their food arrived, the golden chicken crispy. It tasted
as wonderful as it smelled.

Once they'd finished up, when the waitress arrived
with the check, Micha snatched it. "My treat," he said,
ignoring Carly's protests.

Back in the Jeep, Micha fell asleep almost immediately. Carly watched him, slightly concerned, but also
aware sleep helped the body heal.

This time, he only dozed for thirty minutes, waking
and giving her the sexiest, sleepy smile she'd ever seen.

"Sorry about that," he rumbled, stretching. "I promise I'll try to stay awake now. All that food…"

Stifling her own yawn, she nodded. "I know. It's been a struggle."

This made him sit up straighter. "Really? Do you want me to take over?"

She laughed at that. "Nope, I'm good. We only have a few more hours to go."

Finally, a sign appeared announcing they had reached Rawson, Ohio. "Home sweet home," Micha drawled. "Though the farm is really on the outskirts, kind of in between Rawson and Mount Cory."

Shutting off the GPS, Micha gave directions, pointing out where he'd gone to school and some of the places where he and his brother, Brian, had hung out. Since he rarely ever even spoke his brother's name out loud, she caught her breath and waited to see if he'd say more.

"There were city kids and country kids," he mused. "Brian and I desperately wanted to be city, but of course we weren't."

Keeping silent, she nodded. She could hear him trying to rein in the raw emotion in his voice. She wondered if he'd ever properly grieved his brother, or if that, too, was catching up with him as he tried to come to terms with his father's serious illness. In this, she knew she could only be there for him if he needed her. He had to face this on his own, though she planned to be standing by his side.

They left the small downtown and he directed her in what seemed like complicated turns out on a dirt road in the middle of rolling fields as far as the eye could see.

"It's so green," she said. "I didn't know what I expected, but it's…"

"Boring, I know." He gave her a rueful smile. "I couldn't wait to get out of here when I was a teenager. Brian was the same way."

She caught her breath. This was the third time he'd said his brother's name, a major difference for a man who'd struggled to even utter Brian's name. Once, when she'd asked, he'd said there were some things he just couldn't talk about. So she didn't press, even now. Especially now, though Micha appeared to be opening up. It was his story to tell, and she figured he'd do that when he was ready.

Simply nodding, she waited to see if Micha would continue.

"Brian was always the star," he said. "The most popular guy in school, and outstanding athlete, and the girls loved him. His one major flaw was that he would say whatever he thought people wanted to hear, even if it wasn't true. He told my parents he would come back and take over the ranch once he served his four years in the army. They believed him, of course, and it did take a lot of pressure off me."

"How do you know he didn't mean it?" she asked, unable to help herself.

Micha grimaced. "Because he told me and everyone else he knew that he considered the army his ticket out of here. He was right. That's why I enlisted as soon as I graduated high school."

Carly didn't comment, figuring she didn't need to

point out that maybe Brian had simply told Micha what he'd wanted to hear also.

"None of it mattered in the end," Micha continued. "Because Brian went and got himself killed. Damn, I was pissed at him."

Even now, so many years later, she could hear the grief in his voice.

Micha must have noticed it, too. He shook his head and dragged his hand through his hair. "Sorry. Enough of talking about the past. Look around. What do you think? Have you ever been to Indiana or Ohio before?"

"It's pretty," she said. "Very green with lots of trees. And no, I haven't."

Now, she thought. Now would be the perfect time to ask him the question she'd been wanting to ask since they'd left Chicago. Heart pounding, palms sweating, she tried to think of exactly what she wanted to say.

"Let's not talk about anything else that's serious," Micha told her, effectively canceling out her short but to-the-point speech. "Okay?"

What could she do but agree? Her question would have to wait until later, but since they weren't too far from Micha's parents' place, Carly knew she didn't want to wait much longer. She couldn't. She needed to have things clear in her head. And she could only hope once everything was settled, the end results would match her heart.

Chapter Fifteen

During his time as a captive and later while in the hospital recovering, Micha had often wondered if he'd ever see his childhood home again. It had felt odd to feel nostalgic for a place he'd only wanted to escape, but he figured that was part of human nature. Until he'd joined the army, the farm had been the only place he'd ever lived. He even pictured it, most often in the context of him simply driving down the gravel road in his vehicle, looking out over the familiar green fields that would be still unchanged from his childhood, and maybe even taking a picture of the front of the house he'd grown up in. This hadn't ever included him seeing his parents in person.

Surprisingly, seeing his parents again made him feel both nervous and eager. Meanwhile, he took in the familiar scenery and allowed a place inside of him that he hadn't even known was broken to slowly heal.

Then something new and unfamiliar made him sit up straight.

A sign advertising a new housing development sat at the corner of his parents' private drive and the now-paved main road.

"What the…?" he wondered out loud, just as they crested the small hill and he caught sight of several large houses in the area where his family had once grazed cattle.

"Nice houses," Carly said, fidgeting. She seemed antsy for some reason. He put it down to nerves at meeting his mom.

"They are nice," he reluctantly admitted, admiring the clean lines of the houses. "Though they're out of place here."

"Maybe this will soon be an up-and-coming residential area." Hands on the steering wheel, she practically bounced in her seat. "And look at the size of their yards."

He shook his head. Carly always made small talk when she was nervous. It was part of her way of processing stress.

"If I was in the market for a new home in this part of Ohio, I'd definitely consider one of those," she continued. "I bet they're a lot less expensive here than in Chicago."

Though Micha found their presence in what had been unspoiled farmland unsettling, he swallowed hard and agreed.

The road curved, and once they'd left the subdivision behind him, the rolling, treed hills he remembered took over.

Finally, his parents' house came into view. Still painted a cheery yellow—his mother's doing—the single-story ranch house looked a little more weathered than he remembered. Carly pulled the Jeep up in front of the two-car garage and parked. She killed the engine and turned to face him, wiping her palms off on the front of her jeans.

"Nervous?" he asked, wondering if she'd find it comforting that he was, too.

"A little." Carly nodded, fidgeting in her seat. "Though not about what you think. At least not entirely." She took a deep breath, the worry in her wide-eyed gaze making him want to comfort her. "Listen," she continued. "Before we go in there, I need to ask you something important."

"Anything," he said, meaning it. "What is it?"

"Just a second." To his surprise, her hand appeared to be shaking as she reached for a delicate silver chain she wore around her neck. Her gaze locked on his, she pulled it out of her shirt. "This," she told him, showing him what she wore dangling at the end of the necklace.

He caught his breath. "Is that…?"

"Yes. The engagement ring we picked out together before you went back to active duty. I wore it on my finger for a year after I was told you died."

Touched, he swallowed hard. "You kept it."

"Yes. Once I stopped wearing it on my hand, I wore it on this chain, tucked inside my clothes so no one could see. I just took it off and put it in my jewelry box right before you came back. I put it back on this morning. This ring means that much to me. It's a symbol of our love."

Their love. Hope bloomed within him, unfurling in his chest.

Then, while he struggled to figure out the right words to say, she unclipped the chain, removed the ring and held it out to him.

Throat aching, furious with himself for actually daring to hope, he froze, eyeing the ring as if it were dangerous. In a way, it was.

She was giving it back. Now, as he prepared to face one of the most difficult times in a life that hadn't been easy in a long, long time, Carly Colton had decided to stab him in the heart.

"No." He refused to believe it, his chest aching. "It's yours. You keep it. I don't want it back."

"What?" Tilting her head, she eyed him as if she thought he'd lost his mind. "You thought… Oh, Micha. I brought the ring back out to ask you if you wanted me to wear it again." She lowered her hand. "That's what I get for being presumptuous. I wanted you to put it back on my finger."

Thoroughly confused now and almost afraid to dare to believe he'd heard her properly, he looked from her beautiful blue eyes to the sparkling ring and back again. He thought his heart might explode from his chest. "Do you mean…?"

"Yes. I'd like to go back to being engaged," she said primly, though a tiny smile hovered at the corner of her mouth. "That is, if you still want to marry me."

"If I still want…" He sucked in his breath. "Carly Colton, are you proposing to me?" he asked, blood roaring in his ears. "Because if you are, the answer is yes. Definitely, unequivocally yes!"

"Well, technically I'm asking if we can reinstate our engagement," she began. Then her eyes widened. "Yes?" she repeated. "Does that mean we…"

"Have a wedding to plan." Leaning over, he kissed

her. Not a long, deep kiss like he longed to do, but a quick one due to them being parked outside his childhood home. "I love you," he said. He took the ring and, gazing in her eyes, slowly slipped it over her finger. "Back where it belongs. Engagement reinstated."

"You know what?" she asked, her expression suddenly solemn. "I love you, too, Micha Harrison. I always have and I always will."

Now he knew he could face anything. "Let's go inside and meet my mother."

"Yes." She nodded. "Now I'm ready to meet my future mother-in-law."

Her simple choice of phrase made his throat close. The thought that his father might never get to know the wonder and beauty that made up Carly Colton hurt. But he couldn't focus on that now. His mother needed him. And too many years had passed since he'd hugged her.

Pushing aside all raw emotion, he nodded. "Let's go."

They got out of the Jeep at the same time, linking hands to walk up the sidewalk. They made it halfway when the front door of the house opened and his mother stepped out onto the front porch. She wore a pair of faded blue jeans, work boots and a cotton, button-down shirt. She looked the same, he thought, except she now wore her silver hair in a stylish short cut.

"Micha!" She cried out his name and opened her arms.

Micha stepped into them without hesitation. Carly remained a few steps back, quietly watching.

Clinging to him, his mother wept. "It's so good to have you home."

"It's good to be here," he replied.

"What happened to your head?" she asked, pulling back far enough to peer at his bandage.

"That's a long story," he told her. "I'll save it for later, if that's okay with you."

Expression troubled, she searched his gaze, exactly the same way she'd used to when he was a teenager and she was trying to ascertain if he was telling the truth. "But you're all right, aren't you?"

He hugged her tight. "I'm all right, Ma. I promise."

When she finally released him, Micha turned her around and introduced her to Carly. "Mom, this is my fiancée, Carly Colton."

More hugs, more weeping, and finally his mom ushered them both inside the house. She kept checking back over her shoulder to make sure they were following her.

Inside, the place appeared the same as he remembered, untouched by time. The familiar floral wallpaper decorated the kitchen walls, and the same metal-and-vinyl kitchen table and chairs sat under the same stained-glass light fixture. It felt like stepping back into the past.

Except now he knew his father wouldn't come stomping in through the kitchen door, having left his dirty boots on the back stoop, wanting nothing more than a hot shower and a good meal.

Micha waited until they were all sitting around the old kitchen table sipping on his mother's freshly made lemonade before asking about the subdivision.

"We had to sell off some of our land," his mother explained, only slightly apologetic. "With your father slowing down due to age, we were struggling to keep the ranch running. Finally, we decided to just hang on to the house and ten acres. Even that was a lot, though. Right before Al had his stroke, we were even talking about moving into Lima since it's less than a half hour away."

"Dad is considering living in town?" Micha asked. Next, he halfway expected her to tell him pigs could fly.

His mom nodded. "He's sick, but technically he's living in Lima now. He was at Saint Rita's Medical Center, but yesterday they moved him into a rehabilitation facility. They said he'd be there a few weeks."

Rehabilitation. His dad must hate that. Al Harrison had always taken such pride at being a man's man, big and weather-roughened, his large hands calloused from hard work. Micha couldn't imagine how he'd deal with being weakened by a stroke. "Will we be able to visit him?"

"Yes." Expression troubled, his mother placed her hand over his. "But I should prepare you. He's in and out of consciousness. I'm not sure he'll even recognize you."

He hadn't expected that. He swallowed hard. "I hope he does. There are a few things between us that we need to settle once and for all."

Though she nodded, his mother once again started to cry. Carly, with her big heart, got up and went to her, wrapping the older woman in a tight hug. "It's going to be all right," she murmured. "You'll see."

Though she nodded, his mom's bleak expression indicated she wasn't sure anything would ever be all right again.

"We've received an offer on the house and remaining ten acres," she finally said. "By the same people who built that fancy subdivision. Though your father and I were only considering it before he had the stroke, I'm likely going to accept it now."

For a moment, Micha couldn't catch his breath. But then he realized she was right. He hated the thought of the two of them struggling to run the ranch. Who knows, maybe they'd be open to moving closer to Chicago. He decided to bring that up at some point before he left.

After finishing their drinks and refusing his mom's offer to make them something to eat, they got Bridget settled in the kitchen and then they all piled into Micha's Jeep to drive to Lima. After all these years away, Micha would finally see his father again. He only wished it were under different circumstances.

THOROUGHLY CHARMED BY Micha's mother, who'd asked her to call her Beth, Carly kept quiet and stayed in the background while Beth and Micha reconnected. For as long as she'd known and loved Micha, he had buried his emotions deep inside regarding his family. Seeing him now, clearly hurting yet full of love, only made her realize she'd made the right choice in reinstating their engagement.

As if she'd ever doubted. Even when she'd been furious and hurt over the way he'd let her think he'd died, she'd still loved him with every ounce of her being.

Micha had let his mother ride in the front seat and he'd taken the back while Carly drove. Pulling up in front of the rehabilitation hospital, she parked. The single-story brick building appeared welcoming.

Carly glanced at Beth and then Micha. "Should I wait

out here?" she asked, willing to give them all the privacy they needed.

"No," Micha answered immediately. "I want you with me."

Beth wisely stayed out of the discussion, rummaging in her purse for something.

Carly got out, motioned at Micha to do the same. "I think you should talk to your father privately at first. Once you're comfortable, you can bring me in and introduce me."

Opening his mouth as if to argue, Micha considered. He exhaled. "Maybe you're right."

"You and your mother," Carly urged. "I don't want to intrude right now. I'm sure they have some sort of lobby. I'll sit there and wait."

Though Micha still appeared uncertain, he nodded. Inside, he waited until Carly had gotten settled in a chair before offering his mother his arm. Together the two disappeared down one of the hallways.

Her phone chimed, indicating a text. It was Jones, just checking to make sure she'd arrived in one piece. They texted back and forth for a little bit, and right before he said he had to go, he reminded her to let Heath know she was okay. She did that, received a brief, I'm glad, in response, which meant her eldest brother had to be too busy to chat.

She checked social media, scrolling through her feed, when she looked up to see Beth had returned.

"I'm letting them have alone time," the older woman stated, dropping into the chair next to Carly. "Al has been in and out of it since they moved him here. He's sleeping a lot, though they tell me they've been able to get him up out of bed in a wheelchair. Micha is talking to him, hoping his father will respond to the sound of his son's voice."

Carly nodded. "Has he been awake much with you?"

Slowly, Beth nodded. "A little bit," she said. "It's been really frightening, not knowing if my husband is going to recover."

Reaching over, Carly hugged her. "It'll all work out. Sometimes these things just take time."

Once Carly let go, Beth eyed her curiously. "You sound awfully confident. How do you know?"

"Because I'm a nurse." Carly smiled. "Pediatrics, though. I work in the Neonatal Intensive Care Unit. Time, along with modern medicine, often bring about surprising healing. Now I don't know your husband's particular medical situation, but I'm sure his doctor can give you a lot more information."

"Oh, he has. He actually said something similar to what you just did. We need to give Al time and see what functions he regains. The therapy here is supposed to help with all that, too."

"I'm sure it will."

Both women looked up as Micha reappeared. He seemed composed, Carly thought.

"Dad woke up," Micha told his mother. "Not for long, but I'm pretty sure he saw and recognized me."

Beth's gaze searched his face. "Did he say anything? I know it can be kind of hard to understand him."

"No. He just looked at me and smiled. Then he closed his eyes again."

"How long are you staying?" Beth asked, her tone guardedly hopeful.

Micha glanced at Carly. "I'm not sure. We haven't actually discussed it yet."

"I see. Well, you're both welcome to stay as long as you like. Please, at least another day," she pleaded. "We have so much catching up to do."

"We'd planned to spend the night," Micha replied. "Beyond that, I'm not sure."

"I'm glad. That's a start." Beth got up slowly, relief shining in her eyes.

Carly's heart went out to her. If Micha wanted to stay a couple of days, she'd be willing.

Once they arrived back at the farm, Beth informed them she would be making something special for supper, including dessert, so she asked them to please save their appetites. She showed them the room she'd given them to use, asking if they wanted to stay together or in separate rooms.

Micha tugged Carly close. "What do you think?" he asked, only half teasing.

"If you're okay with it, Beth," Carly replied. "Together. We've actually been living that way at my place for a little while."

"I don't mind." Smiling, Beth turned to go. "We'll probably be eating at six. Why don't you two rest up a little and then join me in the kitchen?"

Once she'd left, closing the door behind her, both Carly and Micha dropped down on the bed and sat, legs dangling off the side.

"I haven't heard anyone call dinner supper outside of a television show," Carly mused. "I like it."

"We're country folks," Micha said. He looked around. "This used to be my bedroom growing up," he. "It's been painted and fixed up, but that actually looks like my bed and old dresser."

Unable to resist, Carly wiggled her eyebrows. "I bet you never slept with a girl in it. Or have you?"

He laughed. "No. This will be the first time."

"And the last," she pointed out. "We'd better make it matter."

Hauling her up against him, Micha kissed her. "Oh, we will. I can promise you that."

By the time he released her, she couldn't stop smiling. "I'm so glad we came," she said, resting her head against his shoulder.

"Me, too." He tucked a wayward strand of her hair behind her ear. "Before we go back home, I'd really like you to meet my dad."

Carly nodded. "I'd like that, too."

He hesitated, his expression serious. "I'm thinking of talking to my mom about them both moving to Chicago after they sell the farm. I think it'd be better for everyone if they lived closer to us."

"I agree." Heart full, Carly nodded. "And I'd really love for them to meet my family, too." One large, blended family.

"Me, too." Micha kissed her again, another slow and sensuous promise of what the night would hold later.

From her spot on the floor, Bridget woofed, wagging her tail.

"See, even our dog agrees," Micha said, smiling broadly.

Our dog. Carly liked that.

"Come on." Micha pulled her up to her feet. "Let's go see if there's anything we can help with in the kitchen."

"You go." She shooed him with her hands. "I want to freshen up a bit. I'll be out there shortly."

He kissed her again, a quick one this time, and left. Once the door had closed behind him, Carly dropped back onto the end of the bed. Bridget got up and nudged her with her nose so Carly would pet her.

Stroking her dog's silky fur, Carly exhaled, reflecting on how much her life had changed in such a short time. The love of her life had come back to her, she'd gained a dog and now would be adding in-laws to her family. Maybe even, someday, she and Micha would have children. The thought made her smile.

The only thing that could make her life complete would be for her father's and uncle's killer to be caught and brought to justice.

After washing her face and brushing her hair, Carly headed toward the kitchen with Bridget padding along at her side.

She'd barely reached the end of the hallway when the scent of something heavenly reached her. "Lasagna?" she guessed, stepping into the kitchen.

Beth grinned. "Yes. My specialty from an old family recipe. When Micha was younger, he requested I make it for every birthday."

"That and your amazing cheesecake," Micha added, looking hopeful. "I don't suppose you happened to make one of those, too?"

Instead of answering with words, Beth simply went to the refrigerator and opened it. She held up a beautiful cheesecake decorated with cherries on top.

"Of course!" Micha laughed. "Thank you so much, Mom. I seriously used to daydream about your lasagna and cheesecake."

After closing the refrigerator, Beth turned to face him. Her eyes had filled with tears. "I almost lost you twice. Once at Brian's funeral and then again when the army told me you were killed. Naturally, I'm going to make your favorite foods for you."

Pushing to his feet, Micha hugged her. "I love you, Mom."

She hugged him back. "I love you, too." Holding out her other arm, she met Carly's gaze. "Get over here, Carly. I want a group hug with my daughter-in-law-to-be."

Touched, Carly joined in. To her surprise, she even teared up a little.

"Sit, sit." Beth motioned toward the table. "Lasagna takes time to cook. I've made salad that we can eat beforehand if you're hungry."

"We can wait," Micha said. "Sit with us, Mom. Carly and I want to talk to you about considering a move closer to Chicago."

Stunned, Beth pulled out a chair and dropped into it. She looked from Micha to Carly. "Are you serious?"

"Yes. At least think about it, why don't you? Since you're selling the farm and planning to move, anyway, why not live closer to us?"

"Plus, the Chicago area has a lot of top-notch doctors," Carly added. "I work at one of the hospitals there, so I can help you with referrals. I know how difficult finding a good doctor can be."

After looking from one to the other, Beth covered her face with her hands, crying now in earnest. "I'd love that," she finally said, smiling through her tears. "And I'm sure your father would, too. I'll talk to him about it, when he's able to understand."

Micha nodded. He reached into his pocket and put a small, highly polished carving on the table. "I made this for you," he said.

Beth sniffed, reaching for it. When she picked it up, she began crying again. "This is beautiful," she managed. "And looks just like us, right about the time you left for the army. You say you made this?"

Slowly, Micha nodded. "I kept it with me for years. Now I'd like you to have it."

She smiled through her tears. "I'll treasure it always."

The stove timer dinged.

"Oh!" Beth jumped to her feet, wiping at her eyes with her hand, before grabbing a tissue and blowing her nose. "The lasagna is done. It will need to sit on top of the stove for a few minutes. Carly, do you drink red wine? Would you like to eat your salads?"

Declining Carly's offer to help, Beth bustled around the kitchen, clearly in her element.

Later, after devouring the most delicious lasagna Carly had ever tasted, bar none, along with garlic bread and salad, Carly nearly groaned when Beth got out the cheesecake. "I'm too full," she protested.

"You have to just try a bite," Micha insisted. "Even

if it's just a sliver. I promise you, you've never tasted anything like it."

With a sigh, Carly gave in. Both Micha and Beth watched, beaming, as Carly cut into the fluffy dessert with her fork and opened her mouth. She'd expected good, but this was better. Melt in your mouth, light and sweet and perfect. "That's the best cheesecake I've ever tasted," she said, unable to conceal her amazement.

Clearly pleased, Beth laughed.

"I told you," Micha said, before turning his attention to his own plate. He devoured his own slice, as did Carly.

Then, stuffed and sleepy, Carly finished her wine and jumped to her feet. Ignoring Beth's protests, she began taking care of the dishes. "You and Micha go on and let me clean up," she said. "I'll join you both in the living room when I'm done."

Bridget woofed, reminding Carly she hadn't been fed.

By the time Carly took care of her dog and the dishes and poured herself another glass of wine, thirty minutes had passed. She carried her wine into the living room and took a seat on the couch next to Micha. He put his arm around her and tugged her close.

Beth watched them both with a dreamy smile. "I never thought I'd see this day," she mused. "Thank you, son."

"For what?" Micha asked.

"Forgiving me and your father our mistakes."

Micha appeared stunned. "We all have made choices we regretted later. Me in particular. If Carly hadn't forgiven me…" His voice broke.

Carly kissed him, snuggling into his side. "I think

the best thing to do is keep looking toward the future," she said. "We cannot change the past."

The three of them chatted for a few more hours. They turned on the evening news and watched that, too. Finally, Beth excused herself to go to bed.

"We'll be visiting your father again tomorrow," she reminded Micha, stifling a yawn. "I'd like to go in the morning, so I can bring him doughnuts from his favorite place. I'm thinking we can leave around eight."

Micha used the remote to turn off the TV. He got up, gave his mother a hug and kissed her cheek. "We'll be ready. I'm hoping Dad will feel well enough tomorrow to meet Carly."

Beth's smile never wavered, despite the sadness in her eyes. "Sleep well, you two. I'll see you in the morning."

After Beth left, Micha and Carly turned off the lights. Carly took Bridget outside one last time and then they made their way to their room.

As quietly as possible, they got ready for bed. Bridget turned circles on the dog mat Carly had brought for her, heaved a sigh and settled down to sleep.

"This has gone better than I expected." Micha climbed into bed, propping his pillow up behind his back. "Everything I could ever have dreamed of, with the exception of my father having had a stroke."

"He'll get better," Carly said, hoping she was right.

"I think so, too. I can't wait to introduce you to him as my bride-to-be."

The satisfaction in his voice made her smile.

"Do you want a long or a short engagement?" she asked, getting into bed next to him.

Micha shot her an incredulous look. "Are you kidding me here? I want to marry you as soon as is humanly possible."

Turning to face him, she took both his hands into hers. "I agree, but I'd prefer to wait until your entire family can be there. Your father needs time to heal."

Clearly touched, Micha held her gaze and slowly nodded. "I agree. But I don't want to wait forever. It's already been way too long."

"Let's see how your dad does in rehab. Your mom said she'd keep us posted."

Micha nodded. "That sounds like a plan. But you know what? Your family isn't going to want to wait. As soon as they see that engagement ring on your finger, you know they're going to start planning big-time."

This made her laugh. "You're right. But at least I have a good excuse to make them give us a month or two."

"You do," he agreed. "But before we leave tomorrow, I'm going to tell my dad he'd better work hard so he doesn't hold up our wedding too long."

Carly wasn't sure what to think about this. "Are you sure that won't be putting too much pressure on him?"

"Nope." He kissed her, his eyes lighting up. "He thrives on a challenge. He always used to say what motivated him the most was someone telling him he couldn't accomplish something. He's got this, Carly. I know he does."

She nodded, then reached over and turned off her nightstand lamp. "We got this, too, Micha Harrison," she breathed, nibbling on his ear. "Now turn off your light so we can show each other how much we do."

With a strangled laugh that turned into a moan as her mouth moved lower, he did as she'd requested.

"Turns out you're right, Carly Colton," he murmured as she settled her body over his. "We got this."

* * * * *

COMING SOON!

We really hope you enjoyed reading this book.
If you're looking for more romance, be sure to
head to the shops when new books are
available on

Thursday 29th April

To see which titles are coming soon, please visit

millsandboon.co.uk/nextmonth

MILLS & BOON

LET'S TALK
Romance

For exclusive extracts, competitions
and special offers, find us online:

f facebook.com/millsandboon

🐦 @MillsandBoon

📷 @MillsandBoonUK

Get in touch on 01413 063232

For all the latest titles coming soon, visit
millsandboon.co.uk/nextmonth

WANT EVEN MORE
ROMANCE?
SUBSCRIBE AND SAVE TODAY!

'Mills & Boon books, the perfect way to escape for an hour or so.'

MISS W. DYER

'Excellent service, promptly delivered and very good subscription choices.'

MISS A. PEARSON

'You get fantastic special offers and the chance to get books before they hit the shops.'

MRS V. HALL

Visit millsandboon.co.uk/Subscribe
and save on brand new books.

MILLS & BOON
A ROMANCE FOR EVERY READER

- **FREE** delivery direct to your door

- **EXCLUSIVE** offers every month

- **SAVE** up to 25% on pre-paid subscriptions

SUBSCRIBE AND SAVE

millsandboon.co.uk/Subscribe

MILLS & BOON

THE HEART OF ROMANCE

A ROMANCE FOR EVERY READER

MODERN

Prepare to be swept off your feet by sophisticated, sexy and seductive heroes, in some of the world's most glamourous and romantic locations, where power and passion collide.

HISTORICAL

Escape with historical heroes from time gone by. Whether your passion is for wicked Regency Rakes, muscled Vikings or rugged Highlanders, awaken the romance of the past.

MEDICAL

Set your pulse racing with dedicated, delectable doctors in the high-pressure world of medicine, where emotions run high and passion, comfort and love are the best medicine.

True Love

Celebrate true love with tender stories of heartfelt romance, from the rush of falling in love to the joy a new baby can bring, and a focus on the emotional heart of a relationship.

Desire

Indulge in secrets and scandal, intense drama and plenty of sizzling hot action with powerful and passionate heroes who have it all: wealth, status, good looks…everything but the right woman.

HEROES

Experience all the excitement of a gripping thriller, with an intense romance at its heart. Resourceful, true-to-life women and strong, fearless men face danger and desire - a killer combination!

To see which titles are coming soon, please visit

millsandboon.co.uk/nextmonth

JOIN US ON SOCIAL MEDIA!

Stay up to date with our latest releases, author news and gossip, special offers and discounts, and all the behind-the-scenes action from Mills & Boon...

 millsandboon

 millsandboonuk

 millsandboon

It might just be true love...

GET YOUR ROMANCE FIX!

MILLS & BOON
—— *blog* ——

Get the latest romance news, exclusive author interviews, story extracts and much more!

blog.millsandboon.co.uk

MILLS & BOON

HISTORICAL

Awaken the romance of the past

Escape with historical heroes from time gone by. Whether your passion is for wicked Regency Rakes, muscled Viking warriors or rugged Highlanders, indulge your fantasies and awaken the romance of the past.

Six Historical stories published every month, find them all a

millsandboon.co.uk/Historical

MILLS & BOON

MODERN

Power and Passion

Prepare to be swept off your feet by sophisticated, sexy and seductive heroes, in some of the world's most glamourous and romantic locations, where power and passion collide.

ght Modern stories published every month, find them all at:

millsandboon.co.uk/Modern

MILLS & BOON
DARE

Sexy. Passionate. Bold.

Sensual love stories featuring smart, sassy heroines you'd want as a best friend, and compelling intense heroes who are worthy of them.

Four DARE stories published every month, find them all at:

millsandboon.co.uk/DARE